City Sages

City Sages
BALTIMORE

Edited by
Jen Michalski

Baltimore, Maryland

Library of Congress Control Number: 2010925258

ISBN 978-1-936328-01-7

CityLit Project is a 501(c)(3) Nonprofit Organization

Federal Tax ID Number: 20-0639118

Printed in the United States of America
First Edition
Cover Design: Justin Sirois

CITYLIT
PRESS
c/o CityLit Project
120 S. Curley Street
Baltimore, MD 21224
410.274.5691
www.CityLitProject.org
info@citylitproject.org

Nurturing the culture of literature.

"There is a saying in Baltimore that crabs may be prepared in fifty ways and that all of them are good."

H.L. Mencken
"The Sage of Baltimore"

Table of Contents

Introduction

JEN MICHALSKI

Where are the writers in Baltimore?

It is a question that has haunted me for the last four years and has culminated in my starting a literary journal, a writers' happy hour, co-hosting a reading series, and now editing this anthology. A not-so-brief summary of how this anthology came about: When I began to get involved in the Baltimore literary scene back in 2006, a great many literary scenes had happened in Charm City, and many were yet to come, but the city as a whole seemingly was at an impasse. There were a few literary journals, no conferences, no dedicated fiction reading series, no happy hours or coed literary sports teams, no outlet for writers to meet, to know each other when they crossed paths in Mount Vernon or Hampden or even Timonium. But surely, with its celebrated Writing Seminars at Johns Hopkins and the literary legacies of Edgar Allan Poe, F. Scott Fitzgerald, Gertrude Stein, John Barth, and others, Baltimore was a town with a literary swagger. It had to be. Either way, I was going to find out.

So I began an online literary quarterly, jmww, with the intent of showcasing Baltimore writers and beyond. Some of you may not have heard of it still, even as we have expanded to publishing print anthologies and appearances at CityLit Festival, the Baltimore Book Festival, and regional conferences. But the important thing is that running the journal led me to other folks, the first tendrils of local writers that became an explosion—writers in the Towson Professional Writing Program, editors from the *Baltimore Review*, the celebrated Madison Smartt Bell and Baltimore "Wire" bad boy Rafael Alvarez.

And Gregg Wilhelm, head of Baltimore nonprofit CityLit Project, whose mission remains to "nurture the culture of literature in Baltimore." Gregg and I began collaborating on some meet-ups in an attempt to bring writers together. After all, what was a culture of literature in Baltimore without writers? Our first idea was a monthly Writers Happy Hour, which ran once a month at various Baltimore bars in 2006–2007. Suddenly, all the pieces began to fall in place. We found that there were other writers, ones who had started their own journals and even their own presses. We were all coexisting in a vacuum.

It was at the Writers Happy Hour that I also met novelist and then-New York transplant Michael Kimball. As I had wondered where all the writers were, he wondered where all the reading series in Baltimore were. We began the 510 Reading Series, a monthly fiction series, in January 2008. Since then we've hosted more than fifty writers, many of them nationally known, regionally located, but mostly local. We found, and continue to find, when booking the series, that there are so many good writers in Baltimore that no one knows about.

Which is how this anthology came to fruition. Writer H.L. Mencken may have been our first "Sage of Baltimore," as he was known, but we've had many more since, and I was dumbfounded that they were not collected in one place. I discussed the idea with Michael Kimball (who helped adjudicate what I originally thought would be a modest anthology), and we made a list of all the Baltimore writers we knew, famous and not, dead or alive, who lived or had lived in Baltimore and sent them a call for submissions. We also posted public calls at area colleges, bookstores, coffee shops, and listservs. We searched through public domain for works of older writers we could include. When the submissions began pouring in, we read and read and read. We tried to include as many people as we could, but there are just too many good stories, too many good writers.

But a short list of who did make this cut: writers who are long dead and writers who are living, writers who are well known and writers not-so-well known, not even to us, at first. You'll find Frederick Douglass alongside Jane Satterfield, Anne Tyler alongside Zora Neale Hurston, Laura Lippman, and Stephen Dixon. What they all have in common is that they are writers who, at some point in their lives, took up residency in Baltimore. Or still do. And they have shaped our literary history and will shape our literary future.

Thanks to Michael Kimball, who believed in the project from the start and lent his expertise regarding editorial decisions and other publishing minefields. Also to Gregg Wilhelm, who was equally enthusiastic and immediately offered to publish the anthology through CityLit Project's new imprint, CityLit Press. And, of course, to all the authors who submitted their work and spread the word to make this anthology the beast it became. Finally, I want to thank you for believing in Baltimore writers. Without your support, there would be no *City Sages*, no CityLit Project, no 510 Reading Series, and no jmww. But there will always be writers. Four years later, I know now that Charm City is swimming in them.

Small Blue Thing

MADISON SMARTT BELL

First of all, it wasn't a raven. I am not a raven, thanks a lot. Thank you. No applause, please. They always get it wrong. A raven, an actual raven with a five-foot wing spread and a beak like a samurai sword, probably wouldn't have even fit in the freaking house. I am a crow, thanks very much, an American Common Crow, *corvus brachyrhyncos*, harsh call and a ragged shadow on the lawn.

"Poetic license" is what they call it. When they get it wrong.

Ungainly fowl, he called me. *Stately raven?* Might have been flattering if he'd got the right species. Then, *fiend, devil, thing of evil*, etcetera, etcetera. *Ebony bird*—I could live with that.

House not big enough to swing a cat, much less accommodate a raven. I suppose you might have walled up a cat in there somewhere. One of his fancies: walled-up cats. *Lord have mercy on my poor soul*, he said at the end, and, some time before or after, *the best thing a friend could do for me is blow out my brains with a pistol*. Do I have that right? He also kept asking for someone named *Reynolds*, which was wrong too because the only person he knew named *Reynolds* was not going to be any help to him then or there, not that anybody else was either.

Why did I come to them, the first time? To that house, that place. Far below the spiral of warm air on which I soared, there was a glint, a sparkle: sunlight riding a crack in a window pane. He lied about the weather too. It wasn't even night.

Poetry. Try cutting your tongue up the middle with a pair of rusty dull sewing scissors—I'll give you poetry. Think I'm kidding, do you? Think it's a joke?

We're not buzzards, by the way. Not stinking baldheaded wrinkle-necked puking vultures. We're crows. On the other hand, we do take notice of distress. We do.

Also, *Nevermore*, I never said it. The first word out of my mouth was a simple "Hello." Not fantastically original, I grant you. That bird-trapper, him with the rusty sewing snips, was not the literary type. He didn't teach me any brilliant conversation. So it was just *hello*

hello

hello

hello

just to fill up the dead air and create a distraction while I sidled nearer to the big round shiny thing on the mantel: that cloudy pearl with its curved reflection.

My greeting wasn't getting it for the poet though. The simple *O* sound didn't do it for him. It had to be *ore*, preferably with a few other syllables draped over the front. This was the guy, remember, who declared in one of his lengthy disquisitions that the most beautiful phrase in the English language was *cellar door*. Nutbag, you say? You wouldn't be the first to think so.

But here he comes, first flapping the same quill pen he'd been writing with, then a moldy old feather duster he dragged up from somewhere behind his table. Here he was, the ambitious or formerly ambitious writer, enacting a bunch of stupid feather puns. Can feathers cast out feathers? ...whatever. Of course he didn't expect me to know. I was an animal to him! He thought I was going to crap on his parchment or something, him with the inkstains all over his fingers, and on the cuff of his shirt too, where he'd unconsciously dragged it through his blots and cross-outs. Never get those stains out, never. It looked like an expensive shirt, too.

The cat, meanwhile, was scrunched up in a corner with its eyes bugged out and its fur all sticking up on end. They did have a cat even though there wasn't room to swing it. It was black too, but the adorable little white socks it had on kept it from looking as scary as it probably would have liked. I mean, come on, gimme a break, so you don't see a crow in the house every day, so? Let's wall your skinny ass up somewhere and then see what you have to say.

The poet is flailing the duster around in a way that obscures my objective. The window is open—why won't the crow fly out? It was hard to fly in such a small space without knocking a whole lot of stuff over (*ungainly fowl*, indeed—let's see you try and do better) so I adopted a pose on top of a lamp and tried to change the subject.

Feed me meat, I said. Then, in case he wasn't listening, with the big commotion and all, I said it again. *Feed me meat.*

See, that guy the birdnapper, Mister Scissorhands—I had to expand beyond his vocabulary in the end. It was my ticket out of there. The birdnapper sold my tailfeathers to some early captain of industry who intended me as a gift for his wife. Company for her was the idea I guess, since (as I learned during my transportation, in various hotel rooms and even a time or two on the train) this early capitalist porker expended most of his own social grace on other women: sluts and whores normally, not to put too fine a point on it. Wifey kept me in a cage about big enough for a parakeet, and during her lonely evenings she'd try to chat me up. All this a long time before TV, remember, or even the radio. She didn't read much either, because she was a moron. Well, I thought of some other stuff to say, even if it was really just only quotations of things I had recently happened to hear, such as **** *me! Oh,* **** *me harder, Horatio!* (this was the capitalist porker's name) **** *me in my* **** *right now! Oh, Horatio, your* **** *is so big!* (Horatio had been paying for this dialogue, naturally). These quotations of mine worked a little too well—nearly got my neck wrung for my trouble. Luckily Mrs Horatio Capitalist-Porker was squeamish. Didn't want to touch the nasty crow. So she heaved it out the window, cage and all. Good job for me the door popped open when it hit the pavement.

Feed me meat, I said. Not the worst thing in my repertoire, you see? Besides, I meant it; I was hungry.

The poet has lowered his feather duster, thank God. He's standing there huffing and sweating from that little amount of exertion. He was never really in very good shape. Eyes bugging out at me big as the cat's. That's right, buddy, the crow is talking. Pinch yourself; it isn't a dream. The crow is talking. *Feed me meat.*

You looked at him, you saw the longing. I put my head on one side, then the other. Left eye, right eye, left. Dark hollows painted around *his* eyes. The mouth rather small, reddish, pursed; some might have called it weak. His hair too long and disheveled, pasted this way and that over his spiraling baldness by the cold unhealthy sweat. The little dandy's mustache had been left ungroomed for a long time. But there was a trace of the dandy about him still, gone seedy like the mustache and the shirt. His skin was delicate, pale, translucent. Blue vein beating there on his temple, still another beating in the hollow of his throat. Next to nothing between his blood and the open air! Everything got through to him. He was curious as a child, wanted to know everything. What would it be like to fly?

Then what do you know he went and got me some. Meat, that is. I mean, this was a sympathetic individual if you once got his attention. I felt like I sort of saw the idea form in his mind so I went hopping along after him when he left the room. The cat was still slinking around the baseboards, not getting any too near. Don't even think about it, cat. I clacked my beak, hopping over the threshold. Crows aren't anywhere near the size of ravens, but get close enough to me and I'm bigger than you think.

In the kitchen my man is uncovering the slop pail and what have we got here? Item with a fine high odor, lustrous with slime. A slice of beef, would be my guess, which through the operation of time and neglect had evolved into a choice piece of carrion. Not that they could afford that sort of waste around this joint. They couldn't. But the lady of the house, through no fault of her own, had sort of been letting the housekeeping slide.

Lunch! I chowed on the thing. I'd flown a long way, it seemed all of a sudden. The cat was winding through the table legs the whole time I ate, pink nose wrinkled in feigned disgust, making like it didn't want a bite.

There was some tearing to be done. Got to work if you want to eat. I kept the meat pinned down with a claw (not that it was going anywhere) and tore strips out of it with my beak. There was commotion at the kitchen door. I was concentrating so I hardly noticed. Meat, you know. But a bustle, a gasp, whirl of shawl, sickroom smell, cough, crumple, *Darling, you mustn't exert yourself*, etcetera. He seemed to be guiding her out of the room. Leaving me alone with my meat, and the cat watching with its witch-green eyes. When I was full was when the meat was gone. Then it occurred to me that maybe now there was nothing between me and my goal.

Another thing, there wasn't any *pallid bust of Pallas*. There wasn't any bust at all. What he had on the mantel was a crystal ball. Like for a wizard or a fortune-teller, some gypsy con. I don't know what he was doing with the thing. Nobody in the house ever seemed to play with it. It sat above the fireplace and sucked up everything it could. All the room and its furnishings warped away in its curved reflection, and the window where I'd entered. Where he let me in.

It had been a cloud-blown day, damp, windy and warm. Darkness of the window pane when I landed on the sill. When the cloud passed from the sun the crack on the glass began to glitter once again. I saw the crow floating in the glass, glossy-winged strong black devil. Okay, I pecked a time or two. There's your famous *tap-tap-tapping*. But look—we don't actually think there's another crow behind the mirror! We're not stupid. When you fight your reflection, you know it's yourself you're fighting…

that's the point.

That was when I saw him first, swimming up from the darkness of the pane. His face was inside my reflection. The shining of his eye matched mine. And through this pairing, somehow too, the shining of the crystal ball.

I don't really know why he opened the window. Maybe he thought I was going to break it. One of the panes was already cracked. He'd scrunched his writing table up against the inside sill to get the best of the daylight he could. It was a crooked little house, and poorly angled for natural light, but they had to scrimp on candles and lamp oil and things like that.

Besides, like I said, he was curious.

He used to play with logic like a rubber band. The Gold Bug, *Eureka*, all that stuff. The horrors came from somewhere else, floating upward from the dark depths of the crystal. He was thin-skinned; everything got through to him. There was that goofy story that pasted the logic to the horror. A guy is looking out his window and sees a gruesome arachnid monster laying waste to the surroundings, how absolutely utterly awful, etc. Turns out it's only a spider about the size of a dandruff flake, suspended on its invisible thread a half-inch from his eye.

All a matter of perspective, don't you see?

There was the crow in the crystal ball. I never considered pecking that. It was too beautiful. If only it had been the size of a marble I could have carried it off and hidden it somewhere. If I gaped toward it my craw slid over the surface stretching wide enough to swallow it altogether. But that was illusion. I hopped backward, turned my head from one side to the other. Right eye, left eye, each eye expanding on the globe to cover it completely. I took another hop, sideways on the mantel. The whole room swam inside the crystal, and everything in it. That cat, composed below the fireplace with its four white booties neatly together, looking up at me harmlessly enough, the picture of innocence, yeah, right. The poet struggling with the poker, trying to coax a little warmth from the miserable tiny coal grate. In the background which was more or less the center of the crystal was that one, the little girl, expiring on a divan. Not dead yet. I saw her raise against the cushion, the movement swimming in the crystal. With her fingers she curbed the edges of her mouth. It was unsettling to me somehow. I turned from her reflection to face her.

You always thought of her as a little girl even though she was twenty-four by that time, and a married woman. But she'd been eleven when they met, sixteen when they married. Little Virginia Clemm—not the euphonious sort of name he liked. *Clemm*, come on, get outa here. Call her Ligeia, or Annabel Lee. Something sibilant and whispering.

Consumption, that was her situation. She still went creeping around the house at times. She'd leave her couch and wander, as she'd done this day. But she was already a goner by then. Her round little face turned all cadaverous, turned discreetly aside to catch the proceeds of a wet cough in her lace-edged blood-clotted handkerchief. There's your *lost Lenore* if you like. She was dead meat.

I never *perched upon a bust of Pallas*. I didn't perch on the crystal ball either. Too hard and slick for claws to get a purchase. And if they had, they would have scratched it. I didn't want that.

I perched on the mantelpiece beside it, shuffled my feathers and faced the room. There was fear in her face as she looked up at me. Recoil. Harbinger of her death she was thinking. Her husband's mad fantasies leaking through. *Grim, ungainly, ghastly gaunt and ominous bird of yore*, etcetera. She had reason to be frightened, poor small thing, though not of me. I'm racking my brains for something reassuring to say to her. Something decent, if it comes to that. *Feed me meat* seemed a little risqué. The tongue slit hadn't really made me more articulate. Most all of my phrases came from sailors and whores. Hell's Bells was mildest thing I could think of. Or *Ring my bells!* but in a way that was worse.

Bells, I said. *Bells bells bells bells bells bells bells bells bells.*

When she took her fingers down there was a smile. Dab of blood at the corner of it but still a smile. The crow talks. The crow is talking, what a novelty, *Bells*, it says. The poet straightened from the coal grate, the poker balanced in his fingers light as air. You could see in his face he didn't quite trust it. He was going to get this moment. Smile and never mind the blood, the bloody fingertips. A small orb of warmth swelled into the room. Just for this moment everything would be okay.

It's a crock about how I loomed over him for all eternity, *my soul from out that shadow that lies floating on the floor / Shall be lifted—nevermore!* and blah blah blah. I didn't stay forever and aye. Not perched on this nonexistent bust of *Pallas* nor anywhere else. There was the cat, for one thing. (It had a name but I wouldn't acknowledge it.) I'd have been a match for the thing in a fair fight, and it knew as much. But hey, you got to sleep some time. It was hard to relax with the cat's witch eyes all over me. And the house was too low and cramped for me to find a really secure perch.

So I used to come and go. With weeks between and sometimes months. We've got migration to consider, after all. But whenever I lit on the sill they'd let me in and sometimes they would feed me. A place they let you in and feed you meat—now that's worth something.

I swear she lit up to see me return, the poor small thing. Like I was the first freaking robin of spring.... It proved that something kept on happening. Another day come and she wasn't dead yet.

It took her years and years to die, and she had little rallies. Evenings she'd come down and play the little spinet backed into the wall, opposite his writing desk. Him and her mother and me and the cat all sitting up polite like we were in church, attending her frail melodies. They never lasted long.

Such a bad rap he got later on for those relationships. Like he was a kid-fiddler, and a fiddled kid too, and I don't know what else. Think about it, sixteen was not so young to marry in those days, and raising your bride from a bulb, so to speak, wasn't all that unusual either. As for the mother, old lady Clemm, so, so what? He got along better with her than you're expected to get on with your mother-in-law, and that's it. She was a kindly old stick when you once got used to the fact that she looked like one of the witches out of *Macbeth*, once you understood that the flat line of her toothless mouth was meant to be a smile. I admit it, I used to sit on her finger sometimes. She liked it. She would feed me meat.

Just the three of them trying to make a nest was all it was, with some warmth and softness and some shiny things scattered here and there. You take what you're given and that's what he got. After all the guy was an orphan himself. I'd sit on the old lady's finger and see it her way. Later on people tried to make out it was some kind of child molestation, but really they were like two children clinging to each other and the cold night pooling all around.

He used to sing to her sometimes. I mean he would also read her his poems and essays and stories, though not the most horrible scary ones, but that was when she was lucid, and strong enough to sit up. When she was sick and off her head he would hold her and sing old lullabies, *when you wake you shall have all the pretty little horses* and so on. God love him, his singing voice was worse than mine. The girl was delirious, it was nothing to her, but the cat would slink off into the alley, while old lady Clemm lurked in the kitchen, fingers practically stuck in her ears. Maybe not so much against the racket as...well, it was distressing. They were in a bad way.

Now what's the other verse to that one, *dumda dumda dum* and (can't remember the first line quite but it involves a calf I think and)

...way down yonder in the meadow
Buzzards and flies, pecking out its eyes
Poor little thing cries Mammy......

I mean, quite a choice for your invalid moribund spouse, or for anybody else if you think about it; imagine singing that to some kid or whatever, into the cradle you're rocking. He must have picked that one up down in Virginia. This was still slavery time, don't forget, so some of the songs the Mammies sang were kind of grim.

Eyeballs now, take eyeballs for a minute. The eye of a dying creature is like cloud swimming over the crystal, dull milkiness, occlusion. Makes me hungry, sort of, just to say that. We eat eyeballs. Yes, we do.

Green cat's eyeball on a stick? Thank you, why yes, I will have another. They're good! Besides, you gotta eat.

But joking aside, it's hard to talk about it. The blind calf, yawing with its bloody sockets, is not an edifying spectacle. It's just a need we feed on.

In the crystal when the room was empty, flowed the warped crow figure and beyond: the vacant writing desk, the spinet with its empty bench, and above, her tintype portrait hanging on the wall.

Funny but he'd seem to know when I was leaving. He'd look at me with a sort of envy then. If only he could just shrug on a pair of wings and fly away from that whole death trap till it shrank away to a little tight ball, a marble, a dot, then nothing. With all the crazy stuff he wrote sometimes I think that was the worst he ever thought.

I mean, the poor guy—it was never anything weird or perverted. If not for all the stories he wrote probably no one would have thought so. The guy was into dead stuff, face it! It doesn't mean he loved her any less. Probably he'd seen the future. There's nothing in a crystal ball. No magic. It's empty. Because it's empty, you sit there and you look at it and the thing you're looking for appears in your own mind.

I wanted to fly like a mimosa leaf, one time. Stooping, flirting, drifting down. It was so beautiful even though it didn't really shine. That sadness in the papery dulling of its gold. I tried to follow it, accompany it, imitate its movement. But I couldn't. It's just not a feasible way for a crow to fly.

We all have our little frustrations. I used to see that leaf in the crystal, or just at the back of my own eye. Feathering down to land on water silky smooth as oil. *Dark tarn of Usher.* The yellow fan-shape floating on that tide.

He'd have liked to fly off the handle too. That would have been another way out, go stark raving screaming mad like a hero of one of his grislier stories. But in reality the guy was pretty sane. He stayed that way. He just stood there and took it. Even the drinking and drugging was greatly exaggerated later on. Mostly it was just medicinal use. Of course at the end after she was dead and buried and he was sick himself and in great pain, he needed a lot of medicine.

Bells, I told her. Sometimes when the bells are ringing, I fly so high I can hardly stand it. Till the orb of the world shrinks away from me to the size of a blue-green marble. A dot, then nothing. And still I feel its bright eye watching me, in the night of the universe so black I couldn't pick out the shape of my own wing against it. The lonely distant glittering stars. Nothing but darkness and the darkness is me.

Keeping time time time in a sort of Runic rhyme to the paean of the bells of the bells keeping time time time in a sort of Runic rhyme to the throbbing of the bells of the bells bells bells to the sobbing of the bells as he knells knells knells in a happy Runic rhyme to the rolling of the bells of the bells bells bells to the tolling of the bells of the bells bells bells bells bells bells bells—ah Christ won't somebody make it stop?

I still fly over the place sometimes. It's the projects now, West Baltimore slums. All crack dealers and whores in spandex. Everything's right out there on the street. They lost something when they let go the whalebone and lace. Long fancy opium pipes and hookahs like he sometimes smoked. Something, certainly, has been lost.

How long do crows live? Take a good look at me and figure it out. We live as long as we're given to. *In the original unity of the first thing lies the secondary cause of all things, with the germ of their inevitable annihilation.* The horror and the logic both come out in the same place. I live, I live on, I am still flying.

The Black Cat

Edgar Allan Poe

For the most wild, yet most homely narrative which I am about to pen, I neither expect nor solicit belief. Mad indeed would I be to expect it, in a case where my very senses reject their own evidence. Yet, mad am I not—and very surely do I not dream. But to-morrow I die, and to-day I would unburthen my soul. My immediate purpose is to place before the world, plainly, succinctly, and without comment, a series of mere household events. In their consequences, these events have terrified—have tortured—have destroyed me. Yet I will not attempt to expound them. To me, they have presented little but Horror—to many they will seem less terrible than barroques. Hereafter, perhaps, some intellect may be found which will reduce my phantasm to the common-place—some intellect more calm, more logical, and far less excitable than my own, which will perceive, in the circumstances I detail with awe, nothing more than an ordinary succession of very natural causes and effects.

From my infancy I was noted for the docility and humanity of my disposition. My tenderness of heart was even so conspicuous as to make me the jest of my companions. I was especially fond of animals, and was indulged by my parents with a great variety of pets. With these I spent most of my time, and never was so happy as when feeding and caressing them. This peculiarity of character grew with my growth, and, in my manhood, I derived from it one of my principal sources of pleasure. To those who have cherished an affection for a faithful and sagacious dog, I need hardly be at the trouble of explaining the nature or the intensity of the gratification thus derivable. There is something in the unselfish and self-sacrificing love of a brute, which goes directly to the heart of him who has had frequent occasion to test the paltry friendship and gossamer fidelity of mere *Man*.

I married early, and was happy to find in my wife a disposition not uncongenial with my own. Observing my partiality for domestic pets, she lost no opportunity of procuring those of the most agreeable kind. We had birds, gold-fish, a fine dog, rabbits, a small monkey, and *a cat*.

This latter was a remarkably large and beautiful animal, entirely black, and sagacious to an astonishing degree. In speaking of his intelligence, my wife, who at heart was not a little tinctured with superstition, made frequent allusion to the ancient popular notion, which regarded all black cats as witches in disguise. Not that she was ever *serious* upon this point—and I mention the matter at all for no better reason than that it happens, just now, to be remembered.

Pluto—this was the cat's name—was my favorite pet and playmate. I alone fed him, and he attended me wherever I went about the house. It was even with difficulty that I could prevent him from following me through the streets.

Our friendship lasted, in this manner, for several years, during which my general temperament and character—through the instrumentality of the Fiend Intemperance—had (I blush to confess it) experienced a radical alteration for the worse. I grew, day by day, more moody, more irritable, more regardless of the feelings of others. I suffered myself to use intemperate language to my wife. At length, I even offered her personal violence. My pets, of course, were made to feel the change in my disposition. I not only neglected, but ill-used them. For Pluto, however, I still retained sufficient regard to restrain me from maltreating him, as I made no scruple of maltreating the rabbits, the monkey, or even the dog, when by accident, or through affection, they came in my way. But my disease grew upon me—for what disease is like Alcohol!—and at length even Pluto, who was now becoming old, and consequently somewhat peevish—even Pluto began to experience the effects of my ill temper.

One night, returning home, much intoxicated, from one of my haunts about town, I fancied that the cat avoided my presence. I seized him; when, in his fright at my violence, he inflicted a slight wound upon my hand with his teeth. The fury of a demon instantly possessed me. I knew myself no longer. My original soul seemed, at once, to take its flight from my body; and a more than fiendish malevolence, gin-nurtured, thrilled every fibre of my frame. I took from my waistcoat-pocket a penknife, opened it, grasped the poor beast by the throat, and deliberately cut one of its eyes from the socket! I blush, I burn, I shudder, while I pen the damnable atrocity.

When reason returned with the morning—when I had slept off the fumes of the night's debauch—I experienced a sentiment half of horror, half of remorse, for the crime of which I had been guilty; but it was, at best, a feeble and equivocal feeling, and the soul remained untouched. I again plunged into excess, and soon drowned in wine all memory of the deed.

In the meantime the cat slowly recovered. The socket of the lost eye presented, it is true, a frightful appearance, but he no longer appeared to suffer any pain. He went about the house as usual, but, as might be expected, fled in extreme terror at my approach. I had so much of my old heart left, as to be at first grieved by this evident dislike on the part of a creature which had once so loved me. But this feeling soon gave place to irritation. And then came, as if to my final and irrevocable overthrow, the spirit of PERVERSENESS. Of this spirit philosophy takes no account. Yet I am not more sure that my soul lives, than I am that perverseness is one of the primitive impulses of the human heart—one of the indivisible primary faculties, or sentiments, which give direction to the character of Man. Who has not, a hundred times, found himself committing a vile or a silly action, for no other reason than because he knows he should *not*? Have we not a perpetual inclination, in the teeth of our best judgment, to violate that which is *Law*, merely because we understand it to be such? This spirit of perverseness, I say, came to my final overthrow. It was this unfathomable longing of the soul *to vex itself*—to offer violence to its own nature—to do wrong for the wrong's sake only—that urged me to continue and finally to consummate the injury I had inflicted upon the unoffending brute. One morning, in cool blood, I slipped a noose about its neck and hung it to the limb of a tree;—hung it with the tears streaming from my eyes, and with the bitterest remorse at my heart;—hung it *because* I knew that it had loved me, and *because* I felt it had given me no reason of offence;—hung it *because* I knew that in so doing I was committing a sin—a deadly sin that would so jeopardize my immortal soul as to place it—if such a thing were possible—even beyond the reach of the infinite mercy of the Most Merciful and Most Terrible God.

On the night of the day on which this cruel deed was done, I was aroused from sleep by the cry of fire. The curtains of my bed were in flames. The whole house was blazing. It was with great difficulty that my wife, a servant, and myself, made our escape from the conflagration. The destruction was complete. My entire worldly wealth was swallowed up, and I resigned myself thenceforward to despair.

I am above the weakness of seeking to establish a sequence of cause and effect, between the disaster and the atrocity. But I am detailing a chain of facts—and wish not to leave even a possible link imperfect. On the day succeeding the fire, I visited the ruins. The walls, with one exception, had fallen in. This exception was found in a compartment wall, not very thick, which stood about the middle of the house, and against which had rested the head of my bed. The plastering had here, in great measure, resisted the action of the fire—a fact which I attributed to its having been recently spread. About this wall a dense crowd were collected, and many persons seemed to be examining a particular portion of it with very minute and eager attention. The words "strange!" "singular!" and other similar expressions, excited my curiosity. I approached and saw, as if graven in *bas relief* upon the white surface, the figure of a gigantic *cat*. The impression was given with an accuracy truly marvellous. There was a rope about the animal's neck.

When I first beheld this apparition—for I could scarcely regard it as less—my wonder and my terror were extreme. But at length reflection came to my aid. The cat, I remembered, had been hung in a garden adjacent to the house. Upon the alarm of fire, this garden had been immediately filled by the crowd—by some one of whom the animal must have been cut from the tree and thrown, through an open window, into my chamber. This had probably been done with the view of arousing me from sleep. The falling of other walls had compressed the victim of my cruelty into the substance of the freshly-spread plaster; the lime of which, with the flames, and the *ammonia* from the carcass, had then accomplished the portraiture as I saw it.

Although I thus readily accounted to my reason, if not altogether to my conscience, for the startling fact just detailed, it did not the less fail to make a deep impression upon my fancy. For months I could not rid myself of the phantasm of the cat; and, during this period, there came back into my spirit a half-sentiment that seemed, but was not, remorse. I went so far as to regret the loss of the animal, and to look about me, among the vile haunts which I now habitually frequented, for another pet of the same species, and of somewhat similar appearance, with which to supply its place.

One night as I sat, half stupified, in a den of more than infamy, my attention was suddenly drawn to some black object, reposing upon the head of one of the immense hogsheads of Gin, or of Rum, which constituted the chief furniture of the apartment. I had been looking steadily at the top of this hogshead for some minutes, and what now caused me surprise was the fact that I had not sooner perceived the object thereupon. I approached it, and touched it with my hand. It was a black cat—a very large one—fully as large as Pluto, and closely resembling him in every respect but one. Pluto had not a white hair upon any portion of his body; but this cat had a large, although indefinite splotch of white, covering nearly the whole region of the breast.

Upon my touching him, he immediately arose, purred loudly, rubbed against my hand, and appeared delighted with my notice. This, then, was the very creature of which I was in search. I at once offered to purchase it of the landlord; but this person made no claim to it—knew nothing of it—had never seen it before.

I continued my caresses, and, when I prepared to go home, the animal evinced a disposition to accompany me. I permitted it to do so; occasionally stooping and patting it as I proceeded. When it reached the house it domesticated itself at once, and became immediately a great favorite with my wife.

For my own part, I soon found a dislike to it arising within me. This was just the reverse of what I had anticipated; but—I know not how or why it was—its evident fondness for myself rather disgusted and annoyed. By slow degrees, these feelings of disgust and annoyance rose into the bitterness of hatred. I avoided the creature; a certain sense of shame, and the remembrance of my former deed of cruelty, preventing me from physically abusing it. I did not, for some weeks, strike, or otherwise violently ill use it; but gradually—very gradually—I came to look upon it with unutterable loathing, and to flee silently from its odious presence, as from the breath of a pestilence.

What added, no doubt, to my hatred of the beast, was the discovery, on the morning after I brought it home, that, like Pluto, it also had been deprived of one of its eyes. This circumstance, however, only endeared it to my wife, who, as I have already said, possessed, in a high degree, that humanity of feeling which had once been my distinguishing trait, and the source of many of my simplest and purest pleasures.

With my aversion to this cat, however, its partiality for myself seemed to increase. It followed my footsteps with a pertinacity which it would be difficult to make the reader comprehend. Whenever I sat, it would crouch beneath my chair, or spring upon my knees, covering me with its loathsome caresses. If I arose to walk it would get between my feet and thus nearly throw me down, or, fastening its long and sharp claws in my dress, clamber, in this manner, to my breast. At such times, although I longed to destroy it with a blow, I was yet withheld from so doing, partly by a memory of my former crime, but chiefly—let me confess it at once—by absolute *dread* of the beast.

This dread was not exactly a dread of physical evil—and yet I should be at a loss how otherwise to define it. I am almost ashamed to own—yes, even in this felon's cell, I am almost ashamed to own—that the terror and horror with which the animal inspired me, had been heightened by one of the merest chimæras it would be possible to conceive. My wife had called my attention, more than once, to the character of the mark of white hair, of which I have spoken, and which constituted the sole visible difference between the strange beast and the one I had destroyed. The reader will remember that this mark, although large, had been originally very indefinite; but, by slow degrees—degrees nearly imperceptible, and which for a long time my Reason struggled to reject as fanciful—it had, at length, assumed a rigorous distinctness of outline. It was now the representation of an object that I shudder to name—and for this, above all, I loathed, and dreaded, and would have rid myself of the monster *had I dared*—it was now, I say, the image of a hideous—of a ghastly thing—of the GALLOWS!—oh, mournful and terrible engine of Horror and of Crime—of Agony and of Death!

And now was I indeed wretched beyond the wretchedness of mere Humanity. And *a brute beast*—whose fellow I had contemptuously destroyed—*a brute beast* to work out for *me*—for me a man, fashioned in the image of the High God—so much of insufferable wo! Alas! neither by day nor by night knew I the blessing of Rest any more! During the former the creature left me no moment alone; and, in the latter, I started, hourly, from dreams of unutterable fear, to find the hot breath of *the thing* upon my face, and its vast weight—an incarnate Night-Mare that I had no power to shake off—incumbent eternally upon my *heart*!

Beneath the pressure of torments such as these, the feeble remnant of the good within me succumbed. Evil thoughts became my sole intimates—the darkest and most evil of thoughts. The moodiness of my usual temper increased to hatred of all things and of all mankind; while, from the sudden, frequent, and ungovernable outbursts of a fury to which I now blindly abandoned myself, my uncomplaining wife, alas! was the most usual and the most patient of sufferers.

One day she accompanied me, upon some household errand, into the cellar of the old building which our poverty compelled us to inhabit. The cat followed me down the steep stairs, and, nearly throwing me headlong, exasperated me to madness. Uplifting an axe, and forgetting, in my wrath, the childish dread which had hitherto stayed my hand, I aimed a blow at the animal which, of course, would have proved instantly fatal had it descended as I wished. But this blow was arrested by the hand of my wife. Goaded, by the interference, into a rage more than demoniacal, I withdrew my arm from her grasp and buried the axe in her brain. She fell dead upon the spot, without a groan.

This hideous murder accomplished, I set myself forthwith, and with entire deliberation, to the task of concealing the body. I knew that I could not remove it from the house, either by day or by night, without the risk of being observed by the neighbors. Many projects entered my mind. At one period I thought of cutting the corpse into minute fragments, and destroying them by fire. At another, I resolved to dig a grave for it in the floor of the cellar. Again, I deliberated about casting it in the well in the yard—about packing it in a box, as if merchandize, with the usual arrangements, and so getting a porter to take it from the house. Finally I hit upon what I considered a far better expedient than either of these. I determined to wall it up in the cellar—as the monks of the middle ages are recorded to have walled up their victims.

For a purpose such as this the cellar was well adapted. Its walls were loosely constructed, and had lately been plastered throughout with a rough plaster, which the dampness of the atmosphere had prevented from hardening. Moreover, in one of the walls was a projection, caused by a false chimney, or fireplace, that had been filled up, and made to resemble the rest of the cellar. I made no doubt that I could readily displace the bricks at this point, insert the corpse, and wall the whole up as before, so that no eye could detect anything suspicious.

And in this calculation I was not deceived. By means of a crow-bar I easily dislodged the bricks, and, having carefully deposited the body against the inner wall, I propped it in that position, while, with little trouble, I re-laid the whole structure as it originally stood. Having procured mortar, sand, and hair, with every possible precaution, I prepared a plaster which could not be distinguished from the old, and with this I very carefully went over the new brick-work. When I had finished, I felt satisfied that all was right. The wall did not present the slightest appearance of having been disturbed. The rubbish on the floor was picked up with the minutest care. I looked around triumphantly, and said to myself—"Here at least, then, my labor has not been in vain."

My next step was to look for the beast which had been the cause of so much wretchedness; for I had, at length, firmly resolved to put it to death. Had I been able to meet with it, at the moment, there could have been no doubt of its fate; but it appeared that the crafty animal had been alarmed at the violence of my previous anger, and forebore to present itself in my present mood. It is impossible to describe, or to imagine, the deep, the blissful sense of relief which the absence of the detested creature occasioned in my bosom. It did not make its appearance during the night—and thus for one night at least, since its introduction into the house, I soundly and tranquilly slept; aye, *slept* even with the burden of murder upon my soul!

The second and the third day passed, and still my tormentor came not. Once again I breathed as a freeman. The monster, in terror, had fled the premises forever! I should behold it no more! My happiness was supreme! The guilt of my dark deed disturbed me but little. Some few inquiries had been made, but these had been readily answered. Even a search had been instituted—but of course nothing was to be discovered. I looked upon my future felicity as secured.

Upon the fourth day of the assassination, a party of the police came, very unexpectedly, into the house, and proceeded again to make rigorous investigation of the premises. Secure, however, in the inscrutability of my place of concealment, I felt no embarrassment whatever. The officers bade me accompany them in their search. They left no nook or corner unexplored. At length, for the third or fourth time, they descended into the cellar. I quivered not in a muscle. My heart beat calmly as that of one who slumbers in innocence. I walked the cellar from end to end. I folded my arms upon my bosom, and roamed easily to and fro. The police were thoroughly satisfied and prepared to depart. The glee at my heart was too strong to be restrained. I burned to say if but one word, by way of triumph, and to render doubly sure their assurance of my guiltlessness.

"Gentlemen," I said at last, as the party ascended the steps, "I delight to have allayed your suspicions. I wish you all health, and a little more courtesy. By the bye, gentlemen, this—this is a very well constructed house." (In the rabid desire to say something easily, I scarcely knew what I uttered at all.)—"I may say an *excellently* well constructed house. These walls—are you going, gentlemen?—these walls are solidly put together;" and here, through the mere phrenzy of bravado, I rapped heavily, with a cane which I held in my hand, upon that very portion of the brick-work behind which stood the corpse of the wife of my bosom.

But may God shield and deliver me from the fangs of the Arch-Fiend! No sooner had the reverberation of my blows sunk into silence, than I was answered by a voice from within the tomb!—by a cry, at first muffled and broken, like the sobbing of a child, and then quickly swelling into one long, loud, and continuous scream, utterly anomalous and inhuman—a howl—a wailing shriek, half of horror and half of triumph, such as might have arisen only out of hell, conjointly from the throats of the dammed in their agony and of the demons that exult in the damnation.

Of my own thoughts it is folly to speak. Swooning, I staggered to the opposite wall. For one instant the party upon the stairs remained motionless, through extremity of terror and of awe. In the next, a dozen stout arms were toiling at the wall. It fell bodily. The corpse, already greatly decayed and clotted with gore, stood erect before the eyes of the spectators. Upon its head, with red extended mouth and solitary eye of fire, sat the hideous beast whose craft had seduced me into murder, and whose informing voice had consigned me to the hangman. I had walled the monster up within the tomb!

Ada

Gertrude Stein

Barnes Colhard did not say he would not do it but he did not do it. He did it and then he did not do it, he did not ever think about it. He just thought some time he might do something.

His father Mr. Abram Colhard spoke about it to every one and very many of them spoke to Barnes Colhard about it and he always listened to them.

Then Barnes fell in love with a very nice girl and she would not marry him. He cried then, his father Mr. Abram Colhard comforted him and they took a trip and Barnes promised he would do what his father wanted him to be doing. He did not do the thing, he thought he would do another thing, he did not do the other thing, his father Mr. Colhard did not want him to do the other thing. He really did not do anything then. When he was a good deal older he married a very rich girl. He had thought perhaps he would not propose to her but his sister wrote to him that it would be a good thing, He married the rich girl and she thought he was the most wonderful man and one who knew everything. Barnes never spent more than the income of the fortune he and his wife had then, that is to say they did not spend more than the income and this was a surprise to very many who knew about him and about his marrying the girl who had such a large fortune. He had a happy life while he was living and after he was dead his wife and children remembered him.

He had a sister who also was successful enough in being one being living, His sister was one who came to be happier than most people come to be in living. She came to be a completely happy one. She was twice as old as her brother. She had been a very good daughter to her mother. She and her mother had always told very pretty stories to each other Many old men loved to hear her tell these stories to her mother. Every one who ever knew her mother liked her mother. Many were sorry later that not every one liked the daughter. Many did like the daughter but not every one as every one had liked the mother.

The daughter was charming inside in her, it did not show outside in her to every one, it certainly did to some. She did sometimes think her mother would be pleased with a story that did not please her mother, when her mother later was sicker the daughter knew that there were some stories she could tell her that would not please her mother. Her mother died and really mostly altogether the mother and the daughter had told each other stories very happily together.

The daughter then kept house for her father and took care of her brother. There were many relations who lived with them. The daughter did not like them to live with them and she did not like them to die with them. The daughter, Ada they had called her after her grandmother who had delightful ways of smelling flowers and eating dates and sugar, did not like it at all then as she did not like so much dying and she did not like any of the living she was doing then. Every now and then some old gentlemen told delightful stories to her. Mostly then there were not nice stories told by any one then in her living. She told her father Mr. Abram Colhard that she did not like it at all being one being living then. He never said anything. She was afraid then, she was one needing charming stories and happy telling of them and not having that thing she was always trembling. Then every one who could live with them were dead and there were then the father and the son a young man then and the daughter coming to be that one then. Her grandfather had left some money to them each one of them. Ada said she was going to use it to go away from them.

Fugueur

MAUD CASEY

Albert Walks

When Albert walks, he is astonished. To keep from being afraid, he sometimes says to himself, *Fascinating!* Or, *Magnificent!* Or, *Yet another escapade!* Even when he is lost, he is not lost. No *one fine day he found himself in a public square.* No *it seems* or *it appears* or *not able to say how he got here.* He *is*, he *is*, he *is*. He is here: somewhere on the road to Portiers, Champigny, Meaux, Lonjumeau, Provins, Vitry-le-Francais, Chalons-sur-Marne, Chaumont, Vesoul, Macon.

The gentleman at the French consul in Dusseldorf gave him five marks; the one at the consul in Budapest gave him a fourth-class ticket to Vienna; the one in Leipzig gave him seven florins and a lodging ticket; the French ambassador in Prague took up a collection and gave him eight florins and a pair of shoes. When Albert walks, people treat him like a prince; they are that kind. Even the men who put him in prison—no passport, no livret, Albert is always without papers—have been gentle. *Yet another escapade and yet another escapade and yet another escapade!* The mayor of somewhere else entirely puts his arm around Albert's shoulder and says, "Now, go home to Bordeaux. There's nothing better than returning home." But to Albert, kicking a fallen apple through the tall grass of another cemetery of toppled, crowded gravestones, home is never more itself than when he is leaving.

When Albert walks, he is one of the new railway lines, cutting a path through the French countryside toward Paris. The earth's tremor fills his heels; it rumbles through his battered shoes and up his shins. He cuts a swath through the end of the century full of invention and endless possibility. He is the phonograph. When he walks, he is sound made visible to the human eye; he is the recording of Abraham Lincoln's voice on a piece of paper covered with lampblack. He is the telegraph.

What hath God wrought? Albert!

He annihilates distance like a bicycle—evolved from a mere toy, true, *le draisienne*, a hobbyhorse, but a cyclist is now referred to as *un marcheur qui roule*. Albert has no use for wheels but covers as much distance. When Albert walks, he is the steam engine, powering himself like a great ship. Still faster, he moves faster, faster than time. When Albert walks, he is twelve. He is thirteen. Years pass differently on the road. He is fifteen, sixteen, and then twenty, twenty-one, twenty-six. He is full of all of those Alberts. He is himself and himself and himself again.

He is the prince in the stories his father told him as a child: the prince who went out into the world. When he walks, the whole world, the heavens and the angels, are in his head. Even his lost father and mother and brother are there. When he walks, he is no longer only moving toward death; he is no longer only dying. The gift of life is in his bones. The birds in the sky above him are utterly bird, the shadows cast by leaves totally and completely shadow. Their beauty is indisputable. They *are*. They are *here*. He *is*. He *is here*. Ripe fruit falls to the ground at his feet, offering itself to him. From riverbeds comes the song of frogs. When Albert walks, he has been kissed. When he walks, his existence is complete and his body is divine; he is elemental like the sky drenched with sun, then infused with red dusk, then asleep with night, then sun-bright again. Albert walks seventy kilometers in a day without stopping, without eating, without sleeping, in order to feel that gift.

But when he stops, he doesn't remember where he's been. He doesn't remember that the gift exists. He doesn't remember that he was ever astonished at all.

Albert Observed (St. André Hospital, Bordeaux, 1886)

Albert feels as though he will disappear into the Doctor's eyes. *Fascinating! Magnificent! Yet another escapade!*

Perhaps because the Doctor suggests, "You are disappearing."

The Doctor's words drift out the window, floating up like the smoke from the factory chimneys, up with the sound of the church carillons. There is the far smell of wildflowers and the nearer smell of poultices. The iron rings of bed curtains rattle down the hall.

Albert will disappear—hypnotized into sleep—but before he does, the Doctor will look into Albert's eyes as if he knows everything about him, even the things that are gone: his father who died of a softening of the brain; his mother who died of pneumonia; his brother who died of meningitis; the woman who Albert wanted to marry but who refused to see him after he walked to Brive instead of meeting her at four o'clock for tea on that Saturday.

The Doctor's gaze says *Shhh. Listen*, his eyes say, I know everything you've forgotten. In the public gardens there are Spanish chestnut trees you loved to climb as a child though your mother didn't like it because the rats nested in the soft ground under the drooping branches. Listen, your brother shakes you from your first wandering trance when you were twelve, discovering you, and you discovering yourself, selling umbrellas for a salesman in a neighboring town though your father gave you money to go down the street to buy coke for the gas company.

"Not a very happy story, it seems," Albert says, forgetting that the Doctor isn't speaking out loud. "Still, thank you very much. Not being able to say how I got here, it is good to know all of this."

"Shhhh," the Doctor says, stroking the top of Albert's head. The Doctor's hand smells of pomade, cigars, sausage from his lunch. "Your eyelids are warm. They are getting warmer."

To make sure, Albert flutters them and there it is, the heat. The swirl of skin in the Doctor's fingertips on the top of Albert's head makes him pleasantly dizzy.

"Shhhh. You are sinking. You don't worry about anything anymore. You don't see anything. Your arms and legs are motionless. You are sleeping and you are nothing."

Albert tries to move his arms and legs and for the first time in fourteen years, since his journeys began, he can't. *Yet another escapade*, Albert thinks, but is careful not to say. He tries his best to be nothing so the Doctor will not move his swirling fingers. His warm eyelids flutter open despite themselves.

"Shhh, Albert, shhh." The Doctor's voice is steady and solid, like a tabletop that Albert would like to lay his head on. The Doctor's still, blue gaze continues to speak to Albert through his closed eyelids. Albert was once a gas fitter, like his father before him. He fitted the pipes and lit the lamps along the street and outside the shops. There is magic in gas, his father often said. *Shhh*, Albert, *shhh*. The spirit of coal was revealed after they tried everything else—olive oil, beeswax, fish oil, whale oil, sesame oil, nut oil. Public illumination, Albert! Turning night into day! Safer streets, longer factory hours. People read more, read better. Gas may be the reason for all that is good, his father would say, as if he had invented it.

A dropped basin clatters in the hallway. "Give me that," a nurse says irritably.

"Your eyes are very tired. Very, very tired. They've never been more tired. You are so very, very, very drowsy."

The Doctor's eyes speak Albert's ragged memory for him: It was like flight at first. His mother had forbidden it because of the scrambling screeching rats fighting over the fallen chestnuts. Still, the rats gave Albert's mother great pleasure. The fancy trees—recently planted, overrun by rodents—delighted her, a woman who took in knitting for extra money when her husband became sick and couldn't work. We are not a family getting fat off the triangular trade, she would remind Albert, whenever he asked for things. We do not own a sugar refinery built on the backs of others, she'd say and pinch his ear. But the leaves of the trees sparkled gold through the green when the gas lamps Albert's father had installed shone on them. They called to eight-year-old Albert despite his mother's warning that he would surely die from the bite of a filthy rat, and if he didn't die and she discovered he'd been climbing the trees, he would wish he'd only been bitten by a filthy rat.

The chestnuts rained down when he swung himself up into the spindly arms of the tree. He righted himself on a sturdy branch and looked out over the countryside, beyond Bordeaux, to places he'd never been before, to villages where the prince in his father's stories had seen prophetesses in trembling fits reveal secrets of the future, where wolves sucked the marrow from the delicate ankle bones of once plump children, howling for more. Albert looked up to the sky that went on and on, hovering over all of the oceans and distant lands the prince traveled in order, as his father told it, to witness the exact moment that darkness gave way to light.

"Very, very drowsy. So tired. And now you are asleep."

The lamplight in the hospital room flickers. Albert flickers too, and then he is asleep like he has never been asleep before. The Doctor's voice is the world and there is a sparkle in Albert's dark, forgotten heart, like the lit fuse of a gas lamp, illuminating blood and muscle.

"How old are you, Albert?"

"Twenty-nine? Inquiries could be made."

"Twenty-six."

"Ah! I am astonished to learn this, not even being able to say how I got here. Thank you very much. It is very useful to know my age."

Albert feels the prick, prick, prick of the doctor's pin along his jaw, a dream inside a dream. Across the bridge of his nose, prick, prick, prick, along one arm, and up the other. It disappears: *pric, pri, pr, p, p, p*. He wouldn't know the needle was through his tongue if the Doctor hadn't said, "Albert, the needle is through your tongue. Do you feel it?"

"Well, now that you've told me it's there."

Shhh.

"You are a good sleeper, Albert."

Shhh, Albert, shhh, and it's true, he is a good sleeper.

Shhh, he is thick with sleep and then he is walking again and he is astonished. The clouds float like reefs through the water of the sky. He walks and walks and the leaves he has used to stuff the holes in his shoes rustle.

There were days, before, that vanished into the woods between Bordeaux and Toulouse or splashed over the side of the boat into the deep black water between Marseille and Blidah or flittered away into the sky like the sparrows darting beside him between Geneva and Strasbourg—or was it between Vienna and Budapest? Albert walks into yesterday and finds his finger dipped in a honey pot in the foothills of the Pyrenees. The Pyrenees are magnificent! *Yet another escapade!*

Not being able to say how he got there, he is astonished, his finger in thick amber drawn by industrious bees from the nectar of tiny flowers pushed up through rough soil.

Somewhere in the sky, the birds and the Doctor's voice chirp together: You will stay in Bordeaux. You will keep your appointment with me tomorrow at eleven o'clock. Albert's numbed lips form the words: I will stay in Bordeaux. I will keep my appointment with you tomorrow at eleven o'clock.

How did he arrive in the Pyrenees? He found himself in a public square in Pau, no livret, no passport, always without papers. A well-scrubbed man with large, kind ears gave him a kilogram of bread and twenty sous and told him about the old women in the foothills who ran bony hands along the stones, searching for healing herbs so rare they only have names in Catalan.

"Where have you been that your shoes are so worn?" The man's large, kind ears wiggled when he spoke. "Have you come from Tours or Orleans?" Albert couldn't say. Inquiries might be made. There wasn't time to explain. Wiggle, wiggle went Albert's toes, through the rustling leaves, poking out the holes in his shoes. Wiggle, wiggle went the large, kind ears. They told Albert that the nectar of the tiny, defiant flowers contained an ancient cure, perhaps centuries old. Ancient cure was all Albert needed to hear.

"Why do you cry?"

"I fear that I will leave you, Doctor."

"Already? But you just got here. No need for tears yet."

"I feel the urge coming over me again. I would like to walk far, very far, but with someone to watch over me and bring me back."

"I am watching over you. You will stay in Bordeaux. You will come to see me tomorrow at eleven o'clock."

The surface of the Doctor's tabletop voice expands; Albert could lay his whole body on top of it if he needed to.

On each of the honey pots was written *les petits pharmiciens*. What luck to have discovered himself there! This was not a calamity. This was not an escapade. The Pyrenees are truly astonishing! Truly magnificent! Albert sucked his honeyed finger until it pruned and all traces of the magic sweetness were gone. I am here, Albert thought, and not there or there or there, but soon he would be somewhere else again.

He stirs in his sleep.

"I will not leave Bordeaux. I will come to see you tomorrow at eleven o'clock."

On that stony hill, his own sweet finger in his mouth, Albert thought, *This* is real. The sweetness in his mouth was real. The ache in his teeth was the hope for an ancient cure. That ache hurt more than the first sting of the bee that landed on his lip and then all the bees came, a whole swarm of them. He shouted as he ran—*Make me real!*—trampling the healing herbs he couldn't name.

And then he was here.

"Where are you?"

"I don't know."

"I will find you. I will bring you back."

"Ah, thank you," Albert says. "I'm very glad to hear that."

The Doctor blows gently on Albert's eye to wake him and Albert finds himself once again swirling underneath the Doctor's fingers. Horses clop down the narrow, piss-drenched streets. Another basin clatters in the hall. "Stop that," says the same irritable nurse. To Albert, it all seems quite beautiful.

The Medical Record

The Doctor has drawn a crude map of Albert's peregrinations: the line zigs and zags all over France, through much of the German Empire, along the route Albert took by cattle car from Warsaw to Moscow, where he exclaimed to the baffled Russian soldier who took him prisoner, "Siberia? Magnificent! I've never been," before being marched to Constantinople instead. The line meanders through East Rumelia, Bulgaria, Serbia, Austria-Hungary, and then home again to Bordeaux. His travels would be the envy of any Thomas Cook tourist. In Lyon, he saw the funicular railroad (*Magnificent!*). In Trappe de Staouel, he smelled the delicate fragrance of the rose water manufactured there wafting through the whole town (*Fantastic!*). Somewhere in between polishing copper pots on the ship The Moses, unloading cars of ore in Charleroi, and working in the coastal saltworks in the Midi, he had been to Kassel to the castle in which Napoleon II was once held prisoner (*Yet another escapade!*).

The Doctor connected the dots between the towns and showed Albert the map. "How curious," Albert replied.

On the first page of the Doctor's notebook: *It is difficult to know whether someone is telling the truth in professing oblivion.* Between the first and second page, he slides the note (*I think he is off his rocker*) pinned to Albert by someone trying to be helpful. On the second page, the Doctor writes: *The word travel derives from a Latin word for a three-pronged stake used as an instrument of torture.*

The Doctor knows that three-pronged stake. He has traveled a great distance himself. His mother died of a fever when he was a boy, but first her bedroom filled with unimaginable heat. He hated that his father didn't understand the heat rising off his mother or how to cool it, and he hated himself for hating his father. Even when his father thrashed in the same hot bed a year later, there were particles of hatred in the boy as the smallpox blisters became sheets of their own, pulling the outer layers of skin from his father until he was no longer his father but any body unraveling.

The incompetent country doctor—his unbuttoned cuffs flapping frantically as he leached his father until it seemed there was no more blood left to take—wouldn't let him in the room so he left his home forever. He never knew when his father died exactly. To this day, he feels sure he could have saved them both, his mother and his father, if only they'd waited to get sick until he became a doctor. But first there were the long nights in the Toulouse railway station as a bookkeeper's clerk, and then longer days as a delivery man—carrying heavy chandeliers through streets jammed with basket-carrying kitchen maids and merchants—while going to school at night, then hopping aboard the *Niger* to become a cargo clerk on the Bordeaux-Senegal run. It was there the ship's doctor saw in him what he couldn't yet see in himself: the Doctor. He quickly returned home to take a job as under-librarian for the medical faculty while completing his *baccalaureat* in the sciences. And then, after anatomy, botany, and hygiene, he found himself on this ward and in walked this man, weeping not because he was exhausted from walking seventy kilometers a day without food or rest but because he couldn't prevent himself from doing it again.

I am not real. Make me real. This is Albert's whispered refrain in response to the Doctor's own gentle whisper. In regular sleep, the sleeper dreams alone; in sleep by suggestion the sleeper and the doctor dream together. These are wondrous times: the train, the telephone, the steam engine, the Lumière brothers, the bicycle. The bicycle! The Doctor is the first doctor for the biking team of Bordeaux. He is astounded by the elegance of this supple machine, in awe of the unlikely communion of man and metal, the way the bicycle was almost perfectly evolved from the moment of its birth. And still, in the midst of all of this technological progress, what is most astonishing—*astonishing!*—is the progress in the realm of the mind. *Turning night into day*, Albert mumbled during their session. Albert's mind is a dark street and the Doctor is lighting the lamps, one by one.

Albert Walks

Before Albert walks, his body is all urgency. He must drink water—six, maybe ten, glasses of water in a row. He sweats and he trembles. There is an itch in his feet that finds its way up his legs and then into his cock, which he prefers to refer to as his beautiful instrument. He is compelled to play his beautiful instrument. Always gently at first, as if he is greeting it—hello, *yet another escapade!*— the buzz of *les petits pharmiciens* in his legs, hips, and groin, he achieves a steady cadence, holding the buzz inside, keeping it there as long as he can until the song reaches its crescendo. Sometimes he crescendos six, maybe ten, times in a day.

The urgency in his body is a question. It demands an answer when he wakes up along the road, forcing him to respond before he can continue. He has discovered himself crescendoing in the woods beside desolate roads, clouds casting purple shadows on the trees that make shapes—a hat, a bear; crescendoing behind the black blots of fir-woods near a stone cattle track, the wind carrying dust from a farmer's plough nearby, the thick necks of oxen fixed to their yoke; crescendoing in the dark marshy open, all of nature invaded by a fog and then, finally, he too is erased.

When he was kicked out of Russia, mistaken for an anarchist who had attempted to assassinate the czar, a lovely Gypsy girl cuddled him as they were marched to Constantinople. She rolled on top of him, but all he wanted, despite her loveliness, even as his beautiful instrument put up a fight, was to be alone. He is twenty-six years old and he has never had sex. It is not the pleasure of union and oblivion he wants but the relief of knowing he exists. And besides, he knows best how to play his beautiful instrument. Why would he need any help? It is a song he knows by heart.

It's the silence lurking after the song that he fears. Even as he plays, he dreads sticky hands and that silence. There are days when the sky is smeared with charcoal clouds that darken the whole world and Albert too: harbingers of nothing, reminders that every night the black sky will obliterate even the ominous smears. But when Albert walks, his body's singing keeps him company and his sadness lifts into the air to become part of the clouds, eventually raining back down on him transformed, spilling from the branches of poplars turned pale gold when winter's coming.

Albert walks and walks and he is astonished. Albert cannot walk enough.

The Medical Record

On page three, the Baudelaire that came to the Doctor as he and Albert dreamed together: *"Most of the children want more than anything to see the soul.... The child turns his toy over and over, he scratches it, shakes it, knocks it against the wall, dashes it on the ground...finally he pries it partly open for he is the stronger. But where is the soul?"*

The Doctor swears this is not him. He is not a child playing with toys. He swears he will be careful.

Soon, when Albert becomes known throughout Europe as *the Doctor's voyager*, the Doctor will do things he swore he would never do: You are drowsy, Albert. You are tired. You are very, very sleepy. Your left knee will represent Virtue, Albert. Your right knee, Vice.

The photographer will render Albert in light and shadow as the Doctor touches Albert's left knee and Albert picks up an empty glass on the table and drinks as if there is water and he is parched, as if he will never get enough to drink. He will drink and drink until he falls to the ground. When the Doctor touches Albert's right knee, the blood will rush to Albert's face, he will put his hands down his pants and fall to the ground again, rubbing and writhing. *My beautiful instrument! Mon petit phar-*

micien! Afterwards, he will be despondent. He will seem almost to have died. The Doctor will wonder: What happens if he presses both the left knee and the right knee? Albert will put one hand down his trousers and with the other he will pick up the empty glass and pretend to drink. Instead of blowing on Albert's eyelids, the Doctor will clap his hand sharply to wake him. Studying the pictures later, he will think in amazement: Such a range of facial expressions! It is possible to watch Virtue and Vice write themselves on Albert's body. The series of photographs reveal psychic manifestations, the formation of an idea and then the idea put into action. The Doctor will note that this transformation takes precisely thirty-seven seconds. The three-second delays during which the photographer changed the plates will be imperceptible as if Albert knew how to hold the poses just long enough.

But where is the soul? The question will drift through the Doctor's mind the morning after that session, but he won't recognize it until weeks after the experiment when Albert is back on the road and the Doctor has gone for a walk outside the hospital to breathe air that isn't sick. He'll find himself pressing his face against the cool stones of the cathedral whose shadow looms over the squatting hospital. *I am not real. Make me real.* The Doctor will hear Albert's words as the glow of candles illuminates Jesus on the road to Cavalry. In a dark corner, inhaling the incense of the altar, the Doctor will wish fleetingly that he were a man of the church and not a man of science so that the answer would simply be God. In the Middle Ages, the hospital was a stop on the pilgrimage route to the tomb of St. Jacques and the Doctor wonders if, then, Albert's wanderings might have been mistaken for an effort to better his soul.

Now, the Doctor assures himself he is not interested in the theatrics of the Tuesday Lessons held by the great doctor in Paris, as much a performer as he is a man of medicine. So bold he recently diagnosed a man in a woodcut from the eighteenth century (all the signs of an hysteric, the contracture of the face, the fearful eyes). Albert would not be one of the great doctor's hysterics, who, the great doctor has boasted, are each as recognizable, as predictable, as the back of his own hand.

Diagnoses are stories and Albert is his own story, the Doctor thinks with pride. The first of his kind. Wasn't it the great doctor himself who said that the most difficult thing, the most rarely accomplished feat, even for wide-awake men in medicine, was to look beyond what has already been seen?

The Prince Who Went Out into The World

Every night when Albert was a boy, he watched as his father steadied a fellow lamp lighter's ladder as he lit their street. The lamp lighter and his father both worked for the gas company and Albert listened, waiting, as they talked about the most recent article in *Plumber and Decorator*—"How Water Works," "House Drainage," "Geometry for Plumbers." "I'm going to read that article to Albert tonight," his father would always say, but it was a joke Albert knew by heart.

It was the last step in the ritual before his father settled in to tell him stories of the prince who went out into the world. The prince spoke to magic toads and performed tasks in order to woo beautiful girls who were secretly princesses and possessed all the land in the world and all the riches. The stories about the prince were tales of happily ever after, tales of love, power, and riches. The wicked were punished, revenge and cruelty were a means to a moral end, and fathers and mothers and brothers became ill and died only for a purpose.

Even then, Albert was less interested in the arrival. "Tell me about the long journey the prince had to make," he would say to his father. And his father would add more hills, more dales, more rivers to cross, more forests in which to become lost. Albert loved especially the moments when it became dark, too dark to see, and the journeying prince would light a candle and something would be revealed—the most beautiful face in the world or a hideous poisonous toad. The light was the most magic of all. "And imagine what he would have discovered if he'd had gaslight," his father would say.

The Medical Record

Fugue means flight, the Doctor thinks. The name for Albert will go in the medical record; it will find its way into the annals of psychiatry; it will endure along with the steam engine, the train, the cinema, the phonograph, the bicycle.

On page four, he writes: *Someone comes...someone to whom one wants to give everything, to whom one would willingly sacrifice life itself. There's no need for words—people just find one another—they have glimpsed each other in dreams.*

It is a passage from Madame Bovary. Then the Doctor remembers: this is Rodolphe speaking. Still, thinking of Albert, the Doctor, too, is dazzled.

Albert Walks

Over hill, over dale, crossing rivers, Albert walks, astonished. *Il revient, il revient, il revient,* sings the Garonne, the Gulf of Lyons, the Rhone, the Tarn. The earth's heart rumbles through Albert's rustling feet.

Each time Albert sets out, he looks back on the slated roofs of his home, never more his home than as it disappears behind him. Bordeaux is the size of his forearm, then a finger, then a fingernail. When Albert walks, that darting bird and then that one and then that one are the Doctor watching over him, making him real.

Author's Note: "Fugueur" was inspired by Mad Traveller *by Ian Hacking (University Press of Virginia, 1998), particularly the case notes (1886-1896) of Dr. Philippe Tissie in reference to Albert Dadas.*

Joe Blow

JENNIFER GROW

Larry and Roger live in this abandoned truck like kings, like they own the thing. They bounce on the springs and pass out against the windows while the whole cab gets smelly and fogged with their breath. They sit in the truck all day like they're at the drive-in, the matinee, unaffected by the movie of life. They watch the rest of us through the birdshit windshield and pass their bottle back and forth as casually as if they're sharing popcorn.

We ignore them mostly. We say, "Hey! Larry! Don't throw your bottles on the street!"

He shakes his head. "It wasn't me. Musta been one of those kids."

And we go, "Yeah, right."

But pretty soon, no more bottles on the street, they're in the back of the pick-up. We might mention the cigarette butts, too, but that doesn't change. Little brown and white filters all over the place, like confetti. The more important thing is the broken glass. So now that's O.K. No more flats. Larry and Roger understand the courtesy of this, even if their tires don't roll anywhere.

Instead, they sit behind a glass windshield and forget that we can see them. They watch the neighborhood like drunken sentinels. They wait for the mail lady, hope for their SSI checks, ward off stray dogs and the weather. When it's cold, they huddle in the cab of the truck, don't move, don't talk, tuck their hands under their armpits. "Winter is the bastard who beats his wife," we heard Larry mumble through the glass one day. Surprised, we looked up from the sidewalk. Did he really say that, or did he say something else? It's like the first line of a poem he never finished.

When spring comes and the air is warmer, Larry and Roger climb out of the truck and sit on the front stoop of Carl's rowhouse. The two men are like cats, the way they soak in the sun; cats, except for the preening. Carl, the pill dealer, lets them sit there while he obsessively polishes his car. Every day, it seems, he's out there waxing and polishing his orange GTO with the talking alarm. Then he revs the engine the way another man would flex his muscles. Tina, the pill dealer's daughter, is as thin as a butterfly and flits in circles as she talks to Larry and plays games. "What's the capital of Kansas?" she asks.

"Kansas City," Larry answers. It's amazing what he knows. Tina is not afraid of Larry, of how he looks or smells, or the pee stains underneath him on the steps where he sits. Tina is used to Larry. All the years of her life he has lived outside on her street. She knows him like she knows her dog. Loves them in the same way.

Tina's father, Carl the pill dealer, jokes with Larry and Roger, buys them sodas every so often, or fries. We've seen him bend over a boat of French fries on Roger's lap and squirt ketchup because Roger's hands are too shaky to handle the packets. Carl, the pill dealer, goes, "Now share," and leaves Tina on the steps with Roger and Larry, who are like her uncle and grandfather, sort of.

Tina hops in a square and asks them questions. "What color am I thinking of?" she quizzes them.

"White."

"What?" she squeals. "That's not it!"

Sometimes, their conversations are more searching. We've seen her look to the sky and point, and Larry nods, he points, too. He's explaining something to her. The birds? The clouds? God knows what.

No one asks questions when Carl comes home a few hours later with a bandage on his ear. Sometimes he's got a big white bandage on the side of his head like an East Baltimore Van Gogh. One who'd cut off his ear for the obsessive love of his car, the anguish of birdshit on his polished hood. But we all know Carl gets bandages because someone has punched him in his bad ear again.

"Don't lean on my car!" Carl warns Larry and Roger when they stumble across the street to sleep in their truck for the night.

Other days we've seen some of the neighborhood boys standing outside of Larry and Roger's truck, calling them names and throwing tiny pebbles and handfuls of dirt at the truck.

"Cut it out, you little motherfuckers!" Larry yells at them. He would pick up stones to throw back at the kids, but he can't get out of the truck or bend over without falling on his head.

"They're throwing things at us," Larry says as we pass by. He says it like he's ten years old.

One more pebble the size of a grain of rice bounces off the truck.

"I'll whup your asses!" Larry yells, unable to defend himself in any other way. His eyes are red with the fury of another lost fight. The kids snicker.

"See what I mean?" Larry insists. "They started it."

Except for the kids, most everyone forgets to notice Larry and Roger. Their drunkenness is such a regular sight. It's like if you lived in a place with mountains in the background: everyday of seeing mountains, they wouldn't seem so large anymore, just ordinary, and pretty soon you'd forget to notice them. You'd become bored. That's how we get with the trash on the street. That's how we get with Larry and Roger.

Then Joe moves into the neighborhood and starts with the broom. Up and down both sides of the street, going everywhere with his trash can on wheels. Sweeping the sidewalk, the curb, trying to get every last one of those cigarette butts. Impossible, when those filters multiply as fast as they do. He ignores the dogs in the alley that bark and yap as he pushes his broom.

Soon, Joe starts pounding on his house. We find out he's a carpenter, a rehabber. Before he moved here, he renovated another house a few blocks away in Butcher's Hill, an old, tall German rowhouse on Pratt Street that had once belonged to a family of brewers. Which family? Which brewery? "At one time, this was the neighborhood for beer!" Joe says. He's read up on it, has a yellowed piece of paper that shows a picture of his former house as it looked in the nineteen-twenties. The caption reads, "F. Scott Fitzgerald was known to visit this home with other writers and thinkers." At every opportunity, Joe shows us his article. He unfolds his wallet and pulls the newsprint from its slot.

"Let me see," Larry calls out from the truck. The truck is parked in front of Joe's rowhouse where Larry and Roger can see and hear everything. Joe hesitates, then he walks halfway to the cab window and holds the article carefully out of Larry's reach.

"I can't read that. My eyes are wobbling," Larry complains. His eyes are usually some shade of bloodshot, broken vessels, glassy. Roger just nods. He's wearing a pair of boxy glaucoma sunglasses that he found on the street.

"It says F. Scott Fitzgerald used to visit the house where I lived," Joe tells them.

"Where's that?" Larry asks. "Across from that old lesbian bar?"

Roger laughs.

Joe eyeballs both of them, folds his paper in his wallet and turns toward the rest of us.

It's true. The neighborhood isn't grand anymore. The old homes with marble steps have been hacked into apartments. Across from the house that used to be Joe's, the house that used to welcome writers and thinkers, sits a sad, empty lesbian bar in a building that used to be something else. Everything around us used to be something else.

"That Fitzgerald was some alcoholic," Larry says with a sneer, as if he can hold Joe in the same contempt. An ambulance blows by, its siren blaring, and cuts off Larry's next sentence. His mouth moves, but we can't hear the words.

The next thing Joe does is fashion a long pole with a cutter at the end to snip the blue plastic bags from the trees. Snip snip, and down floats a bag like a long lost balloon. Joe stuffs the bag in a sack with the other bags he's collected, and off he goes with his pole to find more. It's like he's picking berries.

"It's a w-waste of t-t-time," the stuttering man dismisses Joe. The stuttering man lives with his mother who wants to move out of Baltimore; she's put her house up for sale, but so far, no luck. "The trash just b-bl-blows in again," the stuttering man says while Joe balances his aluminum pole in the air. He's concentrating on a knotted bag near the top of the Linden tree. The stuttering man shakes his head like he can't believe his eyes. He doesn't like Joe, but he lets him sweep in front of his mother's house, cut down bags. "A little more to the l-left," he directs from his screen door.

"To the right!" Larry rolls down his window and yells from the truck.

The stuttering man doesn't like Larry or Roger, either. He glares at them. "To the l-left," he insists.

Roger doesn't have an opinion. He's pressed in the corner of the truck, boxed in by his giant sunglasses and his bright orange cap. It's like he's trying to hide from our sight, hide from Joe. Roger forgets his cap is so loud orange. His cap is louder than he is.

But Larry talks to everyone. He's made friends with the mail lady. He calls her Babycakes. "How're you doin', Babycakes?" he asks. The mail lady is friendly, but not too good with the house numbers. She keeps a pint in her bag and stops to take a little nip with Larry almost every morning. She pours some in a cup for him, and they say, "Cheers." "Gotta go now, Larry. Look at all this mail. My feet are killing me," she says, "and it's only nine o'clock in the morning."

"Tell me about it," Larry starts. Larry's got stories about his feet. They puff out of his boots. It's not just Larry's drunkenness that keeps him from walking straight. His feet are swollen, which, according to the street doctors, is a bad sign. Bad like drawing the wrong upside-down card from the fortune teller, something that means death. It's a hush, though, no one will say it out loud.

Somebody gave Larry crutches as an answer. He might as well be walking on stilts for as clumsy as he is. There's a skinny guy in a bandana who sometimes helps Larry cross the street to the liquor store. The bandana guy helps Roger, too, who doesn't have foot problems, except when he's too drunk to walk. We've seen this from the window: the bandana guy steadies them, one at a time, his arm tight around the waist like he's strolling with his granny. Two drunk, weak, stumbling Grandmas, one named Larry, one named Roger. The bandana guy is as gentle as he's ever going to get when he tucks the drunks into their cab to pass out. Because, other than that, he spends a great deal of time shouting with his girlfriend.

"You're an idiot!"

"I hate you!" every Saturday night.

Dogs bark in the alley. Somebody blares rap from his car stereo till the base line vibrates the windows.

Meanwhile, Joe builds flower boxes and starts calling the cops.

The police get to know Larry and Roger on a first-name basis. When the squad car drives up, the cops nod to Larry and Roger, tell them to move on. "Move on," they say over the bullhorn like they're talking to a crowd. "No loitering." Larry makes like he's reaching for his crutches, pretends he's going to stand, and stalls long enough for the squad car to roll away.

A couple of hours later, Joe might call the cops again. The cops drive by, make sure Larry stands all the way up this time; maybe they watch him struggle a few yards on his crutches before they leave. Then Larry sits down and there goes Joe, again, on the phone dialing 911. Three or four times a day. It's not long before everyone involved is annoyed. After a while of this, weeks, months, Larry and Roger stay in the truck. The cops can't cite them when they're inside a vehicle. So they sweat out the summer with the windows rolled down. They wait until Joe leaves for works so they can sit outside and grab a breeze.

Linda, our neighbor down the block, goes, "I never thought of it as loitering before. Larry and Roger are just out here, like the lamp post, like the stop light. I never thought of it as loitering. Roger's parents live around the corner, Larry's wife used to be here. That's not loitering." Linda works for a wholesale place and gives Larry and Roger apples and old produce, which they have a hard time chewing.

But Joe is determined. "Yeah, it's loitering! Let them go around the corner to Roger's house, let them go somewhere else!" he says. He protests not to Linda, but to all of us, to the air.

"Roger's parents don't want him," Linda explains. This is common knowledge, but Joe shakes his head anyway.

Joe is divorced, and the women in the neighborhood can't understand why, as handy as he is, and fully employed. But the men can see the problem clearly: Joe makes all of us look bad; he can't leave well enough alone. His business cards read, "Joe Blozman Home Improvement," like it's part of his name. "Joe Blow," a few people say, not to his face.

"Joe's a renovator," Carl tells us, snidely. "Let him rehab his own life, leave the rest of us out of it." Carl, the pill dealer, is uncomfortable with so many uniforms frequenting the neighborhood.

"They can't stay here like that," Joe insists. We look across the street to where they're sitting, Larry and Roger, propping each other up, both of them bruised with bloody lips from their fight last night over the last drops of the bottle. We've seen it happen plenty of times: Roger is an angry drunk and bigger, so he pushes Larry out of the truck or off the stoop where they're sitting, and Larry can't walk, he falls over like a sack of potatoes, scraping his face on the sidewalk. But the want of vodka can make him abnormally strong. A force wells up in him like a mother rescuing her child. And pretty soon, Larry will pull himself up, bad feet and all, and stumble over to Roger and clobber him in the head. Then they start punching and yelling. "Fuck! Fuck! Fucker!" back and forth, slurring their words, spitting out blood, coughing, until Larry can't move and passes out in a heap. But Roger, drunk as he is, will stumble around the corner to beg another bottle.

The next day, they might sit on opposite sides of the street and not talk. Or one of them will stay inside the truck, the other outside. It's like a domestic dispute, which most of us stay out of, won't call the cops when there's so much yelling between a man and his wife.

Maybe the mail lady will come by and share a nip with Larry while he recounts his grievances, how he's angry and proud. He'll sit like a king on a throne, and maybe pee stains will grow beneath him on the cement steps while he pretends he doesn't notice.

Roger doesn't say a word, just tucks his head under that orange hunting cap as if no one can see him. His shame is so big, he'd like to hide from it. And still, once a month, he sneaks home, back into his mother's heart, begging for some money or some food. When he slips through the alley, the dogs in the neighborhood bark. They jump against their chain link fences and growl.

Soon enough, Roger stumbles across the street, again to sit beside Larry. He doesn't make a sound while Larry holds court with Carl or the bandana man. "I'm fifty-three years old today!" he slurs like he's got mush in his mouth. Roger smiles. We've heard this before; Larry celebrates his fifty-third birthday often.

"I didn't know what else to do," he explains. "I don't have any family. Just this knucklehead," and he elbows Roger who is struggling to keep himself balanced. "All I want is a Pretty Girl and a Million Bucks," Larry muses to no one in particular. "Even if I lost them, I could say I had them once."

Carl snorts at the idea, but the bandana man nods. Roger takes a swig from the bottle. Larry drops his head and looks at the cement. Latin music is broadcast out a window from somebody's radio. "Turn it down!" the bandana man yells. Everyone is quiet a minute while Larry thinks.

"There's something else I want, but I can't remember what it is."

***

The other thing that happens: Joe calls the city about having the abandoned truck towed.

First, the cops stick a couple of tickets on the windshield every few days. The tickets collect under the folded arms of the windshield wipers. They flap in the breeze, get soggy with rain, are ignored. It's September, the color of the sun has changed, the leaves are dark, dark green. Larry and Roger haven't noticed.

Then, maybe a month later, a tow truck pulls up. It makes noise as it idles and the radio plays. Yellow lights spin in a circle on top of the truck. A man in a clean t-shirt climbs on the bed of the tow truck. He lowers some chains and cables that clank on the pavement. He jumps down, bends on one knee and looks underneath Larry and Roger's truck, inspects it, pulls on something. Then he jumps back into the tow truck for the controls. He grinds gears. The platform lowers at a tilt.

Larry and Roger are across the street soaking in the last rays of Indian Summer. They've got their wine goggles on and can't see straight, can't see clearly to the other side of the block.

"Hey, isn't that your truck?" somebody says as they pass by. "Are they taking your truck?"

"What?" Larry says.

Roger puffs up.

Somebody's dog barks from a window, scratches at the glass.

Joe opens his front door and watches the tow truck from his stoop. The stuttering man opens his screen door and watches, too.

"Hey!" Larry yells. He struggles to find his crutches, leans heavily on them but cannot pull himself up.

"Hey!" Roger echoes. "Hey, you!" Roger is having foot problems because he is too drunk.

"Hey, you! Get off!" Larry yells.

We open our windows at all the commotion, lean outside to watch. The tow truck man has already linked cables. Larry and Roger's truck slowly rises.

"You're doing fine," Joe says to the tow truck man. But the tow truck man doesn't hear, or pretends he doesn't hear. He's got a clipboard with paperwork that he checks off as the abandoned truck tilts and rolls toward the bed.

"I'm telling you to get off!" Larry yells. He is up and wobbling on his crutches, trying to pitch himself forward in a walk.

"Motherfucker, get off our truck!" Roger yells. This might be the first full sentence we've heard Roger say in a long time. He is up and stumbling, cannot walk in the direction of his voice. His feet stray in sideways directions.

"Do you want me to call the police?" Joe asks the tow truck man.

The tow truck man shakes his head.

"Stop it!" Roger screams. It's a high pitched wail, really. His vocal chords stretch with the effort. Tears are in his eyes. He grabs the trunk of the Linden tree and holds on for balance, holds on for life as if he is being swept away by a flash flood. He rubs his face against the bark, then starts banging his forehead. "Motherfucker!" he cries and hits the tree with his face. "Stop taking our truck!"

"Oh sh-shut up," the stuttering man dismisses him. No one hears the stuttering man except us.

Larry is quiet. Stooped over his crutches, he stands as straight as he ever will. He watches the tow truck pull away. "God help me," we think we hear him say. Did he say that, or did he say something else? We know this much: Larry is used to losing, has lost everything. So does he cry when his truck is towed? We can't tell. He just watches the tires roll down the street and stop when the truck reaches next red light. Larry waits. His bottle is firm in his hand.

But Roger is younger and furious at the injustice. Hysterical. He's fuming, and his face is red. Spit forms at the corner of his mouth. He's like a rabid dog attacking himself. "Joe, you sissy!" Roger yells and bangs his head into the tree. There are large welts on his face. Roger moves his foot to kick the tree and misses. He loses his balance but wraps both arms around the tree as he falls. He hugs the trunk like he's clinging to his mother's leg. He scrapes his cheek on the bark.

"Joe! You coward!" he yells. His anger, his own words, are all he has.

"He was only doing his job!" Joe yells back.

"You're a coward, Joe!" Roger insists. He's on the ground, throwing handfuls of dirt towards Joe's side of the street.

We shake our heads at the scene below. From our sidewalks and front doors and from our second floor windows, we see all. Like God, almost. There's Joe, there's Roger, opposite sides of the street, hating something about the other. And the tow truck man in the middle, waiting at the end of the block for the light to change green. We could spit on Larry if we wanted to. Hock a lugie on Joe. But when the light turns green, everyone, all of us, watch quietly as the tow truck makes a turn around the corner and drives out of sight. That's it.

Then all the squawking starts again, the circus of back and forth.

And this is the part when we get tired and pull our heads inside. "That's the cause and effect of it," we might say. We keep the windows open for a breeze, maybe prop it up with a stick or a ruler, an empty beer can.

"Shut up!"

"You shut up!" goes on outside.

All we know is, Joe Blow moves in across the street, goes everywhere with his broom and his trash can on wheels. The neighborhood eventually gets better, years later, but we don't know that yet.

Grey

LIA PURPURA

Here's the cathedral, its grey stone, the grey sky, and all the grey, after-rain mottled streets. And the sky is not a cathedral bell, but *also* grey, grey *alongside*, and the icy puddles are not mirrors of sky, though sky resides in bounded ways there. It is not a cathedral tune, this tone, but the way grey wind and grey stone cloud together. These greys make up the *right now* I am in, as does the sharp uncertainty of what to do with these suddenly free few hours and nowhere to be.

All the likenesses that would gather and lash it all up, that would make one thing partake of another, be as one, be the many-in-all: *no*. Here, beside my uncertainty (where to go, what to do), grey underwing, grey stone, ice, and silvery median grass—just stay, each unto yourself. As you're inclined: hover or seep. Crack, harrow or blow. Cruise low in a gust. Chip. Slick. Stay asleep.

I can tell you, in my uncertainty, I won't be tying it all together. I won't be conjuring the sound-cloud in a conch by listening to wind in grey branches. I won't be revising *"here's the grey weight of a cold afternoon"* to *"an afternoon, cold with the weight of grey noon...."* I want no grey, aortal side street contracting with old, fraught scenes, and no, not an absence reconstituted by cold. No snow-sky hardening its stare (and God, not *gunmetal* for that sky, which, really, how many have truly known, buffed to a shine, cleaned of oil and powder and not just wielded for hard, grey effect?) No *"greyly they pitched their way forward in cold"*—how it must have been in pioneer times, grey woolens, grey blankets and buffalo skins—into miles of snowblindness, the dimming-to-grey a relief from the glare, though it meant more snow coming: I do not mean to synchronize their grey anticipation with my grey anticipation.

In this singular moment I'll have no church bells chased to bird-call. No gravely beautiful sidewalk, ice-cracked, with its palette of greys embedded, upriding like headstones. No grey, choric wind-hum. No cloud-spire combo of greys rising up. No parable-like breadth to all this, containing, extending, enlarging by greys.

Just: now.

All the grey things like only themselves.

It's February in Baltimore, on Mount Royal Avenue. I've just dropped my son at his Saturday art class. It's almost snowing. Each grey thing in its time, in its place, stands just as it is.

Here's the cathedral.

And here I am, outside, giving thanks.

I'm starting by noting each singular grey thing.

By *thanks* I mean *I admit I know not what to do, where to go, with the all I've been given.*

Heart Rumors (from *Dinner at the Homesick Restaurant*)

ANNE TYLER

The first few times that Mrs. Scarlatti stayed in the hospital, Ezra had no trouble getting in to visit her. But the last time was harder. "Relative?" the nurse would ask.

"No, ah, I'm her business partner."

"Sorry, relatives only."

"But she doesn't have any relatives. I'm all she's got. See, she and I own this restaurant together."

"And what's that in the jar?"

"Her soup."

"Soup," said the nurse.

"I make this soup she likes."

"Mrs. Scarlatti isn't keeping things down."

"I know that, but I wanted to give her something."

This would earn him a slantwise glance, before he was led brusquely into Mrs. Scarlatti's room. In the past, she had chosen to stay in a ward. (She was an extremely social woman.) She'd sit up straight in her dramatic black robe, a batik scarf hiding her hair, and "Sweetie!" she'd say as he entered. For a moment the other women would grow all sly and alert, till they realized how young he was—way too young for Mrs. Scarlatti. But now she had a private room, and the most she could do when he arrived was open her eyes and then wearily close them. He wasn't even sure that he was welcome any more.

He knew that after he left, someone would discard his soup. But this was his special gizzard soup that she had always loved. There were twenty cloves of garlic in it. Mrs. Scarlatti used to claim it settled her stomach, soothed her nerves—changed her whole perception of the day, she said. (However, it wasn't on the restaurant's menu because it was a bit "hearty"—her word—and Scarlatti's Restaurant was very fine and formal. This hurt Ezra's feelings, a little.) When she was well enough to be home, he had often brewed single portions in the restaurant kitchen and carried them upstairs to her apartment. Even in the hospital, those first few times, she could manage a small-sized bowl of it. But now she was beyond that. He only brought the soup out of helplessness; he would have preferred to kneel by her bed and rest his head on her sheets, to take her hands in his and tell her, "Mrs. Scarlatti, come back." But she was such a no-nonsense woman; she would have looked shocked. All he could do was offer this soup.

He sat in a corner of the room in a green vinyl chair with steel arms. It was October and the steam heat had come on; the air felt sharp and dry. Mrs. Scarlatti's bed was cranked upward slightly to help her breathe. From time to time, without opening her eyes, she said, "Oh, God." Then Ezra would ask, "What? What is it?" and she would sigh. (Or maybe that was the radiator.) Ezra never brought anything to read, and he never made conversation with the nurses who squeaked in and out on their rubber soles. He only sat, looking down at his pale, oversized hands, which lay loosely on his knees.

Previously, he had put on weight. He'd been nowhere near fat, but he'd softened and spread in that mild way that fair-haired men often do. Now the weight fell off. Like Mrs. Scarlatti, he was having trouble keeping things down. His large, floppy clothes covered a large, floppy frame that seemed oddly two-dimensional. Wide in front and wide behind, he was flat as paper when viewed from the side. His hair fell forward in a sheaf, like wheat. He didn't bother pushing it back.

He and Mrs. Scarlatti had been through a lot together, he would have said, if asked—but what, exactly? She had had a bad husband (a matter of luck, she made it seem, like a bad bottle of wine) and ditched him; she had lost her only son, Ezra's age, during the Korean War. But both these events she had suffered alone, before her partnership with Ezra began. And Ezra himself: well, he had not actually been through anything yet. He was twenty-five years old and still without wife or children, still living at home with his mother. What he and Mrs. Scarlatti had survived, it appeared, was year after year of standing still. Her life that had slid off somewhere in the past, his that kept delaying its arrival—they'd combined, they held each other up in empty space. Ezra was grateful to Mrs. Scarlatti for rescuing him from an aimless, careerless existence and teaching him all she knew; but more than that, for the fact that she depended on him. If not for her, whom would he have? His brother and sister were out in the world; he loved his mother dearly but there was something overemotional about her that kept him eternally wary. By other people's standards, even he and Mrs. Scarlatti would not have seemed particularly close. He always called her "Mrs. Scarlatti." She called Ezra her boy, her angel, but was otherwise remarkably distant, and asked no questions at all about his life outside the restaurant.

He knew the restaurant would be fully his when she died. She had told him so, just before this last hospital stay. "I don't want it," he had said. She was silent. She must have understood that it was only his manner of speaking. Of course he didn't want it, in the sense of coveting it (he never thought much about money), but what would he do otherwise? Anyway, she had no one else to leave it to. She lifted a hand and let it drop.

They didn't mention the subject again.

Once, Ezra persuaded his mother to come and visit too. He liked for the various people in his life to get along, although he knew that would be difficult in his mother's case. She spoke of Mrs. Scarlatti distrustfully, even jealously. "What you see in such a person I can't imagine. She's downright ...tough, is what she is, in spite of her high-fashion clothes. It looks like her face is not trying. Know what I mean? Like she can't be bothered putting out the effort. Not a bit of lipstick, and those crayony black lines around her eyes...and she hardly ever smiles at people."

But now that Mrs. Scarlatti was so sick, his mother kept her thoughts to herself. She dressed carefully for her visit and wore her netted hat, which made Ezra happy. He associated that hat with important family occasions. He was pleased that she'd chosen her Sunday black coat, even though it wasn't as warm as her everyday maroon.

In the hospital, she told Mrs. Scarlatti, "Why, you look the picture of health! No one would ever guess."

This was not true. But it was nice of her to say it.

"After I die," Mrs. Scarlatti said in her grainy voice, "Ezra must move to my apartment."

His mother said, "Now, let's have none of that silly talk."

"Which is silly?" Mrs. Scarlatti asked, but then she was overtaken by exhaustion, and she closed her eyes. Ezra's mother misunderstood. She must have thought she'd asked what was silly, a rhetorical question, and she blithely smoothed her skirt around her and said, "Total foolishness, I never heard such rot." Only Ezra grasped Mrs. Scarlatti's meaning. Which was silly, she was asking—her dying, or Ezra's moving? But he didn't bother explaining that to his mother.

Another time, he got special permission from the nurses' office to bring a few men from the restaurant—Todd Duckett, Josiah Payson, and

Raymond the sauce maker. He could tell that Mrs. Scarlatti was glad to see them, although it was an awkward visit. The men stood around the outer edges of the room and cleared their throats repeatedly and would not take seats. "Well?" said Mrs. Scarlatti. "Are you still buying everything fresh?" From the inappropriateness of the question (none of them was remotely involved with the purchasing), Ezra realized how out of touch she had grown. But these people, too, were tactful. Todd Duckett gave a mumbled cough and then said, "Yes, ma'am, just how you would've liked it."

"I'm tired now," Mrs. Scarlatti said.

Down the hall lay an emaciated woman in a coma, and an old, old man with a tiny wife who was allowed to sleep on a cot in his room, and a dark-skinned foreigner whose masses of visiting relatives gave the place the look of a gypsy circus. Ezra knew that the comatose woman had cancer, the old man a rare type of blood disease, and the foreigner some cardiac problem—it wasn't clear what. "Heart rumor," he was told by a dusky, exotic child who was surely too young to be visiting hospitals. She was standing outside the foreigner's door, delicately reeling in a yo-yo.

"Heart murmur, maybe?"

"No, rumor."

Ezra was starting to feel lonely here and would have liked to make a friend. The nurses were always sending him away while they did something mysterious to Mrs. Scarlatti, and much of any visit he spent leaning dejectedly against the wall outside her room or gazing from the windows of the conservatory at the end of the corridor. But no one seemed approachable. This wing was different from the others—more hushed—and all the people he encountered wore a withdrawn, forbidding look. Only the foreign child spoke to him. "I think he's going to die," she said. But then she went back to her yo-yo. Ezra hung around a while longer , but it was obvious she didn't find him very interesting.

Bibb lettuce, Boston lettuce, chicory, escarole, dripping on the counter in the center of the kitchen. While other restaurants' vegetables were delivered by anonymous, dank, garbage-smelling trucks, Scarlatti's had a man named Mr. Purdy, who shopped personally for them each morning before the sun came up. He brought everything to the kitchen in splintery bushel baskets, along about eight a.m., and Ezra made a point of being there so that he would know what foods he had to deal with that day.

Sometimes there were no eggplants, sometimes twice as many as planned. In periods like this—dead November, now—nothing grew locally, and Mr. Purdy had to resort to vegetables raised elsewhere, limp carrots and waxy cucumbers shipped in from out of state. And the tomatoes! They were a crime. "Just look," said Mr. Purdy, picking one up. "Vine-grown, the fellow tells me. Vine-grown, yes. I'd like to see them grown on anything else. 'But ripened?' I say. 'However was they ripened?' 'Vine-ripened, too,' fellow assures me. Well, maybe so. But nowadays, I don't know, all them taste anyhow like they spent six weeks on a windowsill. Like they was made of windowsill, or celluloid, or pencil erasers. Well, I tell you, Ezra: I apologize. It breaks my heart to bring you such rubbage as this here; I'd sooner not show up at all."

Mr. Purdy was a pinched and prunish man in overalls, a white shirt, and a shiny black suit coat. He had a narrow face that seemed eternally disapproving, even during the growing season. Only Ezra knew that inwardly, there was something nourishing and generous about him. Mr. Purdy rejoiced in food as much as Ezra did, and for the same reasons—less for eating himself than for serving to others. He had once invited Ezra to his home, a silver-colored trailer out on Ritchie Highway, and given him a meal consisting solely of new asparagus, which both he and Ezra agreed had the haunting taste of oysters. Mrs. Purdy, a smiling, round-faced woman in a wheelchair, had claimed they talked like lunatics, but she finished two large helpings while both men tenderly watched. It was a satisfaction to see how she polished her buttery plate.

"If this restaurant was just mine," Ezra said now, "I wouldn't serve tomatoes in the winter. People would ask for tomatoes and I'd say, 'What can you be thinking of, this is not the season.' I'd give them something better."

"They'd stomp out directly," Mr. Purdy said.

"No, they might surprise you. And I'd put up a blackboard, write on it every day just two or three good dishes. Of course! In France, they do that all the time. Or I'd offer no choice at all; examine people and say, 'You look a little tired. I'll bring you an oxtail stew'."

"Mrs. Scarlatti would just die," said Mr. Purdy.

There was a silence. He rubbed his bristly chin, and then corrected himself: "She'd rotate in her grave."

They stood around a while.

"I don't really want a restaurant anyhow," Ezra said.

"Sure," Mr. Purdy said. "I know that."

Then he put his black felt hat on, and thought a moment, and left.

The foreign child slept in the conservatory, her head resting on the stainless steel arm of a chair like the one in Mrs. Scarlatti's room. It made Ezra wince. He wanted to fold his coat and slide it beneath her cheek, but he worried that would wake her. He kept his distance, therefore, and stood at one of the windows gazing down on pedestrians far below. How small and determined their feet looked, emerging from their foreshortened figures! The perseverance of human beings suddenly amazed him.

A woman entered the room-one of the foreigners. She was lighter skinned than the others, but he knew she was foreign because of her slippers, which contrasted with her expensive wool dress. The whole family, he had noticed, changed into slippers as soon as they arrived each morning. They made themselves at home in every possible way—setting out bags of seeds and nuts and spicy-smelling foods, once even brewing a quart of yogurt on the conservatory radiator. The men smoked cigarettes in the hall, and the women murmured together while knitting brightly colored sweaters.

Now the woman approached the child, bent over her, and tucked her hair back. Then she lifted her in her arms and settled in the chair. The child didn't wake. She only nestled closer and sighed. So after all, Ezra could have put his coat beneath her head. He had missed an opportunity. It was like missing a train—or something more important, something that would never come again. There was no explanation for the grief that suddenly filled him.

He decided to start serving his gizzard soup in the restaurant. He had the waiters announce it to patrons when they handed over the menu. "In addition to the soups you see here, we are pleased to offer tonight..." One of the waiters had failed to show up and Ezra hired a woman to replace him—strictly against Mrs. Scarlatti's policy. (Waitresses, he said, belonged in truck stops.) The woman did much better than the men with Ezra's soup. "Try our gizzard soup," she would say. "It's really hot and garlicky and it's made with love." Outside it was bitter cold, and the woman was so warm and helpful, more and more people followed her suggestion. Ezra thought that the next time a waiter left, he would hire a second woman, and maybe another after that, and so on.

He experimented the following week with a spiced crab casserole of his own invention, and then with a spinach bisque, and when the waiters complained about all they had to memorize he finally went ahead and bought a blackboard. SPECIALS, he wrote at the top. But in the hospital, when Mrs. Scarlatti asked how things were going, he didn't mention any of this. Instead, he sat forward and clasped his hands tight and said, "Fine. Um ... fine." If she noticed anything strange in his voice, she didn't comment on it.

Mrs. Scarlatti had always been a lean, dark, slouching woman, with a faintly scornful manner. It was true, as Ezra's mother said, that she gave the impression of not caring what people thought of her. But that had been part of her charm—her sleepy eyes, hardly troubling to stay open, and her indifferent tone of voice. Now, she went too far. Her skin took on the pallid look of stone, and her face began to seem sphinxlike, all flat planes and straight lines. Even her hair was sphinxlike—a short, black wedge, a clump of hair, dulled and rough. Sometimes Ezra believed that she was not dying but petrifying. He had trouble remembering her low laugh, her casual arrogance. ("Sweetie," she used to say, ordering him off to some task, trilling languid fingers. "Angel boy…") He had never felt more than twelve years old around her, but now he was ancient, her parent or grandparent. He soothed and humored her. Not all she said was quite clear these days. "At least," she whispered once, "I never made myself ridiculous, Ezra, did I?"

"Ridiculous?" he asked.

"With you."

"With me? Of course not."

He was puzzled, and must have shown it; she smiled and rocked her head on the pillow. "Oh, you always were a much-loved child," she told him. It must have been a momentary wandering of the brain. (She hadn't known him as a child.) "You take it all for granted," she said. Maybe she was confusing him with Billy, her son. She turned her face away from him and closed her eyes. He felt suddenly anxious. He was reminded of that time his mother had nearly died, wounded by a misfired arrow—entirely Ezra's fault; Ezra, the family's rumbler. "I'm so sorry, I'm sorry, I'm sorry," he had cried, but the apology had never been accepted because his brother had been blamed instead, and his father, who had purchased the archery set. Ezra, his mother's favorite, had got off scot-free. He'd been left unforgiven—not relieved, as you might expect, but forever burdened.

"You're mistaken," he said now, and Mrs. Scarlatti's eyelids fluttered into crepe but failed to open. "I wish you'd get me straight. See who I am, I'm Ezra," he said, and then (for no logical reason) he bent close and said, "Mrs. Scarlatti. Remember when I left the army? Discharged for sleepwalking? Sent home? Mrs. Scarlatti, I wasn't really all the way asleep. I mean, I knew what I was doing. I didn't plan to sleepwalk, but part of me was conscious, and observed what was going on, and could have wakened the rest of me if I'd tried. I had this feeling like watching a dream, where you know you can break it off at any moment. But I didn't; I wanted to go home. I just wanted to leave that army, Mrs. Scarlatti. So I didn't stop myself." If she had heard (with her only son, Billy, blown to bits in Korea), she would have risen up, sick as she was, and shouted, "Out! Out of my life!" So she must have missed it, for she only rocked her head again and smiled and went on sleeping.

Just after Thanksgiving the woman who'd been in a coma died, and the tiny old man either died or went home, but the foreigner stayed on and his relatives continued to visit. Now that they knew Ezra by sight, they hailed him as he passed. "Come!" they would call and he would step in, shy and pleased, and stand around for several minutes with his fists locked in his armpits. The sick man was yellow and sunken, hooked to a number of tubes, but he always tried to smile at Ezra's entrance. Ezra had the impression that he knew no English. The others spoke English according to their ages—the child perfectly, the young adults with a strong, attractive accent, the old ones in ragged segments. Eventually, though, even the most fluent forgot themselves and drifted into their native language—a musical one, with rounded vowels that gave their lips a muscled, pouched, commiserative shape, as if they were perpetually tut-tutting. Ezra loved to listen. When you couldn't understand what people said, he thought, how clearly the links and joints in their relationships stood out! A woman's face lit and bloomed as she turned to a certain man; a barbed sound of pain leapt from the patient and his wife doubled over. The child, when upset, stroked her mother's gold wristwatch band for solace.

Once a young girl in braids sang a song with almost no tune. It wandered from note to note as if by accident. Then a man with a heavy black mustache recited what must have been a poem. He spoke so grandly and unselfconsciously that passersby glanced in, and when he had finished he translated it for Ezra."O dead one, why did you die in the springtime? You haven't yet tasted the squash, or the cucumber salad." Why, even their poetry touched matters close to Ezra's heart.

By December he had replaced three of the somber-suited waiters with cheery, motherly waitresses, and he'd scrapped the thick beige menus and started listing each day's dishes on the blackboard. This meant, of course, that the cooks all left (none of the dishes were theirs, or even their type), so he did most of the cooking himself, with the help of a woman from New Orleans and a Mexican. These two had recipes of their own as well, some of which Ezra had never tasted before; he was entranced. It was true that the customers seemed surprised, but they adjusted, Ezra thought. Or most of them did.

Now he grew feverish with new ideas, and woke in the night longing to share them with someone. Why not a restaurant full of refrigerators, where people came and chose the food they wanted? They could fix it themselves on a long, long stove lining one wall of the dining room. Or maybe he could install a giant fireplace, with a whole steer turning slowly on a spit. You'd slice what you liked onto your plate and sit around in arm chairs eating and talking with the guests at large. Then again, maybe he would start serving only street food. Of course! He'd cook what people felt homesick for—tacos like those from vendor's carts in California, which the Mexican was always pining after; and that wonderful vinegary North Carolina barbecue that Todd Duckett had to have brought by his mother several times a year in cardboard cups. He would call it the Homesick Restaurant. He'd take down the old black and gilt sign …

But then he saw the sign, SCARLATTI'S, and he groaned and pressed his fingers to his eyes and turned over in his bed.

"You have a beautiful country," the light-skinned woman said.

"Thank you," said Ezra.

"All that green! And so many birds. Last summer, before my father-in-law fell ill, we were renting a house in New Jersey. The Garden State, they call it. There were roses everywhere. We could sit on the lawn after supper and listen to the nightingales."

"The what?" said Ezra.

"The nightingales."

"Nightingales? In New Jersey?"

"Of course," she said. "Also we liked the shopping. In particular, Korvette's. My husband likes the…how do you say? Drip and dry suits."

The sick man moaned and tossed, nearly dislodging a tube that entered the back of his wrist. His wife, an ancient, papery lady, leaned toward him and stroked his hand. She murmured something, and then she turned to the younger woman. Ezra saw that she was crying. She didn't attempt to hide it but wept openly, tears streaming down her cheeks. "Ah," the younger woman said, and she left Ezra's side and bent over the wife. She gathered her up in her arms as she'd gathered the child earlier. Ezra knew he should leave, but he didn't. Instead he turned and gazed out the window, slightly tilting his head and looking nonchalant, as some men do when they have rung a doorbell and are standing on the porch, waiting to be noticed and invited in.

Ezra's sister, Jenny, sat at the desk in her old bedroom, reading a battered textbook. She was strikingly pretty, even in reading glasses and the no-color quilted bathrobe she always left on a closet hook for her visits home. Ezra stopped at her doorway and peered in. "Jenny?" he asked. "What are you doing here?"

"I thought I'd take a breather," she said. She removed her glasses and gave him a blurry, unfocused look.

"It isn't semester break yet, is it?"

"Semester break! Do you think medical students have time for such things?"

"No, well," he said.

But lately she'd been home more often than not, it appeared to him. And she never mentioned Harley, her husband. She hadn't referred to him once all fall, and maybe even all summer. "It's my opinion she's left him," Ezra's mother had said recently. "Oh, don't act so surprised! It must have crossed your mind. Here she suddenly moves to a new address—closer to the school, she claims—and then can't have us to visit, anytime I offer; always too busy or preparing for some quiz, and when I call, you notice, it's never Harley who answers, never once Harley who picks up the phone. Doesn't that strike you as odd? But I'm unable to broach the subject. I mean, she deflects me, if you know what I mean. Somehow I just never… you could, though. She always did feel closer to you than to me or Cody. Won't you just ask her what's what?"

But now when he lounged in the doorway, trying to find some way to sidle into a conversation, Jenny put her glasses back on and returned to her book. He felt dismissed. "Um," he said. "How are things in Paulham?"

"Fine," she said, eyes scanning the print.

"Harley all right?"

There was a deep, studious silence.

"It doesn't seem we ever get to see him anymore," Ezra said.

"He's okay," Jenny said.

She turned a page.

Ezra waited a while longer, and then he straightened up from the doorway and went downstairs. He found his mother in the kitchen, unpacking groceries. "Well?" she asked him.

"Well, what?"

"Did you talk to Jenny?"

"Ah..."

She still had her coat on; she thrust her hands in her pockets and faced him squarely, with her bun slipping down the back of her head. "You promised me," she told him. "You swore you'd talk to her."

"I didn't swear to, Mother."

"You took a solemn oath," she told him.

"I notice she still wears a ring," he said hopefully.

"So what," said his mother. She went back to her groceries.

"She wouldn't wear a ring if she and Harley were separated, would she?"

"She would if she wanted to fool us."

"Well, I don't know, if she wants to fool us maybe we ought to act fooled. I don't know."

"All my life," his mother said, "people have been trying to shut me out. Even my children. Especially my children. If I so much as ask that girl how she's been, she shies away like I'd inquired into the deepest, darkest part of her. Now, why should she be so standoffish?"

Ezra said, "Maybe she cares more about what you think than what outsiders think."

"Ha," said his mother. She lifted a carton of eggs from the grocery bag.

"I'm worried I don't know how to get in touch with people," Ezra said.

"Hmm?"

"I'm worried if I come too close, they'll say I'm overstepping. They'll say I'm pushy, or… emotional, you know. But if I back off, they might think I don't care. I really, honestly believe I missed some rule that everyone else takes for granted; I must have been absent from school that day. There's this narrow little dividing line I somehow never located."

"Nonsense; I don't know what you're talking about," said his mother, and then she held up an egg. "Will you look at this? Out of one dozen eggs, four are cracked. Two are smushed. I can't imagine what Sweeney Brothers is coming to, these days."

Ezra waited a while, but she didn't say any more. Finally, he left.

He tore down the wall between the restaurant kitchen and the dining room, doing most of the work in a single night. He slung a sledgehammer in a steady rhythm, then ripped away at hunks of plaster till a thick white dust had settled over everything. Then he came upon a mass of pipes and electrical wires and he had to call in professionals to finish off the job. The damage was so extensive that he was forced to stay closed for four straight weekdays, losing a good deal of money.

He figured that while he was at it, he might as well redecorate the dining room. He raced around the windows and dragged down the stiff brocade draperies; he peeled up the carpeting and persuaded a brigade of workmen to sand and polish the floorboards.

By the evening of the fourth day, he was so tired that he could feel the hinging of every muscle. Even so, he washed the white from his hair and changed out of his speckled jeans and went to pay a visit to Mrs. Scarlatti. She lay in her usual position, slightly propped, but her expression was alert and she even managed a smile when he entered. "Guess what, angel," she whispered. "Tomorrow they're letting me leave."

"Leave?"

"I asked the doctor, and he's letting me go home."

"Home?"

"As long as I hire a nurse, he says… Well, don't just stand there, Ezra. I need for you to see about a nurse. If you'll look in that nightstand…"

It was more talking than she'd done in weeks. Ezra felt almost buoyant with new hope; underneath, it seemed, he must have given up on her. But of course, he was also worried about the restaurant. What would she think when she saw it? What would she say to him? "Everything must go back again, just the way it was," he could imagine. "Really, Ezra. Put up that wall this instant, and fetch my carpets and my curtains." He suspected that he had very poor taste, much inferior to Mrs. Scarlatti's. She would say, "Dear heart, how could you be so chintzy?"—a favorite word of hers. He wondered if he could keep her from finding out, if he could convince her to stay in her apartment till he had returned things to normal.

He thanked his stars that he hadn't changed the sign that hung outside.

It was Ezra who settled the bill at the business office, the following morning. Then he spoke briefly with her doctor, whom he chanced to meet in the corridor. "This is wonderful about Mrs. Scarlatti," Ezra said. "I really didn't expect it."

"Oh," said the doctor. "Well."

"I was getting sort of discouraged, if you want to know the truth."

"Well," the doctor said again, and he held out his hand so suddenly that it took Ezra a second to respond. After that, the doctor walked off. Ezra felt there was a lot more the man could have said, as a matter of fact.

Mrs. Scarlatti went home by ambulance. Ezra drove behind, catching glimpses of her through the tinted window. She lay on a stretcher, and next to her was another stretcher holding a man in two full leg casts. His wife perched beside him, evidently talking nonstop. Ezra could see the feathers on her hat bob up and down with her words.

Mrs. Scarlatti was let off first. The ambulance men unloaded her while Ezra stood around feeling useless. "Oh, smell that air," said Mrs. Scarlatti. "Isn't it fresh and beautiful." Actually, it was terrible air-wintry and rainy and harsh with soot. "I never told you this, Ezra," she said, as they wheeled her through the building's front entrance, "but I really didn't believe I would see this place again. My little apartment, my restaurant..." Then she raised a palm—her old, peremptory gesture, directed toward the ambulance men. They were preparing to guide her stretcher through the right-hand door and up the stairs. "Dear fellow," she said to the nearest one, "could you just open that door on the left and let me take a peek?"

It happened so fast, Ezra didn't have time to protest. The man reached back in a preoccupied way and opened the door to the restaurant. Then he resumed his study of the stairs; there was an angle at the top that was going to pose a problem. Mrs. Scarlatti, meanwhile, turned her face with some effort and gazed through the door.

There was a moment, just a flicker of a second, when Ezra dared to hope that she might approve after all. But looking past her, he realized that was impossible. The restaurant was a warehouse, a barn, a gymnasium—a total catastrophe. Tables and upended chairs huddled in one corner, underneath bald, barren windows. Buckling plank footbridges led across the varnished floor, which had somehow picked up a film of white dust, and the missing kitchen wall was as horrifying as a toothless smile. Only two broad, plaster pillars separated the kitchen from the dining room. Everything was exposed-sinks and garbage cans, the blackened stove, the hanging pots with their tarnished bottoms, a calendar showing a girl in a sheer black nightgown, and a windowsill bearing two dead plants and a Brillo pad and Todd Duckett's asthma inhalant.

"Oh, my God," said Mrs. Scarlatti.

She looked up into his eyes. Her face seemed stripped. "You might at least have waited till I died," she said.

"Oh!" said Ezra. "No, you don't understand; you don't know. It wasn't what you think. It was just … I can't explain, I went wild somehow!"

But she raised that palm of hers and sailed up the stairs to her apartment. Even lying flat, she had an air of speed and power.

She didn't refuse to see him again—nothing like that. Every morning he paid her a visit, and was admitted by her day nurse. He sat on the edge of the ladylike chair in the bedroom and reported on bills and health inspections and linen deliveries. Mrs. Scarlatti was unfailingly polite, nodding in all the right places, but she never said much in return. Eventually, she would close her eyes as a sign that the visit was finished. Then Ezra would leave, often jostling her bed by accident or overturning his chair. He had always been a clumsy man, but now was more so than usual. It seemed to him his hands were too big, forever getting in the way. If only he could have done something with them! He would have liked to fix her a meal—a sustaining meal, with a depth of flavors, a complicated meal that would require a whole day of chopping things small, and grinding, and blending. In the kitchen, as nowhere else, Ezra came into his own, like someone, crippled on dry land but effortlessly graceful once he takes to water. However, Mrs. Scarlatti still wasn't eating. There was nothing he could offer her.

Or he would have liked to seize her by the shoulders and shout, "Listen! Listen!" But something closed-off about her face kept stopping him.

Almost in plain words, she was telling him that she preferred he not do such a thing. So he didn't. After a visit, he would go downstairs and look in on the restaurant, which at this hour was vacant and echoing. He might check the freezer, or erase the blackboard, and then perhaps just wander a while, touching this and that. The wallpaper in the back hall was too cluttered and he ripped it off the wall. He tore away the ornate gilt sconces beside the telephone. He yanked the old-fashioned silhouettes from the restroom doors. Sometimes he did so much damage that there was barely time to cover it up before opening, but everybody pitched in and it always got done somehow or other. By six o'clock, when the first customers arrived, the food was cooked and the tables were laid and the waitresses were calm and smiling. Everything was smoothed over.

Mrs. Scarlatti died in March, on a bitter, icy afternoon. When the nurse phoned Ezra, he felt a crushing sense of shock. You would think this death was unexpected. He said, "Oh, no," and hung up, and had to call back to ask the proper questions. Had the end been peaceful? Had Mrs. Scarlatti been awake? Had she said any words in particular? Nothing, said the nurse. Really, nothing at all; just slipped away, like. "But she mentioned you this morning," she added. "I almost wondered, you know? It was almost like she sensed it. She said, 'Tell Ezra to change the sign.'"

"Sign?"

"'It's not Scarlatti's Restaurant anymore,' she said. Or something like that. 'It isn't Scarlatti's.' I think that's what she said."

From the pain he felt, Mrs. Scarlatti might as well have reached out from death and slapped him across the face. It made things easier, in a way. He was almost angry; he was almost relieved that she was gone. He noticed how the trees outside sparkled like something newly minted. He was the one who made the arrangements, working from a list that Mrs. Scarlatti had given him months before. He knew which funeral home to call and which pastor, and which acquaintances she had wanted at the service. A peculiar thing: he thought of phoning the hospital and inviting that foreign family. Of course he didn't, but it was true they would have made wonderful mourners. Certainly they'd have done better than those who did come, and who later stood stiffly around her frozen grave. Ezra, too, was stiff—a sad, tired man in a flapping coat, holding his mother's arm. Something ached behind his eyes. If he had cried, Mrs. Scarlatti would have said, "Jesus, Ezra. For God's sake, sweetie."

Afterward, he was glad to go to the restaurant. It helped to keep busy—stirring and seasoning and tasting, stumbling over the patch in the floor where the center counter had once stood. Later, he circulated among the diners as Mrs. Scarlatti herself used to do. He urged upon them his oyster stew, his artichoke salad, his spinach bisque and his chili-bean soup and his gizzard soup that was made with love.

A Narrative of the Life of Frederick Douglass, An American Slave

FREDERICK DOUGLASS

I had resided but a short time in Baltimore before I observed a marked difference, in the treatment of slaves, from that which I had witnessed in the country. A city slave is almost a freeman, compared with a slave on the plantation. He is much better fed and clothed, and enjoys privileges altogether unknown to the slave on the plantation. There is a vestige of decency, a sense of shame, that does much to curb and check those outbreaks of atrocious cruelty so commonly enacted upon the plantation. He is a desperate slaveholder, who will shock the humanity of his non-slaveholding neighbors with the cries of his lacerated slave. Few are willing to incur the odium attaching to the reputation of being a cruel master; and above all things, they would not be known as not giving a slave enough to eat. Every city slave-holder is anxious to have it known of him, that he feeds his slaves well; and it is due to them to say, that most of them do give their slaves enough to eat. There are, however, some painful exceptions to this rule. Directly opposite to us, on Philpot Street, lived Mr. Thomas Hamilton. He owned two slaves. Their names were Henrietta and Mary. Henrietta was about twenty-two years of age, Mary was about fourteen; and of all the mangled and emaciated creatures I ever looked upon, these two were the most so. His heart must be harder than stone, that could look upon these unmoved. The head, neck, and shoulders of Mary were literally cut to pieces. I have frequently felt her head, and found it nearly covered with festering sores, caused by the lash of her cruel mistress. I do not know that her master ever whipped her, but I have been an eye-witness to the cruelty of Mrs. Hamilton. I used to be in Mr. Hamilton's house nearly every day. Mrs. Hamilton used to sit in a large chair in the middle of the room, with a heavy cowskin always by her side, and scarce an hour passed during the day but was marked by the blood of one of these slaves. The girls seldom passed her without her saying, "Move faster, you black gip!" at the same time giving them a blow with the cowskin over the head or shoulders, often drawing the blood. She would then say, "Take that, you black gip!" continuing, "If you don't move faster, I'll move you!"

Added to the cruel lashings to which these slaves were subjected, they were kept nearly half-starved. They seldom knew what it was to eat a full meal. I have seen Mary contending with the pigs for the offal thrown into the street. So much was Mary kicked and cut to pieces, that she was oftener called "pecked" than by her name.

I lived in Master Hugh's family about seven years. During this time, I succeeded in learning to read and write. In accomplishing this, I was compelled to resort to various stratagems. I had no regular teacher. My mistress, who had kindly commenced to instruct me, had, in compliance with the advice and direction of her husband, not only ceased to instruct, but had set her face against my being instructed by any one else. It is due, however, to my mistress to say of her, that she did not adopt this course of treatment immediately. She at first lacked the depravity indispensable to shutting me up in mental darkness. It was at least necessary for her to have some training in the exercise of irresponsible power, to make her equal to the task of treating me as though I were a brute.

My mistress was, as I have said, a kind and tender-hearted woman; and in the simplicity of her soul she commenced, when I first went to live with her, to treat me as she supposed one human being ought to treat another. In entering upon the duties of a slaveholder, she did not seem to perceive that I sustained to her the relation of a mere chattel, and that for her to treat me as a human being was not only wrong, but dangerously so. Slavery proved as injurious to her as it did to me. When I went there, she was a pious, warm, and tender-hearted woman. There was no sorrow or suffering for which she had not a tear. She had bread for the hungry, clothes for the naked, and comfort for every mourner that came within her reach. Slavery soon proved its ability to divest her of these heavenly qualities. Under its influence, the tender heart became stone, and the lamblike disposition gave way to one of tiger-like fierceness. The first step in her downward course was in her ceasing to instruct me. She now commenced to practise her husband's precepts. She finally became even more violent in her opposition than her husband himself. She was not satisfied with simply doing as well as he had commanded; she seemed anxious to do better. Nothing seemed to make her more angry than to see me with a newspaper. She seemed to think that here lay the danger. I have had her rush at me with a face made all up of fury, and snatch from me a newspaper, in a manner that fully revealed her apprehension. She was an apt woman; and a little experience soon demonstrated, to her satisfaction, that education and slavery were incompatible with each other.

From this time I was most narrowly watched. If I was in a separate room any considerable length of time, I was sure to be suspected of having a book, and was at once called to give an account of myself. All this, however, was too late. The first step had been taken. Mistress, in teaching me the alphabet, had given me the inch, and no precaution could prevent me from taking the ell.

The plan which I adopted, and the one by which I was most successful, was that of making friends of all the little white boys whom I met in the street. As many of these as I could, I converted into teachers. With their kindly aid, obtained at different times and in different places, I finally succeeded in learning to read. When I was sent of errands, I always took my book with me, and by going one part of my errand quickly, I found time to get a lesson before my return. I used also to carry bread with me, enough of which was always in the house, and to which I was always welcome; for I was much better off in this regard than many of the poor white children in our neighborhood. This bread I used to bestow upon the hungry little urchins, who, in return, would give me that more valuable bread of knowledge. I am strongly tempted to give the names of two or three of those little boys, as a testimonial of the gratitude and affection I bear them; but prudence forbids;—not that it would injure me, but it might embarrass them; for it is almost an unpardonable offence to teach slaves to read in this Christian country. It is enough to say of the dear little fellows, that they lived on Philpot Street, very near Durgin and Bailey's ship-yard. I used to talk this matter of slavery over with them. I would sometimes say to them, I wished I could be as free as they would be when they got to be men. "You will be free as soon as you are twenty-one, but I am a slave for life! Have not I as good a right to be free as you have?" These words used to trouble them; they would express for me the liveliest sympathy, and console me with the hope that something would occur by which I might be free.

I was now about twelve years old, and the thought of being a slave for life began to bear heavily upon my heart. Just about this time, I got hold of a book entitled "The Columbian Orator." Every opportunity I got, I used to read this book. Among much of other interesting matter, I found in it a dialogue between a master and his slave. The slave was represented as having run away from his master three times. The dialogue represented the conversation which took place between them, when the slave was retaken the third time. In this dialogue, the whole argument in behalf of slavery was brought forward by the master, all of which was disposed of by the slave. The slave was made to say some very smart as well as impressive things in reply to his master—things which had the desired though unexpected effect; for the conversation resulted in the voluntary emancipation of the slave on the part of the master.

In the same book, I met with one of Sheridan's mighty speeches on and in behalf of Catholic emancipation. These were choice documents to me. I read them over and over again with unabated interest. They gave tongue to interesting thoughts of my own soul, which had frequently flashed through my mind, and died away for want of utterance. The moral which I gained from the dialogue was the power of truth over the conscience of even a slaveholder. What I got from Sheridan was a bold denunciation of slavery, and a powerful vindication of human rights. The reading of these documents enabled me to utter my thoughts, and to meet the arguments brought forward to sustain slavery; but while they relieved me of one difficulty, they brought on another even more painful than the one of which I was relieved. The more I read, the more I was led to abhor and detest my enslavers. I could regard them in no other light than a band of successful robbers, who had left their homes, and gone to Africa, and stolen us from our homes, and in a strange land reduced us to slavery. I loathed them as being the meanest as well as the most wicked of men. As I read and contemplated the subject, behold! that very discontentment which Master Hugh had predicted would follow my learning to read had already come, to torment and sting my soul to unutterable anguish. As I writhed under it, I would at times feel that learning to read had been a curse rather than a blessing. It had given me a view of my wretched condition, without the remedy. It opened my eyes to the horrible pit, but to no ladder upon which to get out. In moments of agony, I envied my fellow-slaves for their stupidity. I have often wished myself a beast. I preferred the condition of the meanest reptile to my own. Any thing, no matter what, to get rid of thinking! It was this everlasting thinking of my condition that tormented me. There was no getting rid of it. It was pressed upon me by every object within sight or hearing, animate or inanimate. The silver trump of freedom had roused my soul to eternal wakefulness. Freedom now appeared, to disappear no more forever. It was heard in every sound, and seen in every thing. It was ever present to torment me with a sense of my wretched condition. I saw nothing without seeing it, I heard nothing without hearing it, and felt nothing without feeling it. It looked from every star, it smiled in every calm, breathed in every wind, and moved in every storm.

I often found myself regretting my own existence, and wishing myself dead; and but for the hope of being free, I have no doubt but that I should have killed myself, or done something for which I should have been killed. While in this state of mind, I was eager to hear any one speak of slavery. I was a ready listener. Every little while, I could hear something about the abolitionists. It was some time before I found what the word meant. It was always used in such connections as to make it an interesting word to me. If a slave ran away and succeeded in getting clear, or if a slave killed his master, set fire to a barn, or did any thing very wrong in the mind of a slaveholder, it was spoken of as the fruit of abolition. Hearing the word in this connection very often, I set about learning what it meant. The dictionary afforded me little or no help. I found it was "the act of abolishing;" but then I did not know what was to be abolished. Here I was perplexed. I did not dare to ask any one about its meaning, for I was satisfied that it was something they wanted me to know very little about. After a patient waiting, I got one of our city papers, containing an account of the number of petitions from the north, praying for the abolition of slavery in the District of Columbia, and of the slave trade between the States. From this time I understood the words abolition and abolitionist, and always drew near when that word was spoken, expecting to hear something of importance to myself and fellow-slaves. The light broke in upon me by degrees. I went one day down on the wharf of Mr. Waters; and seeing two Irishmen unloading a scow of stone, I went, unasked, and helped them. When we had finished, one of them came to me and asked me if I were a slave. I told him I was. He asked, "Are ye a slave for life?" I told him that I was. The good Irishman seemed to be deeply affected by the statement. He said to the other that it was a pity so fine a little fellow as myself should be a slave for life. He said it was a shame to hold me. They both advised me to run away to the north; that I should find friends there, and that I should be free. I pretended not to be interested in what they said, and treated them as if I did not understand them; for I feared they might be treacherous. White men have been known to encourage slaves to escape, and then, to get the reward, catch them and return them to their masters. I was afraid that these seemingly good men might use me so; but I nevertheless remembered their advice, and from that time

I resolved to run away. I looked forward to a time at which it would be safe for me to escape. I was too young to think of doing so immediately; besides, I wished to learn how to write, as I might have occasion to write my own pass. I consoled myself with the hope that I should one day find a good chance. Meanwhile, I would learn to write.

The idea as to how I might learn to write was suggested to me by being in Durgin and Bailey's ship-yard, and frequently seeing the ship carpenters, after hewing, and getting a piece of timber ready for use, write on the timber the name of that part of the ship for which it was intended. When a piece of timber was intended for the larboard side, it would be marked thus—"L." When a piece was for the starboard side, it would be marked thus—"S." A piece for the larboard side forward, would be marked thus—"L. F." When a piece was for starboard side forward, it would be marked thus—"S. F." For larboard aft, it would be marked thus--"L. A." For starboard aft, it would be marked thus—"S. A." I soon learned the names of these letters, and for what they were intended when placed upon a piece of timber in the ship-yard. I immediately commenced copying them, and in a short time was able to make the four letters named. After that, when I met with any boy who I knew could write, I would tell him I could write as well as he. The next word would be, "I don't believe you. Let me see you try it." I would then make the letters which I had been so fortunate as to learn, and ask him to beat that. In this way I got a good many lessons in writing, which it is quite possible I should never have gotten in any other way. During this time, my copy-book was the board fence, brick wall, and pavement; my pen and ink was a lump of chalk. With these, I learned mainly how to write. I then commenced and continued copying the Italics in Webster's Spelling Book, until I could make them all without looking on the book. By this time, my little Master Thomas had gone to school, and learned how to write, and had written over a number of copy-books. These had been brought home, and shown to some of our near neighbors, and then laid aside. My mistress used to go to class meeting at the Wilk Street meetinghouse every Monday afternoon, and leave me to take care of the house. When left thus, I used to spend the time in writing in the spaces left in Master Thomas's copy-book, copying what he had written. I continued to do this until I could write a hand very similar to that of Master Thomas. Thus, after a long, tedious effort for years, I finally succeeded in learning how to write.

Assignations at Vanishing Point

JANE SATTERFIELD

1.

Broiling this morning, I note, the sky silver of fish gone belly-up, suspended in stilled current. Blue skies and breezes are someone else's version of summer. *If I have a taste for anything*, Rimbaud wrote, world-weary and intoxicated as always at the festival of his own insatiable hungers, *it's nothing*.

A repudiation that's consuming and familiar.

2.

Here, in the crawl space called a lover's absence, breakfast coffee's bitter. Empty spaces, I find, are best filled by reading voraciously, and I'm charmed for a time by anecdotes of a group of intense Civil War re-enactors whose less intense peers have dubbed them "hardcores." In their fierce aim to authenticate Civil War atmosphere, these men starve themselves so their abs and pecs are carefully defined—standing out on their frames as if elegantly etched—so that while walking dusty trails toward Shiloh or Gettysburg, they replicate the gaunt and hungry look of near-starved Confederate soldiers. This ascetic impulse engenders a kind of sainthood, I guess, in a world where pleasure's fast and furious. Meanwhile, I upend a bouquet, slosh drowse from the vase into the sink.

3.

Alone in bed, cold, quilt-wrapped, smoking cigarettes to blunt her appetite, Canadian writer Elizabeth Smart, long-enmeshed in a tangled love affair with English poet George Barker, a married man to whom she bore four children out of wedlock, wrote with lyric fury and insight about appetite. Aware at love's inception that the "initial intoxication" of love disappears, Smart admonished herself to remember the fullness of things that "in that hour moved you to tears, and made of an outward gaze through the dining car window a plenitude not to be born." Smart's achievement in the brief but brilliant *By Grand Central Station I Sat Down and Wept* is to create a kind of fever-chart of love's trajectory, an emotional blueprint of exquisite and liberating human contact rather than a linear narrative of marshaled facts. In this way, the lover/writer suspends the temporal moment to savor the memory of erotic delight asserting the centrality of desire, its role as sustenance.

4.

"Who lays the crumbs of food that tempt you? Toward a person you never considered. A dream. Then later, another series of dreams ..." wrote Michael Ondaatje, immersing his readers in the minds of characters consumed by great love affairs. The ample bread, using Emily Dickinson's metaphor, *is* unlike the crumb. Once, in spring, a man called to me through the dusty heat of an urban flat. I answered his call, stepped across the threshold of his bedroom. There were volumes strewn around, a mattress tossed on the worn parquet floor. For a brief season he offered me champagne, fresh fruit; afternoons, all pleasures of the flesh. More than food for thought.

5.

In the French film I watched last night, an unhappy wife labored in the kitchen, a character framed in sunlight, burdened by domestic work. Then the camera cut to a tabletop—as if the centre of this room bonded her to hellish handiwork—there were mussels, wholegrain bread, and mushrooms. Her face, when caught by the camera, reflects her hunger for another life. Her eyes are drawn beyond the open window frame, beyond the present moment to where the memory of a lover's voice is a recipe for minor mayhem.

6.

The radio crackles as the air-conditioning kicks into high gear. The upscale, organic, grocery store announces a summer Singles Mingle night. I try to imagine what it would be like, aisles jammed with hordes possessed by a less than casual hunger, proffered—what? Oysters? Champagne? Artichokes? The usual aphrodisiacs?

Who'd be tempted to enter this brave, utilitarian world, to mask desire and wander the aisles, looking for the possible partner, shrewdly consumerist eyes alert for a bargain, the perfect package to pluck off an orderly shelf?

7.

In his classification of Irish fairies, Yeats noted the presence of the "far gorta" or "man of hunger," an emaciated figure who roams "through the land in famine time begging and bringing good luck to the giver." While Yeats categorized the "man of hunger" within a broad range of malevolent spirits, he neglected to clarify the darker elements of the superstition: a greatly feared spirit of the land, he appears during times of shortage and is often the harbinger of famine.

8.

My mother was born at the outset of the Second World War, into an era of rationing that lasted ten years after the war's official end. She tasted tinned peaches once from a neighbor's Red Cross parcel, American sweetness ever afterward cloying to her tongue. Never in need of dieting or in danger of overeating, she was, however, obsessed with food: the pantry and freezer were always re-stocked and her days were arranged around dinner plans. She kept a small address book on the kitchen counter near the phone, filled it with friends' numbers, with shopping lists and menus.... As her children grew and left her home, these habits failed to diminish. In the absence of recipes passed down, in the absence of exact ingredients, my mother is tireless in her attempts to reconstruct her mother's soups and bread.... Always this hunger for *home*.

9.

Legend says that Clare left the confines of her father's house through "the door of the dead," an unofficial exit, a space through which corpses were jettisoned from the family estate. Captivated by the words of Francis, by her spirit's hunger, she shed gold-coiled hair and silken gowns, choosing poverty and the pure life. Cloistered, she begged Francis for scholarship, a meal. He called the body "brother ass." Morsel or mouthful the same largesse; sermons sent by mail, he claimed, would serve as his stand-in.

When Francis fell sick, Clare wrote of her intention to starve. To die first! So that she might greet him in heaven! He ordered that she eat: a bite of bread a day, enough to keep the taste of this world on her tongue.

10.

Hunger-artists are not unknown in literature: Miss Havisham lived in Satis House, surrounded by the decaying remains of what should have been her own wedding feast. And there's Clarissa Harlowe, chaste maiden who left the confines of her father's home at the prospect of an unsuitable marriage to fling herself upon the mercy of a libertine. She unwittingly traded one prison for another, then, presumably violated, divested herself of flesh in a volley of letters.

"If only I had found the right food, believe me, I should have made no fuss and stuffed myself like you or anyone else," says Kafka's Hunger Artist, explaining his talent to an admiring spectator. This dedication to hunger—a willingness to forego self-nourishment—is clearly a repudiation of life and yet, disturbingly, the starving body also articulates meaning.

11.

Feminist scholarship interprets anorexia as a statement of women's rage at the circumscription of their lives, as if they starve, in Maud Ellmann's words, to "defy the patriarchal values that confine their sex as rigidly as walls of stone or bars of iron." Self-starvation, in this view, is an act of inscription; the body becomes readable—a text. Be that is it may, the terms of this protest are, as Kafka says of the machine script which brands prisoners' crimes on their skin in the story "The Penal Colony," "no calligraphy for schoolchildren."

12.

But I experienced hunger as ecstasy, reveling in the transportive potential of self starvation, which resulted in a deceptively freeing sense of disembodiment. In her essay "Food Mysteries," Joyce Carol Oates comments on the seductiveness of this state,

> ...in the radiance of hunger beyond hunger, every instant flashes with the feel of eternity; the most wayward of lightheaded thoughts is an epiphany; consciousness, heightened to the point of pain, makes the subject a razor, scintillating, deathly sharp, cutting through the dull surfaces of the world. Who has not been in this place, and who does not recall it, half-shamefully, as one of the radiant regions of the soul...?

This was it for me exactly; a glimpse into the other world as the path to divine life. I would like to say I knew how or when the impulse to starve first took hold, that it was political, historical, a reasoned decision. But autobiographical memory is notoriously errant; it is never entirely truthful or objective: my mother filled plates; I pushed them away.

13.

"In Ireland, the 'hungry grass' is said to grow at a place where an uncoffined corpse was laid on the ground on its way to burial. This affects the quality of the place for the worse. Those unfortunate enough to step on such a spot are doomed to suffer insatiable hunger. An infamous place for the "hungry grass" was on a road near Ballinamote. It was activated so frequently that the woman of the house kept a bowl of stirabout in a state of permanent readiness to feed passers-by who stepped on the fated ground" (Pennick, *Celtic Sacred Landscapes*).

14.

"Even after women feel they have recovered from anorexia (in as far as they see recovery as possible), they still restrict their favorite foods strictly...Food that gives pleasure is dangerous food..." (Morag MacSween, *Anorexic Bodies*).

15.

Marguerite Duras described the difficulties of nursing her husband back to life on his return from Belsen in her memoir, *The War.* There had been accidents, she wrote, where refugees of the death camps had been given food too soon. There are practical problems, she learned, to be considered: the stomach would be lacerated by the weight of the food, the weight would have pressed on the starved man's heart which had "grown enormous in the cave of his emaciation." A conundrum, then: this once estranged and newly recovered husband "couldn't eat without dying. But he couldn't go on not eating without dying."

For seventeen days the survivor is beset with fever, swathed in down to prevent him from shearing the skin drawn tight against his bones. One morning he wakes, speaks, says "I'm hungry." From there, Duras reported his hunger took on terrifying proportions; it "grew from what it fed on."

16.

Over lunch, a friend asks if I've satisfied my hunger. He pushes a plate toward me. I look up, meet his eye, and laugh. It's broiling, the sky silver of fish gone belly up, suspended in stilled current. The city's wrapped in an ozone haze; blue skies and breezes are someone else's version of summer. Could this be the start of another season of champagne?

There's coffee, shared crumbs. Questions to consider. The world looks better, I know, when the stomach's full.

Publication note: "Assignations at Vanishing Point" was published in Daughters of Empire: A Memoir of a Year in Britain and Beyond *(Demeter Press, 2009). The essay first appeared in a slightly different version in* Seneca Review.

Mush for the Multitude

H. L. Mencken

Midway between the tales of persecution and passion that address themselves frankly to servant girls, country school-teachers and the public stenographers in commercial hotels and those works of popular romance which yet hang hazardously, as it were, upon the far-flung yardarms of beautiful letters—midway, as I say, between these wholly atrocious and quasi-respectable evangels of amour and derring-do, there floats a literature vast, gaudy and rich in usufructs, which outrages all sense and probability without descending to actual vulgarity and buffoonery, and so manages to impinge agreeably upon that vast and money-in-pocket public which takes instinctively a safe, middle course in all things, preferring Sousa's band to either a street piano or the Boston Symphony Orchestra, and *The New York Times* to either the *Evening Journal* or the *Evening Post*, and Dr. Woodrow Wilson to either Debs or Mellon, and dinner at six o'clock to either dinner at noon or dinner at eight-thirty, and three children (two boys and a girl) to either the lone heir of Fifth Avenue or the all-the-traffic-can-bear hatching of the Ghetto, and honest malt liquor to either Croton water or champagne, and Rosa Bonheur's "The Horse Fair" to either Corot's "*Danse de Nymphes*" or a "Portrait of a Lady" from the *Police Gazette*, and fried chicken to either liver or terrapin, and a once-a-week religion to either religion every day or no religion at all, and the Odd Fellows to either the Trappists or the Black Hand, and a fairly pretty girl who can cook fairly well to either a prettier girl who can't cook a stroke or a good cook who sours the milk.

To make an end, the public I refer to is that huge body of honest and right-thinking folk which constitute the heart, lungs and bowels of this great republic—that sturdy multitude which believes in newspapers, equinoctial storms, trust-busting, the Declaration of Independence, teleology, the direct primary, the uplift, trial by jury, monogamy, the Weather Bureau, Congress, and the moral order of the world—that innumerable caravan of middling, dollar-grubbing, lodge joining, quack-ridden folk which the Socialists sneer at loftily as the bourgeoisie, and politicians slobber over as the bulwark of our liberties. And, by the same token, the meridional, intermediate literature that I speak of is that literature without end which lifts its dizzy pyramids from the book-counters in the department stores, and from which, ever and anon, there emerges that prize of great price, the bestseller. The essence of this literature is sentiment, and the essence of that sentiment is hope. Its aim is to fill the breast with soothing and optimistic emotions—to make the fat woman forget that she is fat—to purge the tired business man of his bile, to convince the flapper that Douglas Fairbanks may yet learn to love her, to prove that this dreary old world, as botched and bad as it is, might yet be a darn sight worse.

I offer *The Rosary*, *Soldiers of Fortune*, *Laddie*, *The Helmet of Navarre*, *Little Lord Fauntleroy*, *Freckles*, *Eben Holden*, and *V. V.'s Eyes* as specimens, and so pass on to the latest example, to wit, *Bambi*, by Marjorie Benton Cooke. By the time this reaches you, I have no doubt, *Bambi* will be all the rage in your vicinage. You will be hearing about it on all sides. You will see allusions to it in your evening paper. You will observe it on the desk of your stenographer. Your wife (if you belong to the gnarled and persecuted sex) will be urging you to read it and mark it well. You yourself (if you are fair and have the price) will be wearing a Bambi petticoat or a Bambi collar or a pair of Bambi stockings or a Bambi something-more-intimate-still. Such, alas, is the course that best-sellers run! They permeate and poison the atmosphere of the whole land. It is impossible to get away from them. They invade the most secure retreats, even the very jails and almshouses. Serving thirty days myself, under the Sherman Act, during the late rage for *The Salamander*, I had it thrust up on me by the rector of the bas tile, and had to read it to get rid of him.

Wherefore, in sympathy, as it were, I have ploughed through *Bambi* in time to tell you what it is about before you have to read it yourself, thus hoping to save you from the dangers of too much joy. It is a tale, as you may suspect, of young love, and the heroine is a brilliant young lady named Miss Francesca Parkhurst, the daughter of Professor James Parkhurst, Ph.D., the eminent but somewhat balmy mathematician. Professor Parkhurst, as Bambi herself says, knows more about mathematics than the man who invented them, but outside the domain of figures his gigantic intellect refuses to function. Thus he always forgets to go to his lecture-room unless Bambi heads him in the right direction at the right hour, and if it were not for her careful inspection of his make-up, he would often set off with his detachable cuffs upon his ankles instead of upon his wrists, and the skirts of his shirt outside instead of inside his pantaloons. In a word, this Professor Parkhurst is the standard college professor of the best-sellers—the genial jackass we know and love of old. The college professor of the stem, cold world, perhaps, is a far different creature: I once knew one, in fact, who played the races and was a first-rate amateur bartender, and there is record of another who went into politics and clawed his way to a very high office. But in romance, of course, no such heretics are allowed. The college professor of prose fiction is always an absent-minded old boob, who is forever stumbling over his own feet, and he always has a pretty daughter to swab up his waist coat after he has dined, and to chase away the ganovim who are trying to rob him, and to fill his house with an air of innocent and youthful gayety.

Naturally enough, this Professor Parkhurst of our present inquest is not at all surprised when sweet Bambi tells him that she has decided to marry young Jarvis Jocelyn, the rising uplifter, nor even when she tells him that Jarvis knows nothing about it, nor even when she kidnaps Jarvis while he is in a state of coma and sends for a preacher and marries him on the spot, nor even when she puts him to bed a cappella on the third floor of the house, and devotes her honeymoon to gathering up and sorting out the flying pages of the Great Drama that he is writing. College professors of the standard model do not shy at such doings. Like babies in arms, they see the world only as a series of indistinct shadows. It would not have made much impression upon Professor Parkhurst had Bambi invited the ashman to dinner or flavored the soup with witch-hazel or come to the meal herself in a bathing-suit. And so it makes very little impression upon him when she shanghais Jarvis and internes the poor fellow in the ganet and kicks up a scandal that shakes the whole town. He is dimly conscious that something is going on, just as an infant is dimly conscious that it is light at times and dark at times, but further than that he reeks and wots not.

Well, well, we must be getting on! What does Bambi do next? Next she grabs a pencil and a pad of paper and dashes off a short story of her own, with herself, Jarvis and the professor as its characters. Then she tires of it and puts it away. Then, one day, she picks up a New York magazine containing an offer of $500 cash for the best short story submitted in competition. Then she gets out her story, has it typewritten and sends it in. Then—what! Have you guessed it? Clever you are, indeed! Yes, even so: then she wins the prize. And then, tucking Jarvis under her arm, she goes to New York and tries to sell the Great Drama. And then she spends a week of sitting in the anterooms of theatrical managers. And then, her story being published under a *nom de plume*, she finds herself an anonymous celebrity and is hospitably received by the genial Bob Davis, editor of *Munsey's*. And then another and much slimmer magazine editor—no doubt G. J. Nathan, thinly disguised—falls in love with her and gives her many valuable pointers. And then Charles Frohman proposes to have her story dramatized, and she lures him into offering Jarvis the job, and then pitches in and helps to perform it. And then the play makes a tremendous hit on Broadway, and she confesses the whole plot, and Jarvis falls desperately in love with her, and we part from them in each other's arms.

A sweet, sweet story. A string of gum-drops. A sugar-teat beyond compare. Of such great probabilities, of such searching reports of human motive and act, the best-seller is all compact. If you have a heart, if you can feel and understand, if your cheers for the true, the good and the beautiful are truly sincere, then this one will squeeze a tear from your leaden eye and send it cascading down your nose. And if, on the contrary, you are one of those cheap barroom cynics who think it is smart to make game of honest sentiment and pure art, then it will give you the loud, coarse guffaw that you crave. But do not laugh too much, dear friend, however hard your heart, however tough your hide. The mission of such things as *Bambi* is, after all, no mean one. Remember the fat woman—how it will make her forget that she is fat. Remember the tired business man—how it will lift him out of his wallow and fill him with a noble enthusiasm for virtue and its rewards. Remember the flapper—how it will thrill her to the very soles of her feet and people her dreams with visions of gallant knights and lighten that doom which makes her actual beau a baseball fan and corrupts him with a loathing for literature and gives him large, hairy hands and a *flair* for burlesque shows and freckles on his neck. And so to other things.

Frog Made Free

STEPHEN DIXON

He suddenly seems to have lost all his marbles. Doesn't know where he is. Dark, feels movement, sounds of movement, so feels he's going someplace. A car, but no seat, just a rough wood floor he's on, so it isn't. Bed of a truck, totally enclosed, shaking back and forth, moving slowly, but not the sounds of one, outside or underneath. A train, bouncing like one. Sounding like it. How could it be? Not a real train. Sure, one with something pulling it and on tracks, but what's he, some bum tramping it in a boxcar? Smells like it, old hay, animal dung. He's sitting on a floor, still a rough wood floor, thick liquid on it where one of his hands touches, back up against someone's back, feet squashed against something like a crate or wall. Where's his family? He's no bum. Has a home, car, job, all small but as much as most, wife and kids he lives with, mother in a nearby city whom he helps support. They were with him just before, had to give away the dog, hours, a day, before he woke up. That's it: was asleep. "Denise? Denise?"

"Shh, go back to your snoring," man whose back he's against says. "It wasn't as loud."

"What's going on? What is it with this train?"

"And I'm going to tell you? Don't worry, it'll all turn out bad. Ha-ha, that's a good one. Sorry, go to sleep. Don't be afraid to, the ride's for a couple more days at least. Believe me, we're all here who were here, even the ones who aren't dead yet. Sorry again. I can't help myself. I don't know what I'm saying. I don't even know if I said anything. Did I?"

"Shh, you too," someone says. "You're making more noise than him now."

"Denise?" Howard yells.

"What's with this guy?" someone else says. "Hey, pipe down."

"We're over here," she says. "Directly across the car from you. The girls are all right, sleeping now. People were kind enough to let us move near the pail so the girls could relieve themselves right into it. You were sleeping. You wouldn't budge. Rest, dear. Take care of yourself. In the morning come over."

He gets up. "Excuse me," he says, feeling bodies with his hands and feet. Stepping on someone. "Get off me," a woman says.

"I'm sorry, really. But I want to get to my wife and children."

"You'll see them in the morning like she says."

"Stay where you are...Go back to where you were...You're upsetting everything," other people say.

"No, now, please, I have to. This might be my last chance before the train pulls in."

"Last chance nothing. Your foot's on my hand." He lifts his foot and puts it down on someone else's or this same man's hand. "Just go back to your spot, will you? Ah, it's likely already filled by three others. Come on, someone light a candle. Let this man get to his family."

Car stays dark. "Come on," the man says, "someone break down and light a candle. This is Grisha Bischoff talking. If it's because you don't want to spare a match, I'll loan you."

A candle's lit about twenty feet away. Little he can see, car's packed full with bundles and people sleeping. Some look at him, one eye, then blink shut. "Over here," Denise says, waving at him. "Excuse me, excuse me," he says. "My wife."

"Better to crawl over rather than step," a woman below him says.

"Right, I just wanted to be quick." Gets down, crawls over people. It takes a long time. "I'm sorry," he says. "I'm very sorry." Someone punches his back as he passes. "Imbecile," a man says. "Let him be," someone else says. "He got permission. Maybe his kids need him like he says." "They need him, I need him—when you're split up you're sunk and that's final, but you have to make it hell for everybody else? OK, OK, I'll get out of his way."

He gets to Denise. "I'm here, thank you, you can put out the candle, whoever it was." Candle goes out.

"There's only room for one adult here," Denise says, on her knees. "Olivia's in a space for someone half her size. Eva's been on my chest. I'll make room somehow."

"Excuse me," he says, feeling for the person next to them and nudging his shoulder. "Could you just give us one or two inches?"

"There's no room to," the man says. "I don't have enough for my family or myself. Go back to your place. It was bad enough when she and your kids came here."

"I can't. I'll never get back. Thanks all the same." He feels for Olivia, picks her up, takes her spot, makes himself small, lays her face down on him, feels for Denise's head, "It's me," he says, kisses her lips, for a while his lips stay on hers without moving, says, "I didn't believe this just before. That we were here. I didn't know where I was, is more like it. Suddenly I was a kid, it seemed—a lost one. Parents gone; no brothers. In the dark, literally and the rest of it. I felt crazy. All I wanted was for you to be—"

"Go to sleep, my darling. Try to."

"I wish I could. We sleep most of the day; how could anyone sleep now? And the infection in my finger's killing me. When I crawled over I bumped it a dozen times and it now feels twice the size it was. It's a small inconvenience, and so what about the pain compared to all the other things, but if I can't soak and treat it it'll—"

"We'll try to do something in the morning. Maybe we can get some hot water, for your finger and to wash the girls. Sleep, though. We have a few hours to."

He kisses her, closes his eyes, head on her shoulder, one arm holding Olivia close, other on Eva's back. Very cold. Smell of shit and piss is worse here than where they were. The fucking slop pail. She had to move here? But the girls won't soil their clothes or less so than if they were over there. "If there was only something I could do for us."

"Like what?"

"Like everything."

"Right now there's nothing. Just stay close. No heroics unless it's a sure thing for us. Stay with us till the end. Wake up when I ask you. Help me keep the girls in a good mood. But now, sleep; not another word."

He doesn't sleep. Snoring of a woman close by keeps him up. Smells and cold. Weight of Olivia. Wailing every so often from people. Weeping, coughing, babies crying. Someone shouting, someone talking in his sleep. But Denise and the girls seem to sleep.

They go on like this for days. People die. No food except a little for the children. Some people share it. Olivia and Eva are always hungry and thirsty and complain and cry a lot about it. A bucket of water for the whole car is given them once a day. Bischoff distributes it in spoonfuls. Howard's finger gets so swollen that he jabs it into a nail in the wall and keeps sucking it and it starts healing. There's a slit in the door and someone during the day is usually telling the car what the weather and scenery are like. Now it's hilly, now it's flat. Lots of big clouds in the sky, but nothing threatening. More people die. Corpses are piled on top of one another in a corner and what little hay can be found is strewn over them.

The bottom ones begin to smell. Now it's clear out, now it's sleeting and looks as if it'll turn into snow. Some people seem to pray all day and night now. Train stops, goes, pulls into stations, drags along mostly, stays still for hours sometimes, one time for an entire night. They pass a pretty village, an oil refinery that goes on for miles, farmers working in fields. "Potatoes they're trying to dig out that they might've missed," the slit-watcher says. "Turnips, cabbages, even a carrot or two. Sounds good, right? Look, a farmers waving his pick at us. Hello, you lucky stiff. Look, a dog's running to the train. Do you kids hear him bark?" Nobody answers. Sunny, rainy. Denise and the girls sleep most of the time now. Olivia always seems to run a low fever and he's afraid it'll suddenly go out of control at night and she'll die. The slop pail's filled and starts running over. Some people talk of killing themselves. Bischoff gives an order. "Nobody kills himself. If you got pills or stuff that can do it, give them to me to use on someone who's really suffering or about to die. But we should be at the place soon we're going to and then let's hope it'll all be much better for us and most of us are even able to stay together as a group. Does anyone have some good stories to tell? Dreams, but interesting ones we can all appreciate? Then anything you want to make up for us or poems you remember from books or school? Does anyone have any food for the children?" Nobody answers. They haven't had a bucket of water for two days. During one stop someone asks a guard through the slit if they can get some water and also empty the slop pail. "Get rid of it through your hole there," the guard says. "You got little spoons. It can be done:" "It'll probably make more of a mess than help us," Bischoff tells the car, "but what do we got to lose?" The pail's moved to the door. Denise wants to follow it, but Howard says "We got a good place together and now not such a filthy one, so let's stay." Someone's always spooning out slop through the slit, except at night. Some cardboard's turned into a funnel and they get rid of the slop faster. The pail keeps running over though, but not as much as before.

The train stops at a station. "I think this is it," the slit-watcher says. "Lots of lights, barbed wire and fences. Dogs, soldiers, marching prisoners in stripes who look like they're on their last leg. I hear lively and music from someplace, but it doesn't look good." "Don't worry, don't worry," Bischoff says. "They might be political prisoners you're seeing; we're not." They stay in the station till morning. Most of the groaning and crying's stopped. More people have died but nobody's piling them up. "It's snowing," the slit-watcher says. "Big flakes, but melting soon as they hit the ground. Plenty of activity outside, everyone being lined up, called to attention, even the dogs. Something's about to happen. A tall man in a great coat and officer's cap is pointing to the train."

The door suddenly opens and several men and women outside start shouting orders. One tells them to hurry out of the car and leave all their luggage on the platform, a second says to go to this or that truck. "What's going to happen to us?" Denise says in the car.

"I don't know," Howard says. "There's air though. Feel it coming in? Olivia, Eva—do you feel it? Already it smells better. Soon toilets, water for drinking and baths."

"Have we really got everything planned fully?" Denise whispers to him. "If they tell you to go one place, me another and the girls a third, or just split us up any other way but where we lose you or both of us lose the kids, what should we do?"

"What can we?"

"We could say no, stay with our children—that we have to, in other words. They're small, sick, need us. We don't want to lose them, we can say, lose them in both ways, and it's always taken the two of us to handle them."

"And be beaten down and the girls dragged away? I don't see it. I think we have to do what they want us to."

"We could ask graciously, civilly. Quick, we have to come to some final agreement. We can plead with them if that doesn't work—get on our knees even; anything."

"We can do that. I certainly will if it comes to that. But we'll see when our turn comes."

"It's coming; it's about to be here. I'm going to beg them first to keep us all together, and if that doesn't work, then for you to go with the girls. You'll last longer than I if it's as bad where they take us as it was in the car."

"One of us then will stay with the girls. If they don't go for it, then each of us with a child. OK, that's what we'll say and then insist on until they start getting a little tough."

There's room to move around now. Half the people have left the car. He gets down on his knees and kisses the girls, stands them up between Denise and him and he hugs her and their legs touch the children. "Should I start to worry now, Mother?" Olivia says and Denise says "No, absolutely not, sweetheart—Daddy and I will take care of you both."

"May it all be OK," he whispers in Denise's ear. "May it."

"Come on out of there," a man shouts. "All of you, out, out yours isn't the only car on the train."

"Good-bye all you lovely people," Bischoff says. "We did our best. Now God be with you and everything else that's good and I hope to see each of you in a warm clean room with tables of food."

Howard hands Eva to Denise, picks up Olivia and their rucksacks. "This is how we'll split the kids if it has to come to it, OK? By weight," and she nods and they walk out.

"All right, you," an officer says to Howard, "bags on the platform and go to that truck, and you, lady, go to that truck with the children." "No," she says, "let us stay together. Please, the older girl—" "I said do what I say," and he grabs Olivia to take her from Howard. Howard pulls her back. "Do that—stop me, and I'll shoot you right here in the head. Just one shot. That's all it'll take." Howard lets him have Olivia. The officer puts her down beside Denise. "What will happen to them?" Howard says.

"Next, come on—out with you and down the ramp, bags over there. Richard, get them out faster. You go that way," to a man coming toward him and points past Howard, "and you two, the same truck," to two young women. "Go, you both, what are you doing?—with your children and to your trucks," he says to Denise and Howard. "No more stalling." She stares at Howard as she drags Olivia along. A soldier tugs at his sleeve and he goes to the other truck. She's helped up into hers with the girls. Some more men and young women climb into his truck. He can't see her or the girls in her truck anymore. It's almost filled and then it's filled and it drives off. "Denise!" he screams. Many men are screaming women's names and the names and pet names of children, and the people in that truck, older people, mothers, children, are screaming to the people in his truck, and a few people on the platform are screaming to one or the other truck. Denise's truck disappears behind some buildings. He can hear it and then he can't. Then his truck's filled and a soldier raps the back of it with a stick and it pulls out. They'll never get our belongings to us, he thinks. What will the girls change in to? It makes no difference to him what he has. They'll give him a uniform or he'll make do. But Denise, the children. Denise, the children. "Oh no," and he starts sobbing. Someone pats his back. "Fortunately, I had no one," the man says.

Benediction

F. Scott Fitzgerald

I

The Baltimore Station was hot and crowded, so Lois was forced to stand by the telegraph desk for interminable, sticky seconds while a clerk with big front teeth counted and recounted a large lady's day message, to determine whether it contained the innocuous forty-nine words or the fatal fifty-one.

Lois, waiting, decided she wasn't quite sure of the address, so she took the letter out of her bag and ran over it again.

"Darling," it began—"I understand and I'm happier than life ever meant me to be. If I could give you the things you've always been in tune with—but I can't Lois; we can't marry and we can't lose each other and let all this glorious love end in nothing.

"Until your letter came, dear, I'd been sitting here in the half dark and thinking where I could go and ever forget you; abroad, perhaps, to drift through Italy or Spain and dream away the pain of having lost you where the crumbling ruins of older, mellower civilizations would mirror only the desolation of my heart—and then your letter came.

"Sweetest, bravest girl, if you'll wire me I'll meet you in Wilmington—till then I'll be here just waiting and hoping for every long dream of you to come true.

"Howard."

She had read the letter so many times that she knew it word by word, yet it still startled her. In it she found many faint reflections of the man who wrote it—the mingled sweetness and sadness in his dark eyes, the furtive, restless excitement she felt sometimes when he talked to her, his dreamy sensuousness that lulled her mind to sleep. Lois was nineteen and very romantic and curious and courageous.

The large lady and the clerk having compromised on fifty words, Lois took a blank and wrote her telegram. And there were no overtones to the finality of her decision.

It's just destiny—she thought—it's just the way things work out in this damn world. If cowardice is all that's been holding me back there won't be any more holding back. So we'll just let things take their course and never be sorry.

The clerk scanned her telegram:

"Arrived Baltimore today spend day with my brother meet me Wilmington three P.M. Wednesday

Love

"Lois."

"Fifty-four cents," said the clerk admiringly.

And never be sorry—thought Lois—and never be sorry—

II

Trees filtering light onto dapple grass. Trees like tall, languid ladies with feather fans coquetting airily with the ugly roof of the monastery. Trees like butlers, bending courteously over placid walks and paths. Trees, trees over the hills on either side and scattering out in clumps and lines and woods all through eastern Maryland, delicate lace on the hems of many yellow fields, dark opaque backgrounds for flowered bushes or wild climbing garden.

Some of the trees were very gay and young, but the monastery trees were older than the monastery which, by true monastic standards, wasn't very old at all. And, as a matter of fact, it wasn't technically called a monastery, but only a seminary; nevertheless it shall be a monastery here despite its Victorian architecture or its Edward VII additions, or even its Woodrow Wilsonian, patented, last-a-century roofing.

Out behind was the farm where half a dozen lay brothers were sweating lustily as they moved with deadly efficiency around the vegetable-gardens. To the left, behind a row of elms, was an informal baseball diamond where three novices were being batted out by a fourth, amid great chasings and puffings and blowings. And in front as a great mellow bell boomed the half-hour a swarm of black, human leaves were blown over the checker-board of paths under the courteous trees.

Some of these black leaves were very old with cheeks furrowed like the first ripples of a splashed pool. Then there was a scattering of middle-aged leaves whose forms when viewed in profile in their revealing gowns were beginning to be faintly unsymmetrical. These carried thick volumes of Thomas Aquinas and Henry James and Cardinal Mercier and Immanuel Kant and many bulging note-books filled with lecture data.

But most numerous were the young leaves; blond boys of nineteen with very stern, conscientious expressions; men in the late twenties with a keen self-assurance from having taught out in the world for five years—several hundreds of them, from city and town and country in Maryland and Pennsylvania and Virginia and West Virginia and Delaware.

There were many Americans and some Irish and some tough Irish and a few French, and several Italians and Poles, and they walked informally arm in arm with each other in twos and threes or in long rows, almost universally distinguished by the straight mouth and the considerable chin—for this was the Society of Jesus, founded in Spain five hundred years before by a tough-minded soldier who trained men to hold a breach or a salon, preach a sermon or write a treaty, and do it and not argue…

Lois got out of a bus into the sunshine down by the outer gate. She was nineteen with yellow hair and eyes that people were tactful enough not to call green. When men of talent saw her in a street-car they often furtively produced little stub-pencils and backs of envelopes and tried to sum up that profile or the thing that the eyebrows did to her eyes. Later they looked at their results and usually tore them up with wondering sighs.

Though Lois was very jauntily attired in an expensively appropriate travelling affair, she did not linger to pat out the dust which covered her clothes, but started up the central walk with curious glances at either side. Her face was very eager and expectant, yet she hadn't at all that glorified expression that girls wear when they arrive for a Senior Prom at Princeton or New Haven; still, as there were no senior proms here, perhaps it didn't matter.

She was wondering what he would look like, whether she'd possibly know him from his picture. In the picture, which hung over her mother's bureau at home, he seemed very young and hollow-cheeked and rather pitiful, with only a well-developed mouth and all ill-fitting probationer's gown to show that he had already made a momentous decision about his life. Of course he had been only nineteen then and now he was thirty-six—didn't look like that at all; in recent snap-shots he was much broader and his hair had grown a little thin—but the impression of her brother she had always retained was that of the big picture. And so she had always been a little sorry for him. What a life for a man! Seventeen years of preparation and he wasn't even a priest yet—wouldn't be for another year.

Lois had an idea that this was all going to be rather solemn if she let it be. But she was going to give her very best imitation of undiluted sunshine, the imitation she could give even when her head was splitting or when her mother had a nervous breakdown or when she was particularly romantic and curious and courageous. This brother of hers undoubtedly needed cheering up, and he was going to be cheered up, whether he liked it or not.

As she drew near the great, homely front door she saw a man break suddenly away from a group and, pulling up the skirts of his gown, run toward her. He was smiling, she noticed, and he looked very big and—and reliable. She stopped and waited, knew that her heart was beating unusually fast.

"Lois!" he cried, and in a second she was in his arms. She was suddenly trembling.

"Lois!" he cried again, "why, this is wonderful! I can't tell you, Lois, how much I've looked forward to this. Why, Lois, you're beautiful!"

Lois gasped.

His voice, though restrained, was vibrant with energy and that odd sort of enveloping personality she had thought that she only of the family possessed.

"I'm mighty glad, too—Keith."

She flushed, but not unhappily, at this first use of his name.

"Lois—Lois—Lois," he repeated in wonder. "Child, we'll go in here a minute, because I want you to meet the rector, and then we'll walk around. I have a thousand things to talk to you about."

His voice became graver. "How's mother?"

She looked at him for a moment and then said something that she had not intended to say at all, the very sort of thing she had resolved to avoid.

"Oh, Keith—she's—she's getting worse all the time, every way."

He nodded slowly as if he understood.

"Nervous, well—you can tell me about that later. Now—"

She was in a small study with a large desk, saying something to a little, jovial, white-haired priest who retained her hand for some seconds.

"So this is Lois!"

He said it as if he had heard of her for years.

He entreated her to sit down.

Two other priests arrived enthusiastically and shook hands with her and addressed her as "Keith's little sister," which she found she didn't mind a bit.

How assured they seemed; she had expected a certain shyness, reserve at least. There were several jokes unintelligible to her, which seemed to delight every one, and the little Father Rector referred to the trio of them as "dim old monks," which she appreciated, because of course they weren't monks at all. She had a lightning impression that they were especially fond of Keith—the Father Rector had called him "Keith" and one of the others had kept a hand on his shoulder all through the conversation. Then she was shaking hands again and promising to come back a little later for some ice-cream, and smiling and smiling and being rather absurdly happy...she told herself that it was because Keith was so delighted in showing her off.

Then she and Keith were strolling along a path, arm in arm, and he was informing her what an absolute jewel the Father Rector was.

"Lois," he broken off suddenly, "I want to tell you before we go any farther how much it means to me to have you come up here. I think it was—mighty sweet of you. I know what a gay time you've been having."

Lois gasped. She was not prepared for this. At first when she had conceived the plan of taking the hot journey down to Baltimore staying the night with a friend and then coming out to see her brother, she had felt rather consciously virtuous, hoped he wouldn't be priggish or resentful about her not having come before—but walking here with him under the trees seemed such a little thing, and surprisingly a happy thing.

"Why, Keith," she said quickly, "you know I couldn't have waited a day longer. I saw you when I was five, but of course I didn't remember, and how could I have gone on without practically ever having seen my only brother?"

"It was mighty sweet of you, Lois," he repeated.

Lois blushed—he *did* have personality.

"I want you to tell me all about yourself," he said after a pause. "Of course I have a general idea what you and mother did in Europe those fourteen years, and then we were all so worried, Lois, when you had pneumonia and couldn't come down with mother—let's see that was two years ago—and then, well, I've seen your name in the papers, but it's all been so unsatisfactory. I haven't known you, Lois."

She found herself analyzing his personality as she analyzed the personality of every man she met. She wondered if the effect of—of intimacy that he gave was bred by his constant repetition of her name. He said it as if he loved the word, as if it had an inherent meaning to him.

"Then you were at school," he continued.

"Yes, at Farmington. Mother wanted me to go to a convent—but I didn't want to."

She cast a side glance at him to see if he would resent this.

But he only nodded slowly.

"Had enough convents abroad, eh?"

"Yes—and Keith, convents are different there anyway. Here even in the nicest ones there are so many *common* girls."

He nodded again.

"Yes," he agreed, "I suppose there are, and I know how you feel about it. It grated on me here, at first, Lois, though I wouldn't say that to any one but you; we're rather sensitive, you and I, to things like this."

"You mean the men here?"

"Yes, some of them of course were fine, the sort of men I'd always been thrown with, but there were others; a man named Reagan, for instance—I hated the fellow, and now he's about the best friend I have. A wonderful character, Lois; you'll meet him later. Sort of man you'd like to have with you in a fight."

Lois was thinking that Keith was the sort of man she'd like to have with *her* in a fight.

"How did you—how did you first happen to do it?" she asked, rather shyly, "to come here, I mean. Of course mother told me the story about the Pullman car."

"Oh, that—" He looked rather annoyed.

"Tell me that. I'd like to hear you tell it."

"Oh, it's nothing except what you probably know. It was evening and I'd been riding all day and thinking about—about a hundred things, Lois, and then suddenly I had a sense that some one was sitting across from me, felt that he'd been there for some time, and had a vague idea that he was another traveller. All at once he leaned over toward me and I heard a voice say: 'I want you to be a priest, that's what I want.' Well I jumped up and cried out, 'Oh, my God, not that!'—made an idiot of myself before about twenty people; you see there wasn't any one sitting there at all. A week after that I went to the Jesuit College in Philadelphia and crawled up the last flight of stairs to the rector's office on my hands and knees."

There was another silence and Lois saw that her brother's eyes wore a far-away look, that he was staring unseeingly out over the sunny fields. She was stirred by the modulations of his voice and the sudden silence that seemed to flow about him when he finished speaking.

She noticed now that his eyes were of the same fibre as hers, with the green left out, and that his mouth was much gentler, really, than in the picture —or was it that the face had grown up to it lately? He was getting a little bald just on top of his head. She wondered if that was from wearing a hat so much. It seemed awful for a man to grow bald and no one to care about it.

"Were you—pious when you were young, Keith?" she asked. "You know what I mean. Were you religious? If you don't mind these personal questions."

"Yes," he said with his eyes still far away—and she felt that his intense abstraction was as much a part of his personality as his attention. "Yes, I suppose I was, when I was—sober."

Lois thrilled slightly.

"Did you drink?"

He nodded.

"I was on the way to making a bad hash of things." He smiled and, turning his gray eyes on her, changed the subject.

"Child, tell me about mother. I know it's been awfully hard for you there, lately. I know you've had to sacrifice a lot and put up with a great deal and I want you to know how fine of you I think it is. I feel, Lois, that you're sort of taking the place of both of us there."

Lois thought quickly how little she had sacrificed; how lately she had constantly avoided her nervous, half-invalid mother.

"Youth shouldn't be sacrificed to age, Keith," she said steadily.

"I know," he sighed, "and you oughtn't to have the weight on your shoulders, child. I wish I were there to help you."

She saw how quickly he had turned her remark and instantly she knew what this quality was that he gave off. He was *sweet.* Her thoughts went of on a side-track and then she broke the silence with an odd remark.

"Sweetness is hard," she said suddenly.

"What?"

"Nothing," she denied in confusion. "I didn't mean to speak aloud. I was thinking of something—of a conversation with a man named Freddy Kebble."

"Maury Kebble's brother?"

"Yes," she said rather surprised to think of him having known Maury Kebble. Still there was nothing strange about it. "Well, he and I were talking about sweetness a few weeks ago. Oh, I don't know—I said that a man named Howard—that a man I knew was sweet, and he didn't agree with me, and we began talking about what sweetness in a man was: He kept telling me I meant a sort of soppy softness, but I knew I didn't—yet I didn't know exactly how to put it. I see now. I meant just the opposite. I suppose real sweetness is a sort of hardness—and strength."

Keith nodded.

"I see what you mean. I've known old priests who had it."

"I'm talking about young men," she said rather defiantly.

They had reached the now deserted baseball diamond and, pointing her to a wooden bench, he sprawled full length on the grass.

"Are these *young* men happy here, Keith?"

"Don't they look happy, Lois?"

"I suppose so, but those *young* ones, those two we just passed— have they—are they—?"

"Are they signed up?" he laughed. "No, but they will be next month."

"Permanently?"

"Yes—unless they break down mentally or physically. Of course in a discipline like ours a lot drop out."

"But those *boys*. Are they giving up fine chances outside—like you did?"

He nodded.

"Some of them."

"But Keith, they don't know what they're doing. They haven't had any experience of what they're missing."

"No, I suppose not."

"It doesn't seem fair. Life has just sort of scared them at first. Do they all come in so *young*?"

"No, some of them have knocked around, led pretty wild lives—Reagan, for instance."

"I should think that sort would be better," she said meditatively, "men that had *seen* life."

"No," said Keith earnestly, "I'm not sure that knocking about gives a man the sort of experience he can communicate to others. Some of the broadest men I've known have been absolutely rigid about themselves. And reformed libertines are a notoriously intolerant class. Don't you think so, Lois?"

She nodded, still meditative, and he continued:

"It seems to me that when one weak reason goes to another, it isn't help they want; it's a sort of companionship in guilt, Lois. After you were born, when mother began to get nervous she used to go and weep with a certain Mrs. Comstock. Lord, it used to make me shiver. She said it comforted her, poor old mother. No, I don't think that to help others you've got to show yourself at all. Real help comes from a stronger person whom you respect. And their sympathy is all the bigger because it's impersonal."

"But people want human sympathy," objected Lois. "They want to feel the other person's been tempted."

"Lois, in their hearts they want to feel that the other person's been weak. That's what they mean by human.

"Here in this old monkery, Lois," he continued with a smile, "they try to get all that self-pity and pride in our own wills out of us right at the first. They put us to scrubbing floors—and other things. It's like that idea of saving your life by losing it. You see we sort of feel that the less human a man is, in your sense of human, the better servant he can be to humanity. We carry it out to the end, too. When one of us dies his family can't even have him then. He's buried here under plain wooden cross with a thousand others."

His tone changed suddenly and he looked at her with a great brightness in his gray eyes.

"But way back in a man's heart there are some things he can't get rid of—an one of them is that I'm awfully in love with my little sister."

With a sudden impulse she knelt beside him in the grass and, Leaning over, kissed his forehead.

"You're hard, Keith," she said, "and I love you for it—and you're sweet."

III

Back in the reception-room Lois met a half-dozen more of Keith's particular friends; there was a young man named Jarvis, rather pale and delicate-looking, who, she knew, must be a grandson of old Mrs. Jarvis at home, and she mentally compared this ascetic with a brace of his riotous uncles.

And there was Regan with a scarred face and piercing intent eyes that followed her about the room and often rested on Keith with something very like worship. She knew then what Keith had meant about "a good man to have with you in a fight."

He's the missionary type—she thought vaguely—China or something.

"I want Keith's sister to show us what the shimmy is," demanded one young man with a broad grin.

Lois laughed.

"I'm afraid the Father Rector would send me shimmying out the gate. Besides, I'm not an expert."

"I'm sure it wouldn't be best for Jimmy's soul anyway," said Keith solemnly. "He's inclined to brood about things like shimmys. They were just starting to do the—maxixe, wasn't it, Jimmy?—when he became a monk, and it haunted him his whole first year. You'd see him when he was peeling potatoes, putting his arm around the bucket and making irreligious motions with his feet."

There was a general laugh in which Lois joined.

"An old lady who comes here to Mass sent Keith this ice-cream," whispered Jarvis under cover of the laugh, "because she'd heard you were coming. It's pretty good, isn't it?"

There were tears trembling in Lois' eyes.

IV

Then half an hour later over in the chapel things suddenly went all wrong. It was several years since Lois had been at Benediction and at first she was thrilled by the gleaming monstrance with its central spot of white, the air rich and heavy with incense, and the sun shining through the stained-glass window of St. Francis Xavier overhead and falling in warm red tracery on the cassock of the man in front of her, but at the first notes of the "O Salutaris Hostia" a heavy weight seemed to descend upon her soul. Keith was on her right and young Jarvis on her left, and she stole uneasy glance at both of them.

What's the matter with me? she thought impatiently.

She looked again. Was there a certain coldness in both their profiles, that she had not noticed before—a pallor about the mouth and a curious set expression in their eyes? She shivered slightly: they were like dead men.

She felt her soul recede suddenly from Keith's. This was her brother—

this, this unnatural person. She caught herself in the act of a little laugh.

"What is the matter with me?"

She passed her hand over her eyes and the weight increased. The incense sickened her and a stray, ragged note from one of the tenors in the choir grated on her ear like the shriek of a slate-pencil. She fidgeted, and raising her hand to her hair touched her forehead, found moisture on it.

"It's hot in here, hot as the deuce."

Again she repressed a faint laugh and, then in an instant the weight on her heart suddenly diffused into cold fear.... It was that candle on the altar. It was all wrong—wrong. Why didn't somebody see it? There was something *in* it. There was something coming out of it, taking form and shape above it.

She tried to fight down her rising panic, told herself it was the wick. If the wick wasn't straight, candles did something—but they didn't do this! With incalculable rapidity a force was gathering within her, a tremendous, assimilative force, drawing from every sense, every corner of her brain, and as it surged up inside her she felt an enormous terrified repulsion. She drew her arms in close to her side away from Keith and Jarvis.

Something in that candle...she was leaning forward—in another moment she felt she would go forward toward it—didn't any one see it?... anyone?

"Ugh!"

She felt a space beside her and something told her that Jarvis had gasped and sat down very suddenly... then she was kneeling and as the flaming monstrance slowly left the altar in the hands of the priest, she heard a great rushing noise in her ears—the crash of the bells was like hammer-blows...and then in a moment that seemed eternal a great torrent rolled over her heart—there was a shouting there and a lashing as of waves...

She was calling, felt herself calling for Keith, her lips mouthing the words that would not come:

"Keith! Oh, my God! *Keith*!"

Suddenly she became aware of a new presence, something external, in front of her, consummated and expressed in warm red tracery. Then she knew. It was the window of St. Francis Xavier. Her mind gripped at it, clung to it finally, and she felt herself calling again endlessly, impotently—Keith—Keith!

Then out of a great stillness came a voice:

"Blessed be God."

With a gradual rumble sounded the response rolling heavily through the chapel:

"Blessed be God."

The words sang instantly in her heart; the incense lay mystically and sweetly peaceful upon the air, and *the candle on the altar went out.*

"Blessed be His Holy Name."

"Blessed be His Holy Name."

Everything blurred into a swinging mist. With a sound half-gasp, half-cry she rocked on her feet and reeled backward into Keith's suddenly outstretched arms.

V

"Lie still, child."

She closed her eyes again. She was on the grass outside, pillowed on Keith's arm, and Regan was dabbing her head with a cold towel.

"I'm all right," she said quietly.

"I know, but just lie still a minute longer. It was too hot in there. Jarvis felt it, too."

She laughed as Regan again touched her gingerly with the towel.

"I'm all right," she repeated.

But though a warm peace was falling her mind and heart she felt oddly broken and chastened, as if some one had held her stripped soul up and laughed.

VI

Half an hour later she walked leaning on Keith's arm down the long central path toward the gate.

"It's been such a short afternoon," he sighed, "and I'm so sorry you were sick, Lois."

"Keith, I'm feeling fine now, really; I wish you wouldn't worry."

"Poor old child. I didn't realize that Benediction'd be a long service for you after your hot trip out here and all."

She laughed cheerfully.

"I guess the truth is I'm not much used to Benediction. Mass is the limit of my religious exertions."

She paused and then continued quickly:

"I don't want to shock you, Keith, but I can't tell you how—how *inconvenient* being a Catholic is. It really doesn't seem to apply any more. As far as morals go, some of the wildest boys I know are Catholics. And the brightest boys—I mean the ones who think and read a lot, don't seem to believe in much of anything any more."

"Tell me about it. The bus won't be here for another half-hour."

They sat down on a bench by the path.

"For instance, Gerald Carter, he's published a novel. He absolutely roars when people mention immortality. And then Howa—well, another man I've known well, lately, who was Phi Beta Kappa at Hazard says that no intelligent person can believe in Supernatural Christianity. He says Christ was a great socialist, though. Am I shocking you?"

She broke off suddenly.

Keith smiled.

"You can't shock a monk. He's a professional shock-absorber."

"Well," she continued, "that's about all. It seems so—so *narrow*. Church schools, for instance. There's more freedom about things that Catholic people can't see—like birth control."

Keith winced, almost imperceptibly, but Lois saw it.

"Oh," she said quickly, "everybody talks about everything now."

"It's probably better that way."

"Oh, yes, much better. Well, that's all, Keith. I just wanted to tell you why I'm a little—luke-warm, at present."

"I'm not shocked, Lois. I understand better than you think. We all go through those times. But I know it'll come out all right, child. There's that gift of faith that we have, you and I, that'll carry us past the bad spots."

He rose as he spoke and they started again down the path.

"I want you to pray for me sometimes, Lois. I think your prayers would be about what I need. Because we've come very close in these few hours, I think."

Her eyes were suddenly shining.

"Oh we have, we have!" she cried. "I feel closer to you now than to any one in the world."

He stopped suddenly and indicated the side of the path.

"We might—just a minute—"

It was a pietà, a life-size statue of the Blessed Virgin set within a semicircle of rocks.

Feeling a little self-conscious she dropped on her knees beside him and made an unsuccessful attempt at prayer.

She was only half through when he rose. He took her arm again.

"I wanted to thank Her for letting as have this day together," he said simply.

Lois felt a sudden lump in her throat and she wanted to say something that would tell him how much it had meant to her, too. But she found no words.

"I'll always remember this," he continued, his voice trembling a little—"this slimmer day with you. It's been just what I expected. You're just what I expected, Lois."

"I'm awfully glad, Keith."

"You see, when you were little they kept sending me snap-shots of you, first as a baby and then as a child in socks playing on the beach with a pail and shovel, and then suddenly as a wistful little girl with wondering, pure eyes—and I used to build dreams about you. A man has to have something living to cling to. I think, Lois, it was your little white soul I tried to keep near me—even when life was at its loudest and every intellectual idea of God seemed the sheerest mockery, and desire and love and a million things came up to me and said: 'Look here at me! See, I'm Life. You're turning your back on it!' All the way through that shadow, Lois, I could always see your baby soul flitting on ahead of me, very frail and clear and wonderful."

Lois was crying softly. They had reached the gate and she rested her elbow on it and dabbed furiously at her eyes.

"And then later, child, when you were sick I knelt all one night and asked God to spare you for me—for I knew then that I wanted more; He had taught me to want more. I wanted to know you moved and breathed in the same world with me. I saw you growing up, that white innocence of yours changing to a flame and burning to give light to other weaker souls. And then I wanted some day to take your children on my knee and hear them call the crabbed old monk Uncle Keith."

He seemed to be laughing now as he talked.

"Oh, Lois, Lois, I was asking God for more then. I wanted the letters you'd write me and the place I'd have at your table. I wanted an awful lot, Lois, dear."

"You've got me, Keith," she sobbed "you know it, say you know it. Oh, I'm acting like a baby but I didn't think you'd be this way, and I—oh,

Keith—Keith—"

He took her hand and patted it softly.

"Here's the bus. You'll come again won't you?"

She put her hands on his cheeks, add drawing his head down, pressed her tear-wet face against his.

"Oh, Keith, brother, some day I'll tell you something."

He helped her in, saw her take down her handkerchief and smile bravely at him, as the driver kicked his whip and the bus rolled off. Then a thick cloud of dust rose around it and she was gone.

For a few minutes he stood there on the road his hand on the gate-post, his lips half parted in a smile.

"Lois," he said aloud in a sort of wonder, "Lois, Lois."

Later, some probationers passing noticed him kneeling before the pietà, and coming back after a time found him still there. And he was there until twilight came own and the courteous trees grew garrulous overhead and the crickets took up their burden of song in the dusky grass.

VII

The first clerk in the telegraph booth in the Baltimore Station whistled through his buck teeth at the second clerk:

"S'matter?"

"See that girl—no, the pretty one with the big black dots on her veil. Too late—she's gone. You missed somep'n."

"What about her?"

"Nothing. 'Cept she's damn good-looking. Came in here yesterday and sent a wire to some guy to meet her somewhere. Then a minute ago she came in with a telegram all written out and was standin' there goin' to give it to me when she changed her mind or somep'n and all of a sudden tore it up."

"Hm."

The first clerk came around tile counter and picking up the two pieces of paper from the floor put them together idly. The second clerk read them over his shoulder and subconsciously counted the words as he read. There were just thirteen.

"This is in the way of a permanent goodbye. I should suggest Italy."

"Lois."

"Tore it up, eh?" said the second clerk.

Dear Everybody

MICHAEL KIMBALL

[1967]

Dear Mom and Dad,

I didn't know that I was two weeks late and that you were waiting for me. But it always made me feel special to know that Ingham County had to send a snowplow out to our house. It always made me feel special to think of Dad driving the car so slowly behind the snowplow and Mom with her hands on top of her stomach as if I were an important, but breakable, package. I always thought that there was some important destiny in that for me. I always thought that the path that was cleared through all of that cold and snow was somehow going to determine the rest of my life.

[1969]

Dear Dad,

Thank you for taking me to the barbershop to get my hair cut for the first time. I know that it was long and curly and that Mom said that it looked pretty, but I didn't like all of the other moms and dads thinking that I was a girl either.

[1970]

Dear Mom and Dad,

I'm sorry that I pulled the stitching out of my feather pillow and then pulled all of the feathers out of it. I thought that I was going to find a bird.

[1973]

Dear Kathy Granger,

Do you remember when I used to stand on the sidewalk outside your house and yell out your name until you came out to play with me? I didn't know that you were just my babysitter and that my mom and dad paid you to watch me. I thought that you really liked me—and not just because I was a cute little boy. I thought that we were going to get married when I was old enough.

[1974]

Dear Grandma and Grandpa Winters,

Thank you for giving me the Etch-a-Sketch for my seventh birthday. I liked drawing with it better than drawing on the walls, but I always felt bad when I shook it and everything on its magic screen disappeared. It reminded me of how my dad would grab me by both of my shoulders and shake me until everything went blank inside of me too.

[1975]

Dear Scott Poor,

I'm not sorry that I hit you over the head with my Scooby-Doo lunch box and cracked your head open with it. You were a lot bigger than I was then and I was afraid of you and I wanted you and your brother to stop picking on me on the way home from school. But here's what I want to know: Did the doctor show you what it looked like inside your head? If he did, I bet it looked mean.

[1977]

Dear Secret Admirer,

Thank you for giving me the Valentine on Valentine's Day that asked me if I would be your Valentine. I would have been. I wanted to be. But I couldn't ever figure out who you were.

[1978]

Dear Dad,

They taught us in our sexual education class that a baby lives in its mother for nine months. So I counted the nine months back from my birthday, added on the two weeks that I was late, and figured out that I must have been conceived around your birthday, which means that one of your birthday presents turned out to be me.

Happy birthday, Dad.

[1981]

Dear Dr. Fritch,

I cried when you told me that I had a cavity because I didn't want you to drill a hole inside one of my teeth and then fill it back in with some kind of metal. I hated the idea that I was already beginning to rot.

[1982]

Dear Dr. Adler:

That test that you asked me to take knew how I felt. I did feel blue. I did feel sad. I did feel bored most of the time. But here is what I need to know: When I feel happy, what color will that be? Because I know that the red pills were supposed to make me feel better. But I stopped taking them because they were red and they made the whole world blurry. Sometimes, I would start to shake even when I wasn't afraid of anything. Other times, I couldn't think or I didn't know where I was. And one time, those red pills gave me red spots on my skin that made me feel prickly and hot. I thought that I had set myself on fire.

[1984]

Dear Michael J. Fox or Alex P. Keaton,

I didn't like your television show even though everybody at school talked about how funny it was. I didn't think it was funny and I didn't even believe that it was true that anybody's family could get along like that. I know that television is made up, but it should at least be believable. I mean, we were supposed to be about the same age, so how could our lives be so different?

[1985]

Dear Jessica Cooper,

I'm sorry that I stood you up for the date that we were supposed to have on Valentine's Day in 1985. Do you think that we could have been happy together?

[1987]

Dear Mom and Dad,

I know that you had to sell the house that we had all lived in for so many years when you got divorced. But I don't think that you should have sold it to that young couple. The same thing was probably going to happen to them.

[1988]

Dear Man in the White Pants and White Shirt Who Looked at Me Through a Face-Sized Window Every Half Hour,

I know that you were just looking in on me to make sure that I wasn't trying to kill myself. I know that you were just checking off that I was still alive at 1:30, at 2:00, at 2:30, etc., but I liked seeing your face in that little window and I started to wait for you to appear. I found it reassuring.

[1990]

Dear Ellen Lipsyte,

You probably thought that it was me who kept calling and hanging up after we broke up. It was. I wanted to see whether you were at home at night or whether you were already going out with somebody else. I was glad that you kept answering the telephone. I'm sorry that I kept hanging up.

[1991]

Dear Weather Satellite,

I didn't know many people when I first moved to Jefferson City. That's why I used to watch you blinking your way across the sky at night and that made me think that you were winking at me and that made me think that we were friends. That's why I climbed up onto the roof of my apartment building every night to look for you—even if it was cold, even if there were clouds. I was comforted to know that you were still traveling in your orbit around me.

[1992]

Dear Sara,

You were so beautiful the first time that I saw you that the first thing I thought was that I wasn't good enough for you. I still don't know why you thought I was, but thank you for smiling at me so that I could smile back at you. I didn't think that I was ever going to meet you.

[1993]

Dear Sara,

Thank you for moving into my apartment and living there with me. I needed somebody else to sit on the couch and the chairs with me. I needed somebody else to watch the television with me. I needed somebody else to eat at the kitchen table with me. I needed somebody else to put their clothes in the dresser drawers and the closet with my clothes.

[1994]

Dear Sara,

Thank you for making me put a sliver of our wedding cake under my pillow on our wedding night. It made quite a mess, but I always had the sweetest dreams of you.

[1995]

Dear Sara,

I know how much that you wanted to have children. I did too. That's why I was always disappointed when your menses came every month. I have always thought of all of that blood as one of my failures. I really thought that we were going to have one kid and then another kid. I thought that the kids would get bigger and that we would eventually move into a bigger house. I thought that our kids would have kids and we would become grandparents together. I thought that we would retire and then take care of each other. I never expected so much of that to never happen to us. I can't believe that my forecast for the rest of our lives was so far off.

[1996]

Dear Sara,

I smashed the television screen with a hammer because I thought that it was watching us. Even when it was off, I could see this faint reflection of somebody in the screen. Also, I unplugged the radio because I thought that it was listening to me and broadcasting everything that I thought outside my head. But even after I unplugged the radio, I could still hear them talking. That's why I threw the radio outside in the rain where it probably got electrocuted.

What I'm trying to say is thank you for holding onto me so tightly when I couldn't hold onto myself anymore. Sometimes, I can still feel your arms around me trying to hold me still.

[1997]

Dear Dr. Gregory,

Thank you for writing a new prescription for me. I think that it helped that the pills were red. That seemed to stop some of the voices from talking to me.

[1998]

Dear Sara,

I used to walk around the house looking for things that you had left behind—clothes, a blow dryer, the pillow that you liked to sleep on—so that I would have an excuse to call you up and see you. But it wasn't long before I couldn't find anything else in the house that was yours. That's when I started buying things that you used to use so that I could pretend that you had left them behind—your favorite shampoo, that hand lotion you used, blue jeans and shoes that were in your size. I didn't mean to be so desperate.

[1999]

Dear Sara,

I didn't sign the divorce papers because I wanted to be married to you for as long as I could. I was even hoping that you wouldn't be able to divorce me at all if I didn't sign them. You didn't have to go to a judge to prove that I was unfit for marriage.

Since we really are divorced now, I think that we should split up our memories too. I want the time when we met and the time when we went to the Grand Canyon. You can have our first date and the day we got married. You can also have the day when you left me, which I have no use for. I want when we moved in together and when we bought our house, though, and I want all of the times that we sat on the couch and watched television together. You can have the times we ate breakfast together, but I want most of the dinners. There are a lot more. Maybe we should talk about all of them.

Family Pics

Leigh Newman

Once Mom was gone, I squinted into the sunlight a lot while Dad took my picture. This was on porch steps with lunch boxes, outside pizza parlors with doggie bags, in front of bronzed presidents and wish-penny fountains and the LA Zoo ticket booth, rubbing at blisters under my sandal straps. This was back when cameras were manual. I was six, maybe seven, fidgeting by the hippo house while Dad focused through the blurred aquarium inside the lens.

"Almost got it now. Don't move"

"You said I got to get a popcorn."

"In a minute. Now where's a smile for your old Dad?"

I used every tooth, even bubbled up a laugh. "Look what a great time we're having" was the smile I had in mind. Just in case Mom was sneaking back into our house while we were asleep—looking around, touching the furniture, taking her left-behind shoes and clothes and necklaces that everyday kept disappearing—and maybe saw my picture up there on the wall.

***

I never worried where Dad was, even in a crowded gym full of fathers and mothers, faces and knees and laps. He was always in the back, bursting into an applause of flashes—the hot white confetti so thick in the air above people's heads, you expected the mothers to shake bits of light from their hair, the fathers to brush it off their shoulders.

Mostly, it went like this: I was sitting up on stage (flash), standing up for French club (flash), walking over to the podium (flash), shaking hands with the principal (flash, flash, flash), sitting back down (flash), waving at Dad from the stage the way the teachers said not to (flash, flash, flash, flash, flash).

The glee club sang. Our fourth-grade class paraded out. Dad switched to indoor/outdoor film and took me at the door of the gym, at the door to the spaghetti restaurant, at the table with a celebration plate of al fredo, then back outside on the sidewalk, "just to finish off the last of the roll."

I strangled myself.

"What kind of face is that?"

I stuck out a gaspy tongue.

"Come on, now. Cut that out now, before you hurt someone."

I smiled, and Dad knew my real smile. But he took me all the same.

***

Nights, he stood at my bedroom door—a shadow Dad in the left-on hall light. I shut my eyes, or shut the crack of them that was open. I kept my breath slow and even. I listened for the oily metal click, the zipper sound of film advancing. His socks made a ragged sound on the carpet. My nose itched.

I daydreamed to keep still, as if I really were asleep. Inside in my head, the postman brought me a letter from Mom asking me to come to France or Canada or farther away places with jungle-bird stamps. Would I live there with her, please, please she begged in green pen. Sometimes I wrote "YES" in magic marker on a postcard. Then scratched it out, wrote "OK." Sometimes I tore up her letters, sent only the paper bits back.

Other times I was older. I hired a private detective who found Mom living in a pioneer cabin, in the forest. When I knocked on the door, a little girl answered with braids and a calico dress, saying, "Mom? Somebody's here for you." Mom's voice said, "Who?" The girl said, "A lady. A stranger." And I ran away.

The film advanced, the button clicked.

I was Mom in the daydream now. And instead of writing that note to Dad, the Mom-me ripped it up and put the suitcases back under the bed and hung the car keys back on the closet hook. Then the Mom-me sat in the kitchen, waiting for the regular me to come home from school so we could leave Dad together. "Hurry," the Mom-me said. "He'll be here soon."

But I could feel the words coming out of my mouth and I had to mumble them into the pillows and not laugh, even when the car made a farting noise as the Mom-me drove us both away down the driveway. Nobody laughs in their sleep.

The film advanced, the button clicked.

***

Not that it makes a difference, but I was in ninth grade or tenth, sitting on the couch, watching television when I felt Dad moving in behind me in that eyes-in-the-back-of-your-head way that he always said was how he caught me in his wallet or over in the neighbor's yard coughing down a practice cigarette. I held still, my chin in my hand, blue wisps of screen-light across my face.

It was a game I played lately. I had to move a little to keep it candid-looking—shifting my weight, re-crossing my legs—but always staring at the television, as if so deep in the show that I didn't notice the plastic shuffles of his zoom telescoping in. Then, casually, I positioned my fingers over the zit on my chin, set my eyes to blanked-out, waited for the click.

Let's Make A Deal was on, or another flashy show with mirrored doors and dinging bells. I waited for the click. The screen went hysterical with clapping. I waited for the click. A blonde woman jumped up and down, her blouse flapping out. And Mom's quilt rose up, up, up over me on the bed—making a parachute, making a rainbow-patched roof for my hideout that fell down over me heavy and black. Her hands smoothed the quilt over my nose and mouth and face out towards the corners of the mattress. "Well, the bed's made. Now where'd that little girl get to? Where could she be?"

Click. I was on the couch, my fingers over my zit. "Dad, who wants a picture of me watching television?"

"Take your feet off the coffee table."

"What do you do? Save them for Mom in case she ever shows up and wonders what she missed?"

"Honey."

On the screen, a man stood panicked, choosing between doors behind which a prize might be hidden. Door 1 or Door 2? Door 1 or Door 3?

"It's my fault, isn't it? I know it. I should talk to you about your mother more, right?"

The man pointed. Door 1 swung open—a model riding a donkey, canned clucks of sympathy from the audience. I turned around, just as Dad reached for my head as if to pat it, his hand hovering out of his sad-sacky bathrobe with the missing belt. I grabbed the camera from him, zoomed in.

"What are you doing?"

"Taking your picture."

"Don't be ridiculous."

"Smile."

"That's enough. If you're upset about your mother, let's discuss it."

"Smile."

"That's enough I said!"

The camera went flying, landed on the hardwood floor in a plastic, metal crunch.

"Dad, you didn't have to hit it out of my hands."

"I didn't. I was reaching for it. It slipped"

"I wanted one of you."

"Well I don't. I don't want me in a picture! Understood!"

"She's a bitch."

"She's your mother."

"Don't even say her name."

"She's your mother."

"Say it one more time and I'll leave you too, for forever. And it's not just me like a kid saying it either."

***

That soft, cottony feeling I had wasn't real, was it? Not if I only had it looking at the one picture of her and me together? I put it back under the mattress, took a shower, got dressed. I still had that feeling just looking at the mattress, just thinking of the picture under the mattress, where I was lying on her chest, pulling on her blond long hair so you couldn't see her face. She was in her nightgown. I was a baby and too young to remember. In fact, I didn't remember. It was the picture, brainwashing my head. I shoved it into the kitchen trash. Somebody put it back under my mattress. I stubbed our faces out, ashtray-style, then left it on Dad's pillow. He grounded me for smoking in the house, again. I snuck out, again—to meet a boy old enough to buy me beer. Without a fake ID.

***

By the end of high school, Dad gave up on pretending to take pictures of me with my friends. He made Peggy Webster, her boyfriend, and her brother, my blind date, stand over in the grass, while he got one of me on the walkway, all dressed up. I was into clothing that suggested heavy-metal weddings and S&M nuns—torn masses of lace, unexplained buckles. I hunched seductively. I coordinated my raised eyebrow with my mysterious, video look.

"Not like that honey."

"Not like what?"

"Just stand up and smile normal and happy."

"Dad."

"Think of how you smiled in that one with the yellow dress."

"I don't have a yellow dress."

"Remember? In that picture of you with your long hair and yellow dress in front of the old green MG?"

I pointed out his car was a Toyota and silver, my dress was fuchsia, my hair short, I didn't remember, and I had a prom and an after-party to get to.

"You had your one hand on your hip. And your hip stuck out a little. And you were waving at me with the other hand. Like this."

"Okay, Dad."

"I love that picture."

I gritted out a smile.

He clicked.

And my friends and I took off—waving at invisible crowds through the open sunroof of our rental limousine.

***

Sightseeing on vacation, there were always people—overweight, Midwestern wives mostly—who would drop out of their couple-couple poses, separating their arms from around their husbands' necks to ask if Dad and me wanted them to take "one of us together."

"No thanks."

"Are you sure? It's so romantic. The Eiffel Tower."

"My daughter and I are fine. Honey, push your sunglasses up so I can see your face."

The wind was blowing. People walked in headlong diagonals, struggling across the viewing deck. My long hair whipped out across the railing—purple-green instead of the purple-black on the drugstore package.

I put a distant, artistic look on my face, stared through my smoky, cat-frame lenses.

"Your glasses, honey."

"Just take it, okay? Push the button."

"You're beautiful under there. Let's see."

"Push the button, Dad. Jesus Christ. Get it over with. Who gives a shit?"

Dad had a new point-and-shoot, a smaller camera than he was used to. It didn't cover enough of his face. The hurt spread down though his cheeks and jaw and into the smile he held onto as if it would blow away.

He didn't take me at the door of the guidebook bistro. He didn't take me by the cage of live doves hanging from the ceiling or at the table with the understated Parisian flower in a vase. We drank champagne. We ordered and didn't eat sweet breads. Dad had a glass of some licorice drink, and another and another.

"I'm telling you and you don't know. And I know, I know, you're into this pissed-off look and all that—off to college, off to fun, screw this. I know, I know, sweetheart. You don't know. You don't."

"Miss?"

"This isn't you. I'm telling you. And I know. You're happy. You're in that yellow dress, okay? In front of the green MG. It never started. It flooded. A crap lemon. You had sunglasses on. But on top of your head. And your hand on your hip. And you were waving at me."

"Miss? Madame? The check?"

"It was like a coat but a dress. It had a belt. And yellow."

"I remember, Dad. I remember."

"You were happy. You were waving. Your sandals were red."

I stopped outside the door to the bistro, smiled. He fumbled with the point-and-shoot as if it were the old manual, trying to focus through his liquor vision. There was a butcher's window across the street. I could see us in it, and the window of the bistro and the cage inside the bistro that looked balanced on my shoulder. I stuck out my hip, put my hand on it. The automatic flash exploded, the doves burst up, I waved through the panic of falling feathers.

***

Parents' day, my college roommate's parents went to the islands with friends instead. Dad adopted her, despite her plan to study up on chemicals. She was a lumpy, misshaped girl with fast sense of humor. She wore sweaters over sweaters. We were friends, but mostly in our room.

At the tailgate and football game, I searched for the guy I was seeing, who was somewhere with his parents who he hadn't asked me to meet. Dad and my roommate disappeared in all the beer cups and elbows. I saw the guy I was seeing. He nodded across the bleachers at me, then worked his eyes back to his mother, who was gesturing out some apparently hysterical story from home with her hands.

Dad and my roommate were already joking about chemicals when I found them at the parent restaurant. My roommate constructed a molecule out of breadsticks. Dad smashed it into crumbs of fission energy. She imitated her professor, down to his Lithuanian accent. He laughed, imitated his Russian grade school teacher. She laughed. I laughed. She went to the bathroom.

"She's a pistol, honey! You lucked out."

"Yeah, she's a funny girl."

"Smart, too."

And sensitive. She didn't mind at all if Dad wanted to take one of me on the sidewalk. She understood completely.

"Dad?"

"Just a minute. I have to change batteries."

"Why don't you take a roommates' picture this time?"

"But—"

"One of the two of us."

"Well, okay. Sure. If that's what you want."

We stood shoulder to shoulder, our arms around each other. I had my long hair and yellow dress on. It was a sundress. I was a daisy. She was a sweater, a molecule, a chemical. I stuck my hip out, waved and smiled, happy and normal.

***

The picture wasn't in the hallway display or in the living room montage or in the extensive collection magneted on the fridge. Upstairs under the bed, Dad had all the extras in shoeboxes. I went through all of them that summer after graduation, while he was off at work and I was at home, "thinking of plans for my future."

Each of the shoeboxes was labeled with the year and the title Family Pics. I went in descending order. There I was in '93 and '92 in yellow halters and mini-skirts, waving in front of the stadium and the history building and the college hotel where Dad always stayed. There I was in '88 in Guess? jeans, expertly ripped across the butt and knees, sitting in the Toyota with my hot-pressed license. There I was in a tutu at a '79 ballet recital, in drab-shorts on a '78 Girl-Scout mountain, in a '77 blue, Snoopy jumper on the steps of nursery school. And there it stopped. The family photos of me ended at age six, with me in a gypsy costume on Halloween.

Maybe Mom took ages one through five with her. Or maybe they just disappeared—along with her coffee mug and bird calendar and ashtray and flower vases and raincoat and purses and lipsticks and books and records and the picture of her and me sleeping on the bed. Unless that was all in a box somewhere too, hidden in a closet or cabinet.

"Where's the one of me in the yellow dress?"

"In the shoeboxes somewhere."

"No it's not. I looked."

"Well you must have missed it."

"I was wearing red sandals and sunglasses?"

"I think so. I don't remember just this minute."

"How old was I? Six? Seven?"

"I guess so."

"Who wears sunglasses when they're seven?"

"What are you so mad about?"

"I'm not mad!"

"What are you then?"

"I don't know what I am! I'm just asking where the picture is!"

Dad sat down at the kitchen table and started sorting through the mail, as if each letter was a present—the envelope a wrapping paper he had to admire before peeling it off, folding it up to reuse later. "If you need to leave this house, don't pick a stupid fight. Just go ahead and go, okay?"

"I will then."

"You're free to. Just leave me a note."

"Dad, you don't have to make me leaving into deja vu."

He opened a credit-card offer, studied the size of the print. "I'm not. Your mother never picked stupid fights."

***

All I brought to San Francisco was a suitcase. It was an uphill, winterish city, un-Californian. But the newspaper was filled with short-term vacancies. My apartment belonged to man who was in Africa feeding starving children. My job belonged to a pregnant woman who was having her baby. Both of these strangers left me instructions that explained how to do everything exactly the way they did.

I read their pictures on the bedside table and desk instead. The man stood at the back of a fishing boat, staring up with a faceful of love at another man who stared straight into the camera, slobbering his attention on some unseen tropical boy behind the lens. The woman (not yet pregnant) sat with family-looking people at a restaurant, but with her chair shoved out as if she was just about to get up, just as their arms landed on her shoulders, hugging her back down into her seat. The man was ironed, focused, khaki. The woman had lipstick smears on her teeth, a distant glaze to her smile. She was daydreaming. I let her in-box fill up with mail, took long lunches the way she would. I watered the man's plants every day, washed his dishes carefully, the way he would, as soon as they were done.

I didn't know them, of course. But the man might be thinking of me, as an African child snapped his picture by a dusty jeep. The woman might be too, as her husband took her and her just born baby, sitting up in the hospital pillows. Maybe she was worried about me standing in for her. She didn't know me either, or that I wouldn't disappoint her, if she gave me a chance.

***

At the one party I went to, nobody seemed to notice me, sitting in a potted cocktail palm, breaking mulch bark into pieces. I tried to see myself the way other people around me might: a yellow girl in a plant, stabbing her straw at an orange garnish—dumped? stood up? waiting for the bathroom?

I had a funny thought. I wondered who I looked like the most. The woman trapped at the family table, or the man on the boat, alone but with someone?

I went home to go call Dad, but didn't. I threw all my clothes out the window, thinking that they'd float down Market in a windy parade of yellow-ghost dresses—landing on the roofs of buses, draping off the arms of streetlamps. It was raining. They hit the sidewalk in a slump of wet, jaundiced fabric.

This left me without enough clothes to show up at the woman's job. The temp agency said it wasn't a problem. I could be replaced, no worries, just like that.

For days, I sat on the sofa, listening to the answering machine.

"I won't call you everyday for forever." Click.

"I went for spaghetti. The waitress asked how you were." Click.

"Did you see that movie about the runaway street girl, the comedy? Funny Girl? Pretty Woman? She looks like you, except for her hair." Click.

"Your old Dad is going on a date. With that lady from the book group. How about that? You aren't upset, are you? I won't go if you say not to." Click.

***

The black motivational outfits I phone-ordered from a catalogue turned out to be so many sizes too big, I was dragging a shadow of fabric behind me through the party. But I managed to keep away from the potted plants. People went on talking to each other, leaving with each other, until there was only one guy left. He had a thing he could do-hold a lit match in his mouth with his cheeks puffed out in a pumpkin face.

"Now your turn."

I held the match in my teeth, smiling through the singe at the roof of my mouth, spitting the ashy cardboard out in his hand. I had nothing I could do back. He said everybody had something. I put on a thinking expression, as if I were going through a mental encyclopedia of accomplishments and tricks. Then flash, a fake decision lit up my face. I put all my hair up with a single olive toothpick—that whole blond mass, ta-da, one olive toothpick.

"Hello," he said. "There you are."

I lit another match.

He blew it out.

He was a photographer. No kidding.

But he didn't take people. Only birds, birds of the world. I learned the names from his calendars, his books—the ruby-throated finch, the

Providence petrel, the frigrate, the cormorant. I slid my motivational outfits into his drawers, made us coffee in his matching sandpiper mugs.

There had been a previous Mrs. Sandpiper. But she was out of the picture, he said. I laughed, even though he didn't get the pun. Everything he said was funny, wonderful. All he had to do was whisper tufted titmouse, tufted titmouse over a dinner menu and I laughed the food right out of my mouth.

"All I'm saying is you could check your machine every few days." Click.

"Just so I don't fill up the tape." Click.

"And get cut off in the middle of." Click.

***

Um. I was trying to be funny too. I packed myself into his suitcase, curled up inside, my legs up to my chest.

"Out," he said.

I said I could warble too. I was an excellent warbler.

He was sure I was, but I had to get out of his suitcase.

I warbled. It was terrible. It sounded like what it was, crying.

He said it had been an amazing few months, he'd had a incredible time, he cared about me, I was beautiful, frighteningly so, smart, kooky but in a fun way, we didn't know each other that well, sure, but he wanted to see me when he got back from shooting the English warblers, unless the Antarctica job with the emperor penguins came through, he moved around a lot for work, it wasn't anything I had done, understand?

I crawled out of his suitcase, went home.

"I know where you are. You're falling in love, aren't you?" Click.

"Don't do this. You're too young for this. He'll break your heart." Click.

"I didn't mean that. Of course you should fall in love. Don't listen to your old Dad." Click.

***

Years passed, but it happened finally. I turned the age Mom was when she had me. I checked into the Hotel St. Francis, into a junior suite I couldn't pay for in the morning. Naked, in the front of the bathroom mirror, I poofed my stomach out with air, cupped my hands on the bulge, until I had to breathe out and flattened.

I shut my eyes, imagined stretch marks on my stomach, crease lines on my forehead, my hair aged to a grayish white. I opened them—smooth, blond, me, twenty-six.

When I tried to find Mom's face in my mind, I saw the picture from under my mattress—a cigarette burnhole on top of her nightgown body, her arms holding a blanket with a burnhole ringed by curls of newborn hair. When I tried to see her face in my face, I saw Dad in my nose and in the tilt of my head and heard his voice in my voice saying, "Cut that out now, before you hurt someone."

The mirror fogged over from the running tub. Next to the shell soap on the counter stood a tray of precious bottles of lotions, foaming salts for the bath. I took my bottle and the bottle of foaming salts into the water with me. My knees flushed red, my tile-numb feet prickled and burned. In each hand, I had a bottle, playing that game with myself where you have to choose between someone's right or left hand to find the surprise hidden in their fist. I picked my bottle. Then I redid it, picking the foaming salts. But I could feel the difference in their shapes.

My bottle was squat, brown, labeled with somebody else's name and a warning about the dangers of combining while drinking alcohol or operating moving vehicles.

The bottle of foaming salts was slender, feminine with a plastic-jeweled cap that reminded me of the diamond doorknob on my old bedroom door—how I used to watch for snowflakes to fall through the rainbowed glass.

Pick a hand.

Pick a hand.

The foaming salts hissed as they hit the bath. The pills drizzled, toppled slowly towards the porcelain bottom. I was too much of a coward to drown myself without them. And too much of a coward to drink the overdosed, foaming-salt bathwater. But I made myself try. And threw up my first sip.

Back at home, the answering machine had no messages. The twin reels of cassette tape made a screeching sound, turning, as I rewound and erased.

***

There were men. And women, always older. And a new apartment in the Mission, a new digital answering machine. A long period of time blurred by, during which I was out all night every night and had to call myself from strangers' bedrooms with my secret access code. Dad's voice sounded like a computer. He was sick, then better, then sick again. He was waiting for tests. He was getting a second opinion. I could never remember my secret delete code.

"Can't wait to see you."

He left me his credit card number to buy a plane ticket. I used it check into the St. Francis. My real name was blacklisted for non-payment. I used the name Dorothy, after the girl in the Wizard of Oz. Did Dorothy have a last name?

The bellboy showed Dorothy Scarecrow a junior suite with a garden view. I stayed in bed, away from the bathroom. I lived off the mini-bar and the turn-down service mints.

Dad was lying, I told myself. Dad had seen into my daydream—an old one, from when I was little and used to make my mother sick. From her cot in a French nun hospital, my mother was asking me to forgive her. She was wearing a nightgown, her hair dead clumps around her face on the pillow.

"It's too late," I told myself to say as she held my hand. "I waited for you. You had your chance."

I gave her tumored diseases. I covered face her in bleeding AIDS welts. But I was me still and even in the daydream I ending up saying, "I love you, Mom. I forgive you, I promise."

Across the hotel wall, a landscape of swans hung in a blizzard of wings and oil paint. I turned around in the sheets, my arms and legs whisky slow and heavy. Everything smelled like feathers. I touched myself, very lightly, like a feather.

I watched the rain glinting on the window from streetlight.

It reminded me of—

The hall light twinkling off on my diamond doorknob at night, when the door opened. The sound of the film advancing. That oily metal click.

The junior suite comes with touch-button technology. I kept hitting the remote control, shutting and the opening the drapes. But the picture in the window never changed—streetlight, sidewalk, rain.

***

At Neiman Marcus, the salesladies didn't even blink. I stood there, dressed only my hotel robe, under a jittery mass of crystal—a chandelier. The salesladies, all professional, understanding women, brought out yellow dress after yellow dress, not this one, not that one, and what did I mean by a dress that looked like a coat but was a dress?

"It has to have a belt."

They huddled around me. Light bulbs went off. A wrap dress! Did I mean a wrap dress! The seventies! Which were back in now! Wait one second!

It was the thinnest silk, translucent, a daffodil petal. They slid me into the sleeves—one arm, then the other—then crossed the two flaps in front and tied the sashy belt around my waist. I stood in front of the butterfly mirror, as the salesladies adjusted the wings, angling them in and out. "You know what I need?" I said, thinking red sandals, sunglasses.

"Don't you worry," one of the salesladies said. She came back with a cashmere coat. It was winter outside, damp. She didn't want me catching anything. Illness starts in the chest and moves to the head.

***

"Yes, it's a very yellow dress."

"Yes. I have a husband. He's a bird photographer."

"Yes. Dad's met him. They're close, best friends."

The aide kept urging me to eat Dad's tray. The nurses too. I was too thin. Besides, the IV kept him fed.

I put my hand over Dad's hand. They were the same size almost. His face was a nose with sockets. His eyelids fluttered, opened—his pupils drug blurry, but he didn't do that sick person thing you read about, calling for someone in his past, confusing me with his mother.

"You look terrible, honey."

"I feel great."

"You look terrible. Do you even eat? Here, eat my tray for me."

I stood up, twirled around. "Well how fucking yellow does the dress have to be, Dad? You didn't even notice my sandals."

"Red. Very nice."

I flipped my sunglasses up, stuck my hip out, waved.

"You look beautiful, honey."

"I look terrible."

He patted my hand. "You look like you're off for a ride in the MG. With the top down. On the highway, by the coast."

I made my voice, flat. "Did I go on one?"

"The car didn't start.

"Did I get mad and take off with some guy with a car that worked?"

He looked out the window. "You laughed. You borrowed a bottle of gin from the neighbor."

"Let me guess. I drank it all myself and called you a bastard."

"We had the martinis in the front seat. You gave one to the MG, poured it into the engine. That was the best thing about you. You were always the happiest person I'd ever met."

I nodded. I couldn't decide—throw up or punch him or weep on his paper-gowned chest. "I sound like a lot of fun."

"You were. Remember?"

"No." And I didn't. I wasn't even born yet then. But I could have said yes, I could have let him go on smiling with his hopeful stained teeth.

"No," he said. "You don't. But you look just like her, your mother."

"You're my father. I'm your daughter. Remember, Dad?"

He shut his sockets. "You hate me."

"Yes," I said. But I was sitting down on the bed, I was leaning back on the pillow, I was resting my head against his head. The aide didn't want to take our picture. But I made her. She zoomed in very close. Both of our eyes are shut. Both of our cheekbones are punching out from our narrow, stick faces. We are smiling, though, with our mouths closed, the same day-dreamy look on our lips.

Fourteen Things My Father Forbade

LUCA DIPIERRO

1. My father forbade me to touch money until the day he could not touch money anymore. You can touch money when there is nobody to touch it for you, he said.

2.

My father was named Trieste after a city where nobody in our family ever lived. He forbade me to say or write his name in any circumstances. With strangers, I had to refer to him as father.

My name is Antonio Reder. I think my full name sounds much better than my father's. I sound like I am the father and he is the son to whom I, the father, gave the wrong name. I would give my son the wrong name to see if and how he would grow out of it.

My father should have changed his name. When people change their names is like entering your bedroom and every object in it seems to have been moved and put back in place, but not exactly in the same place.

3.

One fountain pen I really cared about, a gift from a girl I met during summer camp, kept on moving on my desk for months, until I decided to get rid of it. I could not stand the suspicion. At dinner I saw my father putting his spoon in his mouth. The same way he sucked my fountain pen doing crosswords.

My father noticed my thoughts. He saw them. I was not able to hide them yet as I do now. He forbade me to have thoughts while eating. Eating bore no distraction.

4.

My grandfather's name was Eugenio Reder.

My grandfather had a golden cross shining on his hirsute chest.

When he died the cross was given to me. It was shown to me, but I was not allowed to touch it, then it was put away in a drawer in my father's bedroom.

In fifteen years I was never able to find the bedroom key. My father never forgot to close the bedroom door when he went to work. I still believe the key was somewhere in the house, because I heard the sound of the key being dropped on a surface. The sound of a key falling in a pocket is muffled, often no sound at all.

My father forbade me to enter his room. I never saw the point of his forbiddance, since the key was hidden. I think my father wanted me to look for the key. He wanted me to get tired of looking and give up.

5.

At dinner he made sure we always had apples. He froze them for when they were not in season. Apples came on the table after we finished our meals. There were seven different meals, served on a different day every week.

My father forbade me to eat the apples with my hands. He taught me to use fork and knife the way his father taught him.

I learned to work the knife on the round, slick surface.

Apples shone of buttery gloss.

6.

One night when I was on the verge of sleep, my father whispered in my ear that he loved me so much that he forbade me to sweat.

Running in the park with my friends, I could not help sweating.

He did not want to hear me saying that I could not help sweating. He asked me if I could not help running either.

You walk, he said, you are not a dog like your friends.

Only now, older, can I understand my father's concern with me hanging out with dogs. I see kids in parks with their tongues dangling out of their mouths.

7.

If I will ever have a son, I will love him the same way my father did. I will protect my son's ears like my father did with mine.

My father forbade me to listen to music. I knew it was because of the melody. He mentioned the melody several times, how they make people all shaky.

You know how as a kid you wake up wanting something you never mentioned wanting before. I asked for a radio.

For a year I asked for the radio and my father said: wait and you will get your radio. I was going to be so patient, but I wanted my father to describe to me how I was going to get the radio.

Finally, my father brought one home. I was not expecting it anymore.

There was a store down the street where my father bought everything we needed like that.

I could see the store from my window. I sat there waiting for my father to come out with the radio in a box. My father was able to walk in front of you and not be seen. One day I opened a bottle of grappa to taste it: so transparent, like water glowing. I sat at the window with the bottle, without taking my eyes off the street. I heard the door when it was too late to hide the bottle. My father pushed the back of my head with the palm of his hand and put the other palm under my chin so I could not keep my eyes off his eyes. He kept my head in that position for a minute and said nothing. The glow of the grappa was in my eyes. My father waited until the grappa came out of my eyes, in little drops.

My father did not go to the store to buy the radio. He got it from his brother Raffaele. It was a big silver radio. The radio transmitted nothing but static. I turned up the volume and static became a waterfall.

8.

My father said I had to be grateful to Uncle Raffaele. He meant I had to do something to show how grateful I was, bit did not tell me what. The last time I heard about Uncle Raffaele, he lived in another town that my father called the dump, three hundred miles from us.

One night my father came into my room and, with the palm of his hand, pushed up my head from the pillow. He said, Let's write a thank-you note to Uncle Raffaele. He forbade me to fall asleep before doing what had to be done. We sat at the desk, my father spelling out the words for me to write. My father kept spelling until there was no room for any other word.

9.

One afternoon my friend Tonio came to watch TV at my house.

Tonio put his finger on the TV and said a word that I could not understand. He wrote the word on a piece of paper for me: Fernsehen. He said other words that I could not understand, and they all ended up being written on pieces of paper. We ripped off the paper from the agenda next to the telephone, where my father wrote down names and numbers that I could not read well.

When my father came back from work, he found the pieces of paper in the garbage can that he examined closely every night before going to bed. I do not know if he was able to read the word Fernsehen, but he came into my room that night and spoke in my ear, softly. He forbade me to watch TV by myself.

We watched TV together. We watched programs about serpents and bees, tarantulas, and crocodiles.

One morning when he left I turned the TV on. I watched it for ten minutes and turned it off.

When my father came back that night he entered the living room with his hat still on. I was sitting on the couch reading a book about cows. My father touched the back of the TV set with the palm of his hand.

It is still warm, he said.

Then laid his hand on my forehead to make me feel the fever he got from the TV.

10.

In the house, there were eggs everywhere.

We never ate them. My father said eggs would make us so sick it would be impossible for us to stand up.

My father forbade me to touch the eggs. They make you sick but they are frail, he said, you break them just by looking at them.

My father boiled the eggs and painted them with tiny brushes. He was able to keep his hand steady for two or three hours. He painted what he said were little flowers but looked like letters to me. The letters were connected by the tiniest lines but did not form words I knew.

11.

One day, I started to grow hair on my body. All in a sudden hair covered my cheeks, armpits, chest, arms, groin. I let hair on my face grow, to hide what sweat did to my face in the summer: thinned it, stretched it.

One Sunday afternoon I was reading in my room. I knew my father was in the room with me when I felt his breath on my temple. Stop growing hair, he said. He wanted to see those cheeks clean, and did not want to see hair underneath either. He wanted to teach me, he said.

He shaved me in the bathroom.

This is how you take the razor in your hand, he said.

He taught me how to properly remove any trace of hair. The hair that was visible underneath the skin disappeared after the third shave.

Now this is clean, he said, the back of his hand on my cheek.

12.

There were words my father forbade me to say.

One was funk.

One day I came home from school and said funk. My father put his forefinger on my lips.

Do not say that word, he said.

According to my father certain words, if repeated, made you turn into them. My father did not want my lips to get smeared with the dirt of words like slack, crap, idiot, ass—dirt to enter my mouth and invade my system.

13.

My father forbade me to stay awake in bed.

One night I was awake in bed. My eyes panned over the ceiling. I had taught myself a way to see in the dark. Instead of letting my eyes look I had to let them be fingers and touch the wall, the carpet, the couch, the mirror.

On the couch there was a darker tangle. It was my father.

Sleep, he said.

I cannot help it, I said.

Wake in bed makes you tired during the day and not able to function. All you have to do in bed is sleep, my father said.

14.

One night I was asleep in bed. My father's hand on my forehead woke me up. He asked me if I remembered what he told me when I was born.

I did not answer, because I was taught to think twice before saying no. I remembered words being said to me when I was born, but was not able to put them together in phrases.

Get dressed and leave the house, my father said.

Give me one minute to remember, I said.

Leave, he said.

Outside it was cold. I walked down the street to warm up.

Running brought warmth to my head like a fever and I remembered what it was that he said.

My father forbade me to be in the house when he was going to die.

I waited for what I estimated to be enough time for him to die and then went back into the house.

High Rise

SUSAN MCCALLUM-SMITH

The night before visiting Malky in prison, Allison dreams she flies out of the high rise. She is wee again, and getting ready for primary school, already dressed in her uniform. She steps over the shoebox of paper dolls cut from the *Bunty* comic, leaving behind the cup of hard-boiled egg mixed with butter on the arm of the sofa. She opens the door to her granny's veranda, a toty balcony tucked into the side of the block of flats, thirteen floors up, and the toastiness of the living room is replaced by a nippy autumn morning sawing at her face.

She's not supposed to go out on the veranda alone. The damp concrete is slidey under her socks. The daylight draws a pretend line splitting the floor between the shadowy puddled corners and the blinding sunshiny front. She grasps the metal railing with both hands, and swings one leg up and over, and then the other, and perches on the ledge, balanced on her bum. She lifts a hand and looks at it; the palm is manky already and smells like the swing park. The wind blows up her gray school skirt and flaps the end of the tie that's tucked down her waistband and dangling between her legs.

She sits for a bit. The trees in Pollok Park are stirred together red and gold and orange. The milk floats clank in and out behind the Co-Op, and her pals dribble from the newsagents having spent their lunch money on crisps and sherbet dabs before heading to school. Posh violin music drifts up from the corporation depot where the buses go to sleep at night, next to the vandalized tennis courts in the park.

She shunts her bum of the edge of the veranda and lets go.

As she hurtles toward the ground, Allison struggles to wake up. If she doesn't manage it up before she hits she'll die. Dreaming of being dead meant you were dead, her granny told her that. Her face plummets to meet the pavement; she can almost feel the scrape and splatter and imagine humungous scabs knitting up and down her front, but whoosh!

She swoops, high, high over the top of the high rise, and down its other side, brushing the tips of those red and gold and orange leaves all stirring together in the park, skirting the gravy-brown burn, and the Maxwell's prize winning Highland cows that stop chewing and lift their marmalade heads to watch her. Her heart bounces from her toes up to her throat, then flip-flops to a stop in the middle of her chest. She floats above Glasgow on her back, the sun warming her face and making sparkly confetti shapes under her eyelids.

***

Allison takes two painkillers and washes them down with milky tea. Some wonky cosmic joke has aligned her periods with her monthly visits to Barlinnie. She's leaking away to nothing. She'll be hollow by the time Malky gets out, like an empty nest, all the best bits of her gone. The one time in the month she wants to look half-way decent and her skin mottles with plukes and the blonde drains from her hair. She feels wrung out like a chip wrapper. Her pal, Carol-Anne, says she should get a grip, take herself off to that new spa in Argyle Street. Says she's acting like a widow in mourning, when she's not even married, as if Malky was dead, rather than away working in the Bar-L, as the local saying goes. Allison's having none of it; she's not getting tarted up or the neighbors' will be asking who for, when her man's in the jail?

She gets herself ready in the same thirteenth floor high rise flat that appears in her dreams, passed on to her by the council when her granny died. Malky had promised to buy her a new house in Bearsden, but he never managed it before he was arrested. Allison's sister comes round to wash the windows when they're needing done, because Allison is so afraid of heights she won't go within one foot of any of them, never even lifts the blinds. She's on the waiting list for a council house at ground level, but because she's no weans, Scotland will have won the World Cup by the time she gets it.

She plasters concealer over the bags under her eyes. Her tummy is swollen and taut like a balloon. She slaps on one of those sticky heating pads, then pings her knickers over it to keep it secure. Gordon arrives just as she's leaving, carrying his toolbox, to install the new taps in the bathroom.

Anything you want me to tell him, she says, pulling her gloves on, avoiding his eyes.

No. Well, say hello and that.

When the lift comes, there's a puddle in the corner. She stands well away from it. As likely to be rainwater as piss but you can't risk it. Carol-

Anne had leant Allison a new black Burberry raincoat, and she knots its belt tightly before stepping into the wind tunnel between the flats. A gust snatches her brolly and she spins around and slams her shoulder against it to keep it upright, then staggers across the car-park in her best black stilettos, dodging the puddles and the boys in hoodie jerseys playing keepie-uppie with a deflated ball, oblivious to the teeming rain. Under a bus shelter tattooed with graffiti, Allison puts her brolly down, and pats her newly-washed and now ruined hair. Don't know why I bloody bother, she thinks. The number 23 will arrive in a tick, hiding inside the next convoy, as if the very buses get lonely, as if the very buses are feart to cross the city on their own.

***

On a wet day like today, the visitors' hall in the Victorian wing of Barlinnie Prison reminds Allison of the public swimming baths. The bottom third of the walls are tiled in the same peely-wally green, before switching over to a dirty white paint up to its arched roof, scrolled over with some fancy plasterwork she can barely see. The long windows are opaque so she can't pretend to look at the view when the conversation lags. It's just the M8 motorway out there, but, and she hears the cars whiz past. Must drive the inmates spare, she thinks, hearing people accelerating off someplace else. At the beginning of the visits everyone whispers, trying to keep their business private from the other eleven tables sharing the hall, then they end up yelling at one another because it's like the ceiling steals the voices —does a runner with them like a shoplifter.

The tiles sweat with damp. It's clammy inside and out and Allison feels clammy too, with the heating pad plonked against her stomach. It's only ten past three but it could be the middle of the night under these florescent lights, she's yon sleepy way she used to get at school during double-maths. She tugs her black skirt over her knees and crosses her legs. Her tights are mud-spattered and a ladder has started inside one shoe. She can feel the punctured nylon strangling her big toe.

So, how's work? Malky says.

No bad. Carol-Anne's covering for me the day.

Speak up, hen, I canny hear you.

It's this room. Drives me nuts, Allison says. It's not Malky's fault the hall has the acoustics of a railway station, but she's all riled up inside.

It's like my sentences come out long-ways as normal, she says. And then get sucked up. It's a big Hoover in here, so it is.

She calms down and tries again. Work's same as usual.

It's not the same as usual, but there's no point telling Malky that. As a cook in the local primary school, she used to take turns at serving the lunches, but now she stays in the back, not minding about having to do more of the heavy work—heaving great platters of lasagna and mince pie in and out of the big ovens and chiseling it into slices. She can't stand being around the kids anymore. The wee ones, the primary ones and twos scare her the most, the four and five year olds—if one gives her a funny look over his plate of corned beef and chips, she's frightened she'll snatch him and run, and keep running, to the high rise, to the airport, to Florida, the moon. She'll morph into one of they monsters you read about in the paper, who steal other women's weans, and everyone will think she's a sick perv, when her sickness is only the wanting.

A guard leans against a wall behind Allison with his eyes shut and his hands in his pockets. Another stands behind Malky by the door to the prisoners' wing, playing with a handheld computer toy.

It's the waiting I can't stand, says Allison.

You don't need to tell me about that, hen, says Malky.

I feel like it's too late. She didn't mean to bring it up again, but there, she's said it.

What do you mean?

You know what I mean, says Allison.

No, I don't. Malky crosses his arms. The guard standing behind him curses at his computer game and jiggles it a bit. I don't get your fucking meaning at all.

No need to swear, says Allison. Every time I try and talk about anything important you start swearing at me.

Malky looks at the clock. 3:15. Have you seen Gordon, he says.

No.

***

Malky had told her to stop moaning about the state of the flat and pay someone to freshen it up. So, when the sink got blocked a couple of months back, she gave Malky's younger step-brother, a plumber, a call. While Gordon was there, she told him to take a look at the bathroom and give her a quote for replacing the tiles and the taps with something more modern.

She left him sitting on the closed toilet seat, adding up his sums on a scrap of yellow paper with a bookie's pencil, and went into the kitchen to put the kettle on. Arithmetic was obviously not Gordon's strong point, because the tea was poured, the paper read, and a fag lit by the time he joined her. He gave her the slip of yellow paper and went over to the sink.

So…she said, reading it. These would be the gold taps, then?

You buy cheap, you pay dear, he said, sounding like an old sweetie-wife. He dumped his tools on the floor. Have you been stuffing tattie peelings down this? he said, pointing at the sink.

No, she said. I've been pouring money, I'm made of it, didn't you know?

Aye, right, very funny.

He took a plunger from his tool bag and rammed it over the kitchen drain. He reminded her of Malky, that's what gave her the idea. Even though they were only half-brothers, something in Gordon's pipe-cleaner frame wound around her heart and threatened to yank it straight through her chest. He was about the same height as Malky. Compact—the height to look her straight in the eye standing up or lying down. In tackety-boots, jeans and a Rangers football jersey, he was none too clean, a bit clatty in that not unpleasant style of workies in general.

Or maybe it was his pumping away at that blocked drain with such dogged determination that gave her the idea. She suppressed a snort at the outrageousness of it. Gordon, the little engine that could. Could he? It crossed her mind that she'd need to think up a stormer of an excuse to tell Malky. Claiming a miracle because she glimpsed the Pope on the telly wouldn't quite cut it. If he wanted a wean as much as she did, but, how much could he mind?

Carol-Anne didn't know how Allison could stand it, going without sex for months on end. She was always trying to pair Allison off with some man or other, reminding her that Malky was behind a locked door and a quick shot on the swings does wonders for a girl's complexion. If I was you, I'd be that horny, Carol-Anne said. I swear I'd be standing outside the post office offering to hump any randy old git going in to collect his pension, even the ones with missing legs and nae teeth.

Allison didn't miss sex, she missed sex with Malky. Since his arrest, her body had become dormant, like a wee animal; desire had curled in on itself, smothered its own flames and slept, its heart-beat tamped down to a murmur. She made an effort, but a lackluster one—still plucked her eyebrows but never bothered shaving her legs, the hair was soft on her shins now, like a pelt, and she hadn't bought new underwear for almost three years. She went to bed earlier and earlier every night, reading historical books from the library, watching the telly till she dozed, then dreamed of flying and falling. This is what it must be like to be old, she thought. To not really know if you're a man or a woman. Sometimes her own breasts surprised her. It was only around kids that something stirred, stretching in its sleep.

Stories of Malky's violence had reached her in roundabout ways, not long after she started going about with him. These didn't seem true, airy-fairy as Chinese whispers or the foreign news, because he'd only ever shown her a tremendous tenderness. A stomping, walloping tenderness, as if he'd belted her hard with it and knocked her out, and that's what kept her faithful all this time.

Gordon?

He turned around and looked at her.

How old are you?

Why?

Just wondered.

I'm twenty-three. He went back to rogering the sink with the plunger and swearing.

Gordon?

What? He sounded exasperated now. He put the plunger down.

He looked so like him, and they might only need to do it the once. It wouldn't be cheating, more like substituting from the bench within the same team.

Could you do us a favor? She said.

***

Allison glances at the clock—3:30—she's desperate for a fag. She takes cigarettes and a plastic lighter from her bag. Smoking is not allowed in the visitor's hall, but everybody does it. They'd tried banning it for a while but the ban almost started a riot. The ability to light a cigarette seemed to ensure one half of the room didn't reach over the tables and throttle the other half.

Maybe I did see Gordon, she says. Can't remember.

What's he up to? Malky says.

How should I know? I'm no your brother's keeper.

He's OK, but?

Well, he's no in here for a start, so he must be doing something right.

Allison rustles in her bag again. She pulls out her diary and takes a photograph from between its pages.

Want to see a picture of Carol-Anne's boy?

The guard steps forward to see what she's doing.

Keep your knickers on torn-face, she says, showing him the photograph, then grimaces at Malky. That bampot thinks I'm Holly Golightly in here with the weather report.

She holds it up for Malky to see. He slips his hands in his pockets.

See that, she says, pointing at the baby. I could eat him.

Another talking sausage with a face like a well-skelped arse.

Allison shakes her head and bites her lip. You didn't even look at it, she says.

Your pal fair churns them out.

She returns the photograph to her bag. I've been thinking, she says.

Does it hurt?

Fuck off.

Tut, tut. Language.

I was reading something in a magazine the other day, and I think it's about time you and I found ourselves.

Why? Are we lost?

Allison stood up. She wanted to leave this clammy place right now.

Oh, sit down, for Christ's sake. You could still start a fight in an empty house.

She sits down, and fiddles with the hem of her skirt. Two tables over a woman yelps like an injured dog. The man she's come to visit shakes his head, stands up and nods at a guard. The guard takes him back into the prisoner's wing, leaving his visitor bubbling into her hankie, wiping her eyes and nose, before bundling herself away.

You've yet to tell me the good news, says Malky.

Allison looks at him sharply. What good news?

Malky glances at the clock again. I missed your birthday, he says.

Missed three of my birthdays, you mean.

Thirty-eight. A mature woman. I do like to get my mitts on a mature woman.

Ancient woman, more like.

When I get out I'll buy you something nice. Would you like that?

Allison blows smoke into the air.

Don't you think you should give these up now? he says. Allison frowns at her cigarette, then at Malky.

A cat, he says. You always wanted a cat.

The council doesn't let you have cats in the high rise.

Give us a break, hen. I'm doing my best.

Aye, well.

Malky slams his palms down on the table. Allison jumps, startled. She drops her cigarette onto the floor, and stamps on it to put it out. The guard behind Malky looks up from his computer game and clears his throat.

Calm down son, he says. Yer giving your bird the heebies.

What did you expect me to do? Malky whispers. Wank in an Irn Bru bottle and stick it in the post?

Allison feels like a lump of coal plugs her throat. A noise escapes her, a whimper. Malky thinks it's a laugh. He smiles, revealing his small, even, white teeth, and reaches across the table and takes her hands.

You're a sight for sore eyes, sweetheart, he says. Haven't changed a bit.

Allison shakes her head.

Remember that day in Pollock Park? he says.

She smiles and looks away. What would the guards do if she clambered over the table right now, she thinks, in front of all these people and onto Malky's lap and took him inside her? Clung to him like a limpet on a rock at Rothesey, her arms and legs latched onto his spine. She feels torn and empty, like one of those poly bags she sees tossed around by the wind, snagged on hedges, hooked on pylons, all ripped and holey.

We nearly buggered the suspension in the car, so we did, he says.

Malky glances at the Guards. He begins to sing, softly. *It's just a perfect day, I'm glad I spent it with you. Just a perfect day...*

You keep me hanging on, Allison joins in. *You just keep me hanging on.*

She sees the guards gander at each other over their heads, and knows the inmates and visitors next to them are pulling faces and snorting. She doesn't care—she and Malky used to sing all the time, everywhere—on buses, in nightclubs, pubs, lifts, restaurants, even at the back of the Odeon in Sauchiehall Street. Before he'd got seven years for aggravated assault, half their conversations came with tunes attached. Other folk's stares have no more effect on them than the weather. A glance from Malky always shuts them up, and it works this time, too. He slowly turns his head and surveys everyone around them, until their audience sticks their noses back in their own business.

So, how's life in the high rise?

Allison pulls her hands away. How d'you think?

If you need anything you know you've just got to ask Hugh.

Hugh. Aye, right.

Allison could never work out exactly what Hugh did for Malky, only that it fell under the category of miscellaneous. A bit of this, a bit of that, a bit of the other, Malky said, when asked.

***

On the morning of her thirty-eighth birthday, her plan for Gordon had gone skee-whiff, gone off the rails faster than a reformed alcoholic inheriting a bar. She'd just told Gordon to take his mean mochat self out of her sight, when the doorbell rang. She was still in her dressing gown when she opened it, thinking Carol-Anne had turned up early, and there stood Hugh, in the same leather jacket she remembered him wearing to a Duran Duran concert years before, and his hockey haircut seeping gel.

Oh, she said. It's you.

Happy Birthday, sweetheart, Hugh said. He lugged what looked like a four-litre-vodka-carry-out in an upside-down brown paper bag. He pulled the bag off with a pansy flourish to reveal a Hallmark gift box streaming lilac and yellow ribbons.

Gordon came stomping up the hall behind Allison, and stopped at the door.

I'm away, then, he said, zipping up his donkey jacket. He brushed past her, nodded briefly at Hugh, and belted toward the lifts. Moving that fast, thought Allison, still boiling with rage and embarrassment, like he'd a firecracker up his arse.

Here's your hat, where's your hurry, she muttered at his retreating back.

Adolescent acne had gifted Hugh a face like a dartboard, and this ugly mug was now a stew of questions.

He's fixing my plumbing, Allison said. Did Malky send you over with this? She fingered the streamers, thinking her morning had perked right up.

Eh, no. No, this is from me.

Allison folded her arms. She swithered about what to do next, sniffing trouble in Hugh's generous sloshing of Old Spice.

Her next door neighbor's door opened. Mrs. McFadden beady eyes followed her nose round the corner.

Oh sorry, pet, she said. I thought that was someone at my door.

Hugh glanced at her, then back at Allison. Mrs. McFadden had taken root.

Any chance of a nice cuppa? he said.

I guess you'd better come in, said Allison. And give me that, you look like a twat.

Thanks very much, sweetheart. Appreciate it. I'll no be a minute.

She headed for the kitchen trailing lilac and yellow ribbons, leaving Hugh to shut the door behind him. Words tumbled out of him like a leaky dictionary, all down the hall, and onto the kitchen table, and through the boiling of the kettle, words about his mother, and his ex-wife, and those kids of his that were out of hand, and how lonely he was, and here she was, and Malky said he was to look after her, make sure all her needs were met, and it's her birthday, and did she never get lonely, sweetheart, and who would ever know?

Five minutes later Hugh was out in the corridor again with her handprint on his face and the nice cuppa soaking his trousers, inches from scalding his balls. Not that Allison would ever tell Malky about Hugh's amateur tackling of her tits in the kitchen, he'd lunged at her with his eyes shut and paws up like a blind goalie. Hugh might be a dingbat, but he didn't deserve to end up trussed in a rug at the bottom of the Clyde.

***

The rain had changed direction. Instead of falling down, it's driving along the M8 from Carlisle to Glasgow, needling at the windows as it passes Barlinnie.

Don't know why you don't marry that clock, Allison says, following Malky's glance. You're smitten with it, the day.

Thought I told you to get the flat fixed up.

I did, she says, managing to follow this sudden swerve in the conversation.

And?

Jimmy papered the living room.

And?

And what?

Don't stop now, hen, spit it out.

Gordon's changing the tiles and the taps in the bathroom.

So you have seen him, after all?

***

Allison had bought an ovulation test from Boots the chemist in town, though she didn't need it, she knew exactly when to ask Gordon to make himself useful—on her birthday. He'd arrived early that Sunday morning. She'd been up half the night worried near to death and was still in her bathrobe. Didn't seem any point getting dressed just to take everything off again. She'd considered having a shower, shaving her legs, putting on a bit of make-up but that would have implied that this was something other than a favor, and the truth was, she was beginning to change her mind.

Out of most of the lassies she'd gone to school with, she was the only one who hadn't got pregnant in her teens or early twenties. Little Miss Smarty-pants had determined not to be shackled to a dunderhead and weans while barely an adult, and had taken herself to Dr. Matthews when she turned fifteen. I'll say this for the pill, she thought, it works, right enough.

She slipped her knickers off under her nightdress and lay down on top of her bed. She stared at the ceiling to avoid seeing Gordon get undressed. She heard him kick the tackety boots on the floor then unzip his jeans. Her heart hammered against her chest like someone trying to get out a burning house. If the wean looks a lot like Malky, she thought, maybe he won't mind so much. She risked a glance at Gordon, but Gordon's resemblance to Malky had fallen away with his clothes to the floor. He looked bigger, more muscled, and hard like a bully. His body was in better nick than Malky's, too, the age difference of almost twenty years showed. Suddenly, she felt horrified, horrified at the depth of her wanting and what she seemed prepared to do to feed it, and scared witless of Malky and what he'd say when he found out. And scared, too, of Gordon, scared of him hurting her, or worse, scared of him making her feel good. Oh my God, she thought, what if I can't help myself and I make a wee noise?

It's fuckin freezing in here, Gordon said. Is the heating on?

She nodded.

What you doing on top of the bed? I'm going under the blankets. Are you coming with me, he said. Or am I doing this on my own?

She jackknifed her legs up and scooted under beside him.

By the way, he said, rolling over on top of her, and scissoring her knees apart with his own. This isn't a freebie.

You're kidding? She squirmed and lifted her head to look him straight in the eye.

She couldn't believe it, how he'd waited till her gingham nightie was scrunched around her waist before he mentioned money. Her body, already tense from top to toe, went as rigid as a plank of wood. Any minute now, she thought, he's going to be huffing away like a paratrooper doing press-ups, hammering her to the bed like a nail, and she knew she wouldn't be able to bear it.

Are you planning to lie there like a doughnut? he said. Or are you gonny gie a boy a bit of encouragement?

That did it. It took all her self-control not to start wailing like a banshee on fire. She shoved him off and stumbled sideways, landing on her knees on the floor.

I've changed my mind, she said, pulling her nightdress down.

Fuckin typical, Gordon muttered. He got out of bed and started yanking his clothes back on, swearing under his breath. Women, he said. Would have been as much fun as a wake, anyways. Allison folded her arms and watched him, trying to maintain some self-control, roiling with embarrassment, knowing she had a brass neck and wishing he'd hurry up and get his bloody knickers back on and bugger off.

Not even a thanks for coming, he said, when he was fully dressed.

But you didn't, did ye?

He still wanted money though. Did she think he was some toy free with her packet of Frosties? It wasn't his fault if she chickened out, he'd taken a risk and she wouldn't want Malky to know now, would she? She put her dressing gown on and went to get her purse off the kitchen table. He wiped his hand down his jeans before he took it, as though he'd just touched something dirty. The tosser still wanted paid for doing the bathroom and all; he was reminding her of this when Hugh had rung the doorbell.

***

Alison took another cigarette from the packet and tapped it against the box. She'd hoped she would've got through the last twenty minutes of this visit without coming back to the subject of Gordon, but no such luck.

Aye, I've seen Gordon, she says. Once or twice.

I know, Malky says.

If you know, why'd you ask? Who told you? No, let me guess. Hugh.

She flicks open her lighter.

At least someone hasn't forgotten the meaning of loyalty, Malky says.

Oh, is that what you call it?

Not like Gordon. I used to think Gordon would take over the business from me.

Gordon's always been your favorite, hasn't he? Greedy wee bugger, though.

Greedy? Well, well.

Malky's tone makes Allison decide to back-pedal a bit from slagging Gordon off.

But, he's no a bad boy, really, she says. Tries his best.

He's not a boy. Was old enough to know what he was doing.

What d'you mean?

You should've waited.

I am waiting.

We said we'd wait.

Allison's hand begins to shake. She stubs out her cigarette, and looks around the hall. She knows she'll remember this moment, squirrel it away into her memory box along with those other times in her life that came with a before and an after built in. She smells antiseptic, aftershave, and wet nylon, and something meaty from the prison canteen and even a whiff of Carol-Anne off the borrowed coat, and a tang of herself, of her own bleeding.

Malky leans forward. So, he whispers, you still afraid of heights?

At the Beach

Michael Downs

I. Dog and Not Dog

Rosa's cat was short haired, black and white, with half its left ear torn away and a tail that twitched when the cat meant to do evil. If Rosa failed to notice the tail, the cat might rake claws across her hand as she petted him. She fancied herself a cat lover, but this animal led her to thoughts of betrayal.

She enjoyed the fruits of her thirty-three years: friendships, loving parents, success in property law, and an expensive condominium in a city that valued its magnolias and crepe myrtle. People who knew her saw a woman confident in herself and her powers. She dated, but unmarried men her age proved immature or too damaged to warrant anything more than sex.

One year, in June, she left to spend a week at the beach with a KKG sister and the woman's family. This was an annual retreat, a chance for sun and talk with a friend she saw too rarely. She brought the cat along in a carrier. The house they'd rented had weathered gray and offered a view from all four bedrooms. Molly and her husband took one, put their children in another and Rosa in the third. Her bed was too soft, and she lay in it restlessly, listening through the air ducts to the kids tease each other. The fourth bedroom they gave to a friend of the husband's. The friend owned small-circulation regional magazines Rosa had read in boutiques. He was a transplanted Yankee and, as Molly had promised, single.

Married once, he said. College sweethearts. We both learned things.

Also, he'd brought a dog.

Later his dog met her cat, and it was a day before the cat would come out from under the house. It clawed her when she finally pulled it into her arms, left hot little lines, the blood beading atop the cuts.

None of this made him memorable. She had met single Yankee men before. Some even had dogs. What struck her about him (what would strike anyone) were the scars that marked his arms and legs, chest and back. The jigsaw patterns changed color in different light. In some places his body hair grew out of his scarred skin as it would on any other man, and in other places—where, perhaps, the scars were deeper?—his skin looked papery and bald. The resulting impression was of a man unfinished. Molly had whispered the cause to her when the Yankee was off fishing: a bad fire when he was a boy. Molly believed everyone had a soft spot for wounds.

He apologized for his dog and after that took greater care when she or her cat were nearby. He befriended the cat, and the cat crawled on his lap when he sat on the porch, the two of them fixated on the yellow-blue horizon. The cat never clawed him.

One afternoon Molly sent Rosa and the Yankee to fetch groceries. Molly could wink without moving her eyes.

The dog rode in the backseat. Rosa, looking out the window at the dunes and the high grasses, absently caressed the scratches on her arm and asked about his magazines. She felt comfortable with his driving, which was fast, easy, confident. She had never ridden in a BMW. She liked the sting of salt in the ocean air and the rumble of the tires on the road. At the grocery store, before they released their seat belts, she noticed vending machines at some distance on the store's concrete apron. Sunlight gleamed off the glass and metal fronts of the machines, one of which sold pop and cola. She couldn't say with certainty what the other advertised. She knew what it appeared to offer, and the idea charmed her.

I'm crazy, she said, but I believe that vending machine sells Blind Faith.

He looked.

Maybe, he said. What comes out of a Blind Faith machine?

Probably blind faith.

In a can? In a wrapper?

She said, What faith would you pick? Faith in Allah? Jesus? The almighty dollar?

He said, Blind faith must cost more than a dollar.

She said, I'll buy. She'd been raised Southern Baptist, and though she had strayed she often felt the tug.

She jingled coins in her hand as they passed the soda machine, but there was no blind faith for sale after all, only live bait—worms and maggots—for a dollar. Inside, they filled the basket from Molly's list, and he added a pouch of dried pigs' ears for his dog.

At the beach house that night, she whistled, but the cat gave no answer. Later, as she walked sandswept sidewalks and then to the wharf whistling for her cat, she felt God working in her life. She never saw the cat again.

II. Croakers

The day moved toward dusk and the wind rose, its fiercest gusts scouring them with beach sand. She pushed her hair behind her ears, but dark strands blew loose over her face.

She explained. She said, Rosalyn was the First Lady's name. Mine is Rosalind. Like in Shakespeare's play.

Rosalind is difficult to say, he said. That D.

You have to want to say it.

He'd taken a break from fishing. He had a length of PVC pipe driven into the sand near the water line and his fishing pole propped inside it. He was fishing for anything worth eating but pulling in only croakers. The fish made their croaking sounds as he pried them from the barbs, tossed them underhand back into the sea, then loaded up with bait again.

She told him her age. He was forty-two.

I work long hours, he said.

So do I. And much of my social life is entangled with the firm. Entertaining clients and whatnot. Are you church-going?

No. I'm a lapsed Catholic.

You're looking at a lapsed Baptist.

They each nodded and smiled. He fingered a snail shell out of the sand.

But Sunday morning is pure to me, she said. I don't work then.

He wore a loose sweatshirt that covered many of his scars, but he was in shorts and he was barefoot. She wanted to touch the scars on his leg, to see how they felt. The shape of his legs was right and, in the case of his calves, beautiful. But the skin was all wrong. She showed him her toe that had no nail.

I dropped a microwave oven on that when I was moving once, she said.

Moving out or in?

Out.

Was leaving him worth losing the toe nail?

Oh yes.

He said, There are nights I can't sleep.

Because of the fire?

No. Other things.

Does the fire matter?

To some folks. It was at a circus. Outdoors. A tent burned and killed a lot of people. My mother and I were there. She never talks about it, and I don't remember much.

I remember the microwave oven. A gift from my parents.

He said, My parents came from Poland before I was born. I've heard every dumb Polack joke ever told.

She said, My family's been poor since before the Civil War. But my daddy made some big money. We're new at it. I'm sure sometimes we are crude and offensive. Just like the new money-people in Faulkner. But we don't mean it.

I haven't read Faulkner.

Do you have children?

No.

Do you want children?

Yes. Do you?

Yes.

He checked his bait can. He'd run out. He hauled in the line, found a croaker on the end of it. He took a knife from his pocket and decapitated the croaker and dropped its head in the bait can. Then he sliced the belly and with a finger scooped out the tiny entrails. He spread these among the hooks, added the head to another, then cast it all back into the sea. He rinsed his hands in the salt water and returned to where she sat. He sat so as to shield her from the occasional frenzy of wind and sand. When he spoke her full name, it sounded as if the D came naturally.

She admired how his hands had worked the knife and the fish. She had read Faulkner and studied law and watched her father increase his fortune; from these things she understood that civilization was built and maintained through killing, and she meant to have a civilized life.

III. Turtle

An afternoon of swimming and body surfing and sunbathing led the tired grownups to the porch and to vodka cocktails, as sea gulls laughed overhead and a band played at a nearby beach house. Earlier that day there'd been a wedding; now the party: the bride exchanging her dress for an all-white bikini with a tiara and veil; the groom donning a black Speedo, a bow tie around his neck like a male stripper. She chased him with a paddle, laughing and slapping at his tush.

Did you bring your bow tie? Molly asked her husband.

Only my body oil, he said.

Molly howled. She said to her husband, You're such a pale skin you get out there with body oil and a bow tie and the only thing gonna jump your bones is a penguin! You work best in the dark, honey.

Rosa refused to picture the Yankee in a bow tie and body oil. Though she had just met him, she'd begun to imagine him in her bed, and she felt it necessary to see him dignified, solemn. She did not want the scars sewn across his body to be part of some freak show striptease.

Then the kids thundered up the stairs, back from a night hunting for sand crabs, coming hard and astonished, flashlights waving, with a tale to tell.

There's a turtle! the first cried. There's a turtle on the beach!

A big one!

You can't see it cause it's dark!

It walked right up on the sand!

It crawled!

It's bigger than this!

So the grownups hurried down, chasing the kids to a spot where a dozen or so people had gathered.

Keep your distance, someone said.

She's laying eggs, said another.

Come up at sunset, right between my fishing pole and my buddy's there.

Don't shine that flashlight on her!

Rosa could not see the turtle, but she saw the turtle dig. It kicked backwards with powerful fins, tossing sand into the moonlight with great urgency. Shovelfuls sprayed through the air, and Rosa tried to imagine some backyard swamp turtle big enough to do this. She curled her toes in the sand.

Someone ought to call the ranger, said Molly's husband. He looked around. Might as well be me.

Rosa leaned near the Yankee. Can you see anything? she said.

Just a dark lump.

The ranger, when he arrived, called the turtle a loggerhead. Back to the beach where she was hatched, said the ranger. That's how they do it. They'll come a thousand miles. They mate on the water's surface. The male hooks his foreclaws into the female's shoulders to get a grip. By the end, she's usually scratched and bleeding.

It was dark now, and they could only make out the spot where they knew the turtle to be and what might be a lump. People drifted away. Molly and her husband took their children home except the oldest girl, called Sara, who wanted to stay. Rosa volunteered to watch with Sara, and the Yankee said he would, too.

They stayed three hours. Sara and Rosa sat in the sand, the girl huddling for warmth against the woman's bare legs. The Yankee and the ranger stood, peering into the dark. Late in their vigil, the turtle bellowed: a guttural birthing song.

She'll lay a hundred or more eggs, said the ranger.

Then the turtle shifted. It turned. It pushed thick mounds of sand over the nest. Rosa stared unblinking as she would through a hole in time to the days before Eden. The turtle crawled along as if it and the sand had been born of the same mother. The ranger—at a distance—kept pace. Just before the turtle reached the water, the ranger turned on his flashlight. The turtle looked orange in places, and green, and black, and her beaked head did not turn to the light. Water lapped against her, washing grainy sand from her carapace. She pulled herself deeper. The ocean lifted her. She vanished into the foam. Rosa watched and when the turtle had gone realized that she held Sara's hand with her left and the Yankee's hand with her right.

Then the ranger pounded stakes around the nest, and the Yankee helped tie string to make a border. To the string, the ranger fastened blaze orange tape and signs warning people away.

I'll alert the biologists, he said. They'll want to move these eggs someplace safer. There's a preserve to the south.

Molly and her husband greeted them from the porch with a pitcher of sea breezes. Sara told the tale, and as she spoke Rosa watched the Yankee and dreamed of the turtle. What monstrous beauties. But there was beast in her, too, and she shivered to imagine the small cruelties she and the Yankee might visit on each other's grateful selves.

IV. Turtle Egg

In the morning she crept about the beach house, her brain swollen with vodka and squeezing against her skull, her pulse hammering her neck bone. Over a loud, buttery breakfast, she tried to conceal her suffering. She smiled when the children told jokes, she nibbled toast, accepted gratefully the aspirin Molly sneaked her. Against her better judgment, she agreed to go with everyone to the beach to see the turtle nest.

The Yankee had not kissed her the night before. On the porch, they'd drunk sea breezes, and their mood became one of laughter and flirtation. They let the taste of cranberry juice and lime swirl in their mouths, dreamed of their turtle deep beneath the black waves, sucked ice cubes softened by vodka and TWO AM air. When they parted company, he pressed her hands between his, said good night, then left her wanting more.

Now she kneeled beside him, hung over and pretending otherwise, part of a circle of volunteers crouched around the edge of the turtle's nest. They dug with archaeologist care, ever ready for the alien texture that meant another egg. Already they'd collected dozens, directed by a pretty, young government biologist come to save the unborn turtles.

The eggs didn't seem so fragile. When the biologist had lifted the first one for all to see, Rosa thought it resembled a wet ping pong ball and was surprised to hold it and find heft at its core, the shell like leather, not a wafery plastic.

Ted, Rosa thought. His name. When she'd spoken it the night before, he told her that he liked how she lengthened the vowel nearly to two syllables. He was not then some typical Yankee, puffing himself up by mocking a drawl, acting as if all the world ought to be dull as the Pilgrims. No, he was a man appreciating the music only Rosa could make of his name.

Leaning over the turtle nest, he whispered, How's your head?

He knew. She said, Leathery and wet.

He smiled, so she had somehow the sense that her hangover was precious to him, that hers was the world's loveliest hangover. His kind manner helped her past embarrassment and put her hung-over self at ease. Maybe he'd learned that – how to put people at ease – by living with his scars. Such a skill could fend off staring, help him fit in. Why is it, she thought, that characters in movies and on TV always learn that fitting in is bad, that parading your freakishness is the bravest path, and then, in the end, that the reward for reveling in your strangeness is love? That was untrue to life. Sometimes love came because you could fit in, because you helped people feel at ease with your strangeness.

If this sense of ease was love, she'd never felt a finer one.

He leaned nearer. She could hear his breath soft at her ear.

You can kiss it, she whispered. My head.

She waited. She wanted him to know the things she spoke of with no one. That she ate fast-food burgers to celebrate paydays; that she still believed in God and prayed to Jesus; that one awful rush night she and the others forced a Kappa pledge to dance naked before football players until the girl wept; that she sends the girl flowers every year on her birthday. If he kissed her hungover head, he could share these secrets. With his kiss, she believed, he could ease her through tomorrow and every day after, through all unexplored things, even his own strange embrace.

The biologist, who was a few months out of graduate school, watched him kiss her and thought: that's what it's like to have loved for years.

Downward Drifting

PATRICIA SCHULTHEIS

We cleaned for our mothers. Off boats and kerchiefed, they stood at conveyor belts, boxing brassieres or culling cartridges, their hands growing cramped, their ankles swollen, until, shift over, they scarcely could climb onto buses and ride to third-floor flats whose mean little rooms, we, their daughters, had cleaned.

Nine, ten-years-old, down on our knees, scrubbing linoleum fissured into battlefield maps. Like slender sappers, our arms tunneled under radiators that pocked the backs of our hands with blisters.

Tall and strong, by twelve I can run the carpet sweeper, iron my big brother's shirts, and start the supper before Mama's bus stops. By sixteen, I'm at Bridgeport Brass, taking the early bus home to pull the wash off the line and peel potatoes while Michael, at the kitchen table, his books unopened, listens to the radio. Turning the dial for Glenn Miller one September, he catches instead the static telling his own fate. Jackboots into Poland. Horses against tanks.

So innocent, Michael almost believes himself that night, telling Mama, "I'm going to get a job at Remington Arms, Mom. Or Sikorsky Aircraft. They'll be hiring now." As if the Warsaw cobblestones weren't already calling his name.

Ignorant of life beyond the most elemental but rich with memories and a survivor's genius, Mama knows the wild eyes of cannon-crazed horses, the boot ... the blast. So she lets her son leave that one night to enjoy his vague, boyish dreams under the corner streetlight. "Wash the dishes, Helen," she says.

In June, when the letter for Michael comes, I wear my Sunday shoes to the Brass the morning he leaves. Red ankle straps, they're a protest, partly for him, but more for myself, sixteen and seeing the endless line of my days: Mama, mute at the table, the stovepipe needing polishing.

But, with so many needing miracles, who am I to beg?

Still, one comes. A mean Bridgeport rain. Me, missing the bus, and a car, careful to not splash, pulls up with a grin. "Hey, need a lift?" It is war. People help out. That grin! I jump in. His name is Stanley.

Before the virgin's altar, down on my knees beside Mama who fingers her beads for Michael, while I beg forgiveness for the miracle of Stanley's kiss.

"Wait for me," he gasps the morning he leaves, scarcely able to pull his lips from mine. "Wait for me and write."

Three years, sweeping up toast crumbs. Mama, too worried to wipe them from her own chin, let alone the floor. Then getting on the bus, flattening my bag on my lap. A white sheet. "Dear Stanley ... The landlord says I can plant a lilac bush in the backyard. Kay, that girl I told you about from the Brass, knows where to get white ones." "Dear Stanley ... The foreman wants me to switch to nights. It's more money, but I don't like leaving Mama alone." "Dear Stanley ... It's been raining cats and dogs. No letter from Michael in a while."

Kay's elbow bumps me the morning the foreman comes down the line. Mama won't open the door. The boy with the telegram had knocked until the landlord had called the Brass. When I get to the flat I hear her moans while I fumble for my key, all the while, beneath her moans and my own chittering dread, hearing, too, my own ugly prayer: "Thank God, it's not Stanley."

Lilacs on the altar, Kay my bridesmaid, and a hole beside Mama in the pew at St. Michael's, the morning I, veiled in unnatural white and stunned in my own shining moment, march toward Stanley's grin, so bright it blinds me to the stain of brains blasted into his eyes at Anzio.

I say a vow and give a lie. It's this: that I would foresake all others. And I truly would but for one, my heart's true tyrant, the bud Stanley's planted in my belly. So I vow "foresaking" before the ring slipping down my finger passes my first knuckle.

Beneath a froth of passion and wonder I bury my lie, and we name our bud Michael. Then, as if to balance the scales of love, two girls, one for each of their father's knees. Rosemary and Diane.

So, three bottoms to wipe, six elbows to scrub, six ears, six knees. A yard with lilacs to trim and a three-bedroom rancher to clean. My arm a metronome shining the picture window framing my days. The trucks delivering broadloom to Gladys on the corner. French provincial to Margery across the street. And me, pressing my lips against the meanest of our early American bought on time.

Kay calls: her brother's lost in Korea. I bring a cake and pinch my lips against my own complaint: Stanley's coming home, firing his lunchpail over the counter, "God damn it ... another bill! God damn it!" His grin, a memory carried further away down the line of our lives, his Anzio eyes tacking for a target, usually finding Michael.

Then, John F. Kennedy four weeks dead, and the slaughter of the innocents is on our picture window. A galaxy of diluted Bon Ami Christmas stars sponged by Michael. He squeezes behind the game on TV to raise the blind's metal slats and turns to Mama sitting mute beside Stanley.

"See, Grandma," Michael says, "that big star in the corner is Jesus, and the others are the babies Harod killed looking for him. The slaughter of the innocents. The little stars are supposed to be babies going to Jesus."

And Mama, smiling, nodding, hearing in Michael's thirteen-year-old voice her own boy's eager innocence. But Stanley, a foreman then at Sikorsky Aircraft, hears a bad call in the game and gives a three-beer growl, "For Christ sakes, Michael. Will you get away from the TV? I can't see the game. Just get away, will you?"

So Michael picks up that "Get away. Get away," and shoulders it up the hall to his room. In the kitchen, I tell Rosemary, "Wipe that drip from the gravy boat's lip."

Two years later a knock at the door. Kay with a cake: So sorry about your mother. So sorry. Down in Georgia to see Billy graduate boot camp. So sorry.

I, glad for having run the vacuum that morning, say, "It was time." We eat her cake. Wrapping words around wounds, I repeat how it was: so few in the pews at St. Michael's, Mama's rosary around her fingers. A packet of letters ribbon from my brother.

"I almost put them in with her. But, at the last minute, I didn't," I say.

"In the end, what difference does it make?" Kay says.

Fall and the days are short. Kay stays. The kids come home. But not Stanley. Overtime at Sikorsky Aircraft. Double shifts. Helicopter blades slicing Vietnam's green heat. Chop. Chop. Chop.

"Hope Billy doesn't go over," says Kay.

"A girl's brother in my class already has," says Rosemary.

"In mine too," says Diane.

Michael says nothing, goes up the hall to his room. Chop. Chop. Chop.

When he leaves, the dust in his room defeats me. Rosemary begs me to move Diane out of their room and into his, but I stand, pan in hand, by his bed still littered by his leaving.

"God damn it, Helen, you can't make a shrine of it," Stanley says. But I, mute, think maybe God has damned me to do just that. What but a shrine can atone for the lie I told so long ago?

The morning the knock comes, I squeeze behind the picture window to lift the blind's metal slat. There are two. White caps. Blue tunics. Brass buttons so shiney that new suns must have been pressed into their young chests. Rosemary comes down the hall, lets them in.

In its triangle case, the flag moves. First on top of the TV. Then up the hall to our bedroom. Finally, to Diane's room when she leaves. She brings her boy named Michael from Arkansas when Stanley goes. That morning, almost every pew in St. Michael's is filled with his men from Sikorsky Aircraft.

Now, sometimes Kay calls. I say I should clean the closets. "In the end, what difference does it make?" she says. Rosemary, her condo converted from a third-floor flat two blocks from Mama's old bus stop calls too: "What did you do today, Mom?"

I have my lies ready: "I cleaned the oven." "I scrubbed the floor."

How can I explain the time I spend watching the downward drifting dust? How it rides the slatted light. Downward, homeward drifting. Like souls returning from having been blasted so far away. How can I explain the time I spend watching that?

Their Eyes Were Watching God

ZORA NEALE HURSTON

One day Hezekiah asked off from work to go off with the ball team. Janie told him not to hurry back. She could close up the store herself this once. He cautioned her about the catches on the windows and doors and swaggered off to Winter Park.

Business was dull all day, because numbers of people had gone to the game. She decided to close early, because it was hardly worth the trouble of keeping open on an afternoon like this. She had set six o'clock as her limit.

At five-thirty a tall man came into the place. Janie was leaning on the counter making aimless pencil marks on a piece of wrapping paper. She knew she didn't know his name, but he looked familiar.

"Good evenin', Mis' Starks," he said with a sly grin as if they had a good joke together. She was in favor of the story that was making him laugh before she even heard it.

"Good evenin'," she answered pleasantly. "You got all de advantage 'cause Ah don't know yo' name."

"People wouldn't know me lak dey would you."

"Ah guess standin' in uh store do make uh person git tuh be known in de vicinity. Look lak Ah seen you somewhere."

"Oh, Ah don't live no further than Orlandah. Ah'm easy tuh see on Church Street most any day or night. You got any smokin' tobacco?"

She opened the glass case. "What kind?"

"Camels."

She handed over the cigarettes and took the money. He broke the pack and thrust one between his full, purple lips.

"You got a lil piece uh fire over dere, lady?"

They both laughed and she handed him two kitchen matches out of a box for that purpose. It was time for him to go but he didn't. He leaned on the counter with one elbow and cold-cocked her a look.

"Why ain't you at de ball game, too? Everybody else is dere."

"Well, Ah see somebody else besides me ain't dere. Ah just sold some cigarettes." They laughed again.

"Dat's 'cause Ah'm dumb. Ah got de thing all mixed up. Ah thought de game was gointuh be out at Hungerford. So Ah got uh ride tuh where dis road turns off from de Dixie Highway and walked over here and then Ah find out de game is in Winter Park."

That was funny to both of them too.

"So what you gointuh do now? All de cars in Eatonville is gone."

"How about playin' you some checkers? You looks hard tuh beat."

"Ah is, 'cause Ah can't play uh lick."

"You don't cherish de game, then?"

"Yes, Ah do, and then agin Ah don't know whether Ah do or not, 'cause nobody ain't never showed me how."

"Dis is de last day for dat excuse. You got uh board round heah?"

"Yes indeed. De men folks treasures de game round heah. Ah just ain't never learnt how."

He set it up and began to show her and she found herself glowing inside. Somebody wanted her to play. Somebody thought it natural for her to play. That was even nice. She looked him over and got little thrills from every one of his good points. Those full, lazy eyes with the lashes curling sharply away like drawn scimitars. The lean, over-padded shoulders and narrow waist. Even nice!

He was jumping her king! She screamed in protest against losing the king she had had such a hard time acquiring. Before she knew it she had grabbed his hand to stop him. He struggled gallantly to free himself. That is he struggled, but not hard enough to wrench a lady's fingers.

"Ah got uh right tuh take it. You left it right in mah way."

"Yeah, but Ah wuz lookin' off when you went and stuck yo' men right up next tuh mine. No fair!"

"You ain't supposed tuh look off, Mis' Starks. It's de biggest part uh de game tuh watch out! Leave go mah hand."

"No suh! Not mah king. You kin take another one, but not dat one."

They scrambled and upset the board and laughed at that.

"Anyhow it's time for uh Coca-Cola," he said. "Ah'll come teach yuh some mo' another time."

"It's all right tuh come teach me, but don't come tuh cheat me."

"Yuh can't beat uh woman. Dey jes won't stand fuh it. But Ah'll come teach yuh agin. You gointuh be uh good player too, after while."

"You reckon so? Jody useter tell me Ah never would learn. It wuz too heavy fuh mah brains."

"Folks is playin' it wid sense and folks is playin' it without. But you got good meat on yo' head. You'll learn. Have uh cool drink on me."

"Oh all right, thank yuh. Got plenty cold ones tuhday. Nobody ain't been heah tuh buy none. All gone offtuh de game."

"You oughta be at de next game. 'Tain't no use in you stayin' heah if everybody else is gone. You don't buy from yo'self, do yuh?"

"You crazy thing! 'Course Ah don't. But Ah'm worried 'bout you uh little."

"How come? 'Fraid Ah ain't gointuh pay fuh dese drinks?"

"Aw naw! How you gointuh git back home?"

"Wait round heah fuh a car. If none don't come, Ah got good shoe leather. 'Tain't but seben miles no how. Ah could walk dat in no time. Easy."

"If it wuz me, Ah'd wait on uh train. Seben miles is uh kinda long walk."

"It would be for you, 'cause you ain't used to it. But Ah'm seen women walk further'n dat. You could too, if yuh had it tuh do."

"Maybe so, but Ah'll ride de train long as Ah got railroad fare."

"Ah don't need no pocket-full uh money to ride de train lak uh woman. When Ah takes uh notion Ah rides anyhow—money or no money."

"Now ain't you somethin'! Mr. er—er—You never did tell me whut yo' name wuz."

"Ah sho didn't. Wuzn't expectin' fuh it to be needed. De name mah mama gimme is Vergible Woods. Dey calls me Tea Cake for short."

"Tea Cake! So you sweet as all dat?" She laughed and he gave her a little cut-eye look to get her meaning.

"Ah may be guilty. You better try me and see."

She did something halfway between a laugh and a frown and he set his hat on straight.

"B'lieve Ah done cut uh hawg, so Ah guess Ah better ketch air." He made an elaborate act of tipping to the door stealthily. Then looked back at her with an irresistible grin on his face. Janie burst out laughing in spite of herself. "You crazy thing!"

He turned and threw his hat at her feet. "If she don't throw it at me, Ah'll take a chance on comin' back," he announced, making gestures to indicate he was hidden behind a post. She picked up the hat and threw it after him with a laugh. "Even if she had uh brick she couldn't hurt yuh wid it," he said to an invisible companion. "De lady can't throw." He gestured to his companion, stepped out from behind the imaginary lamp post, set his coat and hat and strolled back to where Janie was as if he had just come in the store.

"Evenin', Mis' Starks. Could yuh lemme have uh pound uh knuckle pudding till Saturday? Ah'm sho tuh pay yuh then."

"You needs ten pounds, Mr. Tea Cake. Ah'll let yuh have all Ah got and you needn't bother 'bout payin' it back."

They joked and went on till the people began to come in. Then he took a seat and made talk and laughter with the rest until, closing time. When everyone else had left he said, "Ah reckon Ah done over-layed mah leavin' time, but Ah figgured you needed somebody tuh help yuh shut up de place. Since nobody else ain't round heah, maybe Ah kin git de job."

"Thank yuh, Mr. Tea Cake. It is kind a strainin' fuh me."

"Who ever heard of uh teacake bein' called Mister! If yo wanta be real hightoned and call me Mr. Woods, dat's de way you feel about it. If yuh wants tuh be uh lil friendly and call me Tea Cake, dat would be real nice." He was closing and bolting windows all the time he talked.

"All right, then. Thank yuh, Tea Cake. How's dat?"

"Jes lak uh ill girl wid her Easter dress on. Even nice!" He locked the door and shook it to be sure and handed her the key. "Come on now, Ah'll see yuh inside yo' door and git on down de Dixie."

Janie was halfway down the palm-lined walk before she had a thought for her safety. Maybe this strange man was up to something! But it was no place to show her fear there in the darkness between the house and the store. He had hold of her arm too. Then in a moment it was gone. Tea Cake wasn't strange. Seemed as if she had known him all her life. Look how she had been able to talk with him right off! He tipped his hat at the door and was off with the briefest good night.

So she sat on the porch and watched the moon rise. Soon its amber fluid was drenching the earth, and quenching the thirst of the day.

Bubbe and Zeyde

Jessica Anya Blau

My sister, Anna, and I decided that our brother, Emery, had to scrape the hardened cloak of bird shit off the TV room couch. The bird, Ace, who liked to perch on the iron curtain rod above the couch, was Emery's, after all. We were cleaning the house for my grandparents' annual December visit. Even my parents were helping out—a fact that made the chores seem festive—like the Friday after Thanksgiving at my best friend Denise's house where the whole family decorated for Christmas. At Denise's, they tacked thick layers of cotton to the porch rails and called that snow. It occurred to me that if we suddenly were transformed into people who decorated for Christmas, we could leave the bird shit on the couch and pretend it was snow.

Anna and I had been given charge of the house and our brother four years earlier, when I was eight, Anna was eleven and Emery was four. Our mother, Louise, had quit. With a cigarette burning in one hand and a cup of coffee steaming in the other she had told my sister and me that she was done being a housewife.

"I quit," she had said. And that was that.

I handed Emery the paint scraper while my sister and I spent a good hour with a wire trash can trying to catch Ace. When he was finally captured, we locked him in his cage where he silently batted against the bars with a painful persistence that drove Louise to put him on top of the washing machine in the garage.

After banning the bird, Louise took on the kitchen floor with a wire brush and bucket whose water I changed for her every five minutes or so. The reveal of the white linoleum under the putty-grey of the kitchen floor was like a magic act, or the miracle of finding a Picasso under the amateur painting of a silo one buys at a garage sale.

On the Saturday morning of Bubbe and Zeyde's arrival, we were all quietly occupied with the final acts of preparing the house. My father, whom everyone called Buzzy, was sitting on the stuffed green chair in the TV room, leaning into the white kitchen trashcan he had dragged in there as he rummaged through the latest stuff Anna had thrown away. I was cleaning the sliding glass door in the family room with Windex and newspaper and Anna was dusting the newly empty surface of the black driftwood coffee table with Lemon Pledge. The room smelled fabulously, chemically, sterile. Emery was organizing the board games in the family room and Louise was sorting sheets she had purchased for the beds (the old sheets hadn't been laundered in a year and were shiny with a slick layer of dirt). As in other years, Emery would sleep with me, or on a nest of blankets on my floor, and Bubbe and Zeyde would sleep in Emery's first floor room on his bed and a fold-out cot, which was kept in the garage between their visits.

Louise gathered up the sheets, a burning cigarette dangling from her mouth. She stared down at my father, who was reading a crumpled piece of paper. Louise shifted the sheets to one arm, pulled her cigarette out and pointed it at my father as she spoke.

"Buzzy, fuck the trash, get the plants."

"She may have thrown out the receipt from when I had the oil changed on the car last week, I can't find—" Buzzy dropped his head back into the trash can.

"GET THE FUCKING PLANTS!" My mother yelled, then she lifted her cigarette hand and pushed a sweaty strand of brown hair out of her eyes. We all looked up at her, silenced by the suddenness of her anger.

"Dad," Anna finally said, "you have to chop down the marijuana plants."

Gardeners had been called in to bring the front yard under control, but the backyard, with the bursting fruit trees and splintering deck had been ignored.

"They never go in the back yard," Buzzy said, "and chances are they won't even recognize that they're marijuana plants."

Emery looked up from the Masterpiece Game; he was separating the painting cards from the value cards.

"We have marijuana plants?" he asked. His eyes were oversized, brown grommets; his hair was a blond rag mop.

My father, mother, sister and I looked down at him, squatting like a monkey in front of the game.

"No," Louise said, calmly, "we don't have marijuana plants."

"Marijuana's against the law," Emery said. "It's illegal."

There was a certain oddness to any moment when Emery spoke while the entire family was present. What I thought of as the original family—Buzzy, Louise, Anna and me—was such a noisy, bickering group, that there never seemed to be room for Emery's tiny voice. He was like Ace, his bird, a vision of constant movement, chaos and mess, but not a vocal part of the family.

"How do you know it's illegal?" Buzzy asked.

"We talked about it in school."

"You talked about marijuana in school? What the hell kind of a school are you in that you talk about marijuana in third grade?" Outrage at our schooling was a common theme for Buzzy.

"We talked about drugs. Marijuana is a drug."

"Jesus-fucking-Christ," Louise moaned, and shifted the weight of the sheets in her arms. "Marijuana is harmless! And yes, we have marijuana plants because I smoke marijuana!"

I turned from the sliding glass door and leaned toward my brother, "Don't tell your teacher or your friends, okay? Or Mom will go to jail."

"For christsakes, Portia!" my mother snapped. "Nobody's going to fucking jail, why put that thought in his head! Now come help me put sheets on the beds, and Buzzy, cut down the fucking plants!"

Buzzy stood from the trashcan. "But the buds are just a few days from being fully ripe—"

"You don't even smoke them!" Louise said. "Portia! Take these!"

My mother dumped the sheets in my arms, then circled the room with her cigarette butt, searching for the abalone shell ashtray that usually sat on the coffee table. There was a perfect cylindrical ash sitting atop the clean white sheets. I walked to the trashcan, tilted the sheets toward it and blew the ash off. It left a streak of grey, like a cartoon drawing of movement beside running legs.

"Where are the marijuana plants?" Emery had a worried little open-mouthed scowl. I imagined the picture in his brain of a drawing by his favorite illustrator, Richard Scarry, whose dog police would pull up in a black and white paddy wagon and haul off our parents.

"They're surrounded by the lemon trees," Buzzy said, "no one can see them."

"Dad," Anna said, "I know you like to grow the best plants you can, but you have to admit that if it doesn't matter to Mom, it's much safer to just chop them down then risk that Bubbe and Zeyde see them and—"

Emery stood and slid open the glass door. He ran out into the back yard toward the lemon trees.

"You think he's going to pull off the buds and sell them at school?"

Anna asked, and I laughed, although I didn't quite know what the buds were.

"Poor little guy," my mother said, and she walked out after him. Buzzy got up and followed, so Anna and I went too, the pile of sheets still in my arms.

Emery was in the middle of the stand of six-foot high marijuana plants pulling one down to the ground as he tried to break it at the base of the stem. The plant bent and bounced as he pushed on it with his dirty, brown bare foot.

"Okay, okay," Buzzy said, and he took my brother by the arm and directed him away from the plant he was attacking.

"Don't worry, I'll pull them out. Okay?" He tugged on Emery so that he would face him. "We're going to lock them in your mother's studio where Bubbe and Zeyde will never see them."

"IT'S AGAINST THE LAW!" Emery wailed, and fat tears began to fall down his face. He broke free of my father's grip, ran to the eucalyptus tree and scaled it before any of us could even reach the base.

"Hey," My sister called up the tree, "Noble Citizen, come on down! Dad's taking care of it!" My mother and I began to laugh. Buzzy groaned and went to the marijuana plants where he dug each one out at the roots.

***

We all piled into the long, blue station wagon to pick up Bubbe and Zeyde from the airport. Even the car was clean—Anna and I had picked up all the old, nearly-petrified McDonald's French fries, the mysterious hairballs fuzzed with dust, the gum wrappers and other detritus off the floor of the car before Buzzy took it to a car wash where they vacuumed and wiped down the inside as well as scrubbing the outside. The car smelled like pink bubblegum—a change from the usual cigarette and gasoline smell that strangely, in my mind, equated the smell of vomit.

At the airport, we stood at the low, stucco wall that separated a grassy courtyard from the runway. Emery scaled the wall and walked along the top of it, his arms extended like the wings of an airplane.

"Hey, Noble Citizen, get down from there," Louise said. The name Noble Citizen had stuck since Anna first used it and my mother, sister and I had completely abandoned Emery's proper name that day. Buzzy took

Emery's hand and held it while my brother leapt from the top of the wall to the grass.

Bubbe and Zeyde's plane came roaring in. I put my hands over my ears; Buzzy picked up Emery and held him up near his shoulder so he could better see the plane touch down then roll along the runway until it stopped not far from where we stood.

We gathered near the wall, our bodies still in anticipation as the moveable stairs were pushed by a small tractor-like vehicle to the white, looming airplane. I watched as movie-star-looking people, men in sports jackets, women in owl-eyed sunglasses, effortlessly glided down the stairs and onto the runway. And then came Bubbe and Zeyde.

Bubbe was the size of kids a grade lower than I. She wore a nifty pink skirt-suit with shiny square-heeled pink shoes. Her curled white hair had a glossy sheen that I could see from the distance. She stopped on the stairs, smiled and waved at us. Emery jumped up and down waving his arms. Buzzy groaned and waved.

"There she is," he said.

The only person who dreaded Bubbe and Zeyde's visits more than my mother was my father. He claimed his parents were looney: his mother a meddler, his father a braggart.

With one hand on the handrail and her face directed down at her feet, Bubbe slowly stepped down the stairs one foot at a time, as if she were doing the wedding march. Zeyde was right behind her. He was the shape of a penguin and wearing his usual bow tie. (After retiring as an accountant for the post office, Zeyde had taken up sewing and painting. The only thing he sewed was bowties—he claimed that his attention to detail was greater than anything one might find in a bowtie from Boscov's department store.) Zeyde's hair was black, slick, his nose looked like a crow's beak, his skin was darker than Buzzy's, as dark as my sister's skin.

"Cookalah!" Bubbe shouted as they crossed through the open arch into the courtyard. My grandmother grabbed me and gave me hollow smacking kisses on the cheeks and the forehead. Then she pulled my head down to her sloping bosom and rocked me back and forth. When she was done, I was passed to Zeyde who had just finished kissing my sister. He was taller than I, but not as tall as Buzzy and not much taller than Louise.

"Look how they've grown!" Zeyde said, and he laughed in a sharp, whining rhythm that sounded like a boat engine working to turn over:

AH heh heh heh, AH heh heh heh heh. It was a sound that belonged to my grandfather in the same way that the bubbly rumble belongs to a Harley Davidson motorcycle.

Emery was kissed last and with far less enthusiasm. Bubbe and Zeyde had never taken to him—as if having my sister and I were enough and Emery was just one child too much for their tastes.

On the drive home, Bubbe and Zeyde sat in the backseat with Anna between them and me on Zeyde's lap. Emery asked if he could sit on Bubbe's lap, but she said no, he'd wrinkle her skirt. And so Emery was tossed into the way-back where he stuck his head over the edge of the seat and watched us, like a dog.

***

I stood in Emery's room as Bubbe unpacked the two hard, blue suitcases. She moved quickly, humming and smiling, like a little wind-up toy. Propped against the mirror on Emery's dresser were two paintings Zeyde had made that he had given us for Hanukah a few years earlier. One was a bald baby in a bath. When we had unveiled the painting Zeyde put a fat brown finger on the canvas and said, "Can you believe I got the water to look just like water?!" When the next painting had been opened my mother gasped.

"Oh, I like that pirate!" I had said, and my parents and grandparents laughed.

"That," Zeyde had said, his finger pointing to the ceiling in a gesture of erudition, "is Moshe Dyan."

"Is he a pirate?" I had asked, and my grandfather chugged with laughter.

"HE," Zeyde had paused to give weight to his words, "was a great leader of the Jewish people."

"A great leader of the Jewish people!" Bubbe had repeated.

We kept the baby in the bath and Moshe Dyan behind Emery's dresser between Bubbe and Zeyde's visits. Anna was the one who always remembered to pull them out.

"Cookalah, Cooklah," Bubbe said, and she grasped my hand with her pointed bony fingers and slipped a twenty-dollar bill in my palm.

"Thanks Bubbe!" I shoved the bill down into my shorts pocket.

"Use it in good health, "Bubbe said, and she smacked some kisses on me again. "Now where's your sister?"

"I'll get her. Do you want Emery, too?"

"No, no, shhhhh…" Bubbe raised a crooked finger to her lips and looked around as if she were a spy on a mission. Knobby gold rings tilted on her hand, as if the rocks were too heavy to sit upright.

I brought my sister back to Bubbe just as my grandmother was about to change into her housecoat. She had removed her bra and stood in the middle of the room with her giant, plummeting breasts sitting somewhere below her waist.

"Cookalah, Cookalah, shut the door!"

Anna and I stepped in and shut the door behind us. We thought she wanted it shut for reasons of modesty, when in fact, we later realized, she was no more modest than our mother who went only to the nude beach and didn't even own a swimsuit. I thought about my own breasts, which had just started to grow and had no fold; my mother's breasts which had a fold but faced forward, staring the viewer in the eye; and then my grandmother's breasts, each like an orange sitting at the bottom of a net bag. I decided just then that I would never go braless: I would bind my growths so tightly against my chest they would never stray, bounce, accordion fold, or release.

Bubbe tucked a twenty into my sister's palm, then went to her suitcase for more goods.

"Do you want your housecoat?" I asked, and I held out the pink shapeless shift that was hanging on a wire hanger on the closet door knob.

"Yes, yes, but first I have presents for you girls!" Bubbe clapped her hands together and flashed her gold teeth at us. I stared at her teeth as a way to not stare at her hipline breasts.

Bubbe lifted some shirts from Zeyde's suitcase and pulled out two white plastic grocery bags.

"One for you," Bubbe said, and she handed my sister a bag and kissed her on the cheek, "and one for you!" She handed me the other bag, kissed me on the cheek and, at last, reached for the pink house coat.

My sister and I moved to the bed. We sat side by side as we opened our bags and peered in.

"Use them in good health! God bless!" Bubbe said, as she buttoned her housecoat. "And share!"

In my bag were white pens, perhaps a hundred, with Bank of Trenton written on the side. In my sister's bag were about fifty plastic folded raincaps that appeared to be little more than Saran Wrap with a string. They also had Bank of Trenton written on them. Anna unfurled a raincap and put it on. It looked like she was wrapping her head for refrigerator storage.

"They fit in your purse, see?" Bubbe said. "I never walk out the door without one."

"That's cool," Anna said.

"Yeah, really cool," I said.

"Use them in good health!" Bubbe said, just as Emery burst into the room.

"Your grandmother's getting dressed!" Bubbe turned to my brother and with a hand on each shoulder, pushed him out the door and shut it tightly behind him before reaching up and pushing in the last button on her housecoat.

"I don't have anything for him," she whispered. "He's a little boy! What can he do with a pen or a raincap?!"

"Yeah, he likes getting wet in all our rain," I said, and my sister nudged me with her knee. California had been in a drought for so long, rain was an event for us—like a solar eclipse or a big earthquake. The last time it had rained all the neighborhood kids ran out into the street, heads tilted toward the sky, tongues out, screaming and jumping around. We had started singing Singin' in the rain, but no one knew the words so we just sang the first line over and over, never even reaching the glorious feeling part of the song. At my friend Julie Tuna's house, the entire family showered together in order to save water. Anna's best friend's house had a saying written in brown ink and taped on the inside of the toilet lid: If it's brown flush it down, if it's yellow, let it mellow. At my best friend, Denise's house, she had to turn on the water in the shower, get wet, turn off the water, soap up and shampoo and then turn the water back on and rinse. She also had buckets in her showers that her mother used to collect water for her house plants and garden. In our home, nothing was watered, Anna was the only one who showered regularly, and there were no demands for when one could and could not flush the toilet. It was as if my parents were too preoccupied to notice the drought. In fact, the only time I ever heard Buzzy or Louise mention the drought was when Denise and I performed our rain dance we had choreographed one Saturday afternoon—leaping and clapping in synchronized fashion over a tin bucket we had decorated with grimy little feathers we had found in our yards and in my family room (thanks to Ace).

"Wait," Buzzy had said, after he and Louise gave a slow, weak applause. "So is the rain dance to stop rain in flooding areas or to bring rain?"

"It's to end the drought, asshole," Louise had said, and she got up and walked into the house.

When we had shown Denise's parents our dance they stood from their lawn chairs and gave us a standing ovation. Then Denise's dad fetched his home movie camera, which was the size of a saxophone case, and asked us to perform the whole thing over again so he could get it on film.

***

After Bubbe finished unpacking, she went into her purse to give my sister and me even more gifts: silverware from the plane that had Pan Am written on the handle (she had wiped it clean with the cloth Pan Am napkin she had also taken from the plane), sugar packets that said Pan Am on them (she wanted to keep the pink Sweet 'n' Low packets for herself), and a folded soft copy of LIFE that had a subscription sticker on it addressed to Ralph Castle.

"Who's Ralph Castle?" I asked Bubbe, while flipping through the magazine.

"Who's Ralph Castle?" Bubbe said.

"Yeah," I said. "Who's Ralph Castle?"

"I don't know Ralph Castle," Bubbe said. "Is he a friend of yours?"

Anna tapped my shin with her toe.

"Thanks for this stuff Bubbe," Anna said, "we love LIFE magazine."

"Your Aunt Rose," Bubbe said, "may she rest in peace, also loved that magazine!"

Once the presents were fully distributed, my sister and I followed Bubbe into the family room. Zeyde had already taken up his usual spot on the big green chair in front of the TV.

"Sweethearts, come here, come here!" Zeyde slapped both his knees with his palms.

Anna went to the couch and sat in the corner closest to Zeyde. I collapsed on his lap, and tucked my head under his neck. At twelve I was still a snuggler, somehow both aware and unaware that my body was no longer a pot-belly-centered ball of flesh. I had slimed out, flattened in the middle, widened at the hips, and had outgrown my training bra of sixth grade, yet I still moved through the world like a child.

Zeyde shifted me onto his left knee as he dug into his right front trouser pocket. He slipped a twenty-dollar bill into my hand and kissed me on the cheek.

"Use it in good health," he said, then he leaned over, shot a glance at Emery who was sitting on a stool at the counter that separated the kitchen and family room and, through a fake handshake, passed off a twenty to Anna. It was a gesture I later recognized in the *Godfather* movies, and even later, in *Goodfellas* and *The Sopranos*. Bubbe had set out a plate of TastyKakes and a glass of milk for each us. TastyKakes weren't sold in California so she loaded her suitcase with them each year, doling out butterscotch to my sister, chocolate to me, and whatever there was an excess of to my brother.

Buzzy and Louise came in through the garage. They looked guilty of something, Buzzy with his black curly hair looking like broken springs, Louise with a dark fan of sweat under each arm of her magenta silk shirt. I assumed they had been wrangling the marijuana plants in my mother's studio, roping them upside down, like bodies hanging from their ankles. That was how the marijuana plants had been stored all the previous years—it was the reason we were never allowed to bring our friends into my mother's studio.

"Sarah," Bubbe said to my mother, "they love the TastyKakes! You want to try one?"

My grandmother was the only person I knew who called my mother Sarah—the name Louise adopted when she converted from Atheism to Judaism in order to marry my near-Orthodox father. There was a three-year period of Shabbot dinners, Yiddish bandied about, and regular attendance of services at the Hillel temple at Columbia University while Buzzy was in law school and Anna was a baby. My father often spoke of that time with a yearning in his voice. By the time they moved to Boston for Buzzy's first job and my birth, Louise had abandoned Sarah but maintained the dinners, services, and even sent Anna to Hebrew school. When I was four and we moved to California where Emery was born, the only remaining Jewishness in Louise was her frequent use of Yiddish, mostly to crack herself up and to baffle Anna, Emery and me. Hers was an Orthodox conversion, however, indelible in the eyes of Jewish law, a one-way street, rendering her permanently Jewish whether she liked it or not and making her children indisputably Jews.

"It's Louise," my mother snapped, "L-O-U-I-S-E."

"Yes, yes." Bubbe was still smiling, clapping her hands together, pacing behind my brother and sister and I who were all three at the counter now, devouring TastyKakes.

"Sarah, sweetheart, you want to try a butterscotch one?"

My mother ignored her and walked into the kitchen where she began pulling out food, knives and a cutting board to prepare dinner. My sister normally cooked dinner, but she didn't know the laws of keeping kosher, so my mother was reinstated as the cook each year during Bubbe and Zeyde's three-week visit.

"Yetta," Louise said to my grandmother, "I put your fleishig dishes over here and your milship dishes here—" My mother pointed to two sets of plates, bowls and silverware stacked up on the counter—one set for dairy foods and one for meats. Zeyde was willing to abandon his kosher diet when he ate at our house or in restaurants, but Bubbe stuck to it like a zealot. She trapped my friends in the kitchen and explained to them what Kosher meant; and she held hostage the non-Jewish wait-staff of Santa Barbara as she placed her orders in restaurants and explained her reason for the tin foil she carried in her purse and handed to them for use when cooking her food. Of course she never explained the reason for the plastic sandwich bags in her purse, which by the end of a restaurant meal were always filled with sugar packets, sweetners, and salt and pepper shakers if my father wasn't paying close enough attention.

"I'm making fish tonight and baked potatoes—"

"Half a potato for me, dear," Bubbe said, wandering into the kitchen and clapping her hands. "And you can use butter with fish—"

"I know," Louise said, "I know, I know." My mother was a good student. There wasn't anything about being Jewish that she didn't seem to know.

Bubbe hovered over my mother and watched her cook, clapping her spindly, bejeweled hands as the tunes she hummed reached a rousing chorus. At one point she started singing "*Beso Me Mucho*," and Zeyde leapt up from his chair in the family room, shuffled into the kitchen and sang harmony with her. He had one arm around Bubbe's miniscule shoulder and his long, dark head was pressed against her little white head as they held the last note, both mouths open—his a cavernous, sunken cave; hers a bed of gold jewels among ivory stones. Louise leaned against the counter and stared at them as she tapped out an unfiltered Camel, lit it and exhaled slowly releasing a cloud that settled over my grandparents.

***

While my mother prepared dinner under Bubbe's supervision, Anna, Emery and I gathered around Zeyde in the family room. He had a quarter in his hand that he was tugging out of our ears, finding in our pockets, pulling out from between Emery's near-black-with-dirt toes.

"Do the math for us!" Emery said, jumping around Zeyde's knees.

"Not yet … not yet." Zeyde brushed off his trouser leg where Emery's little hands had been.

"Can you do the math, Zeyde?" I asked, and he laughed and pulled me onto his knee.

"Okay, sock it to me!" Zeyde said.

"A hundred!" Emery shouted.

"To the third power," Anna added, and she went on giving him instructions that included square roots, multiplication, division, fractions and decimals.

Zeyde amazed us by coming up with an answer that we assumed was correct. Anna topped off the game with something Emery and I hadn't learned yet—multiplying by pi and throwing in an X component. When we challenged his answer, Zeyde told us to get our calculators. Anna and I each had a brick-sized Texas Instrument calculator that we used in school but by the time we brought them out to double check we had forgotten the sequence of the problem. Sometimes Anna would punch numbers in the calculator while we shouted instructions at Zeyde. He took a lot longer on those problems but, invariably, he got them right. We'd seen his routines many times before—they were identical every year, each feat punctuated with his signature laugh at the end—but we loved them nonethe-less. There was something about the ritualization of them, the fact that these acts seemed honed just for us, that made us happily soak up his shtick.

***

The house blissfully remained clean during Bubbe and Zeyde's visit, as Bubbe, who didn't like to go outside, spent most of the day wiping up after the family and doing laundry that she would sort and fold on the couch in front of the TV. She watched soap operas that everyone, including Zeyde, called her shows, as if she had actually produced or written them. Zeyde would watch with her, but unlike Bubbe he was willing to go to the beach, or for a walk on State Street and miss Bubbe's shows.

One morning, as I was eating a bowl of Grape Nuts at the counter, Bubbe came downstairs carrying a laundry basket filled with the family's dirty clothes. Zeyde came out of the bathroom carrying a *Playboy* magazine that he waved in the air behind himself. We didn't have magazines like that in the house, although my best friend Denise's dad had stacks the height and width of a coffee table beside his orange chair in the living room. I looked down at the magazine, blushed and looked away. Zeyde settled on a stool beside me and slapped his magazine onto the counter, cover down. There was an aged Scotch ad on the back with a woman, who looked like she could have been in the magazine, holding the bottle.

My mother walked into the kitchen wearing a red chenille bathrobe. She poured a cup of coffee and, before even taking a sip, pulled a cigarette out of her robe pocket and lit it.

"Want some coffee?" my mother asked me over the counter. Her eyes were always puffy in the morning, little fleshy life preservers that sat like glasses on her face.

"I don't drink coffee," I said.

Zeyde laughed, "In Europe," he said, lifting his pointer finger, "children often drink coffee!"

"I've been trying to get her to drink coffee," my mother said, "but she refuses."

"It's yucky," I said.

"Then how 'bout a cigarette?" My mother tilted her pack toward me and winked to let me know she was kidding.

"In Europe it's very fashionable to smoke cigarettes," Zeyde said. "But not at age eleven!"

"I'm twelve now," I said, and my mother grinned, popped a cigarette out of the pack and tossed it across the counter where it rolled into the side of my bowl of Grape Nuts. Zeyde looked down at it but he didn't laugh, he didn't even smile.

Bubbe was at the couch sorting the colors from the whites. Emery came into the room, he was wearing cotton pajamas with red dump trucks on them. His blond hair stood up in choppy little tufts. He went to the

TV, turned on Sesame Street and sat on the floor, cross-legged, his face only inches from the tiny black and white screen. Anna and my father came into the kitchen. Buzzy didn't drink coffee but Anna did on occasion, so she poured herself a cup and stood beside my mother, cigarette smoke snaking across her face.

"Where are the Grape Nuts?" Buzzy asked.

"Ask her," Louise pointed at me with the cup of coffee she was balancing in her cigarette hand.

"Here," I said, and I handed my father the small box.

"Harry!" Bubbe shouted to my grandfather from the couch. "Look!" Bubbe came to the counter where we were gathered: me, Zeyde and Buzzy on the family room side of the counter; Louise and Anna on the kitchen side.

Bubbe was holding a pair of my pink floral underpants, the crotch turned out and pulled taut.

"Look at this!" Bubbe said. She held the underpants under Zeyde's face and pointed at the white streak across the center of the crotch.

I hoped that she was really pointing at the weave of the cotton, the color of the flowers, the thick bands of pink elastic around the leg holes. If anyone asked whose underpants they were, I decided, I would tell them they were Denise's—left here the last time she had slept over.

My father stopped pouring his Grape Nuts and leaned his head over to see what Bubbe was fussing about. My sister darted her eyes between me and Bubbe. I wanted her to stop looking at me, indicting me in this underpants debacle. I turned toward my cereal, spooned in a mouthful, then swallowed barely-chewed Grape Nuts that scraped against my throat like fish tank gravel. Zeyde slowly pulled his glasses out of his front shirt pocket, put them on, and stared down at my underpants.

"Those are Portia's underpants," Anna said, sharply.

"So!" My head was instantly clogged with a scorching fuzziness. I couldn't think clearly enough to deny the fact.

"She has discharge!" Bubbe said to Zeyde. "Portia's maturing now, God bless, she's in puberty!"

My mother laughed so hard she had to lean over the sink and spit out a mouthful of coffee. It felt as though I were watching her from afar—I was a tiny, burning fire ant, hanging from the ceiling.

"What?" Buzzy said. "You have to examine the laundry before you wash it?! You gonna show him the shit stains in Emery's underpants?!"

"Yetta!" Zeyde said, removing his glasses, "You don't need to look at her underpants to see that she's in puberty, look at her breasts!"

I remained suspended on the ceiling where I could see even myself: motionless, blank-faced, skin flushed from an internal fire that beat away at the outward calm.

"Yes, yes!" Bubbe leaned in and grabbed my cheeks with the underpants still clutched in one hand. She kissed me once, smack on the lips. "She's been blessed with breasts that, God-willing, will grow bountiful like her grandmother's!"

My mother was still laughing over the sink. She stood up straight and poured herself another cup of coffee. Anna's mouth was a thin, stern line. She put her cup down, went to the laundry basket and began digging out her own underwear.

When my sister left the room, her underpants secured in her fists, I dropped back into my smoldering body and casually followed her out, as if I happened to have just finished my breakfast and needed to go upstairs for a shower. My pose fooled no one; I could hear my father scolding his mother as I headed up the stairs.

***

In my dream that night, Zeyde called me to snuggle with him on the chair in the family room. I went to him, as usual, and sat on his lap, my head tucked under his chin. Bubbe's shows were on and she was talking to the characters, "Don't listen to him, he's meshugenah!"

I looked down at my grandfather's lap and saw a crispy, blackened coiled sausage whose starting point was somewhere in his pants. His fly was open. Just as I realized that it was his penis and not a sausage, it began to uncoil, like a snake, undulating its way towards me.

I startled awake, horrified and nauseous.

The next morning when Zeyde called to me to sit with him, I plopped myself down on the corner of the couch nearest his chair.

"I'm too old for a lap," I mumbled, but he didn't seem to hear and continued to pat his knees, beckoning me. "ZEYDE! I'm too old to sit on laps!"

My grandfather cocked his head to one side, just like Ace, the bird. He reached into his breast pocket and pulled out his glasses.

"Sock it to me," he said, punching his fist in a gung-ho arc.

"Nine-hundred divided by seven ..." I started, but my mind was elsewhere—on the beach, with my friends—and I wasn't following the answers as he gave them.

***

The whole family filed into the station wagon to escort my grandparents back to the airport. Bubbe and Zeyde sat in the back seat with Anna in between them; Emery and I were loose in the way-back, tumbling into one another each time Buzzy took a turn too quickly. At the airport, Emery climbed the wall again and Anna and I limply waved our arms in the air as Bubbe and Zeyde ascended the steps to the sleek Pan Am jet. When they reached the top of the stairs, Zeyde put one arm around Bubbe, lifted his hat and waved it. They looked sadly off-color in the blaring Santa Barbara sun, like a Polaroid picture that would eventually fade into a ghostly fog.

Koi Story

ADAM ROBINSON

Jake met Isabelle when the tire on his bicycle had been flat for about twenty minutes. She jogged past him on the dusty road, trotted in place fifty feet away, then stuck her feet in reverse. Jake squinted in the sunlight and heat, watching as she came back to where he stood. He was still miffed at his tire but interested in this turn of events.

She wore running shorts and a wet patch formed on the back of her aqua shirt. Her feet in her sneakers were turned out slightly. Jake took in her legs with an imperceptible glance.

"Hey cowpoke," she said. The road they were on cut through a large field of cows.

"Hey yourself, lady." She walked with him back to the town, taking turns wheeling the disabled bike. She chastised him jokingly about being unprepared, and the walk was generally mirthful. Jake stuck a blade of grass between his teeth. When they arrived at Jake's home, a concise brown rancher in the careless blocks between the country and the city, he told her how delighted he was that she stopped. She said "exercise is exercise, but that was nice talk," and he asked her to dinner.

They met later that night for a dinner that Jake cooked. He spread out fish sautéed in fresh vegetables, laid over couscous. He opened a bottle of wine. Their conversation came in movie segments, witticisms heaped atop each other as an imaginary camera panned across the small house. The dining room was paneled for mixed-use. It doubled as Jake's library, with a low shelf by the door. It was filled with random books. To Isabelle, the house smelled like the neighbors' who lived down the street from her childhood home. She didn't visit them often, but when she did it was a fabric-y lasagna odor that she noticed first. It was a pleasant thing.

Isabelle, who had barely a few extra pounds of baby soft that carried with her into her thirties, wore a loose, cottony dress. Jake had on a cardigan and was balding. Just cracking 40, he donned his age like his corduroys. After they ate, they each sipped a small, cheap Madeira that Jake stocked pretentiously, and he played a Liszt piece for her that he had grown unpracticed at—but Isabelle loved it. Then he played from his book of Elton John tunes and she sang along. They each had a couple fingers of whiskey in what Jake referred to as his "drawing room," and finally he saw her to his door.

"I had a really nice time," Jake said before Isabelle had a chance to worry about how they were going to end the evening. She liked him and would have. She said, "Oh. Me too." Jake reached his arm around to where her back started its arch outward and drew her in and kissed her. She maintained her volition, though, and kissed back only because she wanted to, because it had been one hell of a nice time. She exited into the warm air.

They both went to sleep thinking about bicycles, how they were fickle for goodness sake. Tires are made for popping.

They woke up thinking about sex, wanting it.

Jake went to work at several thrift stores and antique malls and scored a pair of jeans, a ukulele, and a bulky cassette Walkman. Back at home he referenced one of the books from his library-cum-dining room and learned that the ukulele could fetch about five grand. He listed it for sale on the Internet. He made a mix cassette with a special playlist that included Liszt and Elton John, and pulling a phone book from its shelf, looked up Isabelle's address. He mailed the cassette and Walkman to her, with a note that said how much he enjoyed spending time with her the night before.

In the meantime, Isabelle cleared her worklist at the office, at one point having to use her firm voice. She breezed through five cocky cigarette breaks. She hummed a little. She hummed a lot. On the bus ride home she dozed and woke up next to Jake. When she was buying her groceries that night she looked at him and asked did he like Brussels sprouts, it's okay if not, I'm not crazy about them, they're okay. He rang her up as she came in the door with her bags.

"Wait, wait, wait," she said to the ringing phone. "Hello," she said into it.

"Look," came Jake's voice at the other end, "I'd like to see you again."

"What am I, crazy?" she said. "Do you like science?" He didn't dislike science, so she picked him up and drove him to the cow pasture outside of town where they met the day before.

"I'm interested in what sort of science this is going to be," he said when she pulled her car over to the side of the road.

"Well," she couldn't resist. "Chemistry is part of it." And with that

Isabelle gave him a small kiss and hopped from the car.

"Interesting, interesting," Jake said, rubbing his tingling lips together. From the trunk, Isabelle produced an Estes rocket kit.

"Mostly it has to do with the creation of electricity." And she set off up the hill with Jake in tow.

When Jake was a boy he put together model rockets that would launch hundreds of feet into the air, then at the pinnacle the rocket would break in two and a parachute would deploy from the cone, guiding the model safely to the ground. He exhausted every level of difficulty for building these rockets, then started inventing his own from paper towel tubes and balsa wood.

At the top of the hill, Isabelle set up the rocket stand as Jake sat on the grass and watched. She mounted the engine into the tube and slid the device onto the rod. It was their second date. She clipped the remote to the engine and guided Jake a safe distance away. He could hardly suppress his laughter. They counted, laughing and miscounting, "No, on three," "Coffee break," "Wait, at three, or really at four," "No, no, one, two, three, then press the button," "Okay, down from ten," "Right, you're right, down from ten, on zero," "Okay," and finally, as the cows came home, they launched the rocket into the blue dusk, a red dot going higher and higher until it split in two and fell gently back toward them, their necks craned as they watched it fall.

That was nice, for them, to watch a rocket dangle in the sky.

Jake repaired his bicycle tube and on their third date they rode to the city center, where they ate lunch and walked slowly among the shops. They came to a pet store, and since they were both dog lovers from way back, they went in. Bells on the heavy door jangled behind them, and it took a moment for their eyes to adjust to the dim lighting.

There were no dogs at this shop, but there was a barnacled old rowboat anchoring the center of the room. Shelves of fish food lined the walls in small canisters, so the smell of wet kitten wafted through the air. A thin, bald man with a warty forehead and deep-set eyes stood at the register, just a few feet from Jake's elbow. When he caught sight of the man, Jake unconsciously guided Isabelle toward the rowboat.

It was filled with water and pebbles. A dozen large fish swam around a castle sunk into the false bottom. The fish were red and white, orange and white, white and red, white and orange, gold. They glided through the water in quick turns. Jake leaned over and bent his neck to take in their splendor, and Isabelle crouched in her green skirt next to the boat.

"Them's Koi," the proprietor said. His nametag read DWIGHT. "They're about all I ever sell in here."

"They're remarkable," Jake said, then added, "Dwight."

"Nishikigoi," said Isabelle. "A Japanese fish. It means 'brocaded carp'."

"A-yup," said Dwight. "Real hardy, too."

"Biggest goldfish I ever saw," Jake joked.

"Well, they're related to goldfish," said Isabelle.

"A-yup, and they're lucky, too."

"Lucky like how?" Jake asked. Dwight cast a pensive gaze up to the ceiling.

"Well, like say you're feeling pretty down-and-out and things seem they ain't ever about to look bright. But then you got yourself a Koi, so what the heck." He chuckled eerily.

"I see what you mean," Jake said.

"The thing about them is," Dwight went on, "you're set to have that kind of luck for a long time, too. Know why?"

Jake shrugged. Isabelle said, "Because these fish live into their fifties."

"Right," Dwight said, picking at a scab on his forehead. "How old are you?"

"I'll take one," Jake said, reaching into the boat comically, grabbing at a white fish with orange spots.

"Now hold it right there, mister. I got a net for that." The man came around from behind the counter and scooped the Koi into a water-filled bag. The flesh on his elbows was wrinkled and saggy, a few thick wires of hair protruded from the folds.

Isabelle was impressed with Jake's spontaneity and gave him an admiring look. He didn't seem down-and-out to her. In fact, he was the greatest she ever knew. Out of the corner of his eye he noticed her smile and said, "I love that little guy."

She said, "Aren't you coy" and brushed her lips against his cheek. The proprietor looked up from the cash register. "Yick," he said.

"We have to take him straight home and adjust him to the place. Oh, we'll need a cage too."

"I got all sorts of fishbowls, but what your Koi wants is lots of water in a fake pond."

"Okay, I'll take one of those."

Like an ugly dancer, Dwight moved around the room, gathering everything Jake would need to care for his new fish. He helped the couple heave it out the door. It was difficult to get the fish, plastic tub, food, rocks, and water-treatment home on their bicycles, but it wasn't a long ride to Jake's house. Isabelle said she felt like Buster Keaton. Once they arrived, they had a lot of fun installing the new habitat for Slick. Slick is a funny name for a fish.

That evening Isabelle made a salad for dinner. Jake crunched silently.

"You don't have a lot to talk about," Isabelle observed.

"I'm thinking about that man."

"Warty?" Isabelle and Jake laughed.

"Dwight," Jake corrected as he set his fork onto his plate. "Yeah, about the luck he was talking about. I never went in for luck, and I just thought he sort of had an interesting perspective on it."

"Like, how he didn't seem happy, or bright, but he thought he was lucky?"

"Yeah, I guess that's right. He thought he was, so he knew he was. That's a great way to use something that doesn't really exist."

"*Que tal?*" Isabelle said.

"I mean, like you said, Dwight just seemed to know he was lucky. He didn't seem to question it or anything. And despite his condition, his dimness, he does seem to bask in luck. Which is pretty much how he defined it."

"He had all those Koi."

"One thing about Slick, is that he's going to grow old with us," Jake said. He let the word "us" hang there for a second. Isabelle took it in and put her fork down, too, and sat back in her chair. Jake's hands were in his lap and he looked down at them. Isabelle tilted her head and lifted her eyes to catch Jake's. Sitting back, they smiled at each other, then finished eating in silence.

A few months later, Isabelle was moved in. She continued her work at the office, and on weekends she and Jake drove around the county, shopping at yard sales and flea markets. She marveled at his knowledge of what she thought of as trivial junk. What impressed her most was the value of the items he took interest in. A rusted old toy in a free box could be worth eighty bucks. One ragged book he found was worth $300.

He bought a $1200 pair of jeans for three dollars! Isabelle frequently purchased potholders and silverware only to find that she paid for them exactly what they were worth. She thought this game was very exciting, even though she was awful at it.

It was on one of these trips into the far reaches of the county that they came upon a shambling pickup stopped on the abandoned highway. Leaning on the car was a septuagenarian man in bibbed overalls, a shotgun broken open on the hood. Isabelle slowed her car to pull up behind him. Jake and Isabelle met the man when the dog under the truck had been writhing for about twenty minutes. "Howdy cowpoke," Isabelle started to say, but then she saw the dog and turned aside in wretched horror. She tucked her face into Jake's shoulder.

"I s'pose she came out from those trees over there," the old man said, his face red with remorse. "Course, I didna seen her. I see her now though, don't I, with her stinkin' sad black eyes." It was a youthful hound dog, with the matted fur of a stray. Her short hair was brown where it wasn't red with blood. Her neck was turned in horribly underneath her head. Through a patch of stickiness and chunks of pavement in the dog's matte, Jake made out the trace of a broken rib jutting through the flesh. There was nothing for it. Somewhat recovered now, Isabelle knelt beside the dog and heard her trying to whimper.

The dog had a tag.

The tag said, "Hopper."

A wetness formed around Isabelle's eyes. The old man said, "Aw cripes lady." He looked at Jake. "Outta those trees over there. Outta no where. What could I do?"

"We should get her some help," Jake said.

"Hopper," said Isabelle, standing.

"Hey Hopper," Jake soothed. "Good girl. We'll get you some help."

"Hopper, shucks," the man said.

Isabelle said, "I think it's too late for help, Jake."

"It is. It is too late," said the man.

Jake blanched. "But no," he sputtered.

"I was fitting to put the bitch down, put Hopper down, but I couldn't finagle this shell into this gun." With shaking hands, he alluded to the shotgun on the truck. He dragged the sleeve of his flannel shirt across his nose. Everyone was very sad then. Jake walked to the side of the road and vomited into the weeds. He came back and took the birdshot from the man and hoisted the gun up from the hood, loading the shell as he did so. He fitted the pieces together and jockeyed the butt into his shoulder and looked down the barrel at Hopper.

Hopper lowed and whined, his tongue wiped at his mouth. The man and Isabelle watched Jake as he lowered the gun and his eyes. He tried to hand the gun to the old man, but the old man stepped back. Jake put the gun back onto the truck like it was hot and moved toward Isabelle's car. He opened the passenger door and sat down, his head in his hands.

"Hopper, oh Hopper," said the man.

"You should put her out of her misery," Isabelle said. She thought to put it that way, as a merciful act, would catalyze the man. But he just said "oh no, no," and stepped backward again. Because there was another person there, he could absent himself. There was a pause, then the dog sucked in a wheezy breath, underscoring the silence. Quickly, unthinking, Isabelle snatched up the shotgun, aimed it at the dog's head, and fired once.

Jake and Isabelle rode home in silence. They did not go to any flea markets.

A few days passed. When Isabelle came home from work one quiet evening, she found Jake standing over a salad bowl, a dish towel over his shoulder and his shirtsleeves wet up to his elbow. In his hands she saw he had strangled Slick.

Boy Stuff

Jen Michalski

The college on the postcard tacked to his parent's refrigerator grew from where Sean sat in the backseat. Occasionally he would look up from his hand-held video system at the row of trees that flanked the narrow road on which their Subaru traveled. Beams of sun broke through them intermittently like searchlights, bathing his game in patterns of leaves and trunks. Distracted, Sean imagined the manicured greens of the campus, beautiful co-eds lounging in the sun, professors with beards and bow-ties clutching briefcases, an amalgamation of college settings and inhabitants featured in films with PG-13 ratings that had melded in his mind.

Eventually, the trees on each side of the car opened like hands, a tall brick bell tower, the one in the postcard, resting in their palms. A white sign hung from an iron bar that stood modestly by the roadside: Saint Ann's College.

You're going to see a lot of partying this weekend, his father explained, winking at him in the rearview mirror. But do as I say, not as I did.

Pat, his mother began.

What? The boy's getter older, Shelley. He needs to know things.

Sean was just thirteen, his future in college as far away as his death. But his father had wanted him to come and see where he had played tennis as a semi-pro. Where he had been a young man, full of libido and a lust for danger. Where he had met Sean's mother when they had been assigned to a sociology project together senior year. In sum, where Sean had germinated in some abstract way, the eventual byproduct of varsity tennis, beer, and a sociology paper on the variations of regional dialects in southern Maryland.

They parked the Subaru after young, tanned girls with signs navigated them through the various turns and curves of the well-maintained campus. Brick buildings with simple geometrics gave the illusion that they were all fairly modern and welcoming, an amusement park of learning. Not like the stuffy Ivy League schools, his father had explained. His father and mother commented on the existence or non-existence of certain buildings during their tenure, with either disdain (newer structures) or pleasure (old structures). The banners and signs and streamers conveyed a celebratory nostalgia not meant for Sean but exciting nonetheless: SAINT ANN'S COLLEGE REUNION '08: WHEN THE SAINTS COME MARCHING HOME.

Sean's father shuffled his family to the registration booth at the student center, where great concentrations of pink-cheeked girls gave them name tags encased in plastic on lanyards. Sean stuffed his in his pocket, while his father draped it over his heather green Polo shirt. PAT DYE, 1992. Sean's father smiled at the girls, smiled at his wife, smiled at Sean. Sean looked around at the student center, which was fairly modern by his standards: Wi-Fi connectivity, Starbucks, ATM, a sub shop. He wondered what the center looked like in 1992, stripped of its amenities, his parents stripped of their parenthood, their responsibilities, but he just didn't have the imagination. Or maybe he just didn't care. He wanted to get to the room so he could finish playing his game. He hoped he could play his cards right and stay in their assigned housing all weekend while his parents engaged in school-sponsored activities. One of girls gave him a robotic, practiced smile.

Do you think you'll attend Saint Ann's? she asked.

If he keeps his grades up, his father answered, hands in his pockets, springing up and down slightly on his heels. It's a lot tougher to get in these days—1200 SATS, 3.5 GPA. It was a party school when I was here. That's how I got in—I knew how to party.

Have a great weekend, the girl answered, and when Sean opened his mouth to tell her he thought he'd rather go to Duke, she was smiling robotically at the next couple in line.

At the student living space, a long brick block of one-floor apartments with two bedrooms, a bath, and a common living area, Sean looked out the window at the various groups of alumni, much older and much younger than his parents, pulling their wheeled suitcases behind them, pillows under their arms while his mother unpacked the cooler and offered him a juice box. She was pretty, Sean thought, prettier than his friends' mothers, her soft southern voice alluring, her thin hair wheat-colored and straight. Sean inherited her shyness, sought her tempered, thoughtful advice. But he would be his father's soon, he knew. He had seen it in his other friends. He would be passed off, like baton, into the insular, jocular world of golf and football games on Sunday afternoons and other "man" stuff. He would no longer be able to sit in the cool darkness of his room on summer evenings, playing World of Warcraft and reading Tolkein.

Who do you think is here? His father still stood by the window, still rocking on his heels.

I didn't see anybody we knew on the list, his mother answered, piercing a juice box with a straw. Did anybody ever return your phone calls?

You know those guys. Always waiting until the last minute, he mused. I'm sure they're here. Let's go have a look-see.

Sean followed his parents to the common grass, surrounded by approximately twenty similar units in a semi-circle. Sean's father approached a circle of men playing Frisbee. Sean figured they must be recent graduates, as attested to by their hard, small tanned muscles lapping over their legs, the cargo shorts and Abercrombie & Fitch tops and visors. His father stood a few feet from them, observing and waiting to be invited into the circle. No invitation came, and he stuck his hand up, eager for the Frisbee.

Over here, dude, his father said, and Sean cringed a little. Dude was a pretty popular colloquialism. And all of Sean's friends liked his jokey, rough-housing father, felt he was one of them. Some even wanted him for his own. Sean had never questioned his father's place in the grander scheme of things. But these men were different, a breed Sean had yet to encounter. A graduate with expensive sunglasses and the darkest tan flicked it to Sean's father after a long delay.

You guys lived in Huntington? Sean's father asked them. Sean knew all about the mythical Huntington, the place that Pat Dye had lorded over like a fiefdom, where he almost killed a guy while boxing in full lacrosse gear, where he almost killed himself drinking a fifth of rum. Do as I say, not as I did.

Yeah, for a little bit, one of the more diplomatic Frisbee tossers said. He was shorter, with wavy blond hair that poked out around a threadbare, backwards Yankees cap. Then we lived in Seahouse.

Good parties, Seahouse. His father nodded. I could have lived there. But you know, I liked Huntington. That was a crazy place. I almost killed a guy there lacrosse boxing. They had to break up the fight. They still lacrosse box these days?

Yeah, Yankee boy answered, taking a swig of his beer. But nobody tries to kill anybody.

Well, what can I say? Sean's father sailed a Frisbee a little over the third guy's head. Saint Ann's was crazy back in those days. Say, could I bum a beer? The wife didn't want me to bring beer down. We've got our son with us.

Little lacrosse killer, expensive sunglasses man smirked, a little glint of teeth exposed behind soft, full lips surrounded by stubble. Sean looked around for his mother, not realizing she had appeared beside him.

You want to see the campus? She asked him.

Leave him here, Shelley. Let him hang out with the boys. His father took an exaggerated swig of beer.

I'm going to find my old dorm, she said, looking at Sean. He hated that she let him decide, but he also understood this was how it needed to be. Sean, you can come or stay with your father or go back to the room, but I'll have to give you my key and then you can't leave until I get back.

I'll go. He turned, a little too quickly, toward her, not looking at his father or the men. They walked silently for awhile, until the pairs of alumni heading toward the housing thinned and the dormitories that were closed for the summer loomed around them, silently, their memories of energetic students dormant in their walls. His mother pulled the digital camera out of her satchel and snapped pictures of Roseblum Dormitory, which he assumed was hers—he never heard what she did in her dorm back in the days, although he guessed it was lower-key than what his father did—before heading across the way to take pictures of Huntington.

Your father is a sweet man—don't let him fool you. Sean's mother put the camera away. He was so shy in our sociology class. I knew he wanted to pair up with me because he was a jock and didn't study very much, but I didn't mind. I didn't hang out with very many people, and I thought maybe I should try to know some other people before I graduated. He was so quiet, let me do a lot of the work, but then he started kidding me, teasing me. I was part of his group, finally.

Sean nodded. He thought of lacrosse killers, sunglasses man. Knowing his parents had once been young, their wisdom suspect, was something he had been unwilling to consider to this point. How could he rebel against their reasoning if it was just as flawed as his own? He wanted to go back to the housing and play his racing game. He figured he could subsist on the snack-size bags of pretzels and juice boxes his mother had brought in her oversized satchel, never having to leave his room.

Your father would do anything for me, for us, his mother continued, gripping the strap of her satchel. We'd better get back, see what he's up to.

They found Sean's father still with the younger, Frisbee-playing alum, but they had stopped playing Frisbee and were lounging easily on the ground, a bunch of gangly spiders with tanned, hairy legs. They searched for something long and hard in the bottom of their beer cans, either with their tongues or eyes, as his father stood, holding an awkward court: professor and bored students.

Yeah, I liked tennis almost as much as I liked lacrosse, his father explained. But maybe I liked it better because I didn't have to rely on so many assholes to get things done. I was semi-pro here, had a 120-mile an hour serve. But you know what they used to call me?

Pat, do you want to get ready for dinner? his mother asked.

In a few minutes, Shelley. I'm connecting with alum here. He turned back to the men, whose expressions were cloaked by their sunglasses, the lethargy of their bodies in the grass. Anyway, you know what they used to call me, the other guys, because I gave them a hard time? Wimbledick.

The men laughed. Sean's father beamed. His mother tugged him slightly, and the two of them made their way back to their assigned housing without his father. Sean played a racing game on his video system until dinner. Every few minutes, he heard the sound of his mother separating the slats of the aluminum blinds with her hands before letting them fall shut.

Fucking Saints! The sinner is home! Someone outside shouted across the common.

***

Later that evening, the group on the lawn had grown exponentially. Boys in baseball caps and t-shirts with bands or sports teams or brand names emblazoned across them laughed and flicked the white and green saucer to the Frisbee-playing alumni from earlier that morning while their girlfriends or wives made their own slightly more sophisticated circle, drinking box wine from plastic cups. None of this group ate at the college-sponsored cookout, which was held under a large white tent housing picnic tables that overlooked the river and boasted long tables of fried chicken, potato salad, hot dogs, hamburgers, and Maryland blue crabs (slightly undersized, Sean's father had remarked). Everything had a mass-produced, too-salty or too-bland institutional taste to it, Sean's mother had decided, and Sean wondered if the food would be similar when he got to school. His father had gone back for seconds, thirds, boasting that his appetite was just as large as the one he had possessed as an undergrad.

The group on the lawn tended instead to a large meat smoker they had set up under a tent in the middle of the green, along with some picnic tables stolen from the tent and various coolers. A CD player blasted music, a pounding static that engulfed the group like a bee swarm.

Wimbledick! Several voices yelled in unison as Sean passed with his parents. His father made a shallow bow and nodded to Sean to accompany him.

Pat, don't be long. We're going to miss the alumni concert. Sean's mother stood at the door of their housing.

Whatever. We've got music right here. Come here, Sean. His father embraced him with one arm. The college wants you to see what it wants you to see. But you're going to see the college as it is.

Sean and his father rejoined the group on the lawn. Other than the anonymous acknowledgement from a few moments ago, no one paid them any attention. Sean's father plopped down next to expensive sunglasses man, who still wore his sunglasses even though the sky had melted from a crystalline blue to wet waves of orange and brown.

Dude, can I bum a beer? his father asked sunglasses man.

If you don't hit me with your lacrosse stick, he answered, nodding his head toward the cooler.

Son, get me a beer. His father nodded toward the cooler also, crossing his legs Indian style. Sean put his hand in the icy water and pulled out a silver and blue can. His father had let him have sips of beer at cookouts in the past, but Sean didn't understand what was so great about it. He didn't understand what was so great about reunion weekend at Saint Ann's, either. His parents had not run into a single alumnus they knew, and their memories of the college, since they met in their last semester together, never seemed to converge. His mother's memories, told during the cookout and a tour of the college earlier that afternoon, were mostly of hours spent in the science building, of girls who drank hot chocolate in dormitories and had all-nighters, of her hours in student government. His father's, of course, centered on drinking, vomiting, parties, practical jokes. Sean had never questioned the inevitability of his parent's union, being one of its main byproducts.

But his father, here, his legs looked thinner, his skin pastier, his hair sparser. Sean wanted his father to get his own damn beer, or maybe he wanted his father to share a beer with him somewhere else, not among these men, who looked ferocious in their youth, thread-muscled tigers next to an aged, blind gazelle. He handed his father the beer.

Sit down. His father patted the earth next to him. This is my son, Sean.

You thinking about going to Saint Ann's, Sean? The blond boy from yesterday asked.

I don't know, Sean answered.

He's only thirteen, his father added. He hasn't thought about colleges yet.

You want a beer, Sean? Sunglasses boy asked, catching his eye. He was smiling. Sean looked at his father.

Just don't tell your mother. His father winked, nodding toward the cooler. Sean stuck his hand in the icy water again, feeling the cold travel further up his arm, all the way into the pit of his stomach. He wondered what his mother was doing, if he should go in and see whether she needed help. Whether she would come out to check on them.

Should we get ready for the concert? Sean asked.

You don't want to go to that, do you? His father laughed. I mean, we didn't go to any 'concerts' in college. That's for the white hairs.

And mom, Sean answered. The men in the circle snickered and sipped from their beer cans. He felt his neck burn, not meaning to insult his mother.

Ouch, dude. Sunglasses man smirked. You play lacrosse like your old man, Sean?

He's in his second year of lacrosse camp, his father answered. A chip off the old block.

The men made eye contact with each other, but didn't answer. Sean held onto his can tightly, feeling the residual cooler water drip over his palm. His father had finished his first and made a trip to the cooler for a second. Again, the men made eye contact with each other but didn't say anything.

Pat! Sean! His mother's voice sailed easily over the common. Sean placed his beer in the area where his father had been sitting. He watched as his father met up with his mother on the other side of the common, his emphatic arm gestures, his pointing toward the group. The men in the circle talked about some sweet ass they had seen in the housing two doors down from where Sean was staying with his parents. They ignored him. He realized that if he wanted to go to the concert, the best thing to do would be to get up and get near his mother, to not give her any indication that he wanted to stay here, in this circle, with these people, and his father. He shot up and, mindful of not appearing overly eager to escape their company, walked slowly toward his parents. He had not made it before his father turned and intercepted him, grabbing his upper arms in excited confidence.

We got out of it, buddy. His father grinned. Come on.

Was Mom mad? Sean asked. He suddenly felt very bad for her, wished he had been more decisive. He imagined her sitting alone, in her foldout chair, studiously perusing the program and clutching her satchel.

She understands the need for us to hang out with the boys, do boy stuff. His father wiped his hands on his shorts and led the way back to the circle. He felt very bad that he dreaded going back to the circle with his father, just as he felt very bad for his mother. He felt very bad for all of them that they were not the unit they were accustomed to being—Friday nights at the Outback and the movieplex, watching action flicks (even though he felt very bad they never saw any movies his mother wanted to see). He wondered if they would go back to their Friday night activities or whether his social and cultural development would be ceded entirely to his father and his idea of boy stuff.

Sean sipped at the beer, hoping it would taste better as he drank more, but the thin sourness of it made him feel a little tired. He laid back in the grass and watched the stars sharpen in contrast to the darkening sky. He wondered if any of these men had ever felt like he did, or whether they always liked beer and sweet ass and sitting in a circle talking about things they had already done and how awesome they were. He smelled a sharp, skunky herbal odor and sat up. The men were passing around a hand-rolled cigarette. Although he had never seen one before, Sean knew it was marijuana. He looked to his father, who was sitting wordlessly next to him, a few more crushed beer cans by his side.

Dad, Sean said, but did not know what else to say.

No, you cannot have any, his father laughed. But this is college, son. The real deal.

What if somebody sees it? Sean scanned the common for the other groups of alumni. Most were insulated, much like his one, in little groups, the sounds of their laughter muted from the music and random fireworks set off by a crowd in the far corner of the common.

Nobody's going to rat us out, his father answered. Nobody at Saint Ann's is that lame. At least they weren't.

The joint came to Sean's dad. He held it up and appeared to study it.

Boy, in my day we had some good shit, he answered before passing it over Sean to the man sitting next to him.

The shit is still good, sunglasses man said. Try it.

My son's here. Not that he doesn't know what college is all about—he knows how things work. Hell, I was smoking when I was his age.

Here. The man to Sean's right passed it back to Sean's father.

Well, what the hell. The sinner is here! His father shouted.

***

When his father passed out, Sean had been struggling for the better half of the hour whether to leave. He wanted to find his mother at the concert series, but he wasn't sure where to go. The campus had been a blinding maze of tarred and concrete paths, the buildings confusing similar in their height and design. And he was too afraid to ask his father to let him into the room. His father's stories about his days at the school had become progressively louder and stranger, and he thought the men's reactions were shriller and ruder, but he could not be sure. At any rate, their hooting and hollering seemed to energize his father, who jumped up and down and mimicked lacrosse boxing with a tree branch, the tree from which he had snapped it his opponent. Sean laid down again and stared at the sky, hoping maybe he would wake up in his bed at home or, at this point, even the college housing. When he had finally made his decision to try and find his mother, he sat up and found his father snoring loudly, sprawled the length of one side of the picnic table bench.

Dude, you want to help your father home? Sunglasses man nodded his head toward the bench.

Tell us where you're staying. The blond-haired man held his palm up to sunglasses man, seemingly in warning, or truce. We'll help him back.

Sean could not remember the number of the housing. They had all looked the same. He looked at his father, blotch-faced, his right elbow folded under softly where it met the ground, and took a step back.

I need to find my mother, he stammered, and ran off in the direction of her departure. He didn't know what he was going to tell her. He wondered whether she would get mad at him for leaving his father, for letting him become so inebriated, for not getting her earlier. He considered sitting at the picnic bench with his father, waiting for her return. But would she be angry at him for just waiting, for forgetting the room number? Should he have remembered, asked for his own key?

He didn't know what to do. The activity on the campus had died down, and he did not know where he was, only that he was alone. He felt a lump of anger and tears and disappointment and was mad at all of them. The men who were slyly mean to him and his father, his mother for letting his father indulge. His father for encouraging the same in Sean. The entire Saint Ann's college community for being so indifferent to his plight. His grandmother for taking a bus trip to Atlantic City and not being able to watch him. Himself for secretly wanting to be in Atlantic City with his grandmother. He laid down on a bench and tried not to cry, especially now that he heard a cadre of male voices approaching. He sat up and pretended to tie his shoe, hoping they would pass him without incident.

Lacrosse boy, the voice of sunglasses man was like a sunburn all over his back. You find your mommy?

I thought I'd take a walk, he shrugged.

Your mom came back, the blond man in the Yankees cap explained. We helped her get your dad home okay. But she's gone out looking for you. We told her we'd send you back her way if we ran into you.

Where are you going? He asked, not quite believing his own words. He did not want to spend the evening bearing either his mother's wrath or her pity. And anything that either his father or mother could offer him, in the way of advice, or sympathy, seemed left behind, at the dinner table, or by his bedside. It was certainly not here. And, he feared, it would not be waiting when they returned home.

We're going down to the beach, go swimming in the old hole, sunglasses man, who had finally removed his sunglasses spoke. You wanna come, little lacrosse boy?

Fuck yeah, Sean managed with all the apathy and attitude he could muster. The boys roared, a hearty laugh of approval. He moved among them, floated in the aroma of beer and pot that clouded about them, felt the rising moon glint off the hairs beginning to grow on his legs. He carried one end of the cooler when another man wanted to smoke a cigarette. They pushed through brush, talking in sharp, gutteral tones punctuated by "fuck" and "dude," the branches slashing their exposed limbs and trunks. They finally came to a clearing where a small beach met the wide mouth of the river. Sean could see the modular units of the college high on the hill behind them, watching their moves.

Some of the men stripped and jumped in the river. Most seemed surprisingly modest, wading out to their chests, clutching their beer cans and cigarettes. Sean took the Frisbee and skimmed it close to the water. The men were amused at the white disc moving in the moonlight, seeing who could jump the highest out of the water to get it, who could throw it the furthest. Sean waded out and sat on the beach. He had forgotten about his mother, her search. He wondered how he would dry his shorts, how he would get home. She would not be too firm with him, he knew; usually his guilt about disappointing her was the worst punishment he could imagine.

But he did not feel guilt. He felt angry and free and powerful, and angry that he was free and powerful. But there was no turning back on his power now.

Dude, your father is one crazy little man. Sunglasses man sat beside him, rivulets of river veining his chest in the pale light. He really got fucked up.

Yeah, Sean answered, knowing that he could say more, or he could say nothing. He's all right.

You should definitely come to Saint Ann's, sunglasses man said, cupping him in a half-bear hug. You'll have an awesome time. It's a great school.

I'm thinking about it.

The rest of the men waded their way back from the river like worn seamen after a long trip. The walk on the way home was quiet. Sean breathed the smell of the magnolias and evergreens and grass seeping into his skin, filling him up with a life he had never breathed before. He inhaled aggressively, trying to grow his chest and diaphragm with each gulp. At the commons the men fell into their chairs around the smoker, which had been reduced to a low simmer. Yankees-cap man walked with Sean to his housing, where outside two campus security officers were trying to calm his near-hysterical mother. He felt bad that she'd had to worry about her father all weekend and then him, but the usual burden of his sadness was gone. He wondered whether it had really been his.

Oh my god, Sean, thank god you're okay. She took Sean in her embrace.

He just got lost trying to find you, Yankees cap man explained. We took care of him.

Well, I think it's time for Sean to go to bed, she answered tonelessly, not looking at the man. Earlier that day, she'd been offering him juice boxes and Townhouse crackers for the mere fact he was one of their neighbors on the quad.

I hope, uh, your husband is feeling better, ma'am. The man took a step away, tipping his cap.

Well, we all had a little too much fun tonight, she answered, and since there was no one to blame for anything, campus security left as well, leaving Sean and his mother in front of their housing.

I hope everything you learned tonight...will be a valuable lesson to you, she said, dabbing a drip of snot from her nose. She looked very much like a crushed juice box, Sean decided, a feeling that made him sad and sick and angry. We'll talk about all of this tomorrow, when your father is…in better shape.

Sean followed his mother quietly into the housing in the dark and went to this room. He could hear the low murmur and laughs of the men outside, the dried river on his skin. Outside, he heard a faint scrape and plop and, upon investigation, discovered that the men had lost their Frisbee on the roof of one of the housing units across the common green. It was still there when Sean and the Dyes, Class of 1992, left the college on the postcard the next day.

Easy as A-B-C

LAURA LIPPMAN

Another house collapsed today. It happens more and more, especially with all the wetback crews out there. Don't get me wrong. I use guys from Mexico and Central America, too, and they're great workers, especially when it comes to landscaping. But some other contractors aren't as particular as I am. They hire the cheapest help they can get and the cheapest comes pretty high, especially when you're excavating a basement, which has become one of the hot fixes around here. It's not enough, I guess, to get the three-story rowhouse with four bedrooms, gut it from top to bottom, creating open, airy kitchens where grandmothers once smoked the wallpaper with bacon grease and sour beef, or carve master bath suites in the tiny middle rooms that the youngest kids always got stuck with. No, these people have to have the full family room, too, which means digging down into the old dirt basements, putting in new floors and walls. But if you miscalculate—boom. Nothing to do but bring the fucker down and start carting away the bricks.

It's odd, going into these houses I knew as a kid, seeing what people have paid for sound structures that they consider mere shells, all because they might get a sliver of a water view from a top-floor window or the ubiquitous roof-top deck. Yeah, I know words like ubiquitous. Don't act so surprised. The stuff in books—anyone can learn that. All you need is time and curiosity and a library card, and you can fake your way through a conversation with anyone. The work I do, the crews I supervise, that's what you can't fake because it could kill people, literally kill them. I feel bad for the men who hire me, soft types who apologize for their feebleness, whining: I wish I had the time. Give those guys a thousand years and they couldn't rewire a single fixture or install a gas dryer. You know the first thing I recommend when I see a place where the "man of the house" has done some work? A carbon monoxide detector. I couldn't close my eyes in my brother-in-law's place until I installed one, especially when my sister kept bragging on how handy he was.

The boom in South Baltimore started in Federal Hill, before my time, flattened out for a while in the '90s and now it's roaring again, spreading through south Federal Hill, and into Riverside Park and all the way down

Fort Avenue into Locust Point, where my family lived until I was ten and my grandparents stayed until the day they died, the two of them, side by side. My grandmother had been ailing for years and my grandfather, as it turned out, had been squirreling away various painkillers she had been given along the way, preparing himself. She died in her sleep and, technically, he did, too. A self-induced, pharmaceutical sleep, but sleep nonetheless. We found them on their bed, and the pronounced rigor made it almost impossible to separate their entwined hands. He literally couldn't live without her. Hard on my mom, losing them that way, but I couldn't help feeling it was pure and honest. Pop-pop didn't want to live alone and he didn't want to come stay with us in the house out in Linthicum. He didn't really have friends. She was his whole life and he had been content to care for her through all her pain and illness. He would have done that forever. But once that job was done, he was done, too.

My mother sold the house for $75,000. That was a dozen years ago and boy, did we think we had put one over on the buyers. Seventy-five thousand! For a house on Decatur Street in Locust Point. And all cash for my mom, because it had been paid off forever. We went to Hausner's the night of the closing, toasted our good fortune. The old German restaurant was still open then, crammed with all that art and junk. We had veal and strawberry pie and top-shelf liquor and toasted grandfather for leaving us such a windfall.

So imagine how I felt when I got a referral for a complete re-do at my grandparents old address and the real estate guy tells me: "She got it for only $225,000, so she's willing to put another hundred thousand in it and I bet she won't bat an eyelash if the work goes up to $150,000."

"Huh," was all I managed. Money-wise, the job wasn't in my top tier, but then, my grandparents' house was small even by the neighborhood's standards, just two stories. It had a nice-size backyard, though, for a rowhouse. My grandmother had grown tomatoes and herbs and summer squash on that little patch of land.

"The first thing I want to do is get a parking pad back here," my client said, sweeping a hand over what was now an overgrown patch of weeds, the chain link fence sagging around it. "I've been told that will increase the value of the property ten, twenty thousand."

"You a flipper?" I asked. More and more amateurs were getting into real estate, feeling that the stock market wasn't for them. They were the worst of all possible worlds, panicking at every penny over the original estimate, riding my ass. You want to flip property for profit, you need to be able to do the work yourself. Or buy and hold. This woman didn't look like the patient type.

"No, I plan to live here. In fact, I hope to move in as quickly as possible, so time is more important to me than money. I was told you're fast."

"I don't waste time, but I don't cut corners," I said. "Mainly, I just try to make my customers happy."

She tilted her head up. It was the practiced look of a woman who had been looking at men from under her eyelashes for much of her life, sure they would be charmed. And, okay, I was. Dark hair, cut in one of those casual, disarrayed styles, darker eyes that made me think of kalamata olives, which isn't particularly romantic, I guess. But I really like kalamata olives. With her fair skin, it was a terrific contrast.

"I'm sure you'll make me very happy," was all she said.

I guess here is where I should mention that I'm married, going on eighteen years and pretty happily, too. I realize it's a hard concept to grasp, especially for a lot of women, but you can be perfectly happy, still in love with your wife, maybe more in love with your wife than you've ever been, but it's eighteen years and a young, firm-fleshed woman looks up you through her eyelashes and it's not a crime to think: I like that. Not: I'd like to hit that, which I hear the young guys on my crews say. Just: I like that, that's nice, if life were different, I'd make time for that. But I was married, with two kids and a sweet wife, Angeline, who'd only put on a few pounds and still kept her hair blond and long, and was pretty appreciative of the life my work had built for the two of us. So I had no agenda. I was just weak.

But part of Deirdre's allure was how much she professed to love the very things whose destruction she presiding over, even before I told her that the house had belonged to my grandparents. She exclaimed over the wallpaper in their bedroom, a pattern of yellow roses, even as it was steamed off the walls. She ran a hand lovingly over the banister, worn smooth by my younger hands, not to mention my butt a time or two. The next day, it was gone, yanked from its moorings by my workers. She all but composed an ode to the black-and-white tile in the single full bath, but that didn't stop her from meeting with Charles Tile Co. and choosing a Tuscany-themed medley for what was to become the master bath suite. (Medley was their word, not mine.)

She had said she wanted it fast, which made me ache a little, because the faster it went, the sooner I would be out of her world. But it turned out she didn't care about speed so much once we got the house to the point where she could live among the ongoing work—and once her end-of-the-day inspections culminated with the two of us in her raw, unfinished bedroom. She was wilder than I had expected, pushing to do things that Angeline would never have tolerated, much less asked for. In some part of my mind, I knew her abandon came from the fact that she never lost sight of the fact that there was an endpoint. The work would be concluded and this would conclude, too. Which was what I wanted as well, I guess. I had no desire to leave Angeline or cause my kids any grief. Deirdre and I were scrupulous about keeping our secret, and not even my long-time guys, the ones who knew me best, guessed anything was up. To them, I bitched about her as much as I did any client, maybe a little more. "Moldings?" my carpenter would ask. "Now she wants moldings?" And I would roll my eyes and shrug, say: "Women."

"Moldings?" she asked.

"Don't worry," I told her. "No charge. But I saw you look at them."

And so it was with the appliances, the counter-tops, the triple-pane windows. I bought what she wanted, billed for what she could afford. Somehow, in my mind, it was as if I had sold the house for $225,000, as if all that profit had gone to me, instead of the speculator who had bought the house from my mother and then just left it alone to ripen. Over time, I probably put ten thousand of my own money into those improvements, even accounting for my discounts on material. Some men give women roses and jewelry. I gave Deirdre a marble bathroom and a beautiful old mantle for the living room fireplace, which I restored to the wood-burning hearth it had never been. My grandparents had one of those old gas-fired logs, but Deirdre said they were tacky and I suppose she was right.

Go figure—I've never had a job with fewer complications. The weather held, there were no surprises buried within the old house. "A deck," I said. "You'll want a rooftop deck to watch the fireworks." And not just any deck, of course. I built it myself, using teak and copper accents, helped her shop for the proper furniture, outdoor hardy but still feminine, with curvy lines and that verdi gris patina she loved so much. I showed her how to cultivate herbs and perennials in pots, but not the usual wooden casks. No, these were iron, to match the décor. If I had to put a name to her style, I guess I'd say Nouvelle New Orleans—flowery, but not overly so, with genuine nineteenth century pieces balanced by contemporary ones. I guess her taste was good. She certainly thought so and told me often enough. "If only I had the pocketbook to keep up with my taste," she would say with a sigh and another one of those sidelong glances, and the next thing I knew I'd be installing some wall sconce she simply had to have.

One twilight—we almost always met at last light, the earliest she could leave work, the latest I could stay away from home—she brought a bottle of wine to bed after we had finished. She was taking a wine-tasting course over at this restaurant in the old foundry. A brick foundry, a place where men like my dad had once earned decent wages, and now it housed this chichi restaurant, a gallery, a health club and a spa. The old P&G plant is now something called Tide Point, which was supposed to be some high-tech mecca and they're building condos on the old grain piers. The only real jobs left in Locust Point are at Domino Sugars and Phillips, where the red neon crab still clambers up and down the smokestack.

"Nice," I said, although in truth I don't care much for white wine and this was too sweet for my taste.

"Vigonier," she said. "Twenty-six dollars a bottle."

"You can buy top-shelf bourbon for that and it lasts a lot longer."

"You can't drink bourbon with dinner," she said with a laugh, as if I had told a joke. "Besides, wine can be an investment. And it's cheaper by the case. I'd like to get into that, but if you're going to do it, you have to do it right, have a special kind of refrigerator, keep it climate controlled."

"Your basement would work."

And that's how I came to build her a wine cellar, at cost. It didn't require excavating the basement, luckily, although I was forever bumping my head on the ceiling when I straightened up to my full height. But I'm 6-3 and she was just a little thing, no more than 5-2, barely 100 pounds. I used to carry her to bed and, well, show her other ways I could manipulate her weight. She liked me to sit her on the marble counter in her master bath, far forward on the edge, so I was supporting most her weight. Because of the way the mirrors were positioned, we could both watch and it was a dizzying infinity, our eyes locked into our own eyes and into each other's. I know guys who call a sink fuck the old American Standard, but I never thought of it that way. For one thing, there wasn't a single American Standard piece in the bathroom. And the toilet was a Canadian model, smuggled in, so she could have the bigger thank that had been outlawed in interest of water conservation. Her shower was powerful, too, a stinging force that I came to knew well, scrubbing up afterwards.

The wine cellar gave me another month—putting down a floor, smoothing and painting the old plaster walls. My grandparents had used the basement for storage and us cousins had played hide and seek in the dark, a made-up version that was particularly thrilling, where you moved silently, trying to get close enough to grab the ones in hiding, then rushing back to the stairs, which were the home-free base. As it sometimes happens, the basement seemed larger when it was full of my grandparents' junk. Painted and pared down, it was so small. But it was big enough to hold the requisite refrigeration unit and the custom-made shelves, a beautiful burled walnut, for the wines she bought.

I was done. There was not another improvement I could make to the house, so changed now it was as if my family and its history had been erased. Deirdre and I had been hurtling toward this day for months and now it was here. I had to move onto other projects, ones where I would make money. Besides, people were beginning to wonder. I wasn't around the other jobs as much, but I also wasn't pulling in the kind of money that would help placate Angeline over the crazy hours I was working. Time to end it.

Our last night, I stopped at the foundry, spent almost forty bucks on a bottle of wine that the young girl in the store swore by. Cakebread, the guy's real name. White, too, because I knew Deirdre loved white wines.

"Chardonnay," she said.

"I noticed you liked whites."

"But not Chardonnay so much. I'm an ABC girl—anything but chardonnay. Dennis says Chardonnay is banal."

"Dennis?"

She didn't answer. And she was supposed to answer, supposed to say: Oh, you know, that faggot from my wine-tasting class, the one who smells like he wears strawberry perfume. Or: That irritating guy in my office. Or even: A neighbor, a creep. He scares me. Would you still come around, from time to time, just to check up on me? She didn't say any of those things.

Instead, she said: "We were never going to be a regular thing, my love."

Right. I knew that. I was the one with the wife and the house and the two kids. I was the one who had everything to lose. I was the one who was glad to be getting out, before it could all catch up with me. I was the one who was careful not to use the word love, not even in the lighthearted way she had just used it. Sarcastic, almost. It made me think that it wasn't my marital status so much that had closed off that possibility for us, but something even more entrenched. I was no different from the wallpaper, the banister, the garden. I had to be removed for the house to be truly hers.

My grandmother's parents had thought she was too good for my grandfather. They were Irish, ship workers who had gotten the hell out of Locust Point and moved uptown, to Charles Village, where the houses were much bigger. They looked down on my grandfather just because he was where they once were. It killed them, the idea that their precious youngest daughter might move back to the neighborhood and live with an Italian, to boot. Everybody's got to look down on somebody. If there's not somebody below you, how do you know you've traveled any distance at all in your life? For my dad's generation, it was all about the blacks. I'm not saying it was right, just that it was, and it hung on because it was such a stark, visible difference. And now the rules have changed again, and it's the young people with money and ambition who are buying the houses in Locust Points and the people in places like Linthicum and Catonsville and Arbutus are the ones to be pitied and condescended to. It's hard to keep up.

My hand curled tight around the neck of the wine bottle. But I placed it gently in its berth in the special refrigerator, gently as if I were putting a newborn back in its bed.

"One last time?" I asked her.

"Of course," she said.

She clearly was thinking it would be the bed, romantic and final, but I opted for the bathroom, wanting to see her from all angles. Wanting her to see, to witness, to remember how broad my shoulders were, how white and small she looked when I was holding her. When I moved my hands from her hips to her head, she thought was I was trying to position her mouth on mine. It took her a second to realize that my hands were on her throat, not her head, squeezing, squeezing, squeezing. She fought back, if you could call it that, but all her hands could find was marble, smooth and immutable. Yeah, that's another word I know. Immutable. She may have landed a few scratches, but a man in my work gets banged up all the time. No one would notice a beaded scab on the back of my hand, or even on my cheek.

I put her body in a trash bag, covering it with lime leftover from a landscaping job. Luckily, she hadn't been so crazed that she wanted a fireplace in the basement, so all I had to do was pull down the fake front I had placed over the old hearth down there, then brick her in, replace the fake front.

Her computer was on, as always, her e-mail account open because she used cable for her Internet, a system I had installed. I read a few of her sent messages, just to make sure I aped her style, then sent one to an office address, explaining the family emergency that would take me out of town for a few days. Then I sent one to "Dennis," angry and hate-filled, accusing him of all kinds of things. Finally, I cleaned the house best I could, especially the bathroom, although I didn't feel I had to be too conscientious. I was the contractor. Of course my fingers prints would be around.

Weeks later, when she was missing and increasingly presumed dead according to the articles I read in the *Baltimore Sun*, I sent a bill for the things that I had done at cost, marked it "Third and Final" notice in large, red letters, as if I didn't even know what was going on. She was just an address tome. Her parents paid it, even apologized for their daughter being so irresponsible, buying all this stuff she couldn't afford. I told them I understood, having my own college-age kids and all. I said I was so sorry for what had happened and that I hoped they found her soon. I do feel sorry for them. They can't begin to cover the monthly payments on the place, so it's headed toward foreclosure. The bank will make a nice profit, as long as the agents gloss over the reason for the sale; people don't like a house with even the hint of a sordid history.

And I'm glad now that I put in the wine cellar. Makes it less likely that the new owner will want to dig out the basement, risking its collapse, and bringing the discovery of what will one day be a little bag of bones, nothing more.

My Small Murders

RON TANNER

The Problem

Year before last, my wife and I were catching mice in our apartment. As many as three or four daily. We used every kind of trap on the market, as well as dish towels and buckets, grocery bags and brooms. Some catches were painless, and the mice released unharmed to the out-of-doors; others were gruesome, sad sights of broken bodies…

When it seemed we had only a single furry visitor, we contemplated letting it share our space. It was a pretty creature, we thought, its dark gray fur lustrous from meticulous grooming. (One book on mice describes their hygiene as "fastidious.") We joked: People pay good money for these little creatures at pet stores, don't they? And we joked some more: If we made available an exercise wheel, would the mouse give it a spin? This one was remarkably brazen, wandering into the living room to browse and sniff while we sat nearby and watched in disbelief.

Alas, where there is one mouse, there are many more. Soon we found ourselves startled by a furry fleeing flurry whenever we flicked on the kitchen light.

Pets

Teri has never liked animals, one way or the other. This should have given me pause when we first met, and now it's not clear which one of us was more deceiving or self-deceiving, she in her pretense of liking Celeste, my fat aged Tortie, or I in my blindness to her obvious discomfort. Her allergy didn't seem a serious allergy. After we moved in together, she—I thought—had accommodated herself to a compromise of sorts.

I wanted to make her happy. So, after her many complaints, eventually I gave Celeste to a cat-needy family. Teri resented that I had waited so long. Since she had never owned a pet, not even a fish, there was no way I could make her understand the difficulty of losing what was, in essence, a member of my family.

All of this is by way of saying that, soon after Celeste's departure, our place was overrun by mice, though only once had we seen Celeste catch a mouse—which I took from her and released into the alley.

A Man's Job

Although I said "we" were catching mice, the truth is that Teri refused to take any responsibility for their extrication and/or extermination. She didn't have the stomach for it, she said.

I didn't either. But somebody had to take control, I insisted.

"You make a project of everything," Teri had often complained because I am capable of tremendous, sometimes obsessive, focus when I set out to accomplish a task, as when I spackled and painted the apartment in a single weekend. My projects could be intrusive and irritating, I was the first to admit. This was one instance, however, where it seemed Teri didn't mind my "project mode."

No need to get into the touchy gender-typed assumptions we make about hunting and trapping, how it has traditionally been man's work. Suffice it to say, if I were successful—and I would be successful—I would prove to Terri that she had married the right man.

Why did I feel the need to prove anything?

By this time we had been married for only two years, after a dizzying one-year courtship. Friends and family had warned us to slow down because both of us were coming from recent divorces. Our first marriages we put down to youthful ignorance. This, our second, was sure to last because we thought ourselves so well matched. We were both painters, after all: she oils, I acrylics, she still-lives, I landscapes. She painted in the bedroom, I painted in the front room, the apartment reeking of turpentine, linseed oil, and paints.

Still, there were conflicts and misunderstandings we had to negotiate, as every couple must. Our small apartment—bought with a loan from her father—increased the stress of living together as each of us worked our day jobs, painted in the off-hours, sent out slides of our work, and fretted about getting a gallery or a show.

Mice, those small surprises at every turn, only made things worse. Their sudden, startling appearances were like cruel practical jokes

Trapping

As I began trapping—first with Sav-a-Lifes—I kept count of the catch. It seemed a kind of game. But then my captures and later my killings became so numerous that, in disgust and dismay, I stopped counting, with thirty-one dead mice on my conscience. If heaped together, they would have filled a bucket.

Would they never stop coming?

George, the Exterminator

Our Co-op manager sent over his exterminator, a middle-aged fellow who reminded me of former heavyweight world champion boxer George Foreman.

I heard him before I saw him, thumping laboriously up our six flights of stairs. One of his legs was prosthetic, apparently. It was a hot August morning and I felt badly for him.

"You got no weight on you," he said by way of introduction, meaning, I supposed, that I was slim enough to take the stairs lightly or that I was wasting away, maybe from worry over mice.

I introduced myself with a polite nod (Does one shake hands with one's exterminator?), and George nodded in return, smiling his benevolent George-Forman smile, sweat streaking down his hairless scalp.

After I explained my problem, he said, "Mice, you know, got no bones, they slide right under the door, you can't keep 'em out, you've got to discourage them." With poison, he meant.

"No bones?" I echoed.

"You want to find them," he continued, "you look for their drippings."

"Drippings?"

"Like so." With two large fingers he pointed to the baseboard under the living room window.

Droppings, he meant.

Teri and I found a trail of them every morning along the edges of our kitchen counter, which I wiped down with bleach before attempting breakfast.

"You mind?" George asked, raising his thin brows at me and nodding to the open bedroom door.

I motioned him forward, though I must have looked skeptical.

He reached into the plastic garbage bag he was carrying and retrieved a small black plastic box the size and shape of a covered butter dish. He then filled this with poison that looked like bright blue, powdered laundry detergent. The hole at either end of the butter dish would accommodate even the fattest mouse.

"Mice run in here for eats," George explained, "then go off and die."

By the time he was done, he had set those little black boxes of poison along baseboards, in closets, behind furniture, and in every corner of the apartment.

I wondered: Is this blue powder universally appetizing to rodents? I mean, there must be some persnickety feeders out there, a few of the fittest who will survive this attempt at genocide. I imagined mice languishing in the walls of my apartment. The stench of death.

I found George peering behind the gas stove in our tiny kitchen. "Here's where they're comin'." He nodded at a gas-pipe hole in the wall.

"But it's so high," I protested.

He laughed. "Mice can climb."

Jesus Christ, I know nothing about mice, I realized.

George stuffed the hole with steel wool, something mice can't chew through, he informed me.

"That should do," he said. The sweat dripping down his face didn't seem to bother him.

He thumped out of the kitchen. He hadn't been in the apartment for more than ten minutes.

"You got more problems, I'll come back," he promised.

After he left—I was surprised at how well he took the stairs (going down looked harder than going up)—more questions occurred to me: How long does the poison last? How long do I keep the black boxes in our apartment?

Appetite

The way George described them, mice seemed as relentless as cockroaches. Our cockroaches, by the way, those fig-sized waterbugs that occasionally found their way up from the basement, had disappeared. Mice eat cockroaches, though they'll leave the antenna and legs.

Mice, in fact, will eat just about anything. Chew the insulation off your wiring, the bindings off your books, the laces off your shoes, eventually bring the whole damned house down around you. Some of the stunning facts I learned as I began to research the history and habits of mice: mice can live without water. In times of famine, they will submit to a quasi-hibernation. Or they will eat their own excrement.

More Mouse Advantage

Contrary to what George-the-exterminator said, mice do have

bones, but they are capable of remarkable compression. A half inch may be enough for mice to slip through. More disturbing is their prodigious climbing: aided by tiny toe nails, they easily clamber up lamp cords, curtains, couches, chair-backs, you name it. Which is why we found droppings or "drippings," as George called them, on window sills, desk tops, bookshelves. Most disturbing of all is their rate of reproduction. A mature mouse, two months old, can have five to twelve pups every month. Which is why the Romans used to say, "It's raining mice."

Fading Hope

The poison seemed to have no effect. It got to the point where Teri would make plenty of noise before entering a room—she didn't want to see little leathery tails coiling into the darkness or furry humps skittering across the kitchen counter. I tried to be braver than she but, no matter how I prepared myself, a glimpse of a fleeing mouse was always the most unpleasant surprise, like seeing a severed hand wriggling on the floor.

These aren't visitors, I decided, these are parasites. They would keep coming, in ever greater numbers; they would nibble and chew and gnaw and scratch and climb and piss and shit every minute of every hour of every day, the apartment seething with their inexorable, inexhaustible scampering and scavenging until, drained of all resources and patience, Teri and I would flee in terror. The only good mouse, I concluded, is a dead mouse.

My research told me the same. "Mice are a viral reservoir!" cautioned one expert. They carry one of the deadliest of the new hemorrhagic plagues, the Hanta virus, which may be spread through the air. A disturbing thought when, every morning, I was wiping up those little black bullets of excrement from the kitchen counter with a damp paper towel.

New Art

I started putting mice in my paintings. It wasn't a plan, exactly, it was more an impulse—a way of exorcising them.

"Is that a dead mouse?" Teri asked, standing behind me as she surveyed my new work.

"I don't know," I admitted. "Does it look dead?"

"Yes," she said.

I paused to consider this.

I had depicted, in very crude strokes, a mouse lying on a napkin. Its eyes lacked definition. Maybe that was why it looked dead.

Teri said, "So you've moved to still life?"

I turned my head to look in her direction but couldn't quite see her expression in my peripheral vision. "I hadn't thought of it that way," I said.

Did she think I was going to compete with her still-lives of moldy cheese? She had a series of eight and was planning more.

Then the irony of my new work struck me with hilarious clarity: maybe I'd do a series of mice—we could have a joint show, my mice, her cheeses!

I was smiling now, about to suggest this idea, which I was beginning to consider seriously because it could have worked, but then Teri said: "Nobody's going to want to look at dead mice."

This was a hurtful remark. And totally beside the point. Since when had we been worried about what people would or would not want to look at?

I dabbed at the canvas, then rubbed off the dab with my rag. "Do you mind?" I said. "I'm working here."

The Truth About Freedom

During the few months I was freeing my captives, I didn't know that mice have a remarkable ability to find their way home, nor did I understand that, since stray mice are not accepted by other mouse families, I was sentencing these strays to an unfortunate end. So, in my ignorance, I accomplished nothing: either the mice returned to the building, then easily to our apartment (following the scent trails of their predecessors), or they were killed by predators or by other mice. After learning this much, I had to accept my role, finally, as exterminator. This was easier than I'd like to admit.

The Sound of One Hand Clapping

At the height of my exterminations, I often lay awake at night waiting for the snap of the traps. Nothing worked as well as the old fashioned, triggered trap. I could bait it any number of ways. Mice prefer peanut butter to cheese, I learned. I was making a science out of killing.

Sometimes, horror of horrors, the trap only maimed one. I came to dread the mornings when, half blinded by the kitchen light, I stumbled in to clean up the mess. At my most gruesome, I wondered if leaving the corpses out would serve as a warning to other mice, like Vlad the Impaler posting heads of his victims in front of his castle. The most heartbreaking sight I came across was a two-mouse killing in the same area, where one mouse had apparently followed the other into the killing field, perhaps drawn by the sounds of the other's distress.

Mouse Tales

I knew of someone whose infestation of mice grew so overwhelming that, enraged, he sent his housemate away and spent the night batting, swatting, pounding, and pulverizing mice as they poured from the walls. I knew of a couple who set out poison to curtail their infestation but hadn't realized that the mice would return to their nests to die—inside the walls: the stink of dead mice made the house uninhabitable.

Mice have been with humankind from the earliest days, as evidenced by mouse remains found in prehistoric cave dwellings. To call them parasites is grossly inaccurate obviously. It is said that ancient Egyptians domesticated the cat in order to combat the proliferation of mice. And General Rommel, Hitler's Desert Fox, when he was in the midst of the Sahara, found a nest of mice in the tank he was driving.

Definition

A pest is a creature we can neither use nor accommodate.

The Way In Is the Way Out

George-the-exterminator's discovery of the hole behind the stove sent me on an expedition to find more. I spent a day working in the kitchen, seeking these out. I spent another two days sealing the rest of the apartment. When I was done. the place felt as tight as a new sail boat.

A Surprise

Not long after this, Teri announced that our marriage was over. It seemed a cliché, her telling me she needed "space." She felt claustrophobic, she said.

"You mean our apartment's too small?" I asked.

"Our marriage is too small." Having packed her bags, she was going to spend the weekend with Colleen, a friend in Hampden.

Now on my fifth mouse painting, I was holding one of my long brushes. Why had I not seen how unhappy Teri was?

I said: "I know we've been tense lately, ever since the mice—"

"It's got nothing to do with mice."

"The mice haven't helped," I insisted.

"I'm leaving," she said.

"Jesus, Teri, it's not like you're trapped—I mean, what have I done?"

She stared down at her carry-on and pensively wheeled it back and forth as she spoke: it wasn't me, she said; it wasn't another man; it wasn't like we'd done anything wrong as a couple—

"Fuck that," I blurted, "something's gone wrong!"

At last she sighed. "Yes," she admitted, "I've gone wrong. I shouldn't have married you. It just all happened so fast and …."

"And what?" I wailed.

"And I've realized that I've loved you only … as a friend."

That brush upright in my hand like a useless wand, I gaped at her.

I hadn't heard a line like that since I was in high school.

It took Teri two hours to explain that our marriage had been ill advised from the start. At last she said, "Give me six months and we'll see what happens."

Timeline

It had taken us at least six months to realize that we had a mouse problem. And more than six months to rid our apartment of these pests. What could I possibly expect of Teri in a mere six months?

After her return, I moved into an aged high rise nearby. These were inhabited mostly by old folk and college students. The halls stank of insecticide.

I was subletting from a young woman who had moved to Seattle for the fall to see if she and her long-distance boyfriend were ready for marriage.

There were no mice in her apartment as far as I could tell. For this, I was grateful.

Friends No More

Teri and I tried to go out "as friends" but I couldn't manage it and, in anger, I broke off relations. Then we tried marriage counseling, which she broke from, also in anger because she didn't like what the words the therapist was using: "dysfunction" … "transference" … "pathology."

Now we are negotiating our divorce.

I know—and I suspect she knows—that our mutual anger is a product of our profound dismay in ourselves and in each other. It's surprising, and frightening, how much wrong we can find with each other when we look only for the wrong.

The Apartment

Both of us have since given up the apartment, which is now for sale. One of its great selling points is that the place is mouse-free. "You should know," I tell prospective buyers, who tolerate my tour with admirable patience, "that all of these old buildings downtown have mice. There's no way of getting rid of them, you can only shut them out." Then I recount the many, painstaking steps I took to achieve this. "Nothing can get in," I conclude proudly.

And nothing can get out either, I tell myself. The place is like a tomb.

Metaphor

I can't helping thinking it was emblematic of our relationship that Teri refused to have anything to do with the mice, while I was relegated to the role of their executioner. Here I thought we were building something and all the while she saw things crumbling around us. Although, obviously, the mice had nothing to do with the demise of our marriage, the synchronicity of their demise and ours seems too tidy for comfort.

Thankfully, I have been painting new subjects—and, once again, painting outside. Fast-moving Frisbee games have caught my interest of late.

As for my series of mouse paintings—which I stopped at lucky number seven: a few respected galleries downtown have expressed interest but at this point it remains a matter of nibbles, no bites.

Me and My Shadow

Here's a sure-fire way to check for mice after you've moved into a new place: open up the top of the stove and look under and around the burners. See any droppings? They may be old, so clean them out, then check again in a week. I have done this in my new apartment and have learned that the droppings do return—so I have mice. But my new cat keeps them at bay. Whenever I notice him crouching on the kitchen floor and staring intently into the dark gap between the stove and the dishwasher, I know there's a mouse back there, in the darkness, contemplating the possibilities. I try to view this as an acceptable compromise. Just last night, though, I dreamed of seeing a fat mouse darting across the stove top. It was as disturbing a sight as ever, and I had the sense that my life will never be as settled or predictable as I would like. Now, when I think of mice, I imagine them running in exercise wheels, hundreds, thousands, of mice wheeling round and round, and I am appalled at their tireless energy, at their endless turning, as if together they were the world's engine, the strength of their lowly multitude joined in a single, mindless task.

Sister Rafaele Heals the Sick

ROSALIA SCALIA

Sister Rafaele was to be unceremoniously ousted from Josephine's tiny row house in Baltimore's Little Italy; later, she was also to be welcomed into and kicked out of three other houses in the same neighborhood, mostly because their owners had come to believe her to be mad and hateful instead of holy and loving. Sister Rafaele, who had once been known simply as Mrs. Caterina Della Vecchio, former wife of a renowned mobster, had been occupying one of the neighborhood benches, telling anyone who asked that she was awaiting guidance and direction from her boss. She pointed to the sky.

Wearing a navy blue skirt hemmed at her knees, a loose white blouse, no stockings, thick brown sandals, and a huge wooden cross on a rawhide strip around her neck, she looked like one of the nuns from a Catholic grade school, except, surrounded by the large brown supermarket bags filled with her belongings, she also looked homeless. Stained, broken teeth marred what could have been a beatific smile, a smile she flashed when she explained to those who asked that her mission was to be assigned into a household that needed her and that God would, as He would invariably do, guide her to the next assignment.

"I'm being called to this neighborhood," she'd explained, on the early spring day when she showed up on the bench.

Waiting for her "instruction," Sister Rafaele had occupied various neighborhood benches over the spring months, and the neighbors could never discern if she were mentally ill or holy—and so remained content to figure it out from the sidelines, no one coming forth to offer her a place in their homes. Until Josephine.

In all those stories about saints Josephine, or Jody, had read over the years, none of them did normal, everyday things that regular people did. St. Francis of Assisi's own father, embarrassed by his son, considered him a nutcase. St. Lucy plucked out her eyes to avoid marrying a monied, older, non-Christian man, embracing a lifetime of blindness. Joan of Arc, burned at the stake, was considered crazy for putting on armor and riding into battle.

In Sister Rafaele's case, God had spoken, and Josephine, an unlikely candidate, heard.

At 33, Jody smoked cigarettes and pot on the sly. She cursed, the words sliding out of her mouth as easily as breaths. And she loved freely, all kinds of men, saying she was advancing world peace, one man at a time. Pretty, with a head of black curly hair, doe-brown eyes, and olive skin, she loved her twins—two eight-year-old boys, products of her individual world peace campaign, single-handedly raising them with the dedication of a Madonna.

Jody, who hadn't considered either holiness or insanity, merely decided it would be a win-win situation if she provided Sister Rafaele with a home and meals for a few months in return for babysitting the twins after school and doing light housekeeping. On the face of it, when Jody had first thought of the plan, it did sound foolproof. Having a helper like Sister Rafaele around the house could be a boon. Except, Jody hadn't considered all the changes Sister Rafaele would bring about.

Immediately after the nun moved in, she discouraged Jody from listening to CDs and to rock music on the radio. Instead, they listened to Christian radio and endless sermons. When Sister Rafaele noticed the navy blue tapestry with the gold sun and moon border hanging in the second-floor hallway, she encouraged Josephine to remove it, saying the sun and moon designs were evil and frightened her so much she couldn't go upstairs to bathe as long as it hung on the wall. Sister Rafaele also fined Jody a quarter for every time she said the word "shit" and a dollar for every other profanity. And soon, Jody smoked only on the front stoop and not in the house, since the smell of smoke sickened the nun.

"Nothing comes for free," Jody told her neighbors. "I don't mind some of the things, because it sets good examples for the boys, like the cuss cup. I do miss listening to my music, though. She cleaned the basement and mopped the floor. She took a big load off my mind when she caught the laundry up," she said. "She picks the boys up from school, brings them home, and gives them a snack. The boys seem to like her so much."

Sister Rafaele had insisted on prayers before meals. Once the boys had been put to bed, she and Jody would sit in the living room and sing hymns. Jody didn't mind. Having someone to talk to filled an emptiness in the house, too, she'd liked the changes she saw in the boys, who started beginning most of their sentences with "Sister Rafaele says."

Jody started rushing home from work to see the changes Sister Rafaele had made. Sister Rafaele had busied herself by day cleaning the house.

She organized the insurmountable stacks of papers scattered on the dining room table into piles. By the time Jody returned from work, Sister Rafaele would already have overseen the boys' homework assignments, and Jody just had to review them and praise the boys' work.

This was before Sister Rafaele, a woman unattached to any specific community of religious women, established all the house rules, which included no fornication in the house.

"You going out tonight?" Jody asked a coworker. "Let me use your apartment. I need to see Mr. Kung Fu and fuck his brains out."

"You need to divorce Sister Rafaele," her coworker said.

The July heat beat down the streets, cooking the blacktop even though the sun had slowly made its way toward the western horizon. Jody walked home the half block from the bus stop, gazing at the line of people in front of her house and not knowing why it had formed. She thought that perhaps one of the twenty-two neighborhood restaurants was giving away free food to attract such a mangy crowd until she saw Sister Rafaele praying and touching people. Jody approached the line.

"They been waiting in the long line for what seems like hours," one of her neighbors who had come to watch the spectacle informed her. "She's telling them that they're now healed and to go with God."

"Wonder where they all came from. Looks like every homeless person in the city found your place," another neighbor said. "It's a wonder nobody got robbed yet with all these strangers hanging out here for her."

"They ain't staying in front of my house. Sister Rafaele is gonna have to move these fuckers someplace else," Jody said. Her lips formed a straight line across the bottom of her face.

"Looks like they're people coming to be healed. An encounter with soap and water would have one powerful healing effect on them," the same neighbor said. Jody didn't laugh.

The people—unshaven men in raggedy clothes and busted shoes, skinny women with unkempt hair, dragging children with dirty knees and cheap plastic shoes—quietly waited in a queue that stretched across the street into the next block. Some of them held prayer beads. Some of them carried plastic bags that appeared to contain all their worldly possessions.

Hair peeking out from her homemade white linen veil, Sister Rafaele, head bent in prayer, touched them all. She laid her hands on their heads and, eyes shut, prayed in Jesus' name for them to be healed from demons and diseases, from addictions and disasters, and anything that might be plaguing their spirit.

Now the long line of believers, desperate for Sister Rafaele's healing touch, stretched for a block and a half. Embarrassed by the sight, shocked by the diversity of the people in line, confronted by the strangeness of it all, Jody searched for a cigarette.

Another neighbor, old man Mario, face scrunched into an expression suggesting extreme constipation, flashed her angry looks and raised his cane at her.

"What da hella isa dis?" he asked. "Where dese bums come from? I can't get into my house." Jody shrugged.

"Disa no right. We noncha wanna dese people here," another older neighbor said.

Jody waved to Sister Rafaele who stood on the top step of the stoop to her house.

Sister Rafaele waved back and continued on with healing work, this time laying her hands on the dirty gray head belonging to a disheveled man.

"Uh, Sister Rafaele, can I have a word with you?" Jody asked. She stood on the top step of her neighbor's stoop and climbed to the top of her own.

"Not now, dear. I'm doing the Lord's work. The Lord's work doesn't wait," Rafaele said, as if she were talking to a child. She smiled, her broken and stained teeth in need of dire treatment themselves, and turned away from Jody, dismissing her.

"You're going to have to do the Lord's work elsewhere. This crowd is disrupting the neighborhood," Jody said. Her face flushed. She searched her purse for a cigarette and lit one.

Without even looking at Jody, Sister Rafaele said, "Impossible. The Lord has directed me to heal His flock right here."

Jody spotted the twins, their dark heads bobbing and weaving on either side of the line, passing out cups of water.

"You have three minutes to move these fucking people someplace else, other than the outside of my house," Jody shouted.

Sister Rafaele ignored her. Head bowed, she laid her hands on the next seeker of her healing, an obese woman in red polyester shorts and a black striped shirt. "The demon of gluttony leave this woman in Jesus' name," Sister Rafaele intoned. She prayed over the woman, whose eyes fluttered in the back of her head.

Jody disappeared into her house, the door slamming behind her. A few minutes later, she emerged from the basement doorway that fronted the house, hauling a long green hose.

"Time to be baptized," Jody yelled, and pointed the nozzle at Sister Rafaele. A blast of water streamed from the hose and drenched the free-lance nun, who stared in stunned silence. Jody then pointed the nozzle at the long line of disciples and soaked them, walking up and down the long line, wetting them all as they dispersed, unhealed.

Where Hearts Lie

Lalita Noronha

"So, Vinay, it's settled then?"

Vinay nods. He's heard it before—these questions that aren't really questions. Nothing has been settled in his mind, but his wife's mind was made up long before she'd posed the question. As always, Sonia brings things up just days before he's set to leave for America, and today, he's right in the middle of a shave. Can't a man find peace even in a bathroom? He considers his face in the mirror—square jaw, deep piercing eyes, thin lips over straight white teeth, a handsome face by any standards. His eyes drift below his neck to his chest—firm pectoral muscles covered with short curly hair, and a hard abdomen with just a hint of love handles. He'll take care of that, he vows. Once he returns from this trade show, there'll be a lull in his travels. He'll begin a serious work-out regimen. In fact, why not pick up a pair of Adidas in Baltimore? He wants to stay fit for health reasons, certainly, but also for the way women eye him, especially white-skinned American women, who have no false sense of modesty.

Sonia doesn't like Americans at all. Never mind that she doesn't really know any, except perfunctorily from contacts at the Lions Club or the Bombay Gymkhana whereas he, Vinay, knows all types-secretaries, professionals, housewives, people in planes, malls, grocery stores—as well he should. This is, after all, his seventh business trip to America. He's been to England and Germany too, but for his money he'll pick Americans anytime. They're warm, and friendly, if you overlook their quirks. But Sonia's tapered view gleaned from the glitz of TV and magazine ads had led her to a dynamically opposite conclusion.

"They don't mean what they say," she'd once complained.

"How so? Why do you say that?"

"Well, because I know. Like that woman who works out in the gym every Saturday, Eva, Eva-something—can't remember her surname. She'll smile, sweet like halwa, and say, 'how you doing,' then doesn't bother to listen. Why ask and then walk off? It's insulting. Half the time I talk to her backside. And that tall white fellow ..."

"Oh, but it's an expression, for God's sake—a form of greeting like namaste, or hi! You're not supposed to launch into your whole life story.

No one has time to listen."

"Including you. You don't have time, either."

Bitterness seeped from her pores. He'd decided to ignore the comment. He knew that tone; he heard that lorry filled with cement blocks coming full speed, and knew better than to stand there and get crushed.

In the beginning, life with her had been almost intoxicating. Everything about her, the way she carried herself, walked, talked, even scrubbed the floor, exuded an allure, a raw kind of sex, made all the more sexual by the unawareness of her movements. Other times, she was feisty, flirty, a very un-Indian girl, even on her "interview day." Arranged marriages, she would later joke, were interviews for lifelong jobs-no retirement, no benefits, just work! He remembered that day well. Her high cheekbones were like soft contours of desert sand, smooth and brown, tapering to a voluptuous mouth and a small upturned nose. Her eyes were an oasis to drown in. If she'd let you. She was unexplored territory, a handful he knew he'd enjoy handling. And so he had. But now, still childless after ten years, they'd both abandoned their exploration. Disappointed and angry, she'd fed its embers. Her waist thickened, the beautiful angles of her body rounded, and even her lithe spirit was weighted with unspoken words.

Smoothing his jaw with approval, Vinay squints at the triple-headed razor, his newest American acquisition. How he loved these American-made products; loved the variety, choices, competitive prices. Hell, if you shopped around, almost everything was half price. You could practically eat for free-well, not exactly, but you could pig out for a pittance at those all-you-can-eat places. Nice places, mind you, with big smorgasbords-roast beefs, hams, a variety of salads, even mid-Eastern stuff-tabouli, hummus, kebabs. Why, the breads alone were astounding-seven-grain, five-grain, multi-grain, whole wheat, with honey, without honey, sesame, and permutations and combinations, all catered to health nuts and America's changing faces and palates. It was luscious living-opulent and free.

That's why he'd like to migrate to America. It was the place to live. That's why he'd been secretly buying dollars on the black market in Bombay and smuggling them in, sewn safely in the lining of his jacket under his arm pits. He'd even laid away a portion of his salary from each foreign project assignment for a little start-up nest egg, hatched with his sister, Amira, who lived in Baltimore. In fact, he even got her to file immigration papers for him-a bold, perhaps foolish move, considering he hadn't yet broached the subject with Sonia. Still, it was worth getting a head start.

As a mere sibling of an American citizen, his priority rating wouldn't be as high as those of children and spouses. It made perfectly good sense to begin the arduous form-filling, bureaucratic journey. If he was smart, he would sow the seed now, and let it germinate into an idea she could later claim as her own. What did it matter as long as she agreed?

He puts on a pair of well-ironed brown pants and a cream shirt. His fingers riffle along the edges of his ties. Dressing for the embassy, even just to pick up a visa, takes some thought. Important people look important, more important than merited. They carry leather briefcases, smell of Boss cologne, most likely purchased on the black market, and politely excuse themselves to the front of queues.

It is later than he wants it to be. The road through the bazaar is the shortest route to the train station. Dust, dirt, dead leaves, banana peels, lumps and bumps of cement blocks lie in his path. He passes carts piled with pyramids of fruit-papayas, pomegranates, guavas-and vegetables-brinjals, gourds, okra.

He is peripherally aware of the ire of women bargaining down prices. "Oh, bhaiya, give me a final price. Enough of this kit-kit; I'm in a hurry."

One thing about Americans—no one quibbles about prices. Everything is always on sale. Time is precious in their culture; they hurry and get everything done. Past meat stalls with fresh, red, lean sides of beef hanging from clips off a taut wire, his mouth waters for a juicy steak, with a buttery, un-spiced potato, but that will have to wait till he can rip off his vegetarian cloak in America. One thing about Indians—they spice everything. Everything looks yellow or red. He picks up his pace. A vagrant wind churns up loose-leafed newspapers and magazines from a pile lying be-side a heap of coconuts. Passing a circle of women and children crowding the middle of the street, he wonders for an instant if something tragic has happened. But as the lilting, mesmerizing melody of a flute wafts in the air, he knows it's only a snake charmer charming a venomless snake and a gullible audience.

The platform is swarming with people. In the first-class compartment, he finds himself squashed against the window, peering out as the tracks race beneath. Huts, streets, buildings blur past. Vibrantly colored saris hang from balconies, bathed in sunlight. A strong putrid whiff assails his nostrils as the train whistles over a polluted inlet of the bay, bordered with mud huts packed in rows like biscuits in a tin.

He wonders if tonight might be an opportune time to plant the seed.

Amira had estimated a two- to three-year wait before his application would inch to the top. In the meantime, Sonia's waffling could begin—What? Why? Why to go to America? No, never. Then, a toning down, a mulling over, yes, well maybe, then all the obstacles, the buts and what-abouts, regressing back to no, no, never, and the vacillating cycle would begin again. He pulls out his passport nestled in his breast pocket and looks at it-midnight teal, the Ashoka lion seal, The Republic of India embossed in gold. It looks imposing, imperial. Some day, perhaps, he'll carry a different passport-smaller, bluer, with the seal of the United States.

On this trip to America, he thinks, he should splurge for Sonia—buy something beautiful, alluring, a piece of jewelry, heart shaped. Or, perhaps not. American gold was dull, not like India's turmeric-yellow, twenty-two carat. Something she's never seen before, perhaps, sexy underwear, or Elizabeth Taylor's White Diamonds, or a palette of eye makeup with complementary lipsticks. If she could glimpse the differences between Baltimore and Bombay, see beyond the superficialities of boundaries, she'd love Baltimore. Such a city of eclectic rowhouses; ethnic groups—German, Greek, Korean, Italian—who knew, perhaps there might even be a Little India tucked away in one of the neighborhoods. With the steady influx of immigrants it was just a matter of time. It was a smart city, too, bursting with colleges and universities and businesses. The city benches read "Baltimore—The Greatest City in America." And unlike Bombay, people were friendly. They called you hon or sugar and told you to have a nice day. And they named their neighborhoods after parks—Hanlon Park, Druid Park, Roland Park, Park Heights. Amira said they might even rename the whole city-Balti-more-or-less, or Believemore, or just More! Imagine a city with an exclamation point! Maryland had it all, she said, all within the span of a three-hour drive-mountains, a bay, beaches, a harbor, four gorgeous seasons, and a mere hop away from the sheer madness of New York and Washington.

With his American visa tucked safely against his breast, he takes the steps up to the second floor, two at a time, a bunch of yellow roses in his arms. He feels spirited, uplifted. Sonia is dressed in a pretty purple sari with sprays of pink and lavender flowers scattered all over. She has swept her hair to one side, draped it softly over her neck; her lips and the bindi on her forehead are a deep pink, and suddenly she looks younger than she has in years. She stands in front of her dresser, considering a pair of dangling amethyst earrings and a matching bracelet.

His eyes take her in. “Wow! Where are you going? You look beautiful.”

She purses her mouth as if to wince, then smiles instead. “You don’t know? I asked you this morning *if* it was settled, remember?”

He makes a quick, calculated recovery. “Oh, but of course. Yes, you did.”

She grins. “So what was *it*?” He hasn’t fooled her. For once her eyes are shining, playful. “You don’t have a clue, do you?”

He gives in. “No, actually I don’t.” Her flirty flippancy excites him. “So, tell me.”

“We’re going to Meena’s birthday party. She turns forty this year.”

“Oh!” He moves closer, yellow roses still in hand. “I brought you these. I thought we might ...”

“Might what?”

His arms tighten around her. “Stay home tonight.” His fingertips linger on the bare skin of her back, dip into the indent of her spine, slowly swinging up and down along the groove, as if they were on a trapeze. She arches, leans in, the softness of her breasts against his shirt. Her eyelids flicker open and shut like butterfly wings, then close. He lets the roses drop to the floor, freeing both his hands, and in one swift movement undoes the pleats of her sari at her waist. Lifting her gently on to the bed, he loosens the strings of her sari petticoat, unbuttons her blouse and buries his lips in the depths of her neck, moving down slowly. Slowly.

***

At the Baltimore Washington International airport, Vinay hugs his sister. She is wearing a pair of tight jeans and a shirt open at the collar. He holds her at arm’s length. “You look younger every year, *behnji*.”

She hugs him tight. “Oh, poof! Take your pick. I made sandwiches fresh—turkey club, and steak and cheese, just for you. Flattery won’t make them fresher.”

He piles his luggage into her station wagon and gets in beside her. She eases the car through the exiting airport traffic and settles back at a steady cruise. He begins to fidget with the radio knobs. “News, news, everywhere. What happened to songs?”

Amira perks up. “Oh, speaking of news, I have some good news for you.”

He blurts it out before he can stop himself. "What? Are you pregnant? Am I going to be an uncle?"

Her face drops to the car floor. "No. Is that all you think about?"

He kicks himself, yanks his foot out of his mouth, and says nothing. Her eyes veer away from the steering wheel briefly and meet his penitent ones. "Oh, okay, I'm a little testy," she says. "It's just that Anand and I have been really trying, and nothing works. Just like you and Sonia. We have bad luck in our family."

"Oh, I doubt it."

"I've been drinking turmeric milk with almonds, and eating three hundred pomegranate seeds every morning."

"Three hundred?"

"Yeah, people say it helps."

They pull into her driveway. He'll just have to wait for the good news. Perhaps it isn't all that good after all.

It isn't till the next day that Amira brings up the topic again. "It looks like your papers will move quickly—Anand's friend who works at the immigration office has pulled your application to the top of the heap."

He bounds off the sofa he's lounging on. "Really? This isn't going to take three years?"

"More like three or four months."

The news is phenomenal. For the next several weeks, he works long hours, even weekends, eager to return home to India to prepare. Plans glide past his eyes like a movie reel. He won't sell his entire business in India; just one-half, enough to get started in the States. He'll apply for a private import/export license. He'll keep options and operations alive in both countries; he'll hire a manager for the Indian segment. Globalization. What perfect timing!

Vinay glances at his wristwatch. His plane for India leaves in three hours. Chuckling, he makes the sign of the Cross, the way he joked with his Christian school friends, tapping his forehead, groin, left and right jacket pocket, saying, "Spectacles, testicles, passport, ticket."

***

It has been more two months since he's seen his wife. She'd decided not to meet him at the airport—the long cab drive back and forth, the pollution, the crowds, and the noise. "Don't even think about it," he'd said on the phone. "I'll see you soon." Then, unable to restrain himself, he'd burst out. "I have some great news."

As on that night they'd stayed home, she is dressed in the same purple sari with lavender flowers, her hair swept to one side, except that she looks more radiant. She walks into his arms. "I have news for you, too," she whispers. Taking his hands, she directs them to her belly. Her eyes glisten. "Can you guess?"

He steps back. "What? Why didn't you tell me?"

"Not on the phone! Your mother said to wait, to tell you in person. We have a *puja* tonight! And after the ceremony, a big dinner. Everyone is coming! My mama is already planning for me to come home."

"Come home?"

"Of course. Because I'm pregnant, silly! Like Amira would come to her mother's house if she was pregnant."

His heart jumps like a yo-yo in his chest, up and down, the highs and deep lows. He looks at her face—she who has never been abroad, who marks time by the fire of *gulmohur* trees in bloom, and the rolling monsoons in June, who can crack a coconut down the middle with one swing of a hatchet, who cannot fathom that "how you doing" isn't a genuine question. Nothing in his suitcase will allure her away to a distant land, not in the immediate future, if ever. Yet, the timing is perfect. A child born in the United States would be a citizen, and its parents would become citizens, too, before long. It could be ideal, but no, not to Sonia.

She looks up into his face. "Now tell me your great news. Is it greater than mine?" In her eyes, there is an instantaneous burst of light, quick as a firefly, there and gone. "What's wrong? Aren't you happy?"

His voice is high. "Yes, of course!"

On the dresser, past her shoulders, he glimpses a vase of fresh yellow roses, their petals shimmering with water droplets.

Two Plot Devices

RUPERT WONDOLOWSKI

1. Bloody kleenex in the campsite bathroom (turns out to be clay).

2. Driving along the highway, run into traffic jam. Put on bird costume and run up hill clowning (gets shot).

Weddings and Wars

MADELEINE MYSKO

In the spring of 1967—the year I turned eight—we moved to Baltimore, into the house on Frankfort Avenue. By fall of that year, I had become fast friends with Mrs. Hennessy, the widow who lived next door. I called her Miss Loretta, because that was what she told me to call her.

Miss Loretta often invited me to sit on her porch glider in the shade of the dark green awning. It seemed she loved little girls, loved to cut out paper doll dresses, and to contribute her old shoes and costume jewelry for dress-up. It was Miss Loretta who sewed an entire wardrobe for my Barbie doll, mostly modest shirtwaists and ruffled party dresses. Even my mother, who considered Barbie an abomination, said those dresses were lovely.

The view from Miss Loretta's glider is clear in my mind even now: potted geraniums, regimental rose beds, and along the sidewalk, those hedges—her pride and joy—trimmed into the shape of crenellated castle walls with turrets at the corners. Every major holiday, before we left for church, I would parade down our front walk, around the turret of the hedge, and up Miss Loretta's front walk to show off. I can arrange those memories like dresses in a closet—a yellow dotted-Swiss Easter, a dark green velvet Christmas, a white organdy Confirmation.

One happy afternoon in October, that year I turned eight, my mother arrived home from a yard sale with a Halloween costume, a complete bridal outfit exactly my size: white gown and veil, plastic bouquet, shiny plastic shoes with real high heels. I can still see the slightly dented box with the cellophane window, which reminded me of something wonderful you'd bring home from a bakery. I put everything on, dispensed with my mother's approval in the kitchen, and went clacking down the front walk in my high heels, heading for Miss Loretta's.

Miss Loretta was standing out at the curb, talking fast with her hands, while someone took suitcases from a car and settled them on the sidewalk. I clacked back into our house and announced that Miss Loretta had company.

"Goodness, Caroline," my mother said. "That's not company. That's Mary Jo, Miss Loretta's daughter."

Miss Loretta had three children, two sons and a daughter. We saw a lot of Phillip, the quiet older son who lived in Harford County and arrived some Sundays and every important holiday with his red-haired wife and two little red-haired children. And I had immediately developed a crush on Charlie, the handsome younger son, who attended college in Ohio and spent his vacations at home.

But Mary Jo, the daughter in the middle, was something of a mystery. Having once or twice been invited into Miss Loretta's living room, I'd seen the photograph of Mary Jo on the mantle—a smiling, heart-faced young woman with teased blonde hair and perfect spit curls pasted in front of her ears. Atop the hair she wore a pleated white cap, which looked like it might blow off at any moment. Miss Loretta told me that Mary Jo was a nurse. She said "nurse" with a sniff, and readjusted the photograph, angling it slightly behind Charlie's.

My memory of that afternoon in 1967—the first time I saw Mary Jo—is scented by Miss Loretta's roses and accompanied by the sound of a lawn mower. From where I stand on our porch, the view is of trimmed hedges, and beyond them the bungalows across the street—one pale green, one dark brown, one white. In the foreground is Miss Loretta herself, in a polished cotton housedress, white bobby socks, and open-toed heels. Her bangs are rolled on pink sponge curlers. Following her up the sidewalk is the Mary Jo I'd seen in the photograph, but without the cap.

"She's an army nurse," my mother told me later that day. "She's home on leave."

I was an only child, quiet and bookish. I preferred to play alone on the front porch, or occasionally with a friend in the playhouse my father built in our back yard. From inside our chain-link fence I observed the wild games of the other children up and down the alley. As far as I was concerned, Army meant camouflage, the smell of caps, the rattle of toy machine guns, and G.I. Joe. On the other hand, nurse meant a white uniform, a cap like the one Mary Jo was wearing in the photograph, a tray of pills, and Cherry Ames. Army meant boys. Nurse meant girls.

I watched the comings and goings next door, waiting to see Mary Jo emerge in either camouflage or white. But she was always dressed just like everybody else, even at the going-away party Miss Loretta gave for her in their yard, where I remember playing with Miss Loretta's red-haired grandchildren while the grown-ups sat around picnic tables, drinking beer and eating steamed crabs.

The morning after the party, my parents and I watched from the front windows as Mary Jo headed down the front walk, dressed at last in uniform—not in camouflage but in Army green: the straight skirt, the tailored jacket with gold buttons and insignia, the matching hat with the visor down over her eyes, shadowing the spit curls. My father frowned and said that Mary Jo was a very brave girl because she had volunteered to go to Vietnam. It was years before Vietnam meant anything to me other than that uniform going down the front walk. I remember the neighbors across the street came out on their porch and watched until the car pulled away.

Charlie Hennessy went to Vietnam too, but I don't remember much about that. I know he returned, apparently unharmed, attended law school, and later did quite well for himself. He ran for state representative not too many years ago. I know these details only because my parents fill them in for me.

After Vietnam, Mary Jo left the Army and settled in California. Miss Loretta went out there a few times to visit her. I remember those times because Miss Loretta would entrust me with the key to her kitchen door and I would go over there to water her African violets. When she came back, Miss Loretta would always say that Mary Jo was fine, and California was a nice place to visit but who would want to live there?

In June of 1977, Miss Loretta fell in the alley and broke her hip. Mary Jo came home to look after her.

I remember that summer well. I had just graduated from high school, and had taken a summer job waiting tables. Most days I slept late, and then lay around reading or sunning myself until it was time to go to work. The day Mary Jo arrived, I was dozing in the chaise lounge, when my mother put her watering can down beside me and said, "Don't look now, but O my god, I believe that is Mary Jo."

The cab pulled away, and Mary Jo stood at the end of the walk between a duffle bag and a battered suitcase. It was a hot day, but she was wearing a dark, heavy dress that fell well below her knees, and a jacket pieced of crocheted squares. The spit curls were gone. Her hair was pulled loosely to the side of her head in a long, thin ponytail. She looked a good deal older than I thought she ought to look.

"Mary Jo?" my mother called, and Mary Jo looked over and waved.

My mother poked me and told me to go help with the bags.

"Thanks," Mary Jo said simply, when I picked up her suitcase. She came up the walk a few steps behind me, lugging the duffel bag. When we got to the front door, she gave my mother another quick wave, told me I could leave the suitcase where it was on the porch, and went inside.

A few days later Miss Loretta arrived home in an ambulance. They brought her through the front door and into the dining room, where a hospital bed had been set up. My mother insisted I visit that afternoon. She had this crazy idea that I ought to get dressed up in my prom things—gown, jewelry, matching shoes and handbag, the whole works—and sashay next door to show myself to Miss Loretta. She said it would give Miss Loretta such a lift, seeing as she was disappointed to have been in the hospital the night of my prom. I dug my heels in on that one. As a compromise, I carried the gown over there on its hanger.

Mary Jo seemed pleased to see me.

"Come on in," she said, and led me through the living room and into the dining room, where Miss Loretta was sitting royally in her hospital bed. Miss Loretta looked the same as ever—lipstick and rouge generously applied, and the thin gray bangs curled above her penciled eyebrows. She was pleased to see me too, and delighted I had brought the gown. It was a full-length, powder blue satin, with cap sleeves and little rhinestones at the neckline. Mary Jo hung it from the doorframe into the kitchen, where Miss Loretta could look at it.

"I bet you don't even remember Mary Jo," Miss Loretta said to me. "It's been so long since she was home."

I replied that I did remember.

"Well thank God she's here now," Miss Loretta went on, "because poor Phillip has his hands full with his family, and Charlie wouldn't be much good at this. Mary Jo is a nurse, you know—or at least she used to be."

"What do you mean used to be?" Mary Jo said. "Once a nurse always a nurse. You don't forget."

"I thought it was, Once a Catholic always a Catholic," Miss Loretta said, rolling her eyes at me. "But that's another story, isn't it Mary Jo Hennessy? I would think you could forget a good deal about nursing, working in a coffee shop all these years."

"Health food cooperative, Mother." Mary Joe rolled her eyes at me too.

"Health food. If that's what you say."

Miss Loretta loved my prom gown, and went on about how the cut was just perfect for me, with my slim figure. Powder blue, she said, was her favorite color, the same color she had worn on her wedding day, during the war. She pointed to the black and white photograph on the sideboard, in which a very young Miss Loretta wore a little veiled hat and a tailored suit—soft gray against Mr. Hennessy's white sailor uniform.

"That would be World War II," Mary Jo said.

"Well of course World War II," Miss Loretta snapped. "I wasn't even born in World War I."

"But what about the Korean War, Mother? You might have been married during the Korean War." Mary Jo winked at me. "Certainly not the Vietnam War, though. That's my war. And Charlie's. But possibly the Korean."

"Honestly, Mary Jo. Sometimes you pick the dumbest things to argue about. Caroline knows what war I'm talking about. Look at that hairstyle. Look at that suit. Does that look like the sort of thing they were wearing in the fifties?" She pushed herself up on her elbows. "I'll tell you what," she said, nodding in the direction of the photograph on the sideboard. "If I were married in the fifties I wouldn't be wearing any street suit. I'd be wearing a white gown with an empire waist and a full train."

Mary Jo smiled, and went back into the kitchen to make us a pitcher of iced tea.

Sometimes that summer, when I was coming home from work around midnight, Mary Jo would be sitting out front in the dark, always on the steps, never up on the glider. I'd notice the tip of her cigarette, or I'd hear a clink of ice against a glass.

"Hi, Caroline," she'd call over the hedge, making a little tune of my name. "How was work?"

It never seemed she'd intended to say more than a polite goodnight. It never occurred to me to strike up a conversation. After all, she was in her thirties, and I was eighteen. I hadn't the least curiosity about her.

As for my mother, she was dying of the curiosity. Her theory was that Mary Jo had stayed out in California all those years because of the drugs. My mother believed there were only two reasons why anyone would choose to live in California—drugs and the movies. And Mary Jo certainly wasn't movie material. "No personality," my mother said. "No spark in her." It was true that Mary Jo carried herself heavily, like a much older woman, like a woman Miss Loretta's age. And she didn't seem to care about her appearance.

My mother kept coming up with things I had to deliver next door—dishes of custard, jars of soup. "How are they getting along over there?" she'd ask when I returned. I would tell her they were getting along fine. Mary Jo seemed to keep house as meticulously as her mother did. Meanwhile Miss Loretta progressed from the crutches to a walker. In no time at all she was back on the front porch, calling yoo-hoo to the neighbors, directing Mary Jo in the trimming of the hedges.

One night near the end of that summer, as I was coming in from work, Mary Jo called out from the porch steps, and asked me over. I went, and she scooted to the side to make room for me to sit down.

"Caroline. Sweet little Caroline," she said. "Do you know what you were wearing the first time I ever laid eyes on you?"

"I don't know," I said, playing along. "What was I wearing?"

"You were wearing a little bride's dress and a veil."

I laughed. "You remember that?"

"I'll never forget it."

"And did you happen to notice the plastic high heels?"

"I certainly did. The effect was absolutely perfect." She took a drag on her cigarette. "My mother has a picture of you in that get-up. It's still on her dressing table."

"It's probably the same one my mother has," I said. My mother's copy was tucked into the mirror above her bureau, among half a dozen other snapshots of me in various costumes and fineries.

"Weddings," Mary Jo said, shaking her head, which threw me off for a moment, because I had thought we were talking about costumes.

"Would you like to see my wedding picture?" she asked, turning to face me.

I said "Sure," and tried to sound offhanded, but it was news to me that Mary Jo was married.

She reached into the pocket of her skirt and withdrew a thin wallet, the sort a man would carry. "I realize this comes as something of a surprise," she said.

There was only one photograph in the wallet, a small one that appeared to have been cut from a larger one. Mary Jo took the picture out of its sleeve and placed it in my lap. I scooted up a couple of steps, so I could see in the light of the porch lamp. I could make out Mary Jo in her Army uniform, and a man beside her, in uniform too. They were holding hands. There was a palm tree in the background.

I had the sense that I'd been trapped into hearing a tragic story. I was sure that the terrible climax of this story was going to be that the man in the picture was dead, or missing in action all these years.

"That's me, and that's my husband Jerry," Mary Jo said. "That was taken on our wedding day in 1967. We were married in San Antonio, before we went to Vietnam." She dropped the cigarette then, and ground it under her sandal.

"Does Miss Loretta know?" I blurted out, and was immediately embarrassed to have asked such a stupid question.

Mary Jo laughed. "You know," she said, "that's actually a very good question. Mother certainly knew ten years ago. She was mad as hell about it back then. But now I think she's almost managed not to know it anymore. You didn't know I was married, did you?"

"No."

"So she never told any of the neighbors."

"I guess not."

Mary Jo told me that they were married in the post chapel, with only two witnesses present. She told me Miss Loretta had been furious because the ceremony was outside the Catholic Church, and also because they'd cheated her of the wedding she'd always pictured—the wedding of her only daughter.

"For people like my mother," Mary Jo said, smiling wryly, "picturing things ahead of time almost always spoils the way things actually turn out."

As for the husband Jerry, the end of the story was not the tragedy I'd expected, but rather a messy little knot of sorrows, impossible to unravel completely. Jerry had been wounded in a helicopter crash. He had recovered from the injuries, but there were other problems. He drank too much, and when he drank he got mean. In the end, she'd left him. "Technically we're still married," she said. "I can't bring myself to get a divorce. Now that's something my mother really doesn't know."

"Well you don't have to worry about me," I said. "I won't tell."

And I didn't. In fact, it suited me to deprive my mother of that story, even though I knew how much she would have savored it. My mother had her mind on other things anyway. The very next day we began shopping in earnest and packing my things for college. A week later I was living in the dorm, battling homesickness at the University of the South.

I have a box of letters I've saved over the years. Among them is a card from Miss Loretta, dated October 1, 1977. On the front is a picture of a white cat beside a pot of red geraniums. Inside Miss Loretta has written that she knows I will be an A student, and that soon I will make new and wonderful friends. She says she'll see me during the holidays, and P.S. Charlie is now engaged to a girl from Ohio! Details when you get home.

But Miss Loretta died of a pulmonary embolism the day before Thanksgiving of that year. I came for the holiday weekend, and so I got to see her one more time. She was laid out in a blue silk shirtwaist in Ruck's Funeral Home. I knelt before the casket and cried, remembering the days on the glider and the Barbie doll dresses.

My parents and I attended the funeral at St. Anthony's Church, and afterwards were invited with the rest of the neighbors back to Miss Loretta's house. Phillip and his wife and their red-haired children—teenagers by then—were stationed just inside the door when we arrived, like the official greeters. Charlie was sitting on the couch with the new fiancé. Mary Jo came swooping out from the dining room when she saw us.

"Thank you for coming," she said. She was wearing a long hippie-style white cotton dress, which my mother later pronounced as entirely inappropriate.

Mary Jo turned then and introduced the man behind her in the rumpled, dark suit.

"This is Jerry," she said simply.

He had a trembling, damp handshake. He was just shy of handsome, but he had a badly chipped tooth. He asked my father if he'd like a beer, and my father followed him out onto the porch where apparently they had a cooler.

"Who's Jerry?" my mother whispered to me when we got to the kitchen.

I shrugged. The sight of Miss Loretta's African violets had given me a lump in my throat.

My mother sighed and got to work with the other women in the kitchen. She handed me a plate of fancy pastries arranged on a paper doily. "Here, see if you can find a spot to put these."

The neighbors had prepared so much food there wasn't room for another thing on the dining room table. I couldn't decide what to move where.

"Just put them on the sideboard with the coffee service," my mother called out to me.

I saw that Mary Jo and Jerry had stationed themselves in the living room. She glanced over just then and gave me a little wave. Jerry waved too. That long white dress, that dark suit—If you looked at them quickly, and then just as quickly looked away, you might have thought wedding.

They really weren't that much older than I was, and yet it seemed they belonged to another time and place. I rearranged the creamer and sugar on the sideboard. I placed the fancy pastries right in front of Miss Loretta's wedding picture, the one that had been taken during The War.

Small Crimes

ANDRIA NACINA COLE

She's wearing a too-small wedding dress that squeezes her like Aunt Plum when she's drunk and in the mood with no man to touch. From behind, she's a lumpy, lacy thing with shoulders broad as the moon when it's not shamed and shines full. She has nowhere to go, but that's because she's fourteen and the daughter of Lawrence Gaither, who believes in raising a certain kind of woman (six before her—all married, the majority clean), and cannot leave the house except to go inside her own head, even and especially on Saturday mornings when the other neighborhood children are sitting on their porches being common.

Like most days without school or a trip to the branch library, she's sitting in front of the television—black and white and small enough to be carried at her hip if she gets the feeling and dares defy her father to watch it outside on the concrete steps where any and everyone can see. Once, he caught her. And did nothing more than lift his pant leg to climb right past her like she was the railing itself. That and not say her name til the Fourth of July one month later. But today the television's screen is blank and she has nestled her button nose into knotted, praying hands. Over and over again she is chanting the name *Charlie.*

The photograph above the television is almost as tall as the wall it hangs from. *Charlie.* It, like the television, is black and white, but a full thirty years older. Of her parents standing beside a short-stacked, indistinct wedding cake, it folds in at the corners, despite the frame, as if it to hug itself. It has hung, unmoved, through three mistresses not old enough to remember King's murder, through the suicide encouraged by those mistresses, through rape, through an illegitimate child neither named nor kept nor spoken of since. Her father, in a light-colored, well-tailored suit looks satisfied, and her mother, behind him, duped. (Of this picture, he says, "My! Look at Ella. See that look on her face? If that ain't love I don't know what is.)

To the far left of this photograph is a small cut they call the kitchen, but before that is a hallway brief as a blink and beyond it, three bedrooms. In the year of her birth, 1978, they held nine bodies on any given night. *Charlie.* In the bedroom to the west, the biggest, slept her three oldest sisters—each more ugly than the next. In the center bedroom: Her mother and father, and squished between them, she herself, Dot. Pretty enough. In the last and smallest room slept the three remaining girls, on a single queen sized mattress, and well, this arrangement must have been divine, because not one proved less than gorgeous or single past her seventeenth year. Outside the windows of these bedrooms, then and now, pure white wilderness and all the rest of Buffalo sit. Not one girl, ugly or not, has left this house unmarried, let alone a whore. Not one. *Sweet Charlie.*

Dot's suffocating in this wedding dress passed from her mother to one sister after the next to lose her virginity, since it should be spectacular. She is the only one to have been plump in it or not on the verge of marriage, but it's what she has, and she knows enough to give the day some weight. You should have seen how her father used his body to mop the floor when he'd found that Juanita, the third youngest, had been raped.

"What good is she now?" He screamed on all fours.

If not for the Smith boy who cared far less about a spoiled wife (the rape brought the unnamed son) than the roundness of her ass and the utter beauty of her jaw line, the father might've died of grief forty years too soon. *Come here, Charlie.*

If it were Dot's choice, she'd wear a floor-length gown with pencil-thin heels tall as the sun is far away. But her father is careful about his money, sleeps with it shoved in the very center of his box spring, and only ever buys things he can afford flat out. He would never—not for her prom to come, or her mother's funeral passed—consider a new dress when a perfectly suitable one exists. Anyway, what would she ask him? "Can I have a new gown, Daddy? One that teases the floor when I walk and hugs me good in the middle so I can go on and make love with your fine friend, our neighbor, Mr. Charles?" *Charlie.*

They have done everything short of making love, but that's all Charlie's doing. He's tasted her there, with his fifty-year-old mouth, because that can be forgiven, and she knows, because he's told her, that it tastes like pickles or tomatoes, depending on the season. And he loves either. Naturally, she's tasted him back, because that's not sex at all, but when asked, "What's it like?" she's always lost for words and says, "Skin" or if she's swallowed, "Silk." *Dear Charlie.*

According to Melody and Harmony, fraternal twins who live two blocks over—too wide about the hips and so poor they swap two hand sewn shirts—when it comes down to it, Charlie won't want to be bothered with pants. They'll inconvenience him. He'll prefer a skirt. He may walk away if she wears slacks and then where would she be? Exactly where she started. New. He'll want her like a bowl he can dump himself into. Open. And anyway, does she want her virginity tossed away like theirs? On no particular night in no particular way, with no particular clothes worn?

"What about Ella's wedding dress?" Dot asked the twins three days back when the snow was young.

And Harmony said, "How come you call her Ella and not Momma?"

"Because that's her name." Dot looked at Harmony hard, no blinking, but the twin couldn't handle that.

They thought the idea of a wedding dress perfect, but warned her about what to do underneath it.

"Wear panties if you want," Melody said.

"See where that lands you," said Harmony.

And though she is sure Charlie will wait, long as she needs, for her to peel off a pair of pants or panties or anything else, she believes the twins. They were right about kissing—how it's nasty and good all at once; and they were right about his age not making a difference where true love matters. And especially...especially about her body craving his like he was pure sugar. *Charlie.*

He had better hurry. *Charlie, Charlie, Charlie.* Her father will be home in exactly one hour and thirty-three minutes, and won't stop short of gutting him if he's found on top of her where her father thinks only superhero underclothes or sheets or her own hands with toilet paper should be. Charlie knows that as well as she does. He saw, like she and all the rest of Leroy Street, her father drag Bridget's crush out the house by his ankles. And his head hit each step with six thuds that changed things permanently. Charlie knows the boy never spoke good English after that. *Please Charlie. Don't you go chicken on me, Charlie.*

Lawrence works every Saturday, even if there's a graduation to attend or he hits the number for four weeks pay or even if he's bent over sick with pneumonia. He says they need the money, though Dot's counted what's stashed and knows better. What he means is she drives him crazy with her nearly pretty, not necessarily ugly self. She is the mirror image of her mother—dead two and a half years—only shorter and rounder, and looking at her too long means remembering. It creeps Dot out anyway. His staring with that far away look. Who wants to be gawked at knowing the gazer's considering the corpse you resemble? Knowing he's aching to the marrow over his part in the matter?

After seven hundred seventy-six *Charlies*, the man arrives shivering from the cold and Dot can breathe. There are only forty-nine minutes left, and she's turned gray from waiting. She doesn't match as beautifully with the small fair dress as she did forty-four minutes before when she was still honey-colored and horny.

"What happened? I told you two-thirty." She says and raises her shoulders to shrug, but mostly to force her embroidered sleeves down her arms—give him more of her to look at.

He doesn't answer that. Instead he runs up on her like he wants to jump inside her skin and live there. He puts his hands all over her and she cannot keep up. This is exactly why she loves him—for being tangible. She can bite off pieces of his love and hold them in her cheeks to taste later when he's gone. When he's finished making a mess of her lipstick and dress, he tells her he's hungry and thirsty and needs someplace comfortable to sit. By now, her inner thighs are damp. What does he mean hungry and thirsty? Can't he see she's ready and warm?

She pours him homemade juice and chases it with rum, like Lawrence does in the mornings. She's impatient with yesterday's spaghetti—slams the pot, where the noodles and sweet sauce are collected like bits of bone and blood, on the stove. She doesn't do this loudly, but with enough thud that the listener knows there's some anger beneath. He sits there, on the couch, and combs his chest with unsteady hands. He looks her way, but he won't speak.

She wants to tell him to grow up. That in thirty-seven minutes her father will come and blow a hole in his head, and if he wants her at all, he had better take her now, at the stove making his meal. All he needs to do is lift her dress, to move and hold the taffeta with one hand, and there, with the other, he will find nothing at all, just her welcoming bowl, no panties.

Between him and the lonely woman staring down at her from the wedding photo, Dot's ill. Everyone in the room—Charlie, her dead mother, she herself—is damned scared of Lawrence.

He eats as slow as honey pours. Drinks like the juice is lead—as if it should kiss every rift in the roof of his mouth before he swallows.

"What you put in this?"

"Puerto Rican rum."

She never takes her eyes off him. He is the color of wheat bread and unshaven. She sits right close. So close he can't get his fork to his mouth without feeling her titty against his elbow. And when there are only nineteen minutes left and he still has yet to finish his food or take a finger across her thigh, he says, "I can't do this, Dot. Can't do it."

"Don't do that to me, Charlie." Fourteen year old Dot says, as if she is all woman and been here ten times. Charlie says, "I can't do this" as if he hasn't had one year to prepare. As if this is not exactly what they spoke of late last night, in detail, while her father slept and hollered out occasionally from his dreams. When he, Charlie, told her she was more like a woman than not. The chorus of that conversation was "tomorrow at two-thirty," and now he's pretending yesterday wasn't.

He says it again. "Can't do it." And her heart sags low, kissing the stomach. "Can't." Down lower, nearly hanging from the ribs. "I can't do it, Dot." And he gets up to leave her there, with her heart damn near collected her in shoe. She picks up that plate, still heavy with the blood and bones, to throw, but doesn't. It would mean spaghetti slipping down the walls after itself and bits of glass between her toes. It would mean she hates him.

"Don't you remember what we said last night? On the telephone?" She asks and puts the plate at her feet. Intolerance is all in and about those words and there is a thick veil of want over her eyes.

But they must be the ones, intolerant or not, because he turns to her with a tight bulge in his pants, like he is collecting quarters there, and she thinks, This is it.

"I remember," he says and then his eyes gloss over. He is the kind of man that always cries and watching him do so is both amusing and painful.

"I wish I had a camera right now" he says through his mute crying, "so I could take a picture of you in that stupid dress." But he isn't callous. No word has any particular pitch. The sentence is as bland as the spaghetti almost thrown against the wall.

"Don't you do that, Charlie." She sees him picking a fight. "You said you would make love to me."

"What's wrong with you?" He asks.

"I love you."

"This ain't right."

"Sure it is." She says and walks up on him, yanking her dress down over her breasts, big and ripe as honeydew.

"I got no business here."

She takes his old man handsome hand and puts his pointer finger in her mouth.

"How you know to do things like that?" He pretends to want to know, but this is not the time to tell him, "You."

"Well, come on," he says with a chuckle and takes back his finger, "We need to get this thing started if we gonna be done in time to miss Lawrence. He'll be through this door any minute wanting his drink and paper."

He's trying to be cold, trying to make her curse him, but there's no use. There is love clogging his throat and forcing short coughs from him.

She lifts her dress so that it is gathered at her hips in a bunch of pasty ruffles. She stands there with her fat legs exposed all the way to where they meet in a glorious V. She has only had hair there a season and it is not tame. Both she and Charlie find this funny and say things like, "Bet it's enough to braid."

"I know plenty of men slept with girls exactly your age. Some two, three years younger," says Charlie and he pulls his belt back on itself.

"Okay," Dot says, lifting that dress up over her stomach.

"Worst things is going on in this world right now. Things way worse than a man making love with a girl that really want it in the first place."

"Uh hunh."

"It's worst things going on right now while we here *thinking* about what we *might* do."

With the wedding dress hiked she is still round, but soft. Any boy her age would be displeased with her folds; a young boy wouldn't rest his hands between them and tell her how much she feels like home. But Charlie is twenty years past young with eyes that see things in a beige light.

When there are only twelve minutes to go, she pulls him by those handsome hands to the bedroom to the right—the one that is not hers and meant for beauty.

It's difficult making room inside her. First, she's sealed and second he's outsized. Third, he's nervous and therefore unfeeling. He doesn't notice her face clenched tight as a fist and never thinks to kiss even one wrinkle away. Then there's time to think about.

In nine minutes, Lawrence will shuffle through the door, high off of Georgia, the new, peach-smelling woman at the plant. He'll put his hat on the hook beside the door. Pour himself three shots. Drink them like tea. Run his bare feet across every plank of the wood floor, not even knowing his daughter's there, getting grown. If the liquor hits him hard, he just might be fooled, for he'll stand beneath the shade of the photo of him and his wife and see it for what it is. She will look, in his drunken state, as she looks to everyone else: Suicidal. He'll get angry with her and call her "weak" aloud, and decide (this too aloud) that his wife is simply unimportant. Eventually he'll scream, "What I still got you on my wall for anyway?"

While Lawrence is asking his dead wife questions, Charlie can put himself back together and Dot can clean everything away. She won't have to worry about the bedspread so much as she will returning the wedding dress to its plastic shield in her father's bedroom—Lawrence will not go into the beautiful girls' room drunk. All over there are mirrors and he is a short, dull man, shorter and duller when drunk. While he is pretending to search for a hammer to remove the frame from its wall, Charlie can slip right past. He might as well be Lawrence's shadow if the liquor hits quick enough.

Except that Charlie starts up with his crying and slows everything down. The tears open wide all over Dot's breasts. She slams her fists against his back.

"Shut up! Shut up, Charlie! Shut up!"

There are three minutes left and she doesn't know if she's a virgin or not. She can't tell if the pile of skin between his legs where firmness just was means anything. His penis looks discouraged now. Lenient. And for the first time, she feels like a girl with him.

"Get out of here, Charlie!"

Dot sends the crying fool to the wind, not caring if he meets Lawrence on the snow-covered concrete steps and they wrestle like boys. Not caring if they lose their balance and lives over one another.

Squatting on the floor in the beautiful married girls' room, Dot considers Ella. She is as messy as her mother was when they found her, measuring blood with her open mouth (her eyes thrown so far back into her busted head they seemed not eyes at all, but white backdrops wanting painting). Only her mother's mess was cranberry-colored and overwhelming and Dot's is like nectar—translucent and strange. She just almost cries for her mother. Just almost. The tears well up so high it's a wonder they balance. So high if she breathes in the levees will collapse. But she pulls it together and the tears get swallowed backward to live inside her.

By the time her father gets home (he is a full sixty minutes late, and Dot is sure this means Georgia has been fooled onto her back) she is dressed in slacks and a shirt. Her hair is pulled back off her forehead so that she is all eyes and cheeks, and she's standing there on Lawrence's snow-covered concrete porch, with her legs shoulder-width apart and all of her hands inside her back pockets. She's on the top stair and Melody and Harmony skip every other one below her. They are underdressed because they are poor, where Dot is missing hat, gloves and coat because she's a woman now, and warm.

He tries walking past in a way that says, "You're common," but the girls are staggered and he can't give the stairs a straight go. He tries stomping around them but the steps haven't been cleared and his anger is lost on the snow. It must make things worse that Dot's eyes aren't low, evaluating her feet, like the twins'. She has this know-too-much look where her eyelids are pinched and her head tilted just a bit too far left. He can't want to hear her voice.

But she says, "Evening," anyway. And he gives no 'evening' back.

He goes inside to fill himself to the elbows with Puerto Rican rum and the twins look at Dot like she's drowning.

"You crazy?" They say over and over on top of each other.

And Dot is as cool as if she were not the youngest of the Gaither clan. As if she were not a member of the Gaither family at all. She's already told the twins about Charlie. Described the love making as something dying between her legs. Already called the film left across her stomach "sex" and had that description sharpened by them and named "cum." She's already told them about the wedding dress hanging, un-cleaned, back in its plastic cape. Of pounding Charlie's back and falling out of love just that easy.

But not of revelations. Not of finding out first hand what drives your father to cheat. To dictate and cause frail women to hold guns heavier than them to their heads, and use them.

"You not scared?" The twins ask her, staggered.

"Scared of what?" Dot wants to know and stares in their eyes a pair at a time.

"Scared he'll beat you…put you out…never talk to you again."

"Uh uh," she says. And takes the palm of her hand across her hair.

Inside herself, where the twins can't see, she says some things about Lawrence not having the balls to question her. He is a murderer after all and wants no one saying that aloud. She could always say, "You killed my momma, you dirty old dog." She could always point that out. She says some other things about her mother being the weakest, most pitiful thing she knows. At fourteen she knows men are not capable of doing themselves what they require of others. Not capable of keeping their dicks in their pants no matter the consequence. Not a suicidal wife, not an underage girl, not one thing on this whole mighty earth can keep them from giving in.

How Ella live so long and not figure that?

Forty-Five Years Ago

CARYN COYLE

In 1963, I thought everyone went to Mass on Sundays with police officers—arms out stretched—holding people back. I had to wear white cotton gloves and itchy, multi- layered dresses in pastel colors; pink, lavender, lime. I walked up the wide steps to St. Edward's Church in Palm Beach with my hand gripped firmly inside my mother's. She looked straight ahead; her white lace mantilla hid her face.

The Mass wouldn't start until President Kennedy got there.

Forty-five years ago, my father accepted a marketing position and moved us to Palm Beach from Marblehead, Massachusetts. Our new house was on Nightingale Trail and I was disappointed with the gold fish pond in the back yard. It was too small to swim in, and too dark. Orange trees surrounded the small rectangular pool, framed in a stone patio.

Several blocks down from Nightingale Trail, the Kennedy's coral-colored compound was always pointed out to me when we passed it on North Ocean Boulevard. I paid attention to the Kennedys because my parents did.

Yesterday, I was shocked at how my parents struggled to walk down the corridor of their independent living facility. They both use canes. My mother's cane has red tulips and green leaves painted on the steel pole. It is the first time I've seen her use one. Both of my parents' canes have four rubber soled legs that anchor it to the floor each time they put it down.

Our relationship has been reduced to day trips. I drive two hours to see them and take them to lunch.

In the restaurant's booth, I sit next to my dad. He has white hair about a half inch long clustered on his jawbone, below his ear. The bristles around his mouth and chin are uneven. I wonder if he just can't see them anymore or whether he has simply given up and doesn't care.

My mother has brought a deep pink jacket because she is always cold.

"Mom, I like your shocking-pink jacket," I tell her as she pulls her arms through the sleeves.

"My what?"

"Your jacket. It's shocking pink. Jackie Kennedy's color."

"Who's color? Caryn, I don't know what you're talking about."

At Mass, we would choose a spot in the middle of the church. If we occupied the pew in front of the President and First Lady, a Secret Service agent would sit with us. That annoyed my mother. He would peer into her handbag when she opened it, and she would thrust it at him so he could see everything inside.

Because my mother walked me down to the bike trail that overlooked Lake Worth, we watched the President's dark limousine drive up the path where automobiles were forbidden; flags flapping off the front fenders. President Kennedy got out of his limousine and I saw Caroline and John John bound down the ramp toward the Honey Fitz. The First Lady wore dark glasses; a deep pink scarf wrapped around her head billowed over her shoulders.

My dad took me to the bike shop on Palm Beach and I watched him pull twenty dollar bills out of his wallet to pay for a royal blue, ten speed. The bike trail was black asphalt and wide enough for two to ride side by side (or to accommodate the President's limo). Dad would point out the street where we lived, beyond the properties that lined the bike trail and the bridge from West Palm that connected it to Palm Beach on Royal Poinciana Way.

As I peddled beside him, I listened to my dad talk about Mrs. Kennedy and Caroline. He had met them at the Bazaar International, the exotic shopping center he managed in Riviera Beach. It had a small amusement park and Caroline wanted to ride the train. He also took them up in the elevator of the Bazaar's tower overlooking Lake Worth. Mrs. Kennedy had the softest voice he'd ever heard, he said.

My mother moves from one end of her cushioned bench to the other. "Do you feel a draft?" she asks a half-dozen times.

Each time she moves, my dad sighs, "Do you want my jacket?"

She always declines.

"This place reminds me of Creighton's," my dad says.

"World's best apple pie," I say, smiling.

"You remember that?" he asks, his eyes are the color of swimming pool water and he looks at me through glasses he now wears all the time. He didn't wear any for most of his life. In World War II, he flew Corsairs as a Marine pilot, supporting the ground troops in the Philippines.

"Creighton's was at the front of the Bazaar, right? They had 'world's best apple pie' as their slogan," I say.

"Right. They anchored the Bazaar. Remember that, Claire?" he asks my mom.

"No, I don't Charlie," she says it as though he should know that.

He sighs and tells me about my brother, who is designing and building the house he's always wanted. When it's finished, next year, he will move my parents in with him and his family.

At Mass, my mother whispered about the President's brothers. I didn't realize who they were until she'd nudge me, "That's Bobby—or Teddy—the President's brother," when they held long wooden poles—attached to deep rectangular baskets and lined in red velvet—to take the collection for St. Edward's.

My brother was born in Florida. We brought him home from Good Samaritan Hospital in West Palm in a bassinet that hooked onto the back of the front seat. But within a month of my brother's birth, my father's business went bankrupt. We returned to Massachusetts in the summer of 1963.

On Friday, November twenty second, my teacher, Miss Woodberry, ushered us out to the school bus. "Let's hope it's not serious," she said. "Maybe the President's only been shot in the leg."

I sat on the floor of our living room most of the next few days watching the casket being lowered from Air Force One; the horses towing the caisson with the President's coffin on it. Caroline's white gloved fingers under the flag on her father's casket in the Rotunda of the Capital Building.

In the corner of the room furthest from the television, my baby brother was learning how to hold himself up by gripping the sides of his play pen. He had multi-colored plastic donuts he could pile on a bright green plastic pole and a little yellow school bus with small student pegs he stuck into round holes inside the bus. One even had brown braids, like mine.

We wait a half hour for our lunch. My dad notices the people on the opposite side of the aisle, seated after us, are already eating their food. They also appear to have ordered the same thing we have. He gets up from the booth—without his cane—and shuffles off in search of someone to talk to about it. When he comes back, the waiter has appeared with our order and my dad declares, “C'mon. Get up. We're moving.”

The waiter is cheerful and leads us out of the vast room, reconstructed from a barn from somewhere in New England and rebuilt as the largest and tallest of the rooms in the restaurant. We are relocated in another room and seated next to a fireplace with a large portrait of George Washington above it.

“Much better,” he says, shuffling into the new booth. “Where's my cane?”

My mother stops, looks around her, she has her tulip handled cane in her hand and is leaning on it.

“I've got it,” I tell him, holding it up.

When President Kennedy walked down the aisle to Communion, two Secret Service men followed him. One carried a telephone. I wondered who would call him on that phone, but I never heard it ring.

On Thanksgiving, the Thursday after President Kennedy was killed, we hosted a somber dinner. I remember my grandparents, my great-grandmother, my aunts and uncles spoke of the fate of the Kennedy family in the new dining room my mother had remodeled. Someone said, “So much for the torch being passed to a new generation.”

Painted above the chair rail on two walls of the dining room was a large mural of palm trees on a Florida beach. The scene reminded me of waves the color of turquoise we could see as we rode along North Ocean Boulevard. My dad is driving toward Royal Poinciana Way from Nightingale Trail and a convertible pulls out of the Kennedy compound. I watch it follow us and realize the President is driving. His brownish red hair is blowing. There are several people in the car with him.

“Daddy! Daddy! The President's behind us!” I shout from the back seat, tapping his shoulder.

My dad turns slightly, looking at me in the rear view mirror. “Wave at him!” he says.

I turn around and kneel on the seat, raising my right hand and wagging it back and forth in the huge back window. The President is wearing dark sunglasses. His mouth opens and he says something, nodding. He sees me and laughs. One of his hands is on the steering wheel; the other is up in the warm, tropical air.

I turn from the President and see my dad's hand is also up, off our steering wheel. He is waving back.

Charming Billy

ALICE McDERMOTT

Of the (let's face it) half dozen or so basic versions of the Irish physiognomy, they had two of them: Billy thin-faced with black hair and pale blue eyes behind his rimless glasses; Dennis with broad cheeks, eternally flushed, and dark eyes and fair hair that had only begun to thin under his combat helmet, somewhere, he claimed, in northern France. One every inch the poet or the scholar, the other a perfect young cop or barman, the aesthete priest and the jolly chaplain.

But in fact they had both gone to the RCA Institute before the war and had left steady jobs at Con Ed to enlist. In July 1945, they both had plans to return there in the fall, or as soon as the Long Island house was finished, as soon as they were ready to end this hiatus—they called it that—between their lives as they were and whatever it was their lives were to become.

Their charge had been to make the place livable again after nearly a decade of abandonment. To update the plumbing and the electrical, chase out the mice and the wasps, repair or replace whatever parts of the floor or the ceiling, the windows or the doors needed repair or replacement. The directive had come from Holtzman, the shoe salesman, as if an afterthought, over dinner the second night Dennis was home (although it was not home to him, it was the salesman's house, even though he sat at his mother's dining-room table). He offered the project as if in a burst of inspiration, even said something like "Here's an idea for you boys..." although Dennis knew that in his kit in an upstairs bedroom (not his room, although the bed was the one he had slept in as a child) he had the letter his mother had sent him, the laundry list of reasons to remarry. He knew by the anxious glance Holtzman shot her, even as he pretended to be inspired, that the project had been his mother's idea all along.

On the afternoon of their arrival, they parked the car in the rutted and overgrown driveway and in shirtsleeves and fedoras and army boots cut through the knee-high grass and the weeds with the scythe and the clippers Holtzman had lent them. City-bred, they made quite a show of it, testing their arms and the heat and their resolve, and sending the tall grass, the bees and grasshoppers and zithering beetles every which way as they made a good path across the sandy soil to the three peeling steps at the front door. They pulled the screen off its hinges with the first tug.

The key Holtzman had given them was attached to a chain that was attached to a metal shoe horn engraved with the name and the address of his Jamaica Avenue store. It was only this, this awkward key chain, that made them fumble a bit. The door itself opened easily, the way it would in a movie or a dream, as if the lock hadn't been real at all, or as if the hinges had been well oiled. The place was musty and warm, and you could see dust motes in the sunlight that came through the kitchen window as clearly as you could see the sink and the stove and the sagging gray couch.

Now the vague thoughts Dennis had been having about every place he'd been to since his return from overseas took form and he said to Billy, "This has been here," as if Billy would know what he meant. What he meant was, this house has been here, just like this, all the while he had been locked in the adventure and tedium of the war. This had been here, just as it was (like the Chrysler Building, his mother's new home, the Jamaica Avenue El), all the while and at each and every moment he had been away.

"Since the twenties, I suppose," Billy said, not getting it.

"Forever," Dennis told him.

But Billy got it later, after they'd found a restaurant in East Hampton for dinner and then, because neither of them had been here before and because the charm of the village gave them the sense that the roads that led from it offered something more, they toured the place in Holtzman's car. It had all been here. The elegant trees that lined the broad streets, the great green lawns that grew, even as they were slowly passing, greener and deeper in the twilight so you could almost make yourself believe that night was seeping in through their roots, not moving across the sky above them. The houses—when had they ever seen such houses, how was it they hadn't known they were out here? Grand and complex palaces, cottages wood-shingled or white, with gazebos in their gardens and great pillared porches that curved like bows and widow's walks and gabled attic rooms from which you could probably glimpse both the silver spires of the city and the black ocean edge of the earth.

They moaned to see the darkened places that had not yet been opened for the season—"No one even there"—and whispered, "Take a look at that," when one was lit like a steamship from stem to stern. But what killed them, what really killed them, were the houses that looked out over the ocean, that had for their front or back yards a dark lush carpet of beautifully mown grass and then, running down from the other side, as if front and back had been built on different planets, magnificent dunes, sea grass, white beach and sea.

"Leave me there when I'm dead," Billy said of one of them—a large house on a wide lawn with a starry backdrop of sky that even in near darkness seemed to contain the reflected sound and sparkle of the ocean. "Prop me up on the porch with a pitcher of martinis and a plate of oysters on the half shell and I'll be at peace for all eternity. Amen."

They made their way home in darkness, under the thick leaves along Main Street and out toward the sandier and less elegant regions of the Springs and Three Mile Harbor. They made several wrong turns and even in the driveway sat squinting at the little house for a few minutes before they decided it was the right place, after all.

They agreed to sleep in the car that night, since the mattresses were mildewed and the mice well ensconced. With GI resourcefulness they hung t-shirts over the opened windows and secured the edges with electrical tape in order to keep out most of the bugs.

They smoked for half an hour, Dennis in the front seat, Billy in back. "I never knew," Billy said at one point, his glasses in his hand, his hand resting on his forehead, "I never knew what it was like out here." It was what he would write on his postcards tomorrow, creating artifacts. "Isn't that something? I had no idea those places were out here."

"It's something," Dennis said. "Bridie was here once," he added. "She came out to Southampton with someone. She said it was really something."

"It is," Billy said. He paused. "It almost makes you wonder what else you don't know about yet."

Dennis frowned for a moment and then said, "Plenty," with a laugh. But although Billy looked the part he was no poet or scholar and could not explain: what else did he not know about yet that would strike him as the village tonight had struck him—strike him in that very first moment of apprehending, of seeing and smelling and tasting, as something he could not, from that moment on, get enough of and could never ever again live without.

By the end of their first week they had a routine and a sufficient knowledge of the roads to find the dump and the bay beach, the cheaper restaurants and the hardware stores. They did the heaviest work early in the morning and then ducked inside before noon to wire and paint and plaster. Around four or five, when the sunlight began to edge from white to yellow, they took their towels from the clothesline they had rigged between two trees out back and walked with them draped around their necks the mile and a half to the bay. They cleared a shortcut with Holtzman's scythe. The beach there was rocky at the shoreline, littered with shells, but the water was warmer than the ocean, and since neither of them was much of a swimmer, they both welcomed the chance to just float and dive and touch their toes to the bottom at will.

Some nights they stopped into a bar off the Springs road. They both drank too much the first and second time, but only Billy, engaged in long conversation with the bartender and an ugly old Bonacker who could not hear enough about the war, drank too much the third and fourth.

Billy drunk, in those days, was charming and sentimental. He spoke quietly, one hand in his pocket and the other around his glass, his glass more often than not pressed to his heart. There was tremendous affection in Billy's eyes, or at least they held a tremendous offer of affection, a tremendous willingness to find whomever he was talking to bright and witty and better than most. Dennis came to believe in those days that you could measure a person's vanity simply by watching how long it took him to catch on to the fact that Billy hadn't recognized his inherent and long-underappreciated charm, he'd drawn it out with his own great expectations or simply imagined it, whole cloth.

They talked about the war: the characters in their divisions, Midwesterners always the crudest, didn't you notice, something to do with living around farm animals, no doubt; the officers good and bad, the morning just before they returned, when a group coming out of first mess claimed they were serving cake for breakfast, which turned out to be only bread, fresh bread. The tar-paper shack Dennis and two other fellows had constructed, warmer than the tents, the Pilsen Hilton. Their luck in avoiding the Pacific. Their quests for souvenirs. Patton and Ike and F. D. R., the lying old smoothy. The kids begging chocolate and chewing gum. The French girls, all of them beautiful, one coming to Switching Central in Metz, where Billy was operating near the end, to ask if a message could be sent to her fiancé, another GI gone north. She said she even knew his code name, Vampire, which made two or three of the other boys laugh out loud. She was a dark-haired girl with great big dark eyes. She wore a white handkerchief knotted around her neck, as lovely as diamonds. The message she asked Billy to send was simply: "I am still here."

Their shoulders and arm and the backs of their necks burned and freckled and peeled, and after dinner each evening they walked through the village with toothpicks in their mouths or drove past the great houses on the surrounding streets, noticing the changes in them, how they looked in the rain, in clear twilight, how well they bore even the oppressive air of the hotter days and marveling, marveling still, that this Eden was here, at the other end of the same island on which they had spent their lives.

One afternoon just before VJ Day a family was spread across a blanket on the widest crescent of bay beach—at least they thought it was a family as they approached from the road. But as they dropped their towels and bent to unlace their already loosely laced boots, to slip off the socks they wore under them and the pants they wore over their swim trunks, they quickly changed their assessment. Six children, the oldest no more than nine, and two women, girls, actually, who were not old enough to be mothers to them all.

They nodded a greeting to the girls and the children as they made their way to the water and then, swimming out with as much form as they had ever shown for as much distance as they dared to go, floated a bit under the paling sky, glancing as they did, in subtle, sidelong glances, at the group on the shore, at the girls especially, one standing now at the water's edge, a pail and shovel in her hand and two little ones at her feet. The other, only a little plumper, on the blanket still and wearing an old-fashioned swim cap over her curly hair that from the water's distance—at least for Billy, whose glasses were in his pants pock et on the sand—seemed like an aura of royal-blue light.

Five of the children were knee-deep in the water now, dipping their outspread hands just as the one girl was instructing them to do, fingers splayed like starfish, washing off the sand. Then one of the children, the tallest boy, stepped out of the water with his splayed hands held high, as if he were a surgeon, as if the sand might leap up at any minute and cover them again and called, "Eva," toward the blanket, "Eva," although it was impossible to tell if he meant the girl in the swim cap or the sixth child, who sat beside her, because at that moment a huge black touring car pulled up from the road and in a sudden gathering of pails and shovels and shells and picnic baskets and cover-ups and blankets—a sudden momentum that died the minute everything was off the sand and they made, in incredibly slow motion, the trek from beach to car—they were gone.

The two swam a little closer, to a shallower, more comfortable distance from the shore, and then climbed out of the water completely. They reached their towels and in an economy of terry cloth that they had learned in the service dried face and arms and shoulders with one end, chest and legs with the other, and then sat on the dry middle on the sand to smoke a cigarette and then, flicking their feet with one sock and then the other, put on socks and boots for the walk home.

The road was hot and Dennis had both his pants and his towel draped over his shoulders to protect his latest burn. He could feel as he walked the salt drying on his legs and on his face and arms. He could see a line of it on the pale hair of his cousin's calf.

They were virgins, both of them. Before the war, and the girls they'd known had seemed to be another cousin's schoolmate or the daughter of an aunt's best friend, and while desire had presented itself often enough, the tight quarters and the rigorous decorum of that time and place had failed to offer opportunity for more than an accidental brush or a chaste kiss. And later, when opportunity did abound, when they were handsome in their uniforms and perfectly fit, they were only weeks or days away from shipping out and the looming possibility of their own deaths made even the desire to commit, at this late date, that kind of mortal sin seem as foolish and as fleeting as the mad longing to hurl yourself, willy-nilly, from some great height-the parachute jump at Coney Island, for instance, or the observation deck of the Empire State Building—or to raise your head from the mud during a live ammo drill at boot camp, just because you had the urge.

They had bruised girls' lips with kisses then, had learned the pleasure of encircling a waist or running a hand along a stockinged leg, of feeling a heartbeat behind a breast, but the Paulist Fathers had gotten them at an early age and they had studied heaven and hell long before they knew that at the top of a stocking there was only bare flesh, and boys they had known from the basketball court or the K. of C. had already gone over and lost their lives. And even in Manhattan, at midnight, in uniform and as drunk as the girls on their knees, they saw through the bold music and the laughter and the smoky air their foreshortened lives, the nearness of eternity, and so always rode the subway home alone, reeling and laughing and helped by the hands of innumerable smiling strangers, to sleep it off under their mother's own roof.

Raise

Betsy Boyd

My older brother's friend Mike O'Shea used to come to our house every Friday night to play poker in the basement. He won the pot of quarters almost every week, twenty or thirty bucks, unless he was stoned. Even though O'Shea swept the table, the boys and my dad liked to play with him because he made the experience feel important. Even as a kid, he had this built-in confidence—he could read you, but you couldn't read him. My father said O'Shea had a gift for the game like nothing he'd seen.

People called him O'Shea because Mike was also my brother's first name, or sometimes they called him Death, on account of he was six feet tall, skin and bones. O'Shea could have been the thin man in the circus, that's how slim, but he had a boyish face, cute crooked teeth, and dark blue almost black eyes. He'd knock the screen door every Friday night in a pleasing series of beats—not the same pattern everybody uses, but five measured taps, pum-pum, rum-pum-pum—and I would know it was him and run to answer it because I thought I loved him. While the boys played poker, I sat on the stairs and eavesdropped for hours. Just hearing O'Shea say, "Raise," was a turn-on.

He started coming around when he was fourteen, with half his head shaved clean and a rat tail braid down his neck. I was nine, with my own crooked teeth and stick-out bones worse than his. O'Shea got pissed when the basement boys, drunk on beer given them by my father, made fun of his frame. One night, when he had a David Bowie button on his jacket, they called him the Thin White Dong. He told them they'd better watch it or he'd whip out his pocket knife and de-cock the whole small-cocked lot of them. When I ushered him inside my mother's lamp-lit entryway, O'Shea talked nicer, like he was a different person altogether, and let me fit my fingers around his wrist. He let me know some things.

In the summertime, my uniform was short shorts, T-shirts with Culture Club and The Go-Go's ironed on, and blue roller skates with yellow stripes. I had so much blond hair on my legs O'Shea said I was half monkey. He said we were a couple of funny-looking monkeys and, when he did, I felt I might scream with happiness. Once I kissed his knuckles and skated down the driveway to die in shame.

O'Shea used to tell me stories when he came through the door—each one was a test of my gullibility level. He said he didn't want me to get taken advantage of, like most girls. I'd ask a question, and he'd tell me the truth or a lie, and leave it up to me to call it. When he was sixteen and I was eleven, I worked the nerve to ask how his father had died the winter before—my mother had urged me never to bring this up, which made me burn to know. As I traced the dove tattoo on his forearm, O'Shea laid out the scenario. He said that his father, who'd been a trucker, was minding his own business one afternoon, taking a break in a wooded area, when he met a grizzly bear in his path. O'Shea's father had been planning to sit beside a pond and eat his homemade box lunch, but the bear had other ideas.

I yelped in horror.

O'Shea went on.

His father put up a good fight, even broke the bear's paw. But bears will be bears, he said, and this one was hungry and decided to eat his dad's face off.

I linked arms with O'Shea to show my sympathy.

"You believe that?"

I nodded.

"My dad survived two weeks in the hospital," he said.

"Oh, Jesus."

"He kept asking about the whereabouts of his nose and mouth."

"Now, I don't believe you."

"I was using too many details from the start, dummy," he said. "Homemade box lunch?"

Then he gave me a stick of Big Red gum.

"How did he really die?" I asked.

"Remind me to play poker with you sometime."

"How did he really die?"

"He shot himself."

And I knew that was the truth.

***

Three years passed. My brother Mike and O'Shea drifted apart. Mike wasn't nearly as smart as O'Shea, who earned practically perfect scores on every standardized test he ever took, but he was disciplined and industrious, and scared of my father. He made solid grades and set his sights on college because my father wanted him to be the first in our family to go. O'Shea couldn't be bothered to stay in school, especially not Catholic school. He dropped out, despite his mother's threats, and fell into trouble, getting arrested for shoplifting on two occasions. One night, he decided to rip off a pawnshop—they had a drum kit in the window, and he wanted it. Drunk as hell, O'Shea shook his pocketknife at the arresting officer, unraveling the cop's pocket stitching. The cop put a bullet a few inches above O'Shea's kneecap, and O'Shea went to jail for several years. My mother, being the gossipmonger that she is, invited Mrs. O'Shea over for coffee and pound cake several days after O'Shea got locked up. I painted her toenails, as I did all my mother's visitors, and applied tiny silver four-leaf clovers for luck. Though she seemed to hate the effect, mistaking the clovers for sloppy clumps, she gave me a three-dollar tip and said I was a nice girl.

By the time O'Shea got out, my brother Mike had left Baltimore for Ithaca, New York, where he was pre-med, engaged to an education major named Doreen, and a fairly annoying asshole all around. Thanksgiving break senior year, he came home and read MCAT books at the dinner table, even though my mother had spent the day preparing sweet potatoes with toasted marshmallows, green bean casserole, ham, and turkey—all his favorites. My father eventually asked Mike to close his books. The day after Thanksgiving, we sat around the table feeding our faces with leftovers. Mike studied as he chewed.

"Can't you take a break yet?" my mother asked him.

"Not if I want to pass this test," my brother said, and smiled phony.

"Well, okay, but this is a family weekend."

"Well, but this is the fucking MCAT."

"We understand what you're going through," said my father.

"Oh, please," I said. "Can we say fuck at dinner now?"

I was sixteen and no longer skin and bones. My breasts and hips were full—so large they'd slowed me down and cost me a letter jacket in cross country—and I was tall for a girl. I had slight acne, but I was grateful for the breasts, which my mother referred to as future collateral. My main interests were boys—I'd come close to having sex with a kid named Clifton in his little brother's tree house—and doing nails. I wasn't a poor student, but I liked to have a good time more than I liked to crack books. It seemed to me I could get a job doing toes professionally after high school—my trademark was attaching little rhinestone studs or twinkling stars to the big toe. My mother's friends liked the work I did, and I'd saved over two hundred dollars in tip money.

I kept an old Polaroid of O'Shea on my bulletin board, but we hadn't heard from him in three years when he knocked his special knock on the screen door that Friday night. When we heard it, I think we all knew it was O'Shea. My mother's mouth, churning potatoes, went still. My father, buzzed on table wine, raised his eyebrows at my brother, who turned to me.

"Cathleen?" Mike said.

"I'll go." I wiped my mouth. I remember I was wearing a baby blue cashmere sweater purchased that day at an after-Thanksgiving sale, unflattering pants handed down from my mother, and the same buckle-up flats I wore to Catholic school every day. My nails were Geranium Red.

"Go with her, Mike," my mother said.

When I opened the door on O'Shea, I felt like a scrawny kid again, even though I wasn't, and wished I'd been wearing an evening gown, or a dress of some kind, for his homecoming. O'Shea seemed not to know me at first. His hair was short as a soldier's, his body as thin as ever, and when he took a step I could see that he had a limp. He shuffled his feet and wouldn't look at me straight, just sucked his cigarette there in the doorway.

My brother showed up behind me.

"Why, if it isn't Death," Mike said.

The boys shook hands in a vigorous secret way, and I was disappointed to have to share the scene with Mike.

"Hey," I said.

"You look real grown up, Cathleen."

"I do?"

"I thought maybe we could get some cards going," he told my brother.

Our eyes met, but he didn't seem comfortable. I figured that O'Shea had lost confidence during his stint in jail, but I had the thought again that I loved him. I wondered if I could convince him of it.

"Is that Michael O'Shea at the front door?" my mother called. "Has he eaten?"

***

Back at the house, my parents scampered off to bed immediately after dinner, treating O'Shea like he had a bad-luck disease. I think I heard my father ask Mike not to leave me alone with O'Shea, but he had nothing to worry about. While the three of us were down there in the basement watching reruns and smoking pot, O'Shea would barely look at me. I asked him if I could paint his fingernails dark blue and he shrugged. Mike tapped me hard on the back of my head and said, "He's not a fag, Cathleen." O'Shea had lavender circles under his eyes and he hadn't shaved in a day or two. Obviously, things were bad for him, but I couldn't understand why he was acting so cold toward me. The colder he acted, the more I feared he wasn't my friend anymore, and didn't respect me. I was sure he could have told me all kinds of strange stories—he'd done jail time, worked hard jobs—but he wasn't interested in trying to outsmart me anymore. His main priority was hooking Mike in a two-man game of Texas Hold 'Em, but Mike wouldn't comply.

He was high on the pot O'Shea had brought over but still determined to study for his test. It was sad watching him stick to the same page for half an hour at a time, reading with his mouth open.

"One game," O'Shea said.

"I'm not losing any more money to you in this lifetime," my brother said.

O'Shea backed off, but I noticed he was working his knee up and down in frustration.

"Why don't you go to bed, Cathleen?" my brother asked.

"I'm not tired."

"Who do you owe money to?" Mike asked O'Shea.

"Christ, don't worry yourself."

"You owe money to that fucking drug dealer Latrobe?"

Latrobe played poker with them back in the day.

O'Shea smiled crookedly, the way he used to standing in the entryway, like he couldn't help it.

"You know what?" my brother said, letting his book slip to the floor. "I hate getting stoned. It's boring."

Mike left the room in a huff.

O'Shea stood up and paced—I observed his subtle limp. Finally, he sat back down and we stared at a hair-removal infomercial on TV. A woman was saying, "It's so effective. It doesn't hurt a lick!"

After the infomercial, O'Shea cleared his throat and asked me if I might want to play a hand or two. Because I didn't know how to play, I lied and said I just didn't feel in the mood. When he left, I followed him out to his car and knocked on the window with two handfuls of money, tips I'd saved over the year. As he lowered his window, I dropped my two hundred dollars in his lap and waited for him to say something. He tried to give it back, but I refused, shaking my head side to side, my long hair flapping dramatically.

"If we're gonna talk, get in the car," he said. So I did.

O'Shea seemed less broken-down with that money in his hand—he began talking to me like a friend, proposing a plan to drive to Atlantic City by himself, three hours away, play the poker room at the Taj Majal, quadruple the money I'd saved, and return with an extra hundred bucks for me. But I insisted I'd like to go along and watch out for my money. I told him that I had a fake I.D. and I'd learned not to be gullible—learned from the master.

"So, does that mean you got more cash inside?" he asked. "More money going in, that's safer."

I shook my head.

He looked away, said, "What time do your parents wake up?"

We bought Dunkin' Donuts coffee, filled his car with gas, and reached Atlantic City around three a.m. That gave us two hours to win big and hit the road for Baltimore by five. Before we walked into the casino, we stood freezing in the parking garage and O'Shea encouraged me to put on some extra lipstick and eye makeup to look older. It was the first time he'd really stopped to look at my face. A lean orange cat rubbed his leg and he smiled the smile I used to like, but when the cat lingered he gently kicked it away.

"And stay beside me," O'Shea said. "There's lot of hookers around here, not that you look like a hooker, but you know—there's not much difference."

I could tell that O'Shea was feeling guilty about having brought me when he tidied up my lipstick with his fingers. He squinted like somebody had punched him in the gut and asked me what in the world he was doing bringing an underage girl inside a casino.

"I'm not the same person," I told him; "I'm more."

O'Shea put his arm around my shoulder the way my father does at church. It pissed me off—I feared it meant he wasn't going to be able to think of me as anything but a little girl the whole night. We walked inside, into the cigarette air, over maroon carpet, O'Shea limping, and me trying to look glamorous and sophisticated in those polyester pants of my mother's. It wasn't much warmer in here—O'Shea said they kept the AC going to keep people awake, playing their games, breaking their banks.

The middle-aged cocktail waitress in the glass-walled poker room recognized O'Shea and gave him a lit-up smile, which flat-lined as soon as she saw he was with me. She took our drink orders, everything complimentary, and brought me a Bloody Mary, no questions asked. O'Shea tipped her two chips. While I read a stack of brochures I'd picked up in the gift shop, he played a six/twelve table where you can raise your bet by six dollars and later by twelve, and I could see that the men, most of them overweight and over fifty, respected him. It was in the way they watched him, even when he wasn't playing, like they were watching out. I sat directly behind him in a plastic-coated dining room chair and, now and then, scratched his back because he was stressed—working his knee and chewing gum like a hyperactive kid I used to baby-sit.

"Thanks," he said. And I promised myself to outsmart him into making love to me in a hotel, where we would hole up until our winnings needed to be replenished.

"Raise," O'Shea called when the dealer looked at him. The mustached man to O'Shea's right seemed to disapprove. He had a decent-person look like the lumpy science teacher I had freshman year. When the hand finished, the chips got pushed to O'Shea. And then it happened again and again. In a while, O'Shea turned to face me, placed his hands on my knees. He forgot himself and said what pretty fingernails I had—it made me tremble. Meanwhile, a chisel-cheeked older man wearing a silky shirt with ruby cuff links studied me.

"Are we winning big?" I asked O'Shea.

"Not so loud."

He kissed my cheek. I felt twice as drunk.

"How much?"

"We've got four hundred bucks. I think we should keep going, if you think so."

It was almost five a.m., but I couldn't care less. The Atlantic City brochures depicted boats and water, fancy fish restaurants and elegant dress shops, and these were things I could experience when the sun came up. With the money we were making, I could probably get a nice dress full-price.

While the dealer ended his shift and traded out, the cuff-linked guy asked me how much I charge. O'Shea's nostrils expanded—he looked at the man like he might strangle him.

"She's with me."

"How old are you, kid?"

The man leaned over and fingered my sweater sleeve.

O'Shea pulled me onto his lap and held me there—in a tight life-saving way—while the other men at the table tried to act disinterested. Ruby cuffs rubbed his palms on the table like he meant to warm it or charm it. Hands around my waist, O'Shea brushed his lips over my neck. It might sound cheesy, but his breath on my skin was the best thing I'd felt, like my first buzz off Dad's table wine, like skinny-dipping, like every excitement I'd sneaked surging at once.

When the new dealer sat down, the game began all over. O'Shea nudged me off, checked his fresh cards, and gave me a blank look I chose to interpret as care. He seemed more relaxed now—not pumping his leg. In between plays, he attempted to make light conversation, asking me about people from our neighborhood, and how I'd learned to do nails. I wanted to ask him if he liked touching me, or if it was show. Instead, I asked him to describe his worst experience in jail.

"I guess the night my cellmate told me he didn't love me anymore," he smiled, lowering his eyes.

"Liar. What was the worst?"

"Taking a shit in front of someone else."

I noticed that O'Shea kept scanning the room and thought he might be trying to locate the cocktail waitress. He was in a good mood, but I got a worried feeling he wouldn't keep hold of it. He pulled out three pieces of gum, two for him, one for me.

"What do you want to drink?" I asked.

"Re-raise," he told the dealer.

"Drink, O'Shea?" I said.

"Scotch rocks, you mind telling the woman?"

As I started to stand, O'Shea leaned to the lumpy mustached man and asked him discreetly if he knew where he could score some coke.

"Hell if I know," the man said. "That stuff will kill you."

"Thanks anyway," O'Shea said. He lifted his hand to say stop.

"I'm serious. Stuff killed my cousin Benny. I can tell you first-hand—"

By the time I got back with the scotch, O'Shea had shifted to the other empty seat at the table to get away from the guy who wanted to lecture him. As I set down the drink, he looked at the clock and said: "Shit, Cathleen, we have to get you home, little girl."

When he called me little girl, I felt my face slacken, and a rock settle in my throat, but I was determined not to wimp out. I formulated a plan to set him straight.

"You think that albino guy in the basketball jersey sells coke?"

"What, Cathleen?"

"See that guy through the glass? Stocky build?"

"Yes."

"I think he sells."

"No, I don't think so," O'Shea said. "He's a honeymooner probably."

I pointed out the man's expensive gold necklace, his sunglasses—they looked like real Ray Bans—and I compared him to the other men standing around, the sloppy, no-jewelry crew wearing sweat-stained shirts, smoking cigars. If I sold drugs, I'd wear Ray Bans.

"Are you trying to stop me from walking over to talk to him?"

"Cathleen, you're acting stupid."

"You don't think I know a coke dealer when I see one?"

"Maybe you do. But let's drop it."

"You don't think I know."

"That guy's not a dealer, but it's irrelevant to you, got it?"

"Got it."

"Re-raise," said the man in the cuff links.

"Cap it," said O'Shea.

But the chips got pushed to the man because he had a full house.

After another couple of games, I was sleepy and rested my forehead on O'Shea's denim shoulder. On the other side of the glass wall, the fellow in the basketball jersey was talking to a bald Asian in a green casino blazer—they were having an argument of some kind—until finally the bald man pointed his arm like a rifle and sent the jersey guy bounding down the hall.

"Fold," said O'Shea. He'd come down two hundred dollars, and I thought some cocaine would cheer him.

"Could I have fifty dollars for the slots?" I asked.

"It's your money. But we have to leave soon. And don't talk to anybody."

***

The sun was pushing up. Snow poured like sugar and soaked into my cashmere sweater as I followed the stocky man in the jersey to the corner where we'd agreed to meet. He'd assured me that he did have a very reliable gold connection two miles across town. He was an honest person, I gathered from our brief exchange, in which he counseled me not to say anything more to him inside the casino, where cameras were running. He'd been busted once before, and neither of us could be too careful. As we stood on the corner, I planted fifty dollars in his hand when I shook it, and promised him twenty more when he brought me the drugs—that's the way he wanted to work it. I didn't have an extra twenty, but I figured I could flirt my way out of it. My watch read half past six, and the man said he would return no later than seven, probably sooner. I would camp outside.

"Or you could just come with me," the guy said. "Stay warm." He grinned.

"Sure," I said. And we walked down the block.

"I got a young daughter about your age. She's in Hawaii with her mom. She's very beautiful like you—could be a model. Her name's Liliana—"

He kept talking about his girl, and I started not to trust him. It was in the details. His blue van waited parked on the street, and he reached in his pocket and clicked off his car alarm. It sounded to my tired brain like something squealing.

"You know, I think I'll just wait here," I said. "My friend's, you know, inside."

"Come on." He put his hand on the small of my back.

"I'll wait."

"Just get in the van. We're friends, right?"

I ran several steps backward, which made him laugh loud and strong, then spit a ball of phlegm, and shake his head, smiling. He looked mad.

The bus-stop bench outside the casino was stinging cold—gum and bird shit stuck to the seat. I sat there exhaling white gusts, moving my fingers as though grabbing, trying to believe the guy was coming back, but it got hard to keep my eyes open. When O'Shea bumped my shoulder to wake me, I was drooling like a baby and my eye makeup was smeared across the tip of my nose. I could see it each time I looked down. His eyes were red-shot. He wouldn't look at me. He said he'd lost our money by switching seats to an unlucky spot at the table, and he figured we should probably hit the road soon. But O'Shea never lost, and I didn't know whether to believe him when he told me we were broke. I thought he might be testing me.

"I'm not fucking with you, Cathleen," he said. "Let's go home."

"Let me see your wallet."

He opened it—there were a few cards and foil wrappers, but nothing else.

O'Shea sat on the bench and I pulled his long arm around me like a stole.

"Monkey," he said after a minute—he said it the way a man might say, "Darling."

"I've got a surprise for you. The guy in the jersey is bringing coke at seven a.m."

"It's already eight o'clock," he said. "You didn't give him your money?"

***

When we got inside O'Shea's car, he cranked the heater and apologized without looking at me for spending all my cash. I racked my brain to think how I could still trick him into loving me, or at least fucking me. Desperate, I sucked my breath and shimmied out of my fuzzy sweater—I told him I needed to let it dry out.

"Right," he said.

"Jesus Christ," he said, stealing looks at me in my white lace underwire bra. He ripped off his jacket. And I sensed my plan was working.

"The guy with the mustache said we were a couple of doves."

I pressed my breasts together to enhance the effect.

"What?"

"The man at cards, he said the word doves. Maybe he was talking about your tattoo, there on your arm."

Then I realized that O'Shea had been wearing his jacket all night inside the cold casino—no way the man could have seen his bird tattoo. I thought about doves in the Bible. They were a positive image. They symbolized peace. Isn't that why O'Shea had one stamped on his arm? But a pair, like two turtledoves at Christmas, that was most likely a weaker thing to be.

O'Shea rested his head on my shoulder.

"My mom told me you make money doing nails."

He was working his knee, but I put my hand on his leg and stopped it.

"She did?"

"She told me you practically run a nail shop."

"Maybe someday I will."

"Do you get what I'm saying, Cathleen?"

"That's part of why you came over, the money—"

We were packed close but did not turn to look at each other.

"I wanted real bad to see you again."

"I didn't give you all my money," I said. "I kept back eighty."

"Good. That's good."

"Was that a lie about wanting to see me again?" I asked him.

But it wasn't.

When I brought O'Shea's hand to my breast and we exchanged our kiss, it was hungry. Our teeth scraped. My lip got cut. As he moved away, I could taste blood, and I thought I'd convinced him. He reached in his pocket to find more gum.

"You're killing me here, Cathleen," he said. "Put your sweater back on, will you please?"

So I did. You couldn't outsmart him.

Valet Parking

Geoffrey Becker

The Lexus was parked at the farthest end of the lot, near the fence, black finish sparkling in the chalky stadium lighting, and I was sweating by the time I got to it. I drove lots of nice cars in that job, if only for a minute or two: Infinitis, Caddys, BMWs, Mercedes, even Porsches. Some of the other guys turned up the sound systems to see what they could do, but I liked the silence, the way when I rolled up the windows and shut the door, it was like finding the mute button for everything.

I pulled up, got out, and opened the passenger door for the lady. She had a mane of teased blonde hair and wore a big don't-fuck-with-me sticker over her real face. She eased down and in automatically, like a crisp, new bill into a change machine, and I clicked the door shut, then went around the other side.

The guy was in his mid-forties, also blond, dressed all in black, with a chest that strained the buttons of his silk shirt, and worried wrinkles around his eyes. "Fifty bucks, you drive us home," he said. "I'm hammered."

I could see Scotty over by the entrance leaning against the wall, watching. "I don't get off for another half-hour."

"It's not that far. West Paces. Fifty. Plus your cab fare." He was swaying just a bit, I noticed.

I was supposed to pick up Rachel at the wine bar in the Highlands where she worked, but fifty bucks was fifty bucks. I walked over to Scotty. "Cover for me."

"What are you talking about? Cover how?"

"I don't know. Say I'm in the bathroom or something." Our boss, Marvin, took the whole thing pretty seriously, like if he did a good enough job, someday they'd promote him to owner.

"No way, buddy. You're on your own." He grinned, a stupid, go-ahead-and-make-a-mistake kind of grin, then opened up his crossword book again. We'd never been friends, really. I wasn't even sure why I'd asked.

***

For the first few minutes, we drove in silence. The guy rode in the back seat, and in the rear-view mirror I could see him there, sitting in the center, staring straight ahead. In front next to me, the woman leaned her head against the window. She had on a slinky black dress that ended high up her thighs. The top part was off her shoulders, stretched tight across her chest.

"Pepper," the guy said, leaning forward.

"Sorry?"

"I used to know this guy who thought we should do away with money and just use pepper instead. Carry around bags of it. Pepper."

We were on Peachtree, heading north, and I hit the brakes for a red light. "Black?"

"Black. Like what the waiter grinds onto your salad. This was in Brooklyn. Georgie Lopinsky. He had it all figured out—the wealthiest guy would be the one with most pepper."

I couldn't think of anything to say to this, so I just waited, watching the light not change.

"Jesus, Connie," said the woman.

"My wife was in the amateur contest tonight. Didn't win, though. A thousand bucks."

"Don't feel bad. It's almost impossible. They aren't amateurs, just dancers from other clubs on their night off."

"Not all of them. Anyway, I paid for that body." He sort of coughed and laughed at the same time. "Next left."

I signaled and made the turn, heading into a residential area. They were both quiet. I tried to imagine how far things would have to have gone before you'd want to see your wife naked on stage, a bunch of bozos waving dollar bills at her.

Connie was silent the rest of the drive, except to grunt directions. His face was red and a little puffy. The wife began to hiccup, but in a way I'd never heard anyone before, with very long intervals—as much as a minute.

We pulled into a place called Ashley Plantation, a new growth of condominiums hidden among tall pecan and magnolia trees. There was a remote on the visor that opened the huge iron gates with the gold crest in the middle, and I drove through and up a winding drive to their townhouse.

"Come on in," said Connie. "We'll call you a cab."

I hustled around to open the door for the wife. She swiveled and put one long leg out, toeing the blacktop as if checking a pool's temperature, then got unsteadily to her feet. I tried my hardest not to think about her any way but dressed.

"He's a mean bastard," she said to me, her voice cool and even as the surface of a martini. "But he's my mean bastard."

Inside, the place was all mirrors and glass and smelled like guest-bathroom soap. An enormous gold sofa occupied the center of the room, with a triangular glass coffee table in front of it that looked like it could easily have taken out your kneecap. There were fake flowers in a Chinese urn by the door, a floating staircase descending near the back of the living room where glass doors led out onto a deck. The wife took her shoes off by the door, hiccupped, and went upstairs.

"Phone's there," Connie said, pointing to the kitchen. He opened the liquor cabinet and pulled out a bottle.

First I called Rachel at the restaurant, but it was twelve-thirty and she'd already left. I tried her house, let it ring twelve times, then gave up. I'd been pushing her to get a machine, but she claimed she didn't believe in them. *Believe* in them? I said. The idea was to know if people called. I mean, at least sign up for voice mail. I had a hard time getting an answer at any of the cab companies, but finally someone picked up at Cherokee Taxi, the ad for which featured an Indian in full headdress. They told me half an hour to forty-five minutes.

In the middle of all the cab calls, Connie had brought me a scotch on the rocks. Now he was out in the living room sitting on the sofa. I still hadn't been paid and was wondering if I ought to ask.

"You know how old she is? I'm not going to tell you. Those other girls, they're like twenty-two." He had biceps you could crack walnuts with. He examined the palm of one hand, picked for a moment at a callous there. "It was a bad idea."

"Listen," I said, checking my watch. "There was that fifty."

"I don't want to lose her. But I figure that's next. Like fucking dominoes. You know what? Steal my car."

"Do what?"

"I got a court date in the morning—bankruptcy. They won't let me keep a Lexus. Steal it—it's yours. You liked driving it, I could tell."

"You don't know what you're saying."

"It'd be a shame to have it go at auction to some guy with a hairpiece. I'll file for insurance, they'll take that too."

"I don't steal cars."

"Not so far you don't. You know what I think about? A guy could go his whole life doing right, then make one mistake, and forever afterward, that's what he is. You murder somebody, say. You live seventy years, but this thing you did that took maybe thirty seconds, that's what you are. Maybe you coached little league, but when people talk about you, is that what they say? No. They say 'There's that murderer.' Anyway, here's our problem—I don't have any cash. You want a maxed-out credit card? I can give you a couple of those. That chandelier over the dining table? Thing cost five hundred bucks. I'll get you a screwdriver."

I looked at my watch once more. Now it was a matter of damage control. Rachel was going to be unhappy. Sex would be out of the question, and I just wondered if I'd have to sleep on the sofa again. I stood up.

"Sorry about all this, chief," said Connie. "You're welcome to watch TV or something 'til your cab comes."

"That's OK," I said. I tossed down the rest of my scotch, crunched the ice-cube. I noticed his keys sitting on the table by the door, and I grabbed them on the way out.

***

Rachel was sipping red wine and reading *Time* magazine, which her parents subscribed to for her. We didn't live together, but I had a key—I used her phone, too, since I owed Southern Bell $658. Her apartment was over a garage behind a house in Candler Park, a hilly, wooded, residential area. I rented a basement room in a house two miles away that we were both a little scared by, what with bugs the size of Brazil nuts skittering around. All Rachel's neighbors had dogs and kids. It was a tiny apartment, with a rickety flight of stairs outside and she'd decorated it with posters and India print fabrics. We called it the treehouse, because it felt more like that than a real place a person would live.

She'd been sitting around for a while, deciding how to make me feel as bad as possible. She'd taken her hair down. Rachel was skinny and big-breasted, with a freckled, round face and green eyes. Sometimes she reminded me of one of those doctor's office paintings of a kitten. I had met her when she was still at Emory, and I was making pizzas. It was pretty clear to me that I was a kind of statement for her—no college, shaved head, an actual Georgia boy. Rachel was from Bryn Mawr, Pennsylvania, and the following month she would be moving to New York City for a publishing internship. She talked about it like it was no big deal, and she still said "us" quite a bit. She'd be living with two other girls on the Upper West Side, over an Indian restaurant.

"I had to get that grabby assistant manager to give me a ride."

"Sorry," I said. "I was stealing a car."

"And Marcy's opening? You forgot entirely, right?"

Marcy was a girl she worked with who had bought a bunch of disassembled old department store mannequins and painted them and wired them together in unusual combinations. A head with an arm sticking out of it, two legs bound together and decorated with *Peanuts* band-aids. She had a show at Caffiends downtown, and there was a reception I'd said I might go to.

"Oops," I smacked my forehead. "Hey, put something on your feet and come see."

Rachel took her time putting on her sandals, then followed me down to the curb. Hands on hips, she examined the Lexus. I felt an odd pride of ownership about it. It was a nice ride. Not something I'd have bought, probably, but very sharp.

"What's this supposed to be?"

"I did a designated-driver gig for some drunk and his wife. He couldn't pay, so I took his wheels."

"What are you, a gangster? 'Took his wheels'?"

"It was a business transaction. You studied economics."

All I usually had to offer at the end of an evening—apart from the occasional celebrity sighting—was the stuff people left in their cars. Empty food and beverage containers, mostly, which hardly made for a good story. One time, I'd parked an old Cadillac that was decorated inside like some kind of shrine, with pictures of Jesus taped up everywhere, as well as quotes from the Bible and little crosses, but that kind of thing was the exception.

"Don't lie to me. Where'd you really get it? Have you lost your mind?"

"The guy owed me fifty bucks. I took his car." Hearing myself say it, it almost sounded reasonable.

"This is a twenty-thousand-dollar vehicle. I mean, at least."

"Get in and I'll give you a ride."

We drove to where the reception was, but the place was closed up tight. I apologized again, even though I was actually happy, since I'd just as soon have chewed gravel as look at Marcy's art. The streets were deserted except for one crazy-looking bum picking through a garbage can.

"This is a nice car," she said, powering her seat into La-Z-Boy position.

"See? That's what I'm talking about."

We cruised around for a while, enjoying the tight suspension, the smell of the leather seats. At the Krispy Kreme on Ponce, the "Hot Donuts Now" sign was on, so we parked and had one, then stood outside for a while watching the machinery. We did this a lot—it was our thing, because we'd done it on our first date, over a year ago. Hundreds of them, sugared and cooling, traveled slowly around the huge, bright room on conveyer belts. To their left, under the contraption that sprayed on the sugar, a huge pile of frosting had grown. It looked like candle wax. Rachel was convinced that they discarded the stuff, but I told her she was wrong. They shoveled it up, melted it down and poured it over the next batch.

"You want to tell me what the deal is, really?"

"There is no deal."

"I see." To our right, where the donuts began their trip, one was caught in the vat of hot oil, bobbing away there, turning blacker and blacker on the bottom. Our reflections in the plate glass didn't even look familiar. "Why aren't the police out looking for you?"

"They might very well be."

She knocked at the side of my head. "Is there anybody home in there?"

One of the workers inside came over and fished out the burnt donut. He also went along and pulled another six or seven off the belt that looked perfectly fine, tossing them into a big bin.

"Where's your car?"

"Back at the club."

"And whose is this one, really?"

"I keep trying to tell you." I could see there was something else. "What?"

She wiped her mouth with a napkin. "Marvin called. He said you left early, and it wasn't the first time. He said you shouldn't bother coming in tomorrow."

"Just look at all that grease," I said.

"OK, don't tell me about the car. Let's go to the shoe show."

"Yeah?" I couldn't tell if she was serious.

"This was your last night, and I've never even been."

"Right. I never thought you'd be interested."

"Why not? I can appreciate a woman's body—after all, I own one. Besides, I want to know more about you."

I drove us back to the club. 'Shoe show' was my term—I never could get it to catch on with Scotty ("No one looks at their shoes," he explained, searching my face for signs of mental deficiency). The truth was they might as well have had on suits of armor. Partly that was because five of the meanest hunks of meat in Atlanta were on constant patrol for that moment when some drunk businessman tried to reach across the demilitarized zone and actually touch a girl. But it was also mental, a mind-body separation they learned to achieve. Exist in the moment and outside it at the same time like Zen masters. Okay, maybe they just turned off their brains.

On the way, Rachel checked the glove compartment and found a manual, some receipts from Jiffy Lube, a couple of maps, a package of moist towelettes, and a cap gun styled like a miniature old-west six-shooter.

"Your drunk friends have a kid, I guess." She twirled it around her index finger. "What is it with boys and guns?"

"You're joking, right?"

It was two a.m., and the parking lot had emptied considerably, but there were still forty or fifty cars out there. I'd been hoping that Scotty would be on duty so I could make him park the Lexus, but he wasn't. There was no valet parking past midnight, except on weekends, and Scotty was home in bed by now, probably telling his wife about me, how I'd thrown away a perfectly good job this evening over the promise of a fifty-dollar tip. I parked away from the entrance where we wouldn't be seen getting out and left the keys in the ignition.

"Wipe down the steering wheel," Rachel said. "Get rid of the fingerprints."

I gave it a rub with my elbow. We got out of the car.

She was looking over at the entrance, with its green awning, the two-foot-high green neon emerald above it set against the concrete, staring out like an eye.

There was a chill in the air, even if it was still humid. Summer was over. Football had already started up again. That time of year always made me feel anxious, as if there were important things I ought to be doing. I thought about Connie and his wife, how what at first had seemed like a game turned into a real problem.

"I can't go in. I just got fired. It's embarrassing."

"Then I'll go myself."

"Really?" I tried to imagine this. "There's a cover."

"They won't charge me, will they?"

She marched over to the entrance where Bo, the one-armed bouncer, opened the door for her. She didn't look back, just passed on through into the black light and noise.

I got back into the car, turned on the radio and listened to a rebroadcast of a sports phone-in show from earlier in the day. There is a feeling of freedom that comes with losing a job. It was like letting out a really good burp.

She was gone about ten minutes. For a while, I studied one of the maps. When I saw her come out, I pulled up to the front of the building. Some guy on the radio was shouting about the Georgia defense, how you could drive a truck through the holes they left open.

"We're just leaving yours here?" she asked.

"Don't worry about it. Get in."

She didn't have much choice. How else was she going to get home? She settled in beside me. I put it in drive and eased out toward the exit.

"They're all so pretty," she said, after a minute. "I've never seen so many pretty girls in one place."

"Oh, Emerald City has the prettiest girls, ask anyone."

The streets were quiet and I drove too fast. Rachel held on tight to the armrest. I knew she thought that somewhere in me there was a flaw, like a faulty transistor in a stereo that occasionally made it spit and pop. Still, nothing I could say would convince her that I'd stolen a car, and I found this a little disappointing.

I pulled up in front of her place and kept the engine running.

"You're not coming up, then?" she asked.

"I'm going to take this thing to Mexico and sell it."

"Come in and I'll make cookies. I bought dough this afternoon."

"I'm serious."

"If it is borrowed, you need to bring it back. You could get in real trouble."

"Birmingham, New Orleans, Houston, Corpus Christi, Brownsville." The moon was tangled up like a lost balloon in the topmost branches of the big pecan tree across the street. "Want to come? It should be a pretty drive."

"You go back there and get your own car. Then call me in the morning, OK?"

When she was gone, I opened up the glove compartment and took out the toy pistol. It had a cracked, fake-pearl handle. I hadn't seen any evidence of a child at Connie's town house, so I figured it was his, and I wondered what he might have been thinking about doing with it. My taking the car could have been very good for him, considering. Kept him out of trouble. I listened to the cicadas discussing things amongst themselves. *Look, look, look,* they said, and then they said it again, in humming waves. I thought about Ashley Plantation with those ugly, gold gates to keep the riff-raff from wandering in. Like we'd want to.

The River Rushed On

Todd A. Whaley

The body pinned against the spill barge by the river's current wasn't the first Billy Parris had seen, just the first one that summer. From the deck of the DELCO sand dredge, he watched, as the others on board watched, smoking a cigarette and wondering if the men driving the police boat would make the same mistakes the other men had made the summer before.

"Goddamn, look at that guy. He's getting a rope out."

Billy nodded at Jim, who stood beside him and spit into the river.

"Remember those idiots last year?" Jim continued. "They tied a rope to that floater's arm and tried to pull it into the boat? Whole damned arm came off like a turkey leg. Remember that?"

Last year, when the first decomposing body floated past, the police had thought it was early enough, that the body would hold together. It wasn't. Maybe these men would be smarter. Billy took another drag of his cigarette and squinted into the slowly setting sun. He could see both shores of the Ohio, the trees that lined the banks, the spill barge that had been temporarily shut down to allow the police boat freedom to maneuver, and the long snake of floating pipeline that attached to the rear of the DELCO. And, of course, the dead body with one purple arm extending skyward, as if signaling for help. It seemed almost comical.

"Can't these guys hurry up? Goddamn."

Jim shrugged his shoulders and scratched his arm. They were losing money—$16.91 a minute for every minute they were down. If they didn't start dredging again soon, the delays would start to reflect in their paycheck.

"What's going on? Why are we stopped?"

Billy glanced over his shoulder. It was the kid—Curt, the college puke with the impractical Abercrombie T-shirt and steel-toed boots who represented the Corps of Engineers and babysat their operation. Billy had to keep this kid happy—the whole crew did—but that hadn't stopped the other guys from harassing the kid about his shiny hard hat or clean jeans or well-groomed hair. Billy didn't, and for that reason, Curt had taken a liking to him.

"There's a body in the river. Donnie called it in," Billy said and motioned toward Donnie, who operated the small tugboat bobbing a hundred yards away in the middle of the river.

"No shit?"

The kid approached the rail but didn't touch it. They made a line of spectators—Billy, Jim, Rick, Johnny, the kid, and even Billy's father, William, who stood outside the dredge control booth in his untucked, Hawaiian-print shirt and smoothed the black hairs over his scalp—while the police officer leaned over the boat motor and lassoed the purple wrist. With a quick signal to the driver, the police boat began to move slowly upriver, dragging the body with it.

"What are they doing?" the kid asked.

Billy spit into the brown water, and the froth dissipated on the surface.

"They're dragging it to shore or a pier or something. Can't pull it into the boat, not in that condition."

"What are they going to do with it?"

"Why the hell do you care, kid?" Rick said, laughing and exposing the gaps in his smile. "Do you want it? They'll probably give it to ya."

"I don't care what they do with it," Jim said, "as long as they don't bring it over here."

Billy heard a crackle and reached for his radio. The police officer was waving, signaling the all-clear, and Billy watched his father close the door to the control booth. He was eager to get started again. They all were. Soon William would engage the cutterhead that rested on the river bottom, and the sand and silt and rocks and old tires and submerged trees would again be chewed into bits, travel the half mile along the floating pipeline to the spill barge, where it would be sprayed into shallower water, making the shipping channel deep enough to navigate.

"All right, let's go," Billy said into his radio and then turned to Curt. "Mark that in your log, kid. Seven forty-four. That's when we got back online."

Without waiting for a response, Billy walked the deck toward the engine room, throwing his cigarette butt into the river, where it was swept toward Paducah, toward Cairo, toward every river bend and dam between here and the Gulf of Mexico.

***

His head was throbbing.

Late the next morning Billy stood on the shore overlooking the wide expanse of the Ohio. Far downriver the DELCO and the midnight shift were packing up, readying their relief, and even from this distance, Billy could hear the grinding of the cutterhead, feel the motions of the dredge as it pulled on the guide wires and pivoted right, then left, then right, back and forth, advancing southward on two alternating steel piles that rested, in turn, on the riverbed. Like walking through water on stilts. Every hour the dredge advanced a little more in wide, 90-degree arcs that dug the channel deeper for coal barges, sand barges, everything that needed to pass from one place to the next.

He'd return next year to this very same bend in the river, and the summer after, as long as the river continued to flow. His entire life would be spent here. And why not? He made good money for a high-school dropout. One day, if he was lucky, he'd reach his father's age and understand the river as he did—love it, even—and all its depressions and angers and aggressions and destructions. But he'd never respect it. What was the point? His old man acted, at times, as if the river was a man with a soul, a spirit, but Billy never believed it. One day, when William caught Billy urinating from the deck, he warned him: "Piss on the river," William had said, "and one day the river will piss on you."

Billy thought it was a joke. But now that he had started hearing voices, he wasn't quite so sure.

Donnie drove into the dirt parking lot beside Billy's truck, cut the engine, and stepped out. He wore the same jeans he had the day before. They all did.

"Yo, Billy. You made it. Didn't think I'd see you after you hooked up with that girl from the bar. What was her name? Darla?"

"Darla, yeah."

Darla was a local girl, thin, with kinky, black hair, red lips, and a silver ring on every finger of her hand. She couldn't have been more than 25, although the way she had used her body, she had to be older. Old enough, anyway. Billy thought of her leaning over the pool table next to them at the bar, shaking her ass to the music, holding her cigarette with two fingers and carefully, delicately, wrapping her lips around it while Billy watched.

"So, couldn't handle her?" Donnie scratched his red whiskers and smiled. He was a big man, nearly 6'-5", and spent every night of his two-week shift drinking late and sleeping little. Twelve hours on, twelve off. Two weeks on, one off. Seven days a week. Unlike Billy, Donnie could handle anything.

"I don't need to tell you everything."

"Yeah, you do. So, how was she?"

"I slept in my truck."

Billy didn't totally remember what happened before he arrived in the parking lot sometime after eight in the morning. There was the country road at sunrise, a split rail fence, and reeds rising from the drainage ditch like bristles from a hairbrush. Then, somehow, suddenly, he had fallen asleep in the bed of his truck and woken when a train rumbled between the trusses of the railroad bridge that crossed the Ohio at the river's neck. Since then, he had stood on the muddy bank, listening to the gurgling water and watching a plastic bottle become wedged, trapped, in the roots of an overarching tree. Something was bothering him.

"Bullshit," Donnie said. "Then where'd you get them scratches?"

On his forearm Billy saw deep, red gouges from his elbow to his wrist. He was always getting scratched, from maintaining the DELCO's hydraulics to bumping into burred metal. It was nothing new. Yet an image flashed into his mind, of brambles and branches, of current, of desperation.

"Some wildcat, eh?"

Billy ignored him.

Once the rest of the crew arrived, promptly at 11:45 a.m., they'd board the dented fishing boat that would ferry them to where the DELCO roared like a steaming locomotive. Pipes and engines and hosings and steel trusses protruded from the bow to support the massive cutterhead. Flood lights shimmered on the water's surface after sunset, but now, just before noon, the entire dredge was visible. Exposed. Billy smelled, already, the familiarity of oil and electricity. While he squinted toward the tugboat that was busily resetting an anchor buoy, Billy wondered if things were as they always were or if something had drastically changed.

***

"I like you," she said, and Billy saw the glitter of a small jewel on one side of her nostril. A piercing.

They were both weaving. His legs felt like jelly. She was funny, this girl, and he liked the way her black jeans fit around her ass, shaping it.

"I like you too," Billy said.

There was some confusion whether he would finish the last of his beer or kiss her in the bar's parking lot, so he did both. He could hear her nostril whistling, as if she was gasping for air, or perhaps that came from overhead, from the tree branches and rustling leaves. When Darla pulled away, she bit his lip and laughed.

Billy tossed his bottle into the woods. He could still hear the music, muffled, from inside the bar. Everything was glittery—windshields of trucks, the chrome from a motorcycle, Darla's rings when she leaned forward to kiss him again. Stumbling, Darla clung to his waist. Like he was driftwood.

"I love your hair," she said and stroked his lengthy, blond curls.

Her skin was soft against his unshaven face, and, compared to his musky scent—he hadn't showered since his shift ended at midnight, four hours earlier—she smelled like wildflowers.

"I like yours."

But his hand got tangled. She was caught. She had to turn her head. They both laughed about it.

***

After two days of disassembling the pipeline, reassembling it again, setting the guide wires onto the lock walls, clearing the debris caught in the cutter head, adjusting the impeller, and fixing the hydraulic cavitation, they were finally operational. And he could feel the drumming of the motor through his boots. In narrow arcs the DELCO wagged between the lock walls that towered nearly ten stories on either side. Here they had to shout to be heard. Here, while the wall of water remained trapped behind steel doors at the far end, their radios had to be kept at full volume, their legs kept steady as the dredge jostled and sometimes lifted up from a tree log or the concrete foundation.

The impeller was cavitating again, that knocking sound that indicated to Billy that the pump was losing suction. The home connection was spraying water. The dredge had stopped a dozen times this hour already. Even Donnie, in the tug, radioed his answers in sharp, rushed sentences, then checked the cutterhead, once William raised it, like some barbaric dentist.

There would be no drinking tonight. After this they would all be too exhausted.

Rick waddled toward Billy, his gut hanging over the rim of his pants.

"We gotta head back down to Ledbetter after this," he yelled.

"What? Why? I thought we finished up."

"Some barge was runnin' the goddamn red buoys instead of the greens and bottomed out near the shore. Tore up the whole goddamn riverbed trying to get unstuck. Kicked all the old spoils right back into the channel. Goddamn idiot."

"All right," Billy said.

So they'd be heading back down again to the bend in the river, where the sunsets coated the sky with deep orange, where the river ran cool and deep and swift, where his memory had failed him.

***

The beginning was clear enough—climbing into Darla's car, her voice, slurred and twangy like a cliché of itself, saying "I can drive; I'm okay, just get in." And he recalled the ending too—walking with his head down along a tree-lined lane, the softening of morning, the dew collecting on the grasses beside the road and bending them. But somewhere in between, he had lost track. Not long after Darla lit a cigarette in the car and passed it to him. Right after the coke. Holes had formed in his memory.

Until he heard the news.

A car was discovered along the banks of the Ohio—he'd heard about it on the radio. A kid found it while fishing. In ten feet of water, among the brambles, the police had pulled the car out to find a purse, a bundle of clothes, a woman's boot, a single silver ring, and a plastic bag that contained, at one time, trace amounts of cocaine. Other than that it was empty.

The police were dragging the river for a body. They'd never find one, and Billy knew it.

***

"I'll drive," Billy said and fished his keys out of his pocket.

"The fuck you will. How much have you had?"

"I dunno."

Darla stood with her hips to one side. Black pants, black lacy top, black boots that stitched up the front to her knee, curly hair that shined, somehow, from the lights outside the bar. He was in love already. Or at least lust. A body like that was good for one thing only, and the thought of it made Billy smile and lean back against the truck grille.

"All right," he said and crossed his arms. "Darla. Let's see what you got."

Inside her car—a red Z28—Darla lit a cigarette and handed it to him. It tasted hot, like fire, and with the window down, the car blew the smoke over his shoulder. The engine was loud, a desperate growl. They passed a gas station, a red flashing light of Dunbarton Road, a community lodge. The air boomed like thunder until she turned left onto a dark lane where a canopy of trees blocked out the remainder of the moon uncovered by clouds. She put a hand on his leg, sliding it toward his crotch.

"You're a big boy, Billy."

One turn followed another, then another, and Billy finished his cigarette and flicked the butt out the window. When Darla tried to remove her hand, Billy clamped it against his pants. He was ready.

"C'mon, I gotta drive."

"You got another one."

She struggled and pulled, laughing, until her hand came free. They passed under a train bridge with abutments made of stone and finally slowed when the nose of the car dove forward into a grove of trees. The wheels bumped along a dirt trail.

"Where're you taking me?"

Billy was beginning to sober up. Soon he might come to realize more clearly what was happening, who he was with, what he was doing, and decide against it. He just wanted it, that release that comes with a solid screw, and then he could settle back into his routine on the river surrounded by men and machines, and none of it would seem so bad anymore. For a time.

Darla stopped the car and turned the key. It was dark. Dangerously dark. With the car windows down, the tree branches overhead made rustling noises and, to either side, crickets chirped, uninterrupted by their arrival. Ahead, something glowed silver. As his eyes adjusted he began to understand that it was the Ohio, illuminated from above by the bulb of the moon.

"I love this spot. No one ever comes here," Darla said.

She swung her leg over the gear shift and across his lap until she straddled him. Billy was shocked at how small she was. Her head barely grazed the roof of the car, and her hips were narrow and taut between his hands. Like he was holding a basketball instead of a woman.

He heard the glove box open with a click, and Darla held up something shiny that crinkled.

"Want some?"

She dropped the plastic bag into his lap. Holding his face between her palms, she kissed his mouth, his neck, his earlobe; she bit his lip; she thumbed the buttons of his shirt and pushed it off his shoulders; she wiggled back and forth, and he felt her, felt the heat from her body happily smothering him, sensed the sweat beginning to slicken the surface of his skin, ran his hands underneath the black, lacy top until it spilled over her head and onto the driver's seat. He could see the contrast of her bra against her chest.

"Wait, wait," she said and reached down between his legs, fumbling for the plastic bag. "Let's do it like this."

She made him hold his arm still and level, then carefully she dribbled a pinch of powder from the bag—it had no smell, like flour—and arranged it in a line with her nails. With one nostril pressed shut, Darla inhaled sharply and wiped her nose, smiling.

"Now you." Her voice was a whisper, a peaceful quiet.

Billy dribbled it onto her chest, snorting and licking it from her skin, her breasts, wherever the dust had fallen. His body became both numb and highly sensitive, as if he could feel every pore and every electrified nerve. He sensed himself moving both forward and backward, as though on the dredge. Time was irrelevant but existed for him alone, for each of them together, and they could do anything. Like a bottle uncorked, he was open and flowing. Like the river, like the clouds that continuously covered and uncovered the moon.

Things moved fast and suddenly slow. Her boots, unsheathed from her leg. Her bra, falling loose and free. The smell of her—oh, the smell of her—so primal and raw and stale from the cigarettes she had burned.

Panting. Her body—so sweet—moving in rhythm on top of him, around him, on him, above him, in his ear. So loud, her voice. So happy and in pain. Then slowing and petting and growing still. And breathing, in and out.

Then she was gone.

The car door stood open, and Billy saw Darla twirling in the darkness with her head tilted back, giggling like a young girl.

"C'mon," she said, and a cloud uncovered the moon which then revealed Darla. The pale skin, the wild hair, the black ink of a tattoo across her shoulder blades, which he hadn't noticed before, the smooth spheres of her ass. "Come in the water with me."

She was running before he had a chance to catch her. She was wading from the bank before Billy had the chance to tell her to stop, to wait, before he could tell her that he knew this part of the river and it was too fast. *The current,* he tried to shout before she dove, headfirst, into the silty brown. *You'll never be able to swim faster than the current.*

Billy stumbled on tree roots and rocks, slipping on the riverbank to the edge. The water swirled in eddies around a clump of debris, and he thrust his arms into it, certain that he'd find her. Branches and twigs, wet leaves, a plastic bag. It scratched his arms. He yelled her name. The Ohio, in response, covered over its crime with soundless whispers of water. All was quiet. The river rushed on.

For an hour Billy waited. Until he began to notice the sky overhead soften with the coming of morning, Billy remained naked and huddled along the shore. That was when the river first spoke to him.

It's a desecration, it whispered. *She's never coming back.*

He'd be blamed for this. Guys like him always were.

At dawn Billy climbed the embankment and walked to the car. He shouldered his shirt and threaded his legs into his jeans. He slid on his boots. The sun was rising in warm, orange swirls when he disengaged the parking brake of Darla's car, listening to the wheels crack the backs of twigs. The Ohio began to glow from the sunlight once the car's hood splashed into the water, tilted, and bubbled over. At the moment the first freight train thundered through the woods behind him, the car had been swept underneath, and Billy was walking, his head down and sober, along a field of waving grass coated with morning dew.

***

While the sun fizzled behind a heavy blanket of gray clouds, Billy stood on the bow of Donnie's tug, inspecting the pipeline that connected the DELCO to the spill barge. He wiped his forehead. This summer heat was relentless.

In an hour they'd be operational. In an hour, just two miles downriver from where he'd last seen Darla—where her car had been discovered, pulled from the river, identified, labeled a mystery, and forgotten the next day—they'd be back in business, grinding the bottom of the river, pumping it, spewing the debris, pivoting left and right and left, inching downstream slowly. Slowly. By August they were normally much farther upriver in Tell City, Evansville, or even the Uniontown Lock and Dam, far away from this damned river bend.

Now, when the river spoke to him, it called his name.

Billy.

Then it was Donnie on the radio.

"Billy—hey, Billy."

"Yeah, what is it?"

"I think we got another floater."

Billy squinted upriver. Under the direct glow of the tug's floodlights, a black object appeared, bobbing gently on the surface. A long mane of black hair, rounded back, unmoving. The current swept under the floating pipeline near the guide wires. If they had been operational, the cutter head might have gotten it.

"I'm gonna get a closer look," Donnie radioed. "Might have to call another one in."

"Leave it, Donnie, we don't have time," Billy called back. He looked over his shoulder to where Donnie stood behind the steering wheel of the tug, a mere 30 feet away. Donnie ignored him, gunning the motor and sloshing forward.

The tug bounded over the wake of a passing coal barge, and Billy held tight to the railing. Fifty yards away. The floodlights bounced over the muddy, brown water. Forty yards. The tug engine growled underneath his feet. Thirty yards.

It was Darla. Billy could see her black hair fanning to either side, her boots like oil, the silver rings on her fingers. The tattoo.

Twenty yards.

She sat up straight, waving to him.

Billy.

Ten yards.

Donnie eased the throttle of the tug, spun the wheel, and headed in the opposite direction.

"Just a dog," Donnie radioed back.

The DELCO shined silently on the surface of the river, waiting. Pulling alongside the dredge, Billy leaped from the tug to the deck and walked toward the engine room. His hands were shaking. He needed a drink. He needed his shift to be over, to drive somewhere and park beside a quiet field. He needed to be as far from the river as possible. But the impeller needed adjustment, signaling a worsening problem. He could fix it. One hour.

"Hey, Billy."

It was Curt, the kid. He had a job that any capable third grader could handle, yet he still asked Billy a thousand questions a day about the river, the dredge, the complicated hydraulics that were involved. He probably even got paid more. Billy didn't have time for his shit.

"Hey, Billy, why are you guys pointing the spill barge back into the river?"

He stopped. The pipeline extended along the top of the water from the DELCO to the spill barge, where the spoils would spray like a fireman's hose back into the river. The silt, the sand, the rocks, the driftwood. All of it repositioned. Dredge it up here, put it down there. It's how they always did it. Sometimes the spoils were high enough to form an island.

"I don't have time. I gotta adjust the impeller."

"But if you spray it into the river, isn't the sand just going to be looser and slide back down into the channel? You're defeating the whole purpose of dredging. In a month the river will just fill up the low places. This was in my hydraulics course. I know this."

"Well, there's a lot you don't know."

"But this is taxpayer money."

"Shut up."

"I'm not going to shut up. You need to spray into a barge and ship it out of here or maybe spray closer to shore."

"I said shut up!"

With a quick right jab, Billy's fist shot out and sent the kid reeling backward into the metal wall of the engine room. Billy kept walking. He knew the kid was holding his nose, knew the blood was streaming down his chin and onto his Abercrombie shirt, knew the kid would do nothing about it. Not now, anyway. Tomorrow maybe. Tomorrow the supervisor from the Corps would be called, the guy in the white, short-sleeved dress shirt and diagonally striped tie, the guy whose job it was to deliver next year's dredge contract to him and his crew. Billy knew something, eventually, would be done.

Although there was nothing yet to measure, Billy stood at the bow with the metal rod. He could feel their eyes on him—William, Donnie, Jim, Rick, Johnny. And the kid. Billy had ruined everything. He'd be asked to leave. He'd never be able to work with his father again or make his living in the same manner.

The river was all he knew. His whole life was spent near it or on it. Maybe, finally, Billy had come to understand the river, but unlike his father, he knew the river as a beast, a monster. It took things away and seldom gave anything back. It was a murderer, a destroyer, a thief, a devil, and a god. It had given Billy everything and now would take it all away.

He knew what he'd do. He'd go, tonight, to the place where they had found the car. Armed with a six-pack, he'd watch the moonlight flutter on the current, a silver stripe of light, glittering, almost solid enough to walk across. If the river called his name again, he'd go to it. He'd take that first cautious step from the bank and wade to his knees. He'd disrespected the river by dumping that car. He'd disrespected himself by not caring about the girl. If the current didn't take him, he'd swim, naked, under the moonlight and overarching stars. If it did, so be it.

Fri•nd / B••k / Alp•ab•t

Joseph Young

His eyes caught the passing of a bus, orange and broken white, and in a passing moment he left the stage. His hands described a guitar, eyes a bus.

She holds to herself a weed, pulled from the grass. Will you? she says. The weed asks her skin a question he couldn't have fixed.

In certain houses the lights were doubled, late city. She wouldn't have been there—the paling sidewalk—except for the voice: daughter? daughter? She folded her hands, nearly folded.

His glasses are televisions of her, even as he watches his hand. Go home? he asks, but she's already there.

Wait, she said. She was surprised how easily the knife passed through the apple, dull knife, red apple. Wait, she said. The sun pierced the door, family in the drive.

An ant began from the linoleum, crawled past her elbow, shoulder, to the clouded ceiling. She stirred her pot, focused on a dark fog. The ant reached the bulb, vaporous and warm.

When he parks the car, he will not get out. The motor will fall away, snow on the windshield. He'll sleep, then and inside, all the hearts on the block neatly typing.

He is clear, it'll be that metal, no other. It is like a dog: blue, heavy, patient. He pays, and the man at the register—what is it?, his eyes silver filling.

She turns away, one black heel, curled ends of her hair. Her smile is fixed—screwed, small. But then the sun declining, orange and cool, her palms find his eyes.

The Velvet Room

RAFAEL ALVAREZ

"I *can see the Statue of Liberty atop the roof of the ice cream factory, but I cannot see the world unfold inside this velvet cell..."*

***

Leini stepped off the streetcar as a late September morning broke across the Holy Land, a rope and canvas shopping bag in one hand; a book in the other with an address penciled inside the cover.

Below a black house dress, she wore white socks and old shoes; at the bottom of the sack that smelled of onions, an evening dress with evening hours away.

Passing Prevas Brothers lunch counter, Leini gave the diner stools a turn; one after the other, six stools revolving behind her as she swept into the Broadway Market, swinging her satchel like a school kid.

Striding past the butcher, she made her way to the flower stall for carnations.

Not the ones bleeding with stripes for she was aware from her reading—constant, intimate reading, put-the-book-down-before-you-go-blind reading—that a striped carnation symbolizes regret for love that cannot be shared.

Leini ordered a mixed bouquet, red and white, the colors of the flag above the Polish Home dance hall, a fun house of beer and clarinets in which she'd never stepped foot. Not because she wasn't Polish—in 1929 it only seemed like everyone along the Baltimore waterfront was from Polska, the same way the radio made folks believe everyone but them was rich.

But because in all her twenty years, Leini had rarely been anywhere that wasn't sponsored by the Greek Orthodox Church and chaperoned by a thousand sets of eyes. Before today, she'd never ventured beyond her own neighborhood with money and a purpose her own.

Smelling the flowers on her way out of the market, she stopped to consider an Old Country shrew squirting down the sidewalk with a black hose. The woman was dressed the same as Leini, but stooped under four times the years, turning the hose away to let the girl pass.

Spanish sailors stood in boarding house doorways sipping coffee, divining Leini's form beneath her dress. Ducks and hens squawked from coops. The birds would be killed today and eaten tomorrow. It was Friday.

Nusinov's had wedding rings on sale but it was too beautiful a morning for a twenty-year-old married woman pretending to be a widow to stop and admire them.

Turning toward downtown, Leini followed her instructions to an alley of matchbox rowhouses and was just about to head down the lane when glass shattered against the sidewalk in front of a Catholic chapel.

A derelict had thrown a wine bottle at a man leaving morning Mass when the communicant tried to give her a dollar.

"Come on St. Francis. Try and give me a dollar. I'll knock your teeth out. How about your roadster and your Victrola and your gin? Kiss my white ass…."

Gripping the flowers, Leini raced down a cobblestone alley just wide enough for a horse and wagon to rattle through; down to a house whose number she'd committed to heart.

Only two of her neighbors on Ponca Street had Victrolas, roadsters were pictures in magazines and with or without Prohibition, she would not have known gin from ginger ale.

All Leini knew were Greeks willing to work themselves to death to afford things they had no intention of buying.

Deep in the alley—"Just try to give me a silver dollar…." echoing off the walls and in her ears, Leini calmed herself and remembered to take a tunnel that divided 408 Cabbage Alley from 410.

Trembling, Leini was rattled by the rumpot's prophecy of false prosperity and struck dumb, as she ducked into the arched passageway, by a shower of Fatima sunshine at the end of the tunnel.

The tunnel was dark, the yard just beyond its end was brilliant and Leini forced herself to take a moment, realizing for the first time that it was not love that had delivered her here.

This life could not have been what her *mitera* and *patera* wanted when they shipped the smartest girl their village had ever known to live with trusted friends in America.

Leini had wanted to be an author.

A scholar.

A librarian, if nothing else.

Fear led me here, she decided, scooting down a tunnel so narrow that her elbows scraped the walls.

Other people's fear.

Her guardians had forced her into marriage with a man she did not know because they saw the way her tongue filled the gap between her teeth when the junkman came around; terrified that she'd mount a penis before she climbed the altar.

"Life is not what you find in your storybooks," preached Mrs. Ralph, the barren woman who'd raised her in the diner.

"Then where do stories come from?"

"Oh, my ripe little fig," laughed Mrs. Ralph, squeezing Leini's shoulders with a soapy hand as they scrubbed pots together. "They make them up."

***

Leini stepped out of the tunnel and into a garden made of two yards cobbled together; a small, lush park with rosebushes, canopies of fruit trees and herbs going to seed in whiskey barrels sawed in half.

A massive Star of David loomed from a brick wall at the back of the yard, ivy reaching up for it from a cast-iron bathtub filled with dirt. Leini stepped toward the Star and discovered—with her eyes and fingertips—that it was made from broken diner china.

Climbing onto the lip of the tub, feeling it wobble beneath her, Leini touched the shards with her palm—smooth here and jagged there—and remembered a man in the book she'd brought with her.

"A flat-nosed Jew with two fine growths of hair luxuriating in each nostril...his cufflinks made of human molars."

She'd written directions to this house in the front of the book in pencil, to be erased before morning. Hopping down from the tub, she thought: Only one person in the world knows that I am here. And he wouldn't tell a soul.

Leini opened a wooden screen door on the back of the house and entered a large kitchen made from two smaller ones, the wall between 408 Cabbage Alley and 410 Cabbage Alley removed, the space filled with the warmth of an absent family and their recent breakfast.

A soiled bib hung over the back of a highchair, dirty dishes were left in a sink beneath a window looking out on the garden; spice grew on the sill.

"If there is a royalty among herbs, it is she reigns sovereign...no other is so revered for its stubborn beauty and lilting fragrance..."

Leini picked a baby's bowl from the sink, ran a finger around its rim and licked cold farina from her pinky, her own baby—a boy, Jimmy for her father—back on Macon Street with her best friend.

Turning to a pinched set of wooden steps behind the coal stove—every angle at ninety, tighter than the tunnel—she began to climb, her bag of clothes squashed against cracked and curving plaster as she rose beyond the second floor to a splintered door.

Outside the door, a pair of work boots, socks stuffed into the cracked leather. Leini knelt to unbutton her own, leaving them and her socks next to the other pair.

Standing, she stretched her toes, closed her eyes, exhaled and knocked.

"You made it," said a voice as the door opened...

Orlo pulled Leini inside and her bare feet moved across yards of new velvet, alternately gray and then flashing silver depending on which way the sun hit it.

To steady herself, she reached for walls draped with velvet the tint of the quiver between her legs; deep maroon pleated like the flesh below the eyes of women from lands that demanded such lights be veiled.

Velvet beyond her reach as Orlo waltzed her to the bed; Leini spinning in the long, narrow room, arms slipping from her coat, her flowers falling to the floor.

"Orlo," she said. "My God...give me a minute to look."

Eyehooks snagged, buttons popped and Leini's head hung over the side of the bed, the marvelous secret turned upside down.

At the far end of the room—near windows that had looked onto Cabbage Alley before Orlo draped them with dark green velvet—the morning sun warmed a skylight paned with green and purple glass.

Leini tumbled from the bed to feel the length of her arms against the carpet and asked: "Where are we?"

"Alone," said Orlo, falling on top of her.

All alone inside a bruised membrane of sweet and sorrowful velvet, purple streaked with gray and gold in the upper room of a crooked alley house a century old: twelve feet wide and twenty-seven feet long from front to back.

As she twisted her neck to look around, Leini realized that the only color Pio had not included was the color of the sea as she remembered it—undulating sheets of brilliant blue velvet—on her crossing from Thessaloniki to Locust Point.

In her remembering, she paused and Orlo put his lips to her collarbone, ran his thumbs along her ribs and dipped his chin between them, measuring their length of with the tip of his nose, her black dress in a corner.

Downstairs, a door opened and Leini felt the creak of its hinges along her spine as Orlo set his mouth on hers. Sunshine poured down from the skylight. Leini flipped onto her stomach and crawled toward it.

Buckets of color, she thought, the velvet smooth against her limbs, color drenching my body if I allowed it to happen down there.

Reaching after her, Orlo saw money pinned to the inside of Leini's black slip as she wriggled free of it, a pair of twenties and a clutch of fives and tens—a small fortune—fastened with a diaper pin; money skimmed from her milk and butter purse in two years of perfect waiting.

Purple on my neck, she thought, inching toward the light in her bra and panties; Orlo reaching for her calves.

Green on my feet.

Orlo balled up the slip and tossed it aside.

Gold stenciled on my nipples like grape leaves.

Sliding out of his pants, Orlo laughed as he caught Leini under the light; pulling himself onto her back like a sea turtle until she turned to face him, color speckling dark crescents of flesh below her eyes.

Purple and green floating in the space between her front teeth; pink tongue filling the gap.

"It's beautiful," she said, spilling tears a bookworm—an innocent slaughtered upon an altar of pride—cries from a loneliness that books cannot relieve.

A good mother ashamed of resenting motherhood.

An angry wife fucked for two-and-a-half years about to make love for the first time.

"I'll leave tonight," said Leini to herself, pastel sunshine blinding eyes that at last could bear to be open the same time as her legs, between which Orlo could not hear her whispers for the sound of his lover's blood pumping against the sides of his head, his teeth deep in purple so dark it edged upon chestnut.

Turning her head from side-to-side in even rhythm with Orlo's tongue, Leini spied her black widow's disguise in a heap across the room and knew she was about to fulfill its mourning promise.

Until her seventeenth summer, when the junkman found her ladling out bowls of pigs' feet in her guardians' diner at the end of Clinton Street, Leini's patrons believed her only fault was reading too many books.

And then they caught her holding Orlo's hand as he prospected for junk and told her it was time—shut up, they said, and listen—the arrangements made with less care than it took to chop pickles for tuna salad.

Come, Orlo pleaded with her the night before the wedding.

Come…go with me.

But she didn't.

Now, blinking tears from her eyes, ashamed of feeling sorry for herself in the midst of such pleasure, she pulled Orlo up from her thighs and whispered "Come here."

Now is the time to run, she thought as Orlo moved inside of her by degrees so small they could only be measured by touch.

And when the perforations in the film joined the teeth of the sprocket, Leini saw a strobe flicker inside the skylight and glimpsed a raisin lost in white sheets: Mrs. Ralph on her death bed.

Holding onto the girl's arm with a promise that she would save her a place in the world to come, the woman who'd guided Leini from schoolgirl to housewife sent her sweet fig away with dry lips and regret; Mrs. Ralph's last moments of life so vexed by Leini's fate that no other indiscretion smelled like sin; the obsession to control another's life the only one that wouldn't yield to the oil of the priest at her bedside.

Leini sat on the stairs above the bed, laying her head against the bannister as Mrs. Ralph used the last of her strength to summon her husband.

Not for a sip of water or another pillow.

To demand: "How long did you look?"

"Easy," said Mr. Ralph. "Go easy."

But she would go in anger; no longer sorry that God had not given them a child of their own.

"How many coffee shops before you found that *moros* George?"

Until Orlo began taking Leini for rides in his wagon, Mr. Ralph and his wife had welcomed the junk-collecting bachelor into their lives like family.

Couldn't they have measured his love for Leini before hating him like a son?

Watching life slip from his wife, tears stinging the bite marks he'd made in his lip, Mr. Ralph remembered the urgency of the not-that-long-ago day when every alarm in the house went off; when Mrs. Ralph had pushed hard for him to do something and he wasn't sure what that something was until George appeared in the smoke made when fear and pride are rubbed together like sticks.

With her last breath, Mrs. Ralph said: "Help her get away."

Leini's sobs filled the stairway with tears more hot and full than the ones absorbed by velvet now that she was finally joined to the man she loved.

"Orlo," she moaned. "Or…lo."

Less than a month after burying his wife, Mr. Ralph would be dead too.

***

A single room, long and narrow and swathed in velvet: a skylight, a small bed, a tub and a pair of French doors opening onto a balcony above the garden.

Orlo pulled on his pants and opened the spigots as Leini waited; tub and bed so close that a man stretched out in one could kiss a woman sprawled across the other without straining his neck.

While Orlo fiddled with the faucets—not knowing how hot Leini liked her bath, whether she washed with a cloth or a sponge, or, until today, that her breasts disappeared when she lay on her back—Leini walked the perimeter of the room, running her palms along the plush walls, her first good look.

"Tell me how we met," she said.

"You were there," he said.

"Tell me again."

He claimed, and would continue to claim, that he had not noticed her before she served him a steaming bowl of pigs feet simmered in tomato and fennel in the lunch room; how he had asked about the book she was reading and casually mentioned where he'd be scavenging for treasure the next day.

"And you just happened to be there."

How Mr. and Mrs Ralph, his friends for a dozen years, barred him from the diner after reports came back to them that Leini had been seen riding the junk wagon with him, picking through trash in the alleys.

"No," she said, walking back to the tub. "It was earlier than that."

And she told about a day a good four years before she'd come out of the lunch room kitchen with the pig's feet special, the day around which the rest of her life would collapse.

The day she found out that she'd been traded to America for fourteen treadle-driven sewing machines; velvet walls, velvet bed and velvet floor… velvet stained with sex beneath a sparkling skylight.

"I was still a kid," she said. "You were coming down Clinton Street one way and Frannie and I were headed the other way."

"I remember," said Orlo.

"I don't think you do," she said, almost laughing; circling the room until she came to the tub, jet black hull above crimson feet; but a moment to navigate the whole of this clandestine cell, just space enough for Orlo to arch the soles of his feet while Leini touched her palms to the floor.

Slipping down into the tub, water spilling over the side as her body slid under it, Leini saw the water pressure drop. Someone was downstairs.

"Who lives here?"

"Whores, hillbillies, and mavri," said Orlo. "Packing-house Polacks and oyster shuckers."

"Who lives in this house?"

"The Pinchereles. Paul and Teddy."

"Are they artists?"

"Yes."

"Both of them?"

"Hardheads," said Orlo, shaking powdered soap beneath the rushing water. "Teddy cores pineapples down Lord Mott's. The knives cut her hands and the acid seeps in. She has to wear white gloves because they're always infected."

"Him?"

"Harbor rat."

"How do they live?"

"As they please."

Bubbles rose in the tub and Leini laughed beyond her years, leaning against Orlo's shoulder, saying, "No one lives as they please."

"Teddy picks up piece work at the packing house when they need a little extra," said Orlo. "Paul crabs in the summer and sails cook when a tug heads down the Bay. Sometimes he takes women out to ships on anchor."

"What?"

"Sometimes he runs women out to the ships for a dollar a head," he said. "Teddy saves coal in the summer by putting a tub of bath water in the yard to warm in the sun."

"She made the Star?"

"She did."

"She's Jewish too?"

"Catherine Theodora Zaminski?"

Leini disappeared under the water and when she came up, Orlo said: "Teddy had some kind of nerve for a kid from Binney Street. Some of those Polacks from St. Casimir's tie their ornery kids to railings with wet clothesline and leave'em screaming as the rope dries.

"You think her family wasn't good and pissed off when she married a guinea Jew from New Orleans and said they were gonna be artists? Dark enough to pass for colored."

"Stupid."

"They was mad as hell," said Orlo, lathering her hair. "But they got over it."

And they're not Greek, thought Leini, who had not heard her parents' voices for more than eleven years, yet succumbed—out of fear that they would never speak to her again—to the mores of a global family whose reach extended anywhere some stubble-chinned Nick fried onions on a grill.

Orlo dumped a handful of cold water on Leini's head and she pushed him away.

"Teddy and Paul are exiles," said Orlo. "They're willing to pay the price."

"I saw a bum this morning," said Leini, rinsing her hair beneath the faucet. "Someone tried to give him some money and he went crazy."

"Smokehounds," said Orlo. "See'em every day."

"Why wouldn't he take the money if he needed a drink?"

"Some people you can't help," said Orlo. "If it's the one I'm thinking of…."

"Sores on his face."

"One shoe on and one shoe off," said Orlo. "Hangs around the car shop waiting for the boy to crack the denatured alcohol, pissing their pants and going blind."

"Who needs a dollar when you can get poison for a penny a shot. For a nickel they could have a glass of beer."

Orlo wrung out the wash cloth and moved it across Leini's shoulders.

"Did you see the pig?"

"No."

"I'm sure it watched you come down the alley."

Leini, flaring: "Who watched me?"

"A concrete pig, Len, on the side of the slaughterhouse around the corner. Teddy sculpted it in exchange for a lifetime of scraps…that's how they make ends meet. Knuckles, tails, ears. Ever eat a sows' ear? You suck the meat from the husks like an artichoke heart."

Orlo took Leini's head, put his mouth around one of her ears and chewed gently until she squirmed free.

"I made our meal for Paul and Teddy once."

Our ball, thought Leini.

Our chain.

"I mixed it up a little bit," said Orlo. "I simmered the trotters with tripe and celery, spent an hour skimming fat while the knuckles dissolved. Served it with an apricot sauce."

"Why are you telling me this?"

"It made me feel better on a bad day…I was headed for another weekend alone."

I'm alone all the time, thought Leini, who'd left her young son with a friend for the day.

"I'd spent all day hauling these tubs from uptown, squeezing them in here without destroying them. I couldn't bring you to dinner, so I made what we like to eat and pretended you were with me."

Leini pictured the tub in the backyard, just like the one she was soaking in now except that it had been turned into a long, porcelain flowerpot.

"Didn't want to go through your alley," said Orlo, moving a washcloth between Leini's shoulders. "Pretending I had something to do. Hoped I might see you doing dishes at the sink."

"I washed a lot of clean dishes hoping you would," said Leini.

"When they asked me to stay for dinner, I offered to cook because I hated them feeling sorry for me," said Orlo, feeling Leini's back tighten under the washcloth. "Teddy talked to me as I put dinner together. I told her everything but your name."

And pig feet simmered down with tripe and lemon.

On top of spaghetti, all covered with cheese.

Love.

"Paul brought me up here after dinner," said Orlo, standing to get a towel. "They'd just bought the building and it wasn't nothing but crumbling plaster and cobwebs. You couldn't walk across the floor."

Leini looked at the skylight and thought of leaping through it; that maybe she could rise up like a space rocket and break the glass with her head, shaking the shards from her ankles as she flew away.

Leini yanked the plug and the drain gulped bath water as she searched for the opening in Orlo's shorts, savoring one of the delicacies she refused her husband.

Clearing her throat, she asked: "The Jew really ate pigs' feet?"

"When his plate was clean," said Orlo, arching his back. "He leaned across the table and licked the fat from his wife's fingers."

***

Who needs three houses?
They'd lived just as they wanted
Bye, bye baby: one, two, three…

***

Orlo soaped a cloth to wipe the silver lining Leini left behind.

Kneeling in the tub, he turned the water on full and put his head beneath it, his words bouncing off the porcelain and ringing in his ears as he told Leini a story; afternoon light pouring in from the porch behind the bed and sparkling off the water streaming down his back.

"In the summertime, when I was little," he said, "my mother would punch holes in the bottom of a coffee can, hang it from a nail on the back of our house and run a hose through it for a sprinkler. That's how we had our fun."

Stretched out on the bed—arms and legs wide, like a kid pretending to be a starfish—Leini remembered the punctured coffee can of her childhood: the Mediterranean with octopus boiling in kettles on the beach.

She wanted to go dancing: dress up and hear jazz and have someone wait on her.

Orlo kept talking—how the idea to trade in junk came to him in a doughboy trench, he would make good money selling long coats and motorcycle guts after the Armistice—and Leini, naked, slipped beneath the velvet bedspread, his words muffled.

Orlo, believed he would spend the rest of his life roaming the city of his beloved's enslavement to perfect the sanctuary they had just begun to enjoy.

Get Jimmy from Francesca and run, thought Leini, humming herself to sleep. With or without Orlo. Just grab the baby and go.

***

Leini woke before Orlo and slipped from his arm.

She moved quietly around the darkening room, picking up her clothes, letting the wilted carnations lay where they'd fallen. Taking fresh clothes from her sack, she dressed without a mirror, brushed her teeth with water from the tub and walked barefoot onto the balcony, black hair still damp from the bath.

Moving from warm velvet to cold tile, Leini thought of all the nickels she'd saved for a day she never thought would come; pleased with how she'd converted loose change from her husband's drinking pants—any pants on any day—into a day to remember.

"Just like the artists," she thought, leaning with pleasure on a railing cast in grapevines, face open to the rising moon.

[Orlo had put up a Bourbon Street railing on the Velvet Room balcony to make Pincherele feel better about the choices he'd made. Nearly all of the Crescent City's gingerbread had been cast in Baltimore and the junkman never let the exile forget it.]

Down in the garden, the woman for whom Paul had forsaken New Orleans sat in the garden with a book, nude, a pineapple slicing sculptor turning the pages with fingers scarred from coring knives.

"That could be me," thought Leini, reaching inside her gown to touch breasts no different—except for fresh teeth marks—than when she was fourteen; no match for the pale, heavy globes of the Pole reading below shimmering triangles of David made from shattered china and splintered chicken bones.

Teddy caressed her nipples with each turned page and Leini imitated her with fingertips still puckered from the bath.

Teddy was plain and Leini was beautiful.

Teddy made art out of nothing while Leini read the same books over and over, thinking she'd missed something.

Teddy content as the setting sun made the Star rotate above her—a wishbone at its center—and Leini anxious: "What does she know that I don't?"

In the time it would take for her to pull on stockings and buckle her shoes, she and Orlo could be uptown before the orchestras began to play.

The French doors behind Leini opened and Orlo joined her; barechested and barefoot, rope holding up a pair of clean work pants; his hair wet, curls springing free at the sides of his head.

He took the hem of Leini's dress and pinched it, trying to shake the nightmare that had woken him, an old one where his teeth came loose, one by one, from the root, the dream so real he could stick his tongue in the holes of his jaw and feel the empty gum.

"Is that her?" asked Leini.

"That's her."

Leini leaned against Orlo and purred: "Look how she sits."

"Like what?"

"Out in the open like that," she said, moving Orlo's hand inside the front of her dress. "Naked."

Orlo pulled his hand away, wanting to talk about his bad dream.

"Look again," he said.

Paul walked out of the house with the baby in his arms. Teddy closed her book and covered herself. Sitting the boy on a straight-backed wooden chair in the middle of the garden, Paul took scissors and a comb from his pocket and Teddy knelt next to the child with a hand on his lap.

Paul combed the kid's hair down to the tip of his nose, snipping swiftly as Teddy steadied the boy with whispers.

"First haircut," said Orlo and Leini pictured one just like it except that the parent doing the cutting and the one doing the soothing were the same.

[Because her own life seemed so hard, Leini assumed things were easier for other people. Watching the Pinchereles, she wanted to know them better, was fixated, since lying down, with the secret of living as one pleased.]

Slipping the shears in his pocket, Paul brushed away the trimmings and Teddy pressed a curled lock between the pages of her book.

Teddy spread a white cloth over a table near the Star and set the table. Paul picked the last tomatoes of summer and green peppers turning red.

In the potholes of Orlo's missing teeth: resentment not satisfied until it brought someone you love to tears.

Why should he leave Baltimore?

Factory whistles cut across the rooftops and Leini felt the energy of the city change direction for the second time that day.

"Let's go dancing."

"In a horse and wagon?"

"A Yellow cab."

"Where?"

"Johnson's Mecca," said Leini, running down speakeasies she'd heard salesmen talk about at the diner. "Sis's Hole. The Eagle in Bolton Hill."

"You know these places?"

"Drinks on the roof of the Southern Hotel," she grinned. "My treat."

A block away on Caroline Street, light glowed from a Statue of Liberty atop the Tutti Frutti ice cream company; Our Lady of Opportunity raising a 100-watt scoop of light in a stucco cone.

Orlo took a peach and a penknife from his pocket, cut a slice and slipped it into his mouth.

"Hold on to your money."

Leini tried to speak again and Orlo filled her mouth with peach. She chewed, swallowed and said: "Let's celebrate."

Orlo plucked the pit free with the tip of his knife, sucked it clean and spit it over the side. Teddy heard it hit the concrete, looked up and waved.

"The first king of Mardi Gras was a Jew, Len," said Orlo, his voice with an edge to it as Paul built a fire in a shallow pit bordered by flat rocks. "Paul's an apostate."

"How so?"

Teddy brought a fish to Paul on a tray, the baby toddling behind her with napkins.

"I'm not leaving Baltimore," said Orlo.

Leini turned to look at the man who'd spent a thousand hours carting the Jazz Age to Cabbage Alley for her, miles of velvet for one long day of sex and cowardice.

The Great Depression was just a bank of dark clouds sailing toward an ice cream cone's neon glow as folks who soon would not have a pot to piss in threw away fortunes that Orlo scooped up by the wagonful.

The five-sided skylight came from the back of a Lithuanian pool hall near Mencken's house; the French doors lay beneath a pile of cardboard on Eutaw Street and the stained-glass transom shimmering above the lovers was taken from the house of a red-headed trouble-maker on Dillon Street who traded it for a case of beer while his wife was at work.

"I only asked to go dancing."

Down in the garden, Paul rubbed the fish with olive oil and rosemary and slipped it on the searing grate; fire crackling and the scent of silver skin crisping to black wafting up to the balcony.

"Come on Leini," said Orlo. "You can buy a month of groceries with the money you brought."

Paul brought the fish to the table, a spatula under the head, the tail pinched between his fingers. Teddy made the sign of the cross and Paul covered his eyes until she was done, knowing just how long it took her to bless the meal.

Teddy trickled a rivulet of olive oil over a bowl of boiled potatoes and Paul took the spatula to the fish like a knife, cutting off the head and setting it on the side for himself.

"This is our Jerusalem," said Orlo, turning away from the railing to give the family privacy as they ate, Leini unable to take her eyes off of them.

"Our New York," she said, mocking their old saw. "Our Paris."

Teddy worked through the fish with the tines of her fork and the tips of her fingers, picking out the bones before bringing meat to her baby's mouth.

The kid picked up a handful of food and threw it in the air. When Paul grabbed the boy's wrist to scold him, the child squirmed free and pointed at Leini, now alone on the balcony.

"Leini…," said Orlo inside the room and she ignored him.

The first king of Mardi Gras was a Jew and along the fine edge of a harbor wind, seagulls gobbled French fries in the gutter where Cabbage Alley spills into Eastern Avenue.

A sullen mistress, Leini?

You could have been an author, a scholar, a librarian.

Turning toward the room, Leini glimpsed her reflection in the beveled glass and brushed by Orlo to find her shoes.

"Where are you going?" asked Orlo.

"Back to Greece," she said.

Contributors

CITY SAGES: BALTIMORE

For twenty years, **Rafael Alvarez** worked as a city desk reporter for the *Baltimore Sun*, which published two anthologies of his journalism, *Hometown Boy* (1999) and *Storyteller* (2001). His two collections of short fiction are *The Fountain of Highlandtown* (1997) and *Orlo and Leini* (2000). He has also published *First and Forever: A People's History of the Archdiocese of Baltimore* (2006.) His next publication is a collection of Baltimore Christmas stories—both fiction and non-fiction—tentively titled "Deep Fried Anchovies."

Geoffrey Becker's new book of stories, *Black Elvis* (University of Georgia Press, 2009), won the 2008 Flannery O'Connor Prize for Short Fiction. His novel, *Hot Spings* was published by Tin House Books in 2010. He is the author of two previous books, *Dangerous Men*, a collection that won the Drue Heinz Prize, and *Bluestown*, a novel. His other awards and honors include an NEA fellowship, selection for the Best American Short Stories anthology, the Nelson Algren Award from *The Chicago Tribune*, and the Parthenon Prize. He teaches writing at Towson University in Maryland, where he also directs the graduate program in Professional Writing.

Madison Smartt Bell is the author of fourteen novels, including *Soldier's Joy*, which received the Lillian Smith Award in 1989. Bell has also published two fiction collections: *Zero db* (1987) and *Barking Man* (1990). Bell's eighth novel, *All Soul's Rising*, was a finalist for the 1995 National Book Award and the 1996 PEN/Faulkner Award and winner of the 1996 Anisfield-Wolf award. Born and raised in Tennessee, he now lives in Baltimore, Maryland, along with his wife, the poet Elizabeth Spires, and daughter. He is currently Director of the Kratz Center for Creative Writing at Goucher College and has been a member of the Fellowship of Southern Writers since 2003.

Jessica Anya Blau's novel *The Summer of Naked Swim Parties* (2008) was chosen as a Best Summer Book by the Today Show, the *New York Post*, and *New York Magazine*. The *San Francisco Chronicle*, along with other newspapers, chose it as a Best Book of 2008. Her second novel, *Drinking Closer to Home* (Harper Perennial), will be out in February 2011.

Betsy Boyd's short story "Scarecrow" received a Pushcart Prize in 2009. She has published stories most recently in *Shenandoah*, *Upleasant Event Schedule*, and *Verb: An Audioquarterly*. Betsy was born and raised in San Antonio and now lives in Baltimore. She has received an Elliot Coleman Fellowship in fiction and a James A. Michener Fellowship in screenwriting. Last summer, she attended the Klots Artist Residency in Rochefort-en-Terre in Brittany. She writes freelance copy and teaches at the Maryland Institute College of Art.

Maud Casey is the author of two novels, *The Shape of Things to Come*, a *New York Times* Notable Book, and *Genealogy*, a *New York Times* Editor's Choice, and a collection of stories, *Drastic*. She has received international fellowships from the Fundacion Valparaiso and the Hawthornden International Retreat for Writers, and is the recipient of the Calvino Prize and a 2008-2009 D.C. Commission on the Arts and Humanities Artist Fellowship. She lives in Washington, D.C., and is an Associate Professor of English at the University of Maryland, where she teaches in the MFA program.

Andria Nacina Cole is a graduate of Johns Hopkins Writing Program. She has published work in *Ploughshares*, *Urbanite Magazine*, and *Fiction Circus*, among others. She is the recipient of three Maryland State Arts Council grants and is working tirelessly to complete a short story collection titled "Clean Piles of Daughter."

To pay the bills, **Caryn Coyle** writes press releases, speeches, and newsletters. Three years ago, she started writing fiction, and her ninth story was recently accepted for publication in *Gargoyle*. Her stories have been published in *jmww*, *Loch Raven Review*, *The Santa Fe Writer's Project Literary Journal*, *Preface*, and a few other publications. She won the 2009 Maryland Writers Association Short Fiction Contest. A graduate of the College of Notre Dame of Maryland and the Johns Hopkins University, she reviews dives and greasy spoons for the website Welcome to Baltimore, Hon.

Luca Dipierro is a writer, visual artist, and filmmaker living in Brooklyn,

New York. His latest films are the documentaries *I Will Smash You, 60 Writers/60 Places*, and the full-length cut-out animation *Dieci Teste*. His art has been exhibited in galleries in the U.S. and in Italy. His short stories have been published in *The New York Tyrant, Lamination Colony, Gigantic, Harp & Altar, No Colony*, and other publications. His life is based on a true story.

Stephen Dixon is among the most prolific authors of short stories in the history of American letters, with over 500 published. Dixon has been nominated for the National Book Award twice, in 1991 for *Frog* and in 1995 for *Interstate*. He is the author of fourteen novels and numerous story collections.

Frederick Douglass (c. 1818-1895) was born in a slave cabin near the town of Easton, Maryland. Separated from his mother when only a few weeks old, he was raised by his grandparents. At about the age of six, his grandmother took him to the plantation of his master and left him there. When he was about eight he was sent to Baltimore to live as a houseboy with Hugh and Sophia Auld, relatives of his master. It was shortly after his arrival that his new mistress taught him the alphabet. When her husband forbade her to continue her instruction, because it was unlawful to teach slaves how to read, Frederick took it upon himself to learn. In 1838, at the age of twenty, Douglass succeeded in escaping from slavery by impersonating a sailor. An important abolitionist, he published his own newspaper, *The North Star*, participated in the first women's rights convention at Seneca Falls, in 1848, and wrote three autobiographies.

Michael Downs' career in journalism and writing has led him to work in Arizona, Connecticut, Montana, Arkansas, and Maryland. For his life in literature, he is grateful to the Graduate Programs in Creative Writing at the University of Arkansas, where he finished an MFA degree in 1999. His short fiction has appeared in *The Gettysburg Review, The Georgia Review, Michigan Quarterly Review, Five Points, Witness*, and other literary reviews. He was born in Hartford, Connecticut, where he sets most of his writing on the advice of poet and novelist James Whitehead who once told him, "we write from where we get the wound."

F. Scott Fitzgerald (1896–1940) is widely regarded as one of the twentieth century's greatest writers. He finished four novels, *This Side of Paradise*, *The Beautiful and Damned*, *Tender is the Night*, and his most famous, the celebrated classic, *The Great Gatsby*. A fifth, unfinished novel, *The Love of the Last Tycoon*, was published posthumously. When his wife, Zelda Fitzgerald, was hospitalized in Baltimore in 1932, Scott rented the "La Paix" estate in the suburb of Towson, where he worked on *Tender Is the Night*. Both Scott and Zelda are buried in Saint Mary's Cemetery in Rockville, Maryland.

Jen Grow has had her work appear in *The Writer's Chronicle*, *The GSU Review*, *Shattered Wig Review*, *Other Voices Magazine*, *The Sun Magazine*, *Indiana Review*, and others. She's received two Individual Artist Awards from the Maryland State Arts Council. "Joe Blow" was previously nominated for the Best New American Voices of 2001. Another story of hers earned a 2005 Pushcart Prize nomination. She holds an MFA from Vermont College and writes the blog "An Open Window" about daily life, dog walking, and the Divine. She lives with the artist, Lee Stierhoff, and their two dogs and cats.

A novelist, folklorist, and anthropologist, **Zora Neale Hurston** (1891-1960) was the prototypical authority on black culture from the Harlem Renaissance. Her novels include *Jonah's Gourd Vine*, *Mules and Men*, *Their Eyes Watching God*, *Moses, Man of the Mountain*, *Seraph on the Suwanee*, and the travelogue and study of Caribbean voodoo, *Tell My Horse*. Her autobiography, *Dust Tracks on a Road*, was published in 1942.

Michael Kimball's third novel, *Dear Everybody*, was recently published in the U.S., U.K., and Canada. *The Believer* calls it "a curatorial masterpiece." *Time Out New York* calls the writing "stunning." And the *Los Angeles Times* says the book is "funny and warm and sad and heartbreaking." His first two novels are *The Way The Family Got Away* (2000) and *How Much Of Us There Was* (2005), both of which have been translated (or are being translated) into many languages. He is also responsible for the collaborative art project "Michael Kimball Writes Your Life Story (on a postcard)."

Laura Lippman was a reporter for twenty years, including twelve years at the *Baltimore Sun*. A *New York Times* bestselling novelist, she is the author of the award-winning Tess Monaghan series and several stand-alone crime novels. Her fifteenth novel, *I'd Know You Anywhere*, will be published in 2010.

Susan McCallum-Smith is a writer and freelance editor. Her work has been featured in, amongst others, *Urbanite, The Scottish Review of Books, The Philadelphia Inquirer*, and *The Gettysburg Review*. She is an editor of *The Baltimore Review* and a contributing reviewer to Maryland Public Radio. McCallum-Smith earned her degrees in creative writing from Johns Hopkins University and Bennington College. Entasis Press published her short story collection, *Slipping the Moorings*, in early 2009. She was born in Glasgow, Scotland, and lives in Baltimore.

Alice McDermott is Johns Hopkins University's Richard A. Macksey Professor of the Humanities. Her short stories have appeared in *Ms.*, *Redbook, Mademoiselle, The New Yorker*, and *Seventeen*. Her novels include *A Bigamist's Daughter* (1982); *That Night* (1987), a finalist for the National Book Award, the Pen/Faulkner Award, and the Pulitzer Prize; A*t Weddings and Wakes* (1992), a finalist for the Pulitzer Prize; *Charming Billy* (1998), the winner of the 1998 National Book Award; *Child of My Heart: A Novel* (2002), nominated for the International IMPAC Dublin Literary Award; and *After This* (2006), a finalist for the Pulitzer Prize.

Henry Louis "H. L." Mencken (1880–1956), was an American journalist, essayist, magazine editor, satirist, acerbic critic of American life and culture, and a student of American English. Mencken, known as the "Sage of Baltimore," is regarded as one of the most influential American writers and prose stylists of the first half of the 20th century. Among his many publications are *Happy Days, Newspaper Days*, and *Heathen Days*. Mencken might be best known for his reporting on the 1925 Scopes trial, which he dubbed the "monkey" trial.

Jen Michalski's first collection of short fiction, *Close Encounters* (2007), is available from So New Media, and her second, *You Were Only Waiting for This Moment*, from Dzanc (2013). Her chapbook *Cross Sections* (2008) is available from Publishing Genius. Her work has appeared in more than sixty publications, including *McSweeney's Internet Tendency, failbetter, storySouth, 42 opus, Gargoyle, The MacGuffin, The Potomac Review*, and *Baltimore* magazine. She is the editor of the lit journal *jmww* and co-organizer of the 510 Readings Series.

Madeleine Mysko was born and raised in Baltimore, where she attended parochial schools and graduated from Mercy Hospital School of Nursing. She later received advanced degrees in literature and writing. Presently she teaches in the Advanced Academic Programs of The Johns Hopkins University, and coordinates the "Reflections" column for *American Journal of Nursing*. Her poetry and prose have appeared widely in journals that include *The Hudson Review*, *Shenandoah*, and *Bellevue Literary Review*. Her first novel, based on her experiences as an Army nurse on the burn ward, is *Bringing Vincent Home* (Plain View Press).

Leigh Newman's stories and essays have appeared in *Tin House*, *One Story*, *Fiction*, *The Northwest Review*, *The Madison Review*, *New York Tyrant*, the *New Orleans Review*, National Public Radio's "Sound of Writing," and the *New York Times* "Modern Love" column. Her memoir about growing up in Baltimore (and Alaska) will be published in 2011 by Dial Books.

Born in Bombay, India, **Lalita Noronha** is a research scientist, writer, poet, and teacher. Recipient of a Fulbright travel grant to the U.S., she earned her Ph.D. in microbiology. Her literary work has appeared in over fifty journals, magazines, and anthologies, including the *Baltimore Sun*, *The Christian Science Monitor*, *Catholic Digest*, *Crab Orchard Review*, *Get Well Wishes* (Harper Collins), and *Yellow as Turmeric, Fragrant as Cloves* (Deep Bowl Press). She has twice won the Maryland Literary Short Story Award, Maryland Individual Artist Award, and the Dorothy Daniels National League of American Pen Women award. She is the author of *Where Monsoons Cry*, and a fiction editor for *The Baltimore Review*.

Edgar Allan Poe (1809-1849) was an American poet, critic, short story writer, and author of such works as *The Fall of the House of Usher*, *The Tell-Tale Heart*, and "The Raven." He lived in Baltimore during the 1830s, and mysteriously died there in 1849. Poe continues to slumber in the graveyard at Westminister Church.

Lia Purpura's recent books include *On Looking* (essays, Sarabande Books), a finalist for the National Book Critics Circle Award, and *King Baby* (poems, Alice James Books), winner of the Beatrice Hawley Award. Her awards include the AWP Award in Nonfiction, the OSU Prize in Poetry, NEA and Fulbright Fellowships, two Pushcart prizes, and five "Notable Essay" citations in *Best American Essays*. Recent work appears in *AGNI*, *Field*, *The Georgia Review*, *Orion*, *The New Republic*, *The New Yorker*, and *The Paris Review*. She is Writer-in-Residence at Loyola University Maryland and teaches in the Rainier Writing Workshop MFA Program.

Adam Robinson lives in Baltimore, where he runs Publishing Genius, writes, and plays music with his band, Sweatpants. His first collection of poetry, *Adam Robinson and Other Poems*, was published by Narrow House Books in 2010.

Jane Satterfield is the recipient of a National Endowment for the Arts Fellowship in Literature and the author of *Daughters of Empire: A Memoir of a Year in Britain and Beyond* (Demeter, 2009), *Assignation at Vanishing Point* (Elixir, 2003) and *Shepherdess with an Automatic* (Washington Writers' Publishing House, 2000). Born in England and educated in the U.S., she holds an MFA from the Iowa Writers' Workshop. She has received three Maryland State Arts Council grants in poetry, and her nonfiction awards include the Florida Review's Editors' Prize, The Heekin Foundation's Cuchulain Fellowship, the John Guyon Literary Nonfiction Prize, and the Faulkner Society's Gold Medal. She lives in Baltimore with her husband, poet Ned Balbo, and her daughter Catherine, and teaches at Loyola University.

Rosalia Scalia's stories have appeared or are forthcoming in *North Atlantic Review*, *Pebble Lake Review*, *Taproot Literary Review: The Healing Tree #20*, *Pig Iron Press*, *Quercus Review*, *The Portland Review*, and *Spout*, among others. "Sister Rafaele Heals the Sick" was nominated for the Pushcart Prize and "Picking Cicoria" won first prize in the Taproot annual literary fiction competition. The first chapter of her novel-in-progress, "Delia's Concerto," was a finalist in a 2003 National League of American Pen Women competition. Scalia earned a master's degree in writing from Johns Hopkins University.

Patricia Schultheis has had several essays and short stories published in national and international literary journals. A member of the Author's Guild and a voting member of the National Book Critics Circle, she serves on the editorial board of *Narrative*. Her pictorial local history titled *Baltimore's Lexington Market* was published by Arcadia Publishing in 2007, and her collection of short stories was a finalist for the Flannery O'Connor Award and Snake Nation Press Award.

Gertrude Stein (1874-1946) moved to Baltimore in the 1890s after the death of her parents. There she enjoyed Saturday evening salons hosted by art collectors Claribel and Etta Cone, a social ritual that she replicated upon moving to Paris. While in Baltimore, Gertrude enrolled at the Johns Hopkins Meidcal School, but left in 1901 without a formal degree. In 1903, Stein moved to Paris with Alice B. Toklas, her lifelong companion and secretary. Her first book, *Three Lives*, was published in 1909, followed by *Tender Buttons* in 1914. Her other influential works are *The Making of Americans* (1925), *How to Write* (1931), *The Autobiography of Alice B. Toklas* (1933), and *Stanzas in Meditation and Other Poems [1929-1933]* (1956).

Ron Tanner has published stories and essays in such magazines as *The Iowa Review*, *The Massachusetts Review*, *The Literary Review*, *Story Quarterly*, *West Branch*, and dozens of others. His work has been anthologized in *Best of the Web*, *The Pushcart Prizes*, and *Twenty Under Thirty: Early Work of America's Influential Writers*, among others. Awards for his short fiction include a James Michener Fellowship from the Iowa Writers' Workshop, first prize in the New Letters national fiction competition, gold medal in the Pirate's Alley Faulkner Society national competition for short fiction, and many others. His first collection of short stories, *A Bed of Nails*, won the G.S. Sharat Chandra Prize and the Towson Prize for Literature.

Author of eighteen novels, **Anne Tyler** was born in Minneapolis, Minnesota, in 1941 and grew up in Raleigh, North Carolina. Her eleventh novel, *Breathing Lessons*, was awarded the Pulitzer Prize in 1988. A member of the American Academy and Institute of Arts and Letters, she continues to live in Baltimore.

A 2008 finalist for The Flannery O'Connor Award for Fiction, **Todd A. Whaley** lives in Baltimore and works for an international architectural firm in Washington, D.C. He has stories in a number of journals, including *Berkeley Fiction Review*, *Louisiana Literature*, *The Baltimore Review*,

Fourth River, Pisgah Review, REAL: Regarding Arts and Letters, Licking River Review, and others. He has been honored as a finalist in *Glimmer Train Stories* and nominated to the Best New American Voices.

Rupert Wondolowski recently returned to the small silver screen in Michael Kimball and Luca DiPierro's film *60 Writers/60 Places*. He is the author of *The Origin of Paranoia as a Heated Mole Suit* (Publishing Genius Press) and *The Whispering of Ice Cubes* (Shattered Wig Press). His writing has most recently appeared in the *i.e. Series Reader, Lamination Colony, Fell Swoop*, and *Mud Luscious Press Stamp Stories*. He is the editor and publisher of The Shattered Wig Press.

Joseph Young lives in Hampden. His book of microfictions, *Easter Rabbit*, was released by Publishing Genius in December 2009. Stories from the book have appeared in *Caketrain, Lamination Colony, FRiGG, jmww, wigleaf, Keyhole*, and elsewhere. He often collaborates with visual artists, most recently with painter Christine Sajecki at Minas Gallery in March 2010.

Publication Credits

City Sages: Baltimore

The publisher and editor have made every effort to trace the ownership of all stories. We apologize if we have misrepresented any publication and will be happy to make a correction in future editions of this book.

"The Velvet Room," by Rafael Alvarez, first appeared as "Orlo's Velvet Room," Macon Street Books, 1998, and in *Hometown Boy*.

"Valet Parking," by Geoffrey Becker, first appeared in *failbetter*, Summer 2004.

"Small Blue Thing," by Madison Smartt Bell, first appeared in the June 1, 2000, issue of *Harper's Magazine*.

"Bubbe and Zeyde," by Jessica Anya Blau, first appeared in the *Urbanite*, No. 50, August 2008.

"Fugueur," by Maud Casey, first appeared in *Bellevue Literary Review*, Vol. 8, No. 1, Spring 2008.

"Small Crimes," by Andria Nacina Cole, first appeared in the *Urbanite*, No. 50, August 2008.

"Forty-Five Years Ago," by Caryn Coyle, first appeared in *Loch Raven Review*, Vol. IV, No. 2, Summer 2008.

"Fourteen Things My Father Forbade," by Luca Dipierro, first appeared in *No Colony*, Vol. 2, 2009.

"Frog Made Free," by Stephen Dixon, first appeared in *Frog*, Holt Paperbacks, 1997.

Frederick Douglass, from *Narrative of the Life of Frederick Douglass, An American Slave*. Boston, Anti-Slavery Office, 1845. This work is available via the public domain.

"At the Beach," by Michael Downs, first appeared in *The Missouri Review*, Vol. 29, No. 2, Summer 2006.

"Benediction," by F. Scott Fitzgerald, from *Flappers and Philosophers*, 1920. This work is available via the public domain.

Zora Neale Hurston, from *Their Eyes Were Watching God*, Harper Perennial Modern Classics, 2006.

Michael Kimball, from *Dear Everybody*, Alma Books, 2008.

"Easy as A-B-C," by Laura Lippman, from *Baltimore Noir*, edited by Laura Lippman, Akashic Books, 2006.

"High Rise," by Susan McCallum-Smith, first appeared in slightly different form in *Slipping the Moorings*, Entasis Press, 2009.

Alice McDermott, from *Charming Billy*, Dell Publishing, 1999.

H.L. Mencken, "Mush for the Multitude," first appeared in (rv) *The Smart Set*, December 1914. This work is available via the public domain.

"Where Hearts Lie," by Lalita Noronha, first appeared in the *Urbanite*, No. 33, March 2007.

"The Black Cat," by Edgar Allan Poe, first appeared in *The Saturday Evening Post*, August 19, 1843. This work is available via the public domain.

"Grey," by Lia Purpura, first appeared in *Southern Review*, Vol. 44, No. 1 Winter 2008.

"Assignations at Vanishing Point," by Jane Satterfield, from *Daughters of Empire: A Memoir of a Year in Britain and Beyond* (Demeter Press, 2009). The essay first appeared in a slightly different version in the *Seneca Review*.

"Sister Rafaele Heals the Sick," by Rosalia Scalia, first appeared in *Pebble Lake Review*, Vol. 3, Issue 1, Fall 2005.

"Downward Drifting," by Patricia Schultheis, first appeared in *Fiction Magazine*, Vol. 54, 2008.

"Ada," by Gertrude Stein, from *Geography and Plays*. Boston, Four Seas Company, 1922. This work is available via the public domain.

"My Small Murders," by Ron Tanner, first appeared in *Wheelhouse Magazine*, No. 1, Summer 2007, and the *Urbanite*, No. 34, April 2007.

Anne Tyler, from *Dinner at the Homesick Restaurant*, Knopf, 1982.

"Two Plot Devices," by Rupert Wondolowski, from *The Whispering of Ice Cubes*, Shattered Wig Press, 2008.

"The River Rushed On," by Todd A. Whaley, first appeared in *Louisiana Literature*, Spring/Summer 2009.

CityLit Press's mission is to provide a venue for writers who might otherwise be overlooked by larger publishers due to the literary quality or regional focus of their projects. It is the imprint of nonprofit CityLit Project, founded in Baltimore in 2004.

CityLit nurtures the culture of literature in Baltimore and throughout Maryland by creating enthusiasm for literature, building a community of avid readers and writers, and opening opportunities for young people and diverse audiences to embrace the literary arts.

Thank you to our major supporters: the Maryland State Arts Council, the Baltimore Office of Promotion and The Arts, and the Baltimore Community Foundation. More information and documentation is available at www.guidestar.org.

Additional support is provided by individual contributors. Financial support is vital for sustaining the on-going work of the organization. Secure, on-line donations can by made at our web site, click on "Donate."

CityLit is a member of the Greater Baltimore Cultural Alliance, the Maryland Association of Nonprofit Organizations, and the Writers' Conferences and Centers division of the Association of Writers and Writing Programs (AWP).

For submission guidelines, information about CityLit Press's poetry chapbook contests, and all the programs and services offered by CityLit, please visit www.citylitproject.org.

Nurturing the culture of literature.

LaVergne, TN USA
16 April 2010
179550LV00004B/97/P